THE

FIERY
CROWN

Jeffe Kennedy

St. Martin's Paperbacks

This is a work of fiction. All of the characters, organizations, and events portrayed in this novel are either products of the author's imagination or are used fictitiously.

First published in the United States by St. Martin's Paperbacks, an imprint of St. Martin's Publishing Group.

THE FIERY CROWN

Copyright © 2020 by Jeffe Kennedy.
Excerpt from *The Promised Queen* copyright © 2020 by Jeffe Kennedy.

All rights reserved.

For information, address St. Martin's Publishing Group, 120 Broadway, New York, NY 10271.

www.stmartins.com

ISBN: 978-1-250-19433-6

Our books may be purchased in bulk for promotional, educational, or business use. Please contact your local bookseller or the Macmillan Corporate and Premium Sales Department at 1-800-221-7945, ext. 5442, or by email at MacmillanSpecialMarkets@macmillan.com.

Printed in the United States of America

St. Martin's Paperbacks edition 2020

10 9 8 7 6 5 4 3 2 1

To my family, both that I was born to and that marriage brought together. Mom, Dave, Hope, Galen, Brett, and Henry: love you all!

~Acknowledgments~

Big love to my editor, Jennie Conway, who made this book so much better in so many ways. It's truly a joy to work with you.

To the team at St. Martin's Press: Thank you for working so hard on behalf of this series. I've been so thrilled at all you do, the attention to detail and the joy with which you embrace the books you publish. To my publicity team in particular: Thank you so much for launching *The Orchid Throne* in such a wonderful way. Working with you makes everything so easy.

Much love and gratitude to my agent, Sarah Younger, who is the absolute best. You are my rock and my guiding star.

Many heartfelt thanks and love to my writer friends who are always there for me at the other end of the phone or internet connection. I'd be lost without you! Virtual hugs and chocolate to Amanda Bouchet, Grace Draven, Jennifer Estep, Thea Harrison, Darynda Jones, Leslye Penelope, Kelly Robson, and Minerva Spencer. Thanks in particular to Megan Hart for an emergency read.

Special thanks to Sage Walker and Jim Sorenson for brunches, to Megan Mulry for cocktails, and to Emily Mah and Trent Zelazny for coffee.

Many thanks to my professional writers organizations, the Science Fiction and Fantasy Writers of America (SFWA) and the Romance Writers of America (RWA)—especially my local RWA chapter, the Land of Enchantment Romance Authors—for being a port in the storm, a rising tide that floats all boats, and fellow travelers on the sea of publishing. Special shout-out to the SFWA Slack chat for daily advice and nonsense.

As always, immense gratitude to my fantastic assistant, Carien Ubink, who does it all.

Finally—first, last, and always—love to David, who is there every day.

"Good morning, Conrí! I must congratulate myself—how did I know I'd find you here?"

I glanced at the wizard, not revealing that he'd surprised me and not bothering to return the empty pleasantries. I hadn't asked him to find me. In fact, I'd come to the portrait gallery to be alone—not easy in the crowded and convivial court of Calanthe. "I don't know, Ambrose. Probably one of the many dark arts you practice."

Ambrose, cheerfully undaunted, shook his head with a smile. He'd decorated his light-brown curls with a garland of flowers in the Calanthean style, and he wore a deep-blue robe lavishly embroidered with glittering silver moons floating in a field of stars in pinprick jewels of every color imaginable. Even his familiar, Merle, a very large raven, sported a silver chain about his neck studded with small jewels that winked even in the dim light from the glass-paned, narrow slits of windows. The raven, perched on the enormous emerald stone topping the wizard's staff, cocked his head at me and opened his beak in a croak that could be interpreted as a laugh.

"Ah, Conrí, I wouldn't waste my prodigious magical talents on locating you when simple logic tells me you'd be lurking here in the shadows while Her Highness holds formal court."

"Shouldn't *you* be lurking in your tower, muttering spells over boiling cauldrons?"

Ambrose laughed. "You really know nothing at all of how wizardry and magic work."

I only grunted, returning my gaze to studying the portrait above me. It was too much to hope that Ambrose would go away, but maybe if I ignored him he'd get bored of poking at me and spit out whatever he wanted to say and then get gone.

But no, he stepped up beside me, keeping his counsel for the moment, and gazed up also. The ornately framed portrait of Oriel's last, doomed ruling family dominated this section of wall. That wasn't just me, either. Anyone would be drawn to the portrait for its size and artistic execution, attracting the eye even among the many paintings that had been crowded into the gallery. The long arcade held hundreds, maybe thousands of drawings, etchings, and paintings. They hung shoulder-to-shoulder, like warriors out of history marching in frozen formation, relics of kingdoms scattered to ash.

Lia—and her father before her—had collected these works of art, smuggled out of the many forgotten empires and kingdoms, saving them from the self-styled Emperor Anure's destruction and greed, bringing them to the island kingdom of Calanthe, to hang quietly in the shadows. It made sense, on one level, to keep the paintings in the dark, preserving them from the tropical sunlight, but a morbid part of me couldn't help comparing the place to a tomb.

Of course, a tomb was the right location for interring this portrait among the others, along with the dead people it portrayed. My father, as broad-chested and vital as he'd been in my boyhood, stood behind my seated mother, both wearing the crowns of Oriel. He had one big hand braced on the back of her chair, the other on my shoulder. Or rather, on the boy prince of Oriel, a child who'd effectively died along with the rest of his family. That kid grinned with cocky confidence and the innocent joy of a stranger. Nothing at all like the man who looked back at me from Calanthe's thousands of shining and unflinching mirrors.

I'd visited the painting enough times now that I could make myself look at my mother's face, her light-brown eyes holding laughter and warmth. The painter had been the best for several kingdoms around—and she'd exactly captured my mother's keen intelligence, her lips curved in a smile as if she might burst out laughing at any moment. My sister and I had inherited her black hair and tawny eyes, not our father's bold blond, blue-eyed looks.

My sister . . . I hadn't yet been able to make myself look at her face.

I tried. I visited the portrait several times a day as a kind of penance, and to test my will. It was the least I could do, when I'd survived and they'd all been consigned to unmarked graves, my mother and sister moldering when they should've been cleanly burnt to ash. My sister stood between my father and mother, so I should be able to slide my gaze over a few inches from my mother's face . . . but my will collapsed, the sick grief grabbing me, and I had to look away, taking a deep breath.

"There's no bringing back the dead," Ambrose said philosophically, though with a note of compassion in his voice. "Not those who've been dead a long time, anyway. It almost never works out well. I could tell you about—"

"Did I ask?" I retorted.

"I just thought I should mention," he replied reproachfully, more of his usual bite to it. "Since you seem to have such a high opinion of my wizardry. In case your brooding and obsessive study of this painting led your thoughts in that direction."

I set my teeth, resisting the urge to grind them. "I'm not brooding or obsessive. This is a good place to think. *Normally* no one bothers me here." If I had to kick my heels in this oppressively cheerful paradise, growing softer with each wasted moment, I could at least contemplate next steps, anticipate Anure's strategy to take his own revenge on Calanthe and her queen. "It's not like I have anything else to do."

"You could attend court, as consort to Her Highness," Ambrose pointed out blandly, and I suppressed a growl of frustration. At least my throat hurt less, since Healer Jeaneth had been treating me—one positive of having time on my hands. My voice still sounded like a choked dog most of the time, however.

"Court." I snarled the word. "I don't get how Lia can waste time on diplomacy and posturing when she promised to discuss defense."

"She does have a realm to govern."

"She won't if Anure arrives to destroy it while she drags her feet. The woman is uncommonly stubborn."

"A perfect match for you." Ambrose narrowed his eyes at my clenched fists. "Isn't she gathering intelligence from her spies?"

I didn't answer that. That's what we waited on, theoretically, but I knew there were things Lia was avoiding telling me. I also suspected that she hoped it would all just go away. Both of us knew that Calanthe couldn't withstand a full-out, devastating attack. When nothing happened immediately after our wedding, it seemed that Lia began to hope that nothing ever would.

I knew better. The painting helped remind me of all

the dead waiting to be avenged—and what happened to those who fell before Anure's might.

Unfortunately, I was at a loss to find a way out of our current predicament.

If Anure was smart—and the Imperial Tyrant might be greedy, arrogant, ruthless, and devoid of redeeming human qualities, but he wasn't stupid—he'd simply surround the island with battleships loaded with explosive vurgsten and bombard Calanthe until nothing remained. He wouldn't care about salvaging anything; he never had. Even with the ships I'd captured and Calanthe's fleets of pleasure skiffs and fishing boats, we didn't have anywhere close to the numbers to effectively surround and defeat Anure's navy. Besides, our own supplies of vurgsten had to be vanishingly small compared with what the emperor would have stockpiled over nearly two decades at his citadel at Yekpehr.

We had to deploy our few strengths with strategic care, and being trapped on an island while the Imperial Toad scoured us off it with superior force wouldn't allow for that. Not only wasn't I closer to destroying Anure and taking my final revenge, I'd put myself and my forces in an even more tenuous position than before. I'd followed Ambrose's prophecy, and taken the tower at Keiost.

Take the Tower of the Sun,
Claim the hand that wears the Abiding Ring,
And the empire falls.

Claiming the hand that wears the Abiding Ring? I only wish it had been as simple as conquering an impregnable ancient city. Instead I'd had to find a way to convince Queen Euthalia of Calanthe to marry me. Against all probability, I'd succeeded. We were duly wed, though saying I'd claimed anything about Lia would be a stretch, and I sure didn't see the empire falling anytime soon. The reverse seemed far more likely.

Doing nothing while my enemy mustered a crushing attack was driving me out of my mind.

"Lia's spies can maybe tell her how much vurgsten Anure has, yes," I finally replied to the wizard's expectant silence. "She might find out exactly how many ships and troops he can send against us, how well fortified his citadel is, and we'll know nothing more than we do now. We'll be no closer to defeating Anure. I thought claiming the hand with the Abiding Ring would lead to the empire's fall." I leveled an accusing glare on him.

"You claimed Her Highness's hand in marriage all right, but the wooing doesn't stop there," Ambrose replied with mild reproof. "You can't order about a queen like you can your soldiers."

"Don't I know it," I muttered. Since Ambrose had destroyed what little peace I'd found, I turned and strode down the long gallery. The wizard glided alongside me, making no sound though my bootsteps echoed on the polished marble of Lia's pretty palace. Ambrose could move silently as a cat when he wished, which was how he'd managed to sneak up on me. No one else could. I'd learned early on in the mines of Vurgmun to duck the ready lash of the guards, a habit that had stuck—and served me well in the years of battle since.

I'd have liked to say I'd gotten used to Ambrose's strange skills, but even I didn't delude myself that much.

We emerged from the shadowed portrait gallery, a place thick with ghosts and the stale smells of hundreds of destroyed kingdoms, and into the bright, flower-scented sunlight of the main hall. Lia's palace didn't have much in the way of walls. With the eternal summer of Calanthe's tropical weather, they didn't need them.

Open arcades of carved pillars framed the lush gardens, pools, and lawns surrounding the palace, with the gleaming turquoise sea beyond. Flowers bloomed constantly from lawns, flower beds, shrubs, and towering trees, with vines coiling over all of it. Butterflies of hues I hadn't known existed lifted in clouds, then drifted on the breeze, and everywhere birds sang, all sweetly, of course. I hadn't figured out yet if Lia had an army of gardeners to tend it all or if it just . . . did that on its own.

I'd made a deal with myself that I wouldn't ask. Not that Lia would laugh at my question—not out loud, anyway— but I didn't like to remind Her Highness of what an ignorant lout she'd married.

A stream burbled its way through the palace from a lagoon on one side to a pond on the other, meandering through in a trough cut into the marble floors and inlaid with little tiles in all shades of blue and green. Arching bridges crossed it in places, more for show than anything, because all but the most mincing courtier could easily leap across the narrow channel. I might not have much in the way of fine manners, but even I knew it would be rude to actually jump over the thing, however, and I didn't much feel like changing my path to cross over the nearest dainty bridge. So I turned and followed the stream outside.

Ambrose, of course, tagged along as if we were out for a companionable stroll.

"What do you want, Ambrose?" I finally asked, capitulating to the inevitable.

"Me? Oh, what a question." He let his staff thunk on the path of crushed stone, leaning on it as we walked, Merle rising and falling with the movement, like the carved masthead of a ship on stormy seas. "I want different things now than when I was an apprentice wizard," he continued conversationally. "Those ideas change over time, have you noticed? The expectations of youthful idealism give way to more mature dreams and goals. Not in a bad way. It's just that what we thought we wanted comes from not really knowing what we could have. Once I learned more about what the world offered me, I discovered I wanted entirely different things. And you?"

"I have no idea what you're talking about." Or how I'd gone from leading armies, with every conquest increasing the momentum of my vengeance, to strolling through a garden, having a conversation like the pretty lads and ladies we passed. Most of the courtiers were in court, naturally, kissing Lia's gorgeously garbed ass and passing their fancily folded notes, but the other denizens of the palace seemed to spend most of their time looking decorative in the gardens. In my black garb—granted, finer than what I'd arrived on Calanthe wearing—and carrying my weapons, I felt like a scarred monster by comparison. Given the askance looks the courtiers gave me before they deflected into other directions, they thought so, too.

"I'm talking about changing expectations," Ambrose replied, lifting his face to the sun and smiling like that one painting of a saint back in the gallery. "You, for example, can expect very different things from your life now that you're king of Calanthe and no longer the Slave King."

"The consort of the queen of Calanthe," I corrected, hating the testy edge to my voice, already so rough compared with the wizard's fluid tones. "Not the same thing. I'm not king of anything, never have been."

Ambrose waved that off as irrelevant. "My point is, it's time for you to stop moping about in the shadows. You can't afford to do nothing. Time to take action, my boy!"

I stopped next to a tiered fountain of roses, glaring at

it while I mastered the urge to throttle the wizard. The roses at the top were bright white, then they got pinker lower down. The blooms progressed through all shades of pink and red, until the bottom ones that were as dark as the blood that pours out when you strike a man in the liver.

Tiny purple bees buzzed around them, making a hypnotic sound that somehow seemed part of the heavily sweet scent of the blossoms. I kept an eye on the bees to make sure they planned to stay occupied with the flowers rather than attacking us. "What action do you want me to take?" I asked, sounding more or less calm. "Lia refuses to convene her Defense Council and *you* agreed with her, saying we should wait to see how Anure responded when he received news of the wedding."

Ambrose sighed heavily, then settled himself on a stone bench that circled the flower fountain, heedless of the bees that investigated the garland in his hair, though Merle snapped at one curiously. "That's what I'm telling you, Conrí," the wizard said with exaggerated patience. "We did have to wait. Now we don't. Must I forever explain these things?"

I wrapped my fingers into my palms, making them into fists so I'd be less likely to forget that I needed Ambrose and accidentally strangle him. Also, he was Lia's court wizard now, and she'd be put out with me if I killed him.

Ours wasn't a marriage of affection. Exactly the opposite, in fact, as we'd started out trying to kill each other before we ever met face-to-face. But the ritual had been done properly, tying us together for the rest of our lives, like it or not. Aside from the sexual consummation, where we seemed to get along just fine, we mostly seemed to piss each other off. Like two bulls in a small pen, one of Lia's pet scholars, Brenda, had called us. Not a bad comparison, if unflattering. I wouldn't mind having horns to wave at Ambrose in menace.

"What changed?" I asked. My voice growled with frustration when the wizard got that sly look of his and raised a chastising finger as he opened his mouth. "And *don't* say everything changes all the time."

Ambrose closed his mouth again and raised his brows. "Well, everything does change. Change is the one dependable element of the world," he pointed out, almost primly, then hastily added as he caught the look on my face, "but I'll address the question I believe you meant to ask, which is why now is the time and not yesterday, or even earlier today. That's a complicated answer, because there are many factors you won't understand, even if I had time to explain them all."

"Ambrose."

"Patience, Conrí. What I'm saying is that Queen Euthalia has received a message from Anure."

"It took you *this* long to tell me that?" I snapped, incredulous. My blood surged hot, but not with anger and frustration as usual. Excitement and bold purpose filled me. Enough of delays and arguing in circles. At last I could embark on the final phase of my mission to destroy Anure, everything he'd built, and everything he cared about. If the Imperial Toad was capable of caring about anything at all.

And the empire falls.

"What did the message say?"

"Oh, I don't know exactly. But the currents of possibility and probability have shifted. It's fascinating to see."

I bit back my impatience. "*How* have they shifted— have you seen how we can counter Anure's certain attack?"

A chorus of music blasted from the direction of the palace proper, along with cheers and shouts. I knew that fanfare well enough, as it always heralded the approach of the queen. Her people behaved as if her every appearance was a cause for joyous celebration. Ambrose stood, using the staff to pull himself up, a delighted smile on his face. "Aha! Here comes Queen Euthalia. She'll be able to tell you what the message says. Then you'll see."

"Something you could have told me long since."

"If you'd bothered to attend court, you'd have known already," he shot back, dropping all hint of playfulness, his words short and full of disapproval.

I didn't reply, setting my teeth together with a satisfying bite instead. Lia's court drove me out of my mind with their fancy dress and pretty posturing. I'd gone to court with Lia that first day, thinking that we'd get actual work done. We did have a war to plan, right? But no—she'd expected me to dress up and then sit there while fancily dressed idiots simpered and offered fake compliments, begging for favors in the guise of offering congratulations on our marriage.

When I lost all patience and suggested—politely, I thought—that we call the Defense Council into session, all hell had broken loose. How was I supposed to know Lia's Sawehl-cursed Defense Council was a *secret*? With everyone in an uproar, Lia had adjourned court and accused me of sabotaging her authority and precipitating panic. I'd had to point out that the threat of incipient attack by an overwhelming force *should* upset people. The argument went downhill from there.

We'd more or less gotten back on friendly, if formal, terms since. But I also hadn't gone back to court. And she still hadn't convened the Defense Council.

The music and cheering grew closer, so I stayed where I was. No doubt the purple bees had told Lia where to find me—or however her elemental magic worked. I only knew a few things about her for sure. One was that Lia was as much flower as flesh. She kept her head shaved because if she didn't, her hair grew out like vines. So she told me—I hadn't seen that part, though I'd seen the plant-like patterns on her skin, surprisingly erotic.

She possessed magic, too, but I didn't know how much, or what she could do. Lia had a lifelong habit of concealing her nature, so she didn't discuss the specifics easily, certainly not in public. And when we were alone . . . well, we didn't talk much.

She came around the bend of the garden path, preceded by two spritely children tossing flower petals in the air to flutter down and decorate the rocks before her. Smooth, colorful stones already gleamed throughout the rougher white gravel, so the petals seemed especially redundant. But the Calantheans never saw anything they didn't try to make even prettier.

Lia led a phalanx of attendants, five ladies-in-waiting instead of her former six—she also refused to discuss replacing Tertulyn, who'd suspiciously disappeared on our wedding day and had yet to be found—along with Lord Dearsley and a few others of her various advisers. Two of my own people, Sondra and Kara, accompanied the entourage, gazes alert for trouble. They were dressed for court, too, though more severely than the extravagant Calanthe styles, so they also stood out as invaders among the blossoms.

I hadn't seen Lia since I'd vacated the bed we shared, leaving her to dress for the day. A weird Calanthean ritual dictated that the "Morning Glory," a young virgin, should assist the queen from her bed. Apparently Lia's father, old King Gul, had also divested the glories of their innocence. When Lia had arched a brow and asked if I'd like to take up that tradition, my answer had been an easy and immediate *no*.

So, since our marriage, Lia had changed the years-old routine by having Lady Ibolya assist in getting me gone before Lady Calla brought the Glory in and pretended to wake the queen all over again.

After that, the Glory helped Lia's ladies complete the extended ritual of dressing her for the day, something I was fine with escaping. I preferred my wife—uncanny still to even think those words—without the adornments of her rank. I knew most noble ladies used their clothing and makeup as a kind of armor in their battles with the world, but Lia elevated dressing to a full-scale war. A lot of the costume and makeup served to disguise her nature. She had to shave her head, so she wore elegant wigs to hide that fact. The elaborate gowns and thick paste covered everything else.

One useful aspect of her complicated attire: Though she rarely revealed much emotion otherwise, her choice of dress absolutely announced her mood. Today she was lethal.

She wore a stiff-boned corset, which pushed up her breasts to distracting levels and narrowed her waist to a wisp I could span with my hands. The underpart of the gown exactly matched her skin tone, with an overlay of sheer material with angular black lines of gleaming black beads in spiky patterns. The skirt sleeked over her hips then flowed long and full behind her, a ruff of black at the bottom that scattered the petals as she walked. Even though there was a lot of it, the gown overall gave the impression that she was mostly naked, wearing only thin black lines of tiny beads. In fact, the more I squinted at it, the better I could see that some of the skirt was sheer, giving glimpses of her long, slim legs, made even longer-looking by the sparkling high heels on her feet.

She'd forgone her usual high collar, leaving her shoulders bare, the covering of her breasts more thickly beaded than the rest, though they hardly needed to be any more emphasized. Another ruff of lace coyly feathered over her cleavage. Even though I knew she'd have her exposed skin covered with thick makeup, the sight of her exquisite bosom tantalized me with memories of how she tasted. Gleaming black silk sheaths covered her arms from wrists to shoulders, her fingers tipped with sharp-looking nails, white with gleaming black at the ends, as if she'd dipped them in ink.

On her left hand, the orchid ring—the Abiding Ring I'd supposedly claimed along with her hand in marriage, for all the good it did me—bloomed in splendor, ruffled petals somehow sexual and magical.

The wig she'd donned to match the outfit was also ebony black—possibly the same one she'd worn for our wedding ball—but elaborately styled so that a long curl draped over one shoulder, the rest forming a coiling nest for the glittering crown of Calanthe. Lia's makeup was all in stark black and white also. Even her lips had been painted glossy black, diamonds glittering at the corners of her mouth, at the two top points, and with a larger one centered in the full lower lip. The crown of jewels in the blues and greens of Calanthe's gentle seas was the only point of color, besides the orchid on her hand.

Well, and the blue-gray of her eyes, a color that should have been misty but came across as crystal-shard-sharp as the beads on her gown when she assessed me from beneath diamond-tipped black lashes. Lia moved with swaying grace toward me, apparently unhurried, her expression as coolly composed as always. But I didn't miss the tension simmering in her.

She paused a decorous distance before me, and I restrained the urge to bow. Yet another reason I'd hated court—or being with her in formal settings—was that I didn't know the rules for how to behave. When it was just us, man and woman, me and Lia, preferably naked, I knew how to handle her. With Her Highness Queen Euthalia . . .

"Good morning, Conrí," she said, her smoothly cultured voice sweet as flowers. "I trust you're enjoying My gardens? It's a lovely day for it."

I barely managed not to wince, or apologize—especially not for refusing to waste time in court when it would only lead to another argument between us. Instead I gave in to the urge to acknowledge her beauty by taking her hand, the one without the orchid ring, bending over it and pressing a kiss to her fingers. As always, she smelled of flowers or the inside of a leaf, as if her petal-soft skin emanated the scent naturally. She curled those nails, sharp as thorns, against my palm in subtle warning. I straightened and gave her a long, cautious look.

"Good morning, wife," I replied, not above needling her in return. Her eyes narrowed in smoky ire. "I understand there's news from our illustrious imperial overlord?"

That narrow gaze flicked to Ambrose and back to me. "Indeed, Conrí," she replied with decorous boredom. "His Imperial Majesty Emperor Anure has sent Me a letter." She lifted her free hand, flicking the black-tipped nails with languid demand, the orchid ring's petals billowing with the movement, and her lady Ibolya set an envelope in the cage of them. The light-gray paper had been folded in intricate lines, then embossed in darker gray with an image of Anure's citadel at Yekpehr, the rocks jagged and menacing.

She spun the envelope to extend it to me, as Sondra might flick one of her blades. Lia's expression remained opaque, eyes guileless. "While I hate to interrupt your idyll in the garden, perhaps I could trouble you with your attention to this."

Oh yeah, Lia was pissed as hell. I could only hope it wasn't all aimed at me.

2

With a wary look, Con took Anure's envelope from me. I had to control the impulse to scrub my hand against my skirt to rid myself of Anure's taint. Even though I'd kept his letter pinned in my nails and not touching my skin, I'd loathed having the vile thing near me, and I'd been hard-pressed not to show how much its contents had shaken my already tenuous composure. The ice I'd been carefully layering around my heart all these long years of ruling alone had begun to fail me. Too much stress. Too much Con and his hotheadedness.

Too many feelings I didn't know how to control.

Thus, I was more than happy to hand the letter into Con's keeping. If only I could as easily rid myself of Anure's words. I'd been reading his crazed and cruel missives for years, but this one had exceeded them all somehow, crawling under my skin like a filth I could never remove. They corroded my already fragile barriers, making me feel weak.

I hated feeling weak.

And now Con just stood there, holding Anure's letter instead of instantly reading it—assessing me as if he expected something more. Why wasn't he reading the cursed thing? He'd been waiting for this moment, practically frothing at the mouth for action since our hasty wedding. Now, when he could act, he did nothing, staring me down.

I kept my chin high and expression composed, refusing to let him intimidate me. My wolf king hadn't tamed much in the days since our marriage. Not that I'd expected him to, really.

As my consort, however, he could damn well spend a few hours in court to demonstrate he cared about Calanthe and respected my rule. Or at least give the appearance of doing so, to silence the snickers of the courtiers who already spun tales that I'd been coerced into this marriage and used by the erstwhile Slave King as surely as Anure had planned to do.

As Anure still planned to do. *For every moment you make me wait . . .*

If I had to be married, I should at least have the comfort of feeling a little less alone. There had been moments, brief glimpses here and there, when it seemed possible Con and I could be a team. When we actually understood each other. Those flashes of harmony shone with bright promise—usually during sex, admittedly—but vanished in the harsh light of morning.

In the final analysis, the two of us came from different worlds and I should have realized Con wouldn't fit into mine. Even now he stood out in the gardens like a bloody sword thrust through a garland of jasmine. Scowling and seething, dressed in unrelieved black, and as always with his rough rock hammer strapped to his back and his bagiroca hanging heavily from his belt, Con was a warrior spoiling for a fight.

I could tell by the look in those golden eyes that he'd happily take that fight with me if I offered the opportunity. I toyed with the idea. I could needle him further to draw him into the argument he so clearly wanted.

No, I wouldn't give him that satisfaction. He had no business acting like the wounded party. He'd made me have to come to him, so it was up to him to make it up to me. As he'd yet to reply to me, I waited him out with cold expectation. He might have the strength to break me in half with those big hands if he chose, but politics were a familiar battleground for me and I knew how to wield my silences like a master.

"Perhaps, Your Highness," Con finally said in his smoke-ruined voice, gravelly and deep, "we should discuss the contents of this letter in private." He still held the envelope, not moving to open it, steady gaze on mine.

I jilted to a halt in my mental dance of triumph. I'd gained the upper hand by forcing him to speak first, but something was off. The beat of silence extended awkwardly while everyone waited on my reaction, their avid interest practically a scent in the air. Con and I were still new enough together that our protocols weren't well worked out. It didn't help that he'd turned out to be so obstinate about appearing in any formal capacity with me. Our public interactions were rare, frequently contentious, and apparently, endlessly fascinating to those around us.

When he'd first entered my court—had it only been a week? It seemed like forever ago—he'd requested a private audience and I'd used that impertinence as a weapon against him. No one had forgotten it, naturally. Then there'd been the very public argument over the Defense Council, which had added new fuel to the gossip wildfire. My court, ever lustful of new entertainment, watched all interactions between Con and me with gleeful anticipation of more juicy tidbits. I was loathe to fuel their hunger further.

The silence extended, this one not at all under my control.

Con still returned my gaze with wariness, the leashed violence in his posture betraying his agitation. That was nothing new. How much was aimed at me, however, I couldn't be sure. Great green Ejarat, why wouldn't he— With a sour crush of chagrin, I realized my error.

Con didn't read well. In my terrible mood and upset at Anure's promised retaliation—which was arguably entirely Con's fault—I'd forgotten about that. An unforgivable error, really, as Con couldn't read because he'd been ripped from life as crown prince of Oriel and forced to labor in the mines of volcanic Vurgmun.

Did he think I'd intended to humiliate him as payback for his various transgressions? Not that I was above such tricks, but I wouldn't use his past against him. I doubted Con knew that, however. I needed to resolve this détente immediately.

"Of course, husband," I said, as if no lapse had occurred. I added a coy smile and a flutter of lashes to distract our observers. The anticipation sighed out of my entourage, a breath of disappointment that there would be no fireworks to describe at the festivities of the Night Court.

I drew nearer to Con, watching his gaze fire with the hunger we had yet to sate between us. At least there was that. "You know I treasure time spent in private with you." I reached up and trailed my nails over the short, surprisingly silky hair of his dark beard, partly to make a show, partly to indulge myself—and partly to feel the thrumming tension of his response to me. A moment of perfect harmony shimmered into place. He closed his hand over mine in shared understanding, the hot, rough skin a reminder of his touch in more intimate places. I suddenly felt much better. Yes. Only sex, but at least there was that. "Leave us," I airily told the others.

We wouldn't be fully private, of course. Not unless we retired to our rooms, and even there I couldn't be certain. Anure's spies were everywhere, and even those loyal to me couldn't resist feeding their curious interest in us when they thought they could escape notice. As Calanthe's crown princess since my birth, and confirmed Her queen in my teens, I was accustomed to the constant attention. Con . . . not so much. The pervasive crowds made his skin twitch like a hunted animal's, his golden gaze going feral as he constantly scanned every movement for potential danger. Giving him the illusion of privacy would help calm him.

Indeed, he relaxed fractionally as my ladies politely herded everyone away, until only my adviser, Lord Dearsley, and Con's people remained. Kara and Sondra hung back, as if unsure if they should post a perimeter guard. I hadn't yet gotten a good read of General Kara. He hailed from Soensen, a realm that had fought more fiercely than most kingdoms, held out longer against Anure than many, and fallen the hardest because of it. The tall, dark-skinned, and rawhide-thin man had barely spoken two words to me without Con present.

Sondra would speak to me, though she didn't like me much. The warrior woman wore her pale-blond hair long and straight, always washed and brushed to a shine, although she paid no attention to any other part of her appearance. Ambrose did the opposite, making up for them all with his adoption of elegant attire. He stood beside Con, smiling genially, forest-green eyes alert with amusement, power shimmering around him with nearly palpable heat. The orchid on my hand shimmied its petals, as if coquettishly waving at him.

"You look very well in your garb as court wizard of Calanthe," I told Ambrose. I'd stepped back slightly from

Con, to give us some polite distance, but he retained hold of my hand, and I was unwilling to make a show of tugging it away, even if only in front of our closest advisers.

"Is that what that outfit is meant to be?" Con raised his brows dubiously, looking Ambrose up and down. "I thought maybe a night sky puked on you."

Behind me, Sondra snickered and Kara cleared his throat. Lord Dearsley, who'd been my father's adviser before me, and was easily three times my age, looked pained at Con's coarseness. Ambrose only cocked his head at Con, his raven familiar echoing the gesture with uncanny similarity. "Such petulance. I pity Queen Euthalia in having to deal with you. Lady Sondra, General Kara, I believe we're not wanted."

At last. Though Sondra and Kara didn't move until Con dipped his chin in permission. I wouldn't let their fealty to Con first and foremost annoy me. Much.

"What are Your wishes for me, Your Highness?" Dearsley inquired, bowing to me with pointedly elegant manners.

"Please see to any of the petitions that don't need My personal attention." The ones that did . . . who knew when I'd get to them? Every day I seemed to fall further behind. The grind of the intensifying nightmares and fretting about Anure's retaliation, on top of dealing with Con, made me inefficient and weary. Dearsley bowed again, more deeply than he had to, making a further point of showing respect, and departed.

"Walk with Me, Conrí," I said, moving away from the many hiding places of the dense flower beds and hedge mazes, and out to a semi-enclosed folly on the cliff overlooking the sea. With a short grass meadow all around, at least no one could hide close enough to overhear, and the surf against the rocks made for a decent noise screen.

Con strode beside me, scanning the area in his hyper-vigilant style, ever ready for the least hint of danger. It irritated me. He was the enemy who'd come to my island, cornered me, and manipulated me into this marriage. Effectively he'd conquered me and Calanthe both. I tried not to let that stick in my craw, as we were supposed to be allies now, but I couldn't so easily forget who posed the most immediate danger to everything I'd built and tried to protect. Con had a different agenda, and I harbored no illusions that he'd sacrifice Calanthe to get what he wanted.

"I don't think Anure will leap out of the bushes to attack," I said, more tartly than I'd intended.

"Forgive me if I take your safety seriously," he retorted. "I recall making vows to protect you."

I bit back a sigh, regretting my words, and my resentment. No matter how we'd begun, the two of us needed to find ways to agree, not argue. Besides, I was the jumpy one, feeling the press of the dread future and Anure's hot breath on the back of my neck. That had been true long before I even knew Con existed. "Thank you for that. Though My gardens are quite safe." I said it to reassure myself as much as him.

Con glanced down at me, a brow quirked meaningfully. "No venomous snakes in paradise, then?"

"Just Me," I replied. "I apologize for taking out My anger on you—and for My misstep in handing you the letter to read. I truly forgot. I did not intend to embarrass you." Not for his inability to read, anyway. I'd wanted to call him out for his absence in court, for all the ways he'd turned my life and rule upside down. I didn't often misfire that way. Except that I'd done it more often with Con than ever before. I had no idea what to make of that.

"I have thick skin," he replied, his rough voice softer.

We entered the folly, and he turned to face me, gaze going to my mouth. "It wasn't your fault—I should've said something." He paused, an odd expression on his face as he stared at me. "You look nice today," he said, as if that explained something.

I raised one brow at the non sequitur. "How poetic."

"Yeah." He snorted at himself, then frowned, thinking. "I mean, you look . . . gorgeous. And dangerous. Seeing you walk down that path, so beautiful and sexual—it made me stupid."

Unexpectedly, my heart fluttered with pleasure, despite his less-than-elegant phrasing. I'd heard plenty of flowery phrases, and that sort of court flattery rolled off me. Con's words struck me to the core, probably because he meant what he said. But I tried not to let him see how susceptible I could be to his compliments, how his heated attention melted the ice around my heart. I couldn't afford to be vulnerable to him or anyone right now. I had to be cold, sharp, and strategic if I was to save Calanthe. No room for weakness.

"Thank you," I replied, sounding far too stiff. To mitigate it, I added, "I was in a mood when I dressed this morning."

"Some presentiment of this?" he asked, holding up the missive from Anure. Not an idle question, either. Con was consumed with curiosity about my magic and nature—and I had yet to decide how much to tell him. My father would've said to tell Con nothing at all, that I had no reason to trust this man who cared nothing for Calanthe. A man who might use my secrets against me, if it served his revenge. Still, it hardly seemed like a workable plan to keep him in the dark with all we faced. Trust him or not?

I didn't know, so I said as little as possible.

Besides that, I didn't like to give voice to the forewarnings of death and destruction that plagued me nightly. The nightmares had gotten worse in the last few days, and that was saying something, as I'd already found them nearly unbearable. Then I'd begun to see omens of my own death in them, and that would be enough to unsettle anyone.

Con didn't know about the nightmares, and I intended to keep it that way. Something about the crashing and abandoned passion of sex with Con made our mornings-after strangely intimate. I was vulnerable in those moments before I'd armored myself for the day, my soft underbelly painfully exposed.

Con didn't seem to notice the effects of the dreams' tumult. I must sleep peacefully enough, only shaken and drenched in a cold sweat when I woke just before dawn. To keep him from noticing then, I'd established a routine to take advantage of the Morning Glory's imminent arrival. My ladies woke Con early and immediately spirited him out of my bed. He left thinking me still asleep, which gave me time to steady myself in the dreamthink. In that calming state of neither sleeping nor waking, I could find my center again, and rebuild the careful walls of thick ice that protected me.

If only I could banish the nightmares as easily as I ordered Con removed from my bed.

"Lia?" Con was studying me, trying to discern what I couldn't afford for him to see. "Is it only the letter, or is something else wrong—what aren't you telling me?"

"Isn't the letter enough?" So perceptive, Ejarat take the man. "Nothing else is wrong," I added. A mistake, as he looked even more unconvinced, so I shrugged, deliberately raising my breasts in order to distract him.

Sure enough, his gaze went to my bosom and rose

again to my mouth. He seemed to consider a moment, then tossed the letter onto the nearby bench. Facing me, he settled his hands on my waist, his grip firm and nearly encircling me, the heat burning through my gown. He studied my lips. "I'd kiss you but that stuff on your lips looks poisonous as any snake."

"While I'm sure you'd be charming with your masculine beauty highlighted here and there with a bit of color, I don't think this look would work smeared on your mouth." I'd meant to take control of this exchange, to be lightly taunting, but I'd gone breathless from the moment he touched me. The corset bones bit into my ribs as I reached for a deeper breath, my breasts feeling as if they swelled in the tight confines, my nipples peaking. "Don't look at Me like that, Con."

Dammit, I'd meant to chastise him, not make a breathless plea.

"Like this?" He took his time scanning me, that fulminous gaze wandering over me, his smile lazy and full of hunger. His eyes came back to mine still seeking to penetrate my masks. From the beginning he'd been able to see through me far too well. I was fighting a losing battle, trying to keep him at a comfortable emotional distance. Just as I'd lost the battle to get him off Calanthe. And now, here we were, dancing this high-stakes waltz together.

I returned the scrutiny, studying the strong-boned face, the eyes that should be brown but looked gold in most lights, the thick black brows and pitted skin. He wore his hair long and loose as usual, but it failed to soften him in the least. He looked dangerous, too, and sensual—and like he wanted to eat me alive. Ejarat help me, I was no longer just teasing him, but had grown warm with my own need. Tempting, to forget everything but wanting him. Something else I couldn't afford to do.

He shifted one big hand to the small of my back, and raised the fingers of the other to my throat, laying them on the pulse there. My heart thudded hard, so he no doubt felt it. "So lovely and cool on the surface," he murmured. He trailed his rough, callused fingers down my throat, then traced the upper curve of my breast beneath the lace ruff where the fabric met skin. "And volcanic beneath." A shiver ran through me, and he watched my face intently. "Are you angry or are you more—"

"Oh, I'm angry." No way I'd let him finish that question.

"At me—or at Anure?"

"It can be both," I tried to snap.

Making a tsking sound, he bent closer, lips grazing my ear. "I know I piss you off, but I'm not the villain Anure is."

"No, but you're closer and you—" I broke off as his teeth closed on my ear in a nip that arrowed straight to my groin.

"Not as close as I could be," he replied in a soft, meaningful growl.

"We have observers."

"I know." His words had a cryptic edge that gave me pause.

"What—" I gasped as his fingertip grazed my nipple beneath the bodice, then moaned when he pinched it. "Con . . ."

"They can't see this." Watching my face still, he slid his hand deeper into the cup of fabric, cupping my breast, his palm rough on my swelling nipple, a hint of a smile on his lips at my reaction. I was hard-pressed not to move in or yank away. He was testing me in some way, perhaps the extent of my anger and his. I'd only ever known sex with my ladies, which had always been a kind of tending, full of soothing caresses and gentle pleasure.

With Con, our fiery natures tended to fan the flames in the other. I wanted to rage at him in my fury, tear at him with my nails and teeth—and I wanted to cling to him, to take him inside of me and have him hold me safe from the world and Anure's threats. A distressing discovery about myself, and yet another development I didn't understand at all.

"Not now," I said, asserting control with a bit of desperation. I pulled away, collecting my thoughts and purpose again. He didn't protest, only examined his fingers, rubbing them together.

"I wondered how far down the makeup went," he said with a smile that passed for charming with him.

I gave him an incredulous look. "How can you flirt with Me at a time like this?" Never mind that I'd started it. But I'd done that to derail his line of questioning while he . . . Realization dawned. "You were deliberately distracting Me."

"You needed a moment to regroup."

When I only glowered, he continued. "In a pitched battle, even the best soldiers can lose perspective. They can get rattled, making emotional decisions instead of calculated ones. Taking a moment to regroup can tip that balance back."

Rattled. Struggling to regain the upper hand in the conversation—wondering how the hell I'd lost it—I reached for my usual icy reserve. "I am *not* one of your soldiers."

Tipping his head, he smiled slightly. "Fair enough." He nodded at the letter, all business again. "What does the Imperial Toad have to say?"

I snatched up the envelope, using the movement to adjust my bosom and make sure my dress covered me as intended, then flicked my nails to undo the intricate folds of the missive. It unfurled in my hands like a carnivorous blossom, but one gone gray from rot. Oddly enough, I felt better able to face it now. Which I would not give Con the satisfaction of admitting. I read aloud.

Darling Wilted Flower of My Wounded Heart,

Oh, My rosebud—or should I call you a crushed blossom? Used up, soiled, chewed, and devoured by the worst of dogs. I can only hope you suffer for betraying your vows, and with the one you promised to capture for Me, a traitor who dares call Me an upstart emperor of a false empire.

I feel confident you have many regrets, given that cur you married, and in a whore's gown. You'll never cleanse yourself of his taint, of your own guilt and perfidy, and Yilkay will never welcome you into the afterlife. On the bright side, you won't face the goddess's judgment for many years to come, because once I lay my hands on you—and that will be sooner than you think, My ruined former fiancée—I'll keep you alive and remind you hourly of how you hurt Me.

I'll purge you of your false loyalties by scouring your precious Calanthe until only bare rock remains. Then will you come back to live with Me, and you will give me what is Mine. Sooner than you think.

You could have been an empress. Instead you'll be skinned and shredded, then fed alive to my dogs.

All My fury,
His Imperial Majesty

Proud of myself for making it all the way through the vicious words without pause or my voice quavering in the least, I cast the thing aside. It lay there on the colorful silk pillows of the bench, fluttering in the sea breeze. If I'd had a dagger on me, I might've impaled the paper with it.

Con had begun idly pacing as I read and now stood, his back to me, hands folded behind him as he stared out at the sea. "He meant to frighten you," he said at last.

"Oh, do you think so?" I replied with hair-curling sarcasm.

He turned at last and looked at me, a different expression on his face than I'd expected. Not pity for my weakness, but a kind of compassionate respect. "Yes," he said simply. "More, I think he succeeded. There's no shame in being afraid, Lia."

I took a breath to retort, reaching for my pride and anger to shore up my shell of reserve. But his grave concern undid me, and I hiccuped instead. To my horror—and, yes, shame at my weakness—a small sob wrenched out of me.

"Here now." In a few strides, he had his arms around me again, pulling me close against him. Nothing sexual in it this time, no teasing, only comfort. And so help me, I clung to that solid strength as if he could save me. I wouldn't weep—my heart had long ago frozen too solid to allow for tears—but the emotions tore at me with claws of grief and rage and . . . fear. I was so afraid. And a queen couldn't afford fear.

"You're not alone, Lia. Everything will be all right," Con murmured. "I won't let any of that happen."

"This is your fault," I managed to say while clamping down on the sobs. And still I held on to him like he could keep me from being swept out to sea, though the coming storm was so much greater than either of us.

"His Imperial Nastiness never sent you horrible

letters before?" He sounded gently amused, rubbing his big hands up and down my back, strangely soothing.

"Of course he did." Oddly, I laughed. And it loosened the tightness in me. "And always awful." But Tertulyn and I had read them together, mocking them like girls pretending Anure's threats would never come to pass. Now Tertulyn had disappeared and I'd shared the letter with Con. This was the first time, I realized with a wave of disorientation, that anyone but she knew the things Anure wrote to me.

Con hadn't laughed. He'd understood how I felt, maybe even before I did.

"It's a horrifying letter. It got under my skin, and I've been through terrible things," he replied, holding me against him with unaccustomed gentleness, as if I might break.

"I shouldn't have read it in court," I said, admitting the error. "Normally, I read his letters in private." With a glass of wine or a generous pour of brandy to ease the pain.

"Why did you?"

With a sigh, I pulled away, determined to stand on my own feet. Calanthe depended on me. If I allowed myself to lean on a man who didn't care about Her, then She would fall with me if—when—he sacrificed us in his game of vengeance.

Con had crushed the netting at my bosom and I straightened it, thinking of how to defend my actions. I'd been in a foul mood, and seething with annoyance that Con refused to attend court, and furious with myself for even caring. It had also occurred to me that the missive might contain information I'd want to keep from Con. I didn't doubt he'd use Calanthe as a tool to get to Anure. "The messenger who brought it said that—"

"What messenger?" Con shot out the question, startling me. "Didn't the letter come by bird?"

"No. That style of envelope is too big for a bird to carry. The messenger came by ship from Yekpehr. He arrived just as court convened."

Con swore and strode to the edge of the folly, cupping one hand to focus his strained voice. "Kara!"

General Kara popped out from behind a tree at the edge of the meadow. Con gave him a series of hand signals—and the man saluted and ran off.

"What did you tell him?" I demanded. I hadn't known they could use signals like that—or that Kara was there—and I didn't like not knowing things. *Add it to the list*, a wry voice in my head suggested.

Con faced me again, eyes glinting with anger. "I sent him to the harbor to investigate and make sure all is secure."

"You knew he was there." No wonder he'd sounded cryptic, and knowing, when I warned him we had observers.

"Of course," Con growled. "You're guarded by my people at all times."

"I have guards," I pointed out with acid disdain.

"You have pretty boys and girls in fancy uniforms better for looking good than deflecting weapons."

"And I have My ladies," I added, "whom I seem to recall defeated you handily."

He curled his hands into fists, jaw tightening. "With magic."

"Well, yes." I smirked at him. "Not all weapons are made of metal."

"Magic alone can't protect you," he ground out. "You admitted that."

No denying that, curse it, so I acknowledged the point with a curt nod.

"I told you that I'd protect you, that my people would

help protect Calanthe, so why in great green Ejarat didn't you tell me a messenger from Anure had arrived?" He finished on a near roar.

I opened my mouth, but he plowed on, face taut. "For that matter, why the hell did your people let a boat through? We discussed this, that no new boats would be allowed into the harbor."

"Oh, we did not 'discuss,'" I hissed. "You issued an order. I modified it, since this is *My* kingdom."

"Then you put your kingdom in jeopardy, out of a foolish need to spite me."

"Don't pretend that you actually care about Calanthe," I fired back. "And I'm not stupid. I've been queen of Calanthe for years and kept Her safe *long* before you arrived to throw orders around as if you're My keeper."

He loomed over me. "You *need* a keeper, Lia," he snarled, emotion making his voice even rougher. "What if that had been an attack? No, you just welcome Anure's man with open arms."

"I. Know. The. Difference." I spaced out my words so they'd penetrate his thick skull. "Do you think I'm so oblivious that I can't tell a sloop from a battleship? That I can't discern a single, letter-carrying messenger from an attacking army? Because I assure you, I can. I captured *you*, after all."

"Through enchantment and trickery," he snarled through clenched teeth, clearly still sore about that one.

"Exactly," I replied, allowing myself a smile of triumph.

He glared back, white makeup smudges on his dark shirt from holding me. Which had been kind of him, and unexpectedly compassionate. And somehow we'd gone from that to battling each other once again. I took a moment to gather my composure. "Why are we fighting with each other?"

He raked a hand through his hair, looking past me with a grim expression. "I suppose because we can't yet kill the guy that deserves it."

"And never can."

"I will. Mark my words."

"You can issue arrogant proclamations all you like, but words are easy. Killing Anure is impossible."

He glared at me, incredulous. "If you believe that, then what are we even doing?"

"I ask Myself that hourly."

Setting his teeth, he spoke through them. "Why did you agree to marry me and work as a team to defeat Anure if you never believed we could win?"

"I had no choice, did I?" I bit out in the same tone. "Marrying you was the only viable option amid far worse choices."

"But you did make that choice," he pointed out grimly. "So why not work with me on this?"

"Because you're hotheaded and reckless," I spat.

"That may be true, but it's worked for me so far, sweetheart."

Our glares meshed, simmering between us. For a moment I thought he might kiss me after all. Then, when he didn't, I kicked myself for feeling disappointed.

Instead, he took a step back, hooking his thumbs in his thick belt and drumming his fingers. "I interrupted you before," he said in a neutral tone, as if the argument hadn't occurred. "Why did you read Anure's missive in court when you usually read the letters alone?"

I stuck with the most innocuous truth. "The messenger said that it contained news about Tertulyn."

Con frowned, and I took it for confusion. "My oldest

friend," I clarified. "My first lady-in-waiting, who has been missing these last days."

"I remember who she is. What I don't understand is why a ruler as savvy as you are hasn't figured out that Tertulyn was a spy who fled to Anure."

I laughed. An absurd suggestion. *Or was it?* "That is the last thing she'd do."

"The two of them clearly have been playing you."

"You're wrong. Tertulyn would never betray Me. She's My *friend*."

"Or she was Anure's spy, planted to keep you on his hook all this time."

"How was she recruited then?" I countered. "Tertulyn never even met the emperor." Though she had frequented the Night Court without me, so she would've have had opportunity to meet with other spies. Except that didn't bear considering because Tertulyn simply wouldn't betray me. *Would she?*

"I don't know," Con answered in a neutral tone. "I don't need to know those details. They're irrelevant."

"The details are not irrelevant, because those are the pieces you're missing," I insisted. I would not let him plant his doubts in my heart. "You're new to Calanthe, and you don't understand. Tertulyn and I were children together. Until recently, never a day passed that I didn't see her on waking, that I didn't retire to her good nights." And sometimes retire with her, as Tertulyn had always been solicitous of me, and generous in giving me pleasure or comfort as I needed. I wouldn't tell Con that. It was private and he didn't need to know that Tertulyn was the one person in the world I'd called friend, who'd loved me for the person I was, not the crown I wore. No, she couldn't have been a spy. I would have known. Surely I couldn't have been blind to something like that.

Con studied me as I spoke, discerning what I hadn't said. "Anure visited Calanthe."

"Only once. My father took care of that."

"Once is enough," Con pointed out with relentless logic, "if you need proof that they could've met."

"So your theory is that he somehow managed to get Tertulyn alone and subverted My dearest friend into only pretending to love Me, so she could one day disappear. Not much of a long game."

"Anure left Calanthe engaged to you, yes?"

"Betrothed. I was only twelve, Con. Far too young to be formally engaged."

"You're mincing words."

"No, it's a vital difference. Betrothal is a promise of engagement. I was never Anure's fiancée, no matter what you or he may believe."

"It's not an important difference for this conversation. Anure left your island believing he'd eventually make you his empress. Why *wouldn't* he leave a spy behind to ensure that everything happened according to his plan?"

"Of course he has spies. I just know Tertulyn wasn't one." I lifted my chin, aware of my eroding position as Con gave me an exasperated look.

"Lia, I know you don't trust me, so—"

"Just like you don't trust Me."

He didn't acknowledge that and forged on. "—so you don't want to tell me much about your magic. But you admitted before that you are connected to Calanthe, that you sense the birds and fishes."

"True," I replied. No sense denying that, but I wouldn't elaborate if I could help it. My father had always been so adamant that I shouldn't talk about my nature and abilities. *If people guess, from the old stories, so be it. But we don't need to hand them power over you and Calanthe.*

"Can you sense the people on Calanthe, too?" he asked, watching my expression with keen attention. I suspected very few people could get away with lying to him. I probably could—I have a deft hand at it—but I decided not to.

"Yes." No need to admit to the rather glaring exceptions to that ability.

"Then is Tertulyn on Calanthe?" he persisted with relentless logic. "You should know."

I hesitated—and visibly so, curse it—because he immediately spotted it, gaze sharpening like a wolf on the scent. Bright Ejarat, I should've been able to spin a lie without thinking. This being vulnerable to someone confused me on many levels. Con had neatly trapped me in this, too. I'd have to admit to this blind spot in my abilities, something I'd really hoped to keep from him a bit longer.

"How about we agree to something?" Con said, gently enough that his voice lost its rough edge, and I could hear how it might have been before the toxic fumes in the mines robbed him. "Instead of lying to me, just say you're not going to answer. That way I'm only fighting my own ignorance, not deliberate misdirection."

I firmed my lips over several replies. He waited me out, a mocking glint in his eyes challenging me to deny it. "Agreed." I really hated that he was right. I'd asked him to use his brutality and ruthlessness to help me save Calanthe. I had to trust him far enough to do that. But not so far that I didn't keep a close eye on his plans—nor would I relinquish my power to him. "I'll answer, but you must promise to keep this a secret."

I'd have liked to ask him not to use the knowledge against me, but ha to that.

To my surprise, he went down on one knee, lifted the black netting at my hem, and kissed it. He looked up at me, the golden flecks in his eyes catching the light like the sun glinting on the sea. "Euthalia, my queen and lady wife, I swear to keep your secrets as my own." His hand slipped under my skirt to caress the spot high on the back of my thigh where he knew a pattern of golden bark and spring leaves twined over my skin. He'd traced it with his tongue the night before, a sensation my body remembered distractingly well. "I promised this already," he continued, pointedly stroking the marks that revealed my nature, "since your secrets protect you. But I ask you to think about this: What about Tertulyn, who knows so much about you?"

Somehow that hadn't occurred to me. My ladies all knew something of what I hid beneath the heavy makeup and elaborate clothing. But Tertulyn knew the most of anyone. Here I'd been so worried about what Con might do with my secrets when I might already be doomed. All because of a woman I'd thought was my friend.

3

Lia's crystal-clear gaze rested on me, in astonishment at my vow and gesture—good for me, that I surprised her—and in dawning horror as she followed my meaning. She sagged a little, and I firmed my grip on her leg, in case she fainted.

But my Lia wasn't the fainting type. Still, she glanced at the bench with longing. "Why don't you sit?" I stood and took her hand to guide her to it.

She resisted. "I can't sit." She sounded annoyed about it, too, and gestured at her elaborate gown. "I'm dressed for court," she added, as if that explained anything.

"You sit on your throne," I said, not understanding at all, and she threw me a look I figured meant she pitied how dense I could be. Fortunately, as much as my idiocy about everything to do with the formal customs of Calanthe irritated me, I had no illusions about my failings that way. "You're going to have to explain things to me, Lia. I think I've proved myself an eager student of your other lessons," I added, reminding her of how much she'd already taught me in bed—and how much we both enjoyed it.

It was the right thing to say—despite Ambrose's wry insults, I was getting better at finding honeyed words for courting—and for the first time that day, Lia smiled at me with some of the genuine warmth of the woman inside the queen. "My ladies help Me sit," she answered on a sigh.

I moved behind her. "All right, what do I do?"

She glanced up, over her shoulder at me, clearly astonished. "You don't mind?"

"Why would I?"

"I know that you . . . think the Calanthean styles are frivolous."

Ah. They were, compared with what I'd known. I didn't want her to think she couldn't ask me for help, though. Whatever I could do to get her to stop seeing me as the enemy. "So, I pull this fluffy bit to the side?"

She muffled a laugh. "Yes, and then sweep that section smooth, and hold this part out."

I did, and she sat with a tiny but grateful moan. "These shoes are not meant for standing in for very long." She toed off the offending slippers. With their pointed ends and jeweled heels that looked more like rapier tips than anything meant to support body weight, I wasn't surprised.

I sat beside her. Then on impulse picked up her silk-stocking-clad feet, propped them on my knee, and started massaging them. The memory flooded back of my father doing this for my mother during family time after balls and receptions. She'd sat with her feet on his lap and he'd rubbed them as they dissected how the event had gone.

It was the right thing to do—I was on a roll—because Lia groaned. She sounded like she did during sex, which had the same arousing effect on me, and she closed her eyes. She had feet as lovely as the rest of her, soft and well tended, her unadorned toenails gleaming through the sheer material, looking like petals from those roses, in all shades from white to bloodred.

"Thank you," she murmured, a note of surprise in it. Then she narrowed her eyes, the elaborate fake lashes nearly screening their glint. "Why are you being nice to Me?"

"I'm your husband. We're supposed to be good to each other." I didn't tell her about my father, but I liked remembering that my parents had loved each other. Not that I deluded myself about my own marriage. Still, there was a lot of ground between a loving marriage and wanting to kill each other—surely we could find *something* in the middle. "And you've had a rough morning," I said instead. "As to your clothes . . . Yeah, it's true I like you better naked, but I get it. I have my armor, you have yours."

Her eyes opened wider as she considered me. "That's exactly how I think of it." She seemed surprised that I understood. "All right," she said, seeming to come to a decision. "The reason I don't know whether Tertulyn is on Calanthe or not is because she isn't from here. She's from Keiost." Lia arched one elegant black brow, the diamond at the point winking as it lifted, and she paused to add significance to the information.

Aha. I took a moment to think through the ramifications. "You only sense people born on Calanthe?"

"Not just people—any living creature—and not just *on* the island, but for some distance around Her. And I know what you're thinking: You are correct that I'm not able to feel where you and your people are." She dipped her chin, acknowledging that she'd handed me a potential weapon. One I might've used against her when I arrived on Calanthe bent on conquest, had I known. Then she smiled, both sweet and lethal. "Though I am able to discern a great deal through other sources."

"You're a scary lady," I commented, leaving it at that.

"But you didn't 'discern' where Tertulyn went—through these 'other sources'?"

"I was otherwise occupied at the time," she replied in the driest of voices, reminding me of the chaos of that afternoon that resulted in our wedding, and the frenzy to plan a party to cover the truth. How we'd spent that night. "And I didn't suspect anything. It never occurred to Me that she might disappear so completely. I only thought she couldn't bear to see Me married and apparently celebrating it."

Lia let out a small sigh of regret, the sound the barest hint of the heartbreak that might go deeper than I'd suspected, a crack in that carefully maintained armor. Lia had held Tertulyn in great affection—and Tertulyn had clearly exploited that blind spot, using and abusing Lia's trust. At least Lia was finally willing to discuss Tertulyn's disappearance. It seemed so obvious to me that Tertulyn had been in a position to know everything about Lia and report on it, and also to subtly influence how Lia viewed Anure. If I pushed on this, though, I risked alienating Lia, again. Better to storm this particular fortress from a different direction.

"Tell me more about how being 'otherwise occupied' affects you," I suggested. Her expression shuttered in that forbidding way I'd come to recognize. "Your ability to sense what happens on Calanthe could be critical in the days ahead," I explained. "I need to know your limitations. If you have any."

She didn't smile at that, instead sighing and tilting her head subtly one way, then the other. Releasing tension from her neck without disturbing the wig and crown, I realized. "I have to be able to concentrate," she said in a quiet voice. She really hated admitting to any weakness, I could tell, and could sympathize with. "The farther something is from My physical location, the more focus I need. It's best when I'm all alone, in the quiet. Ideally, I need to be awake but not thinking."

I frowned, confused. "How does that work?"

"I call it the dreamthink." She hesitated again, this time as if she expected me to laugh or scoff. When I only listened, she continued. "It's easiest when I first wake up—I can kind of drift? And then the sights and sounds of Calanthe come to Me vividly, like taking an inventory of My body."

"Hmm." I considered that. Not that I knew anything about magic. "Did your father teach you to do that?"

She shook her head. "No. He could access Calanthe, I think through the orchid ring, but in a different way than I can." She studied the blossom on her finger. "I'm having to learn on My own."

"Sounds difficult."

Her crystal eyes rose to mine, wary and uncertain. "Yes? And no. I think . . . I think the orchid is trying to help Me learn." Another sigh. "For a really long time, I tried not to listen to it. When it transferred to Me, my father had just died. I was only sixteen, betrothed to a monster, swamped with grief, and . . . I felt so very alone."

I held her feet in a reassuring grasp. She'd never opened up to me like this before. I nearly said I thought we could grow to love each other, as my parents had, but it seemed unlikely that we'd have the time—and an impetuous declaration like that might just put her walls up again. "You're not alone anymore, Lia. We're bound to each other, forever." I braced for a cutting reply, but she gazed back at me with eyes full of doubt.

"We don't work well together," she finally said.

"'Two bulls in a small pen,'" I replied, quoting Brenda with a grimace.

To my surprise, Lia laughed, a musical sound, like well-tuned chimes. "I didn't think you'd heard that particular quip."

"More than once. And there's truth in it. We both like to be the one giving the orders."

"In My case, it's more than liking it—I have a responsibility to put Calanthe first."

"Yeah, but that doesn't mean we can't make decisions in harmony."

"It does mean that if what you want goes against Calanthe's best interests."

True. I didn't get her single-minded devotion to a piece of land, but I respected it. "We can balance our decisions—take both sides into account."

"At least after fighting it out first," she commented wryly.

"I'm willing to try if you are."

She considered me. "As long as you're ready to be a graceful loser. No withdrawing to sulk."

I winced. "Fine. I'll try. But you agree to listen to my side. *Really* listen," I emphasized when she opened her mouth to argue.

She closed her mouth again, then smiled sweet as honey. "I'll try," she mimicked.

Laughing, I squeezed her feet. "Fair enough. Here's some practice: I think Tertulyn betrayed you and left the island."

"She could be hurt or dead," Lia countered with that regal calm I'd begun to identify as one of her weapons. "Have you considered *that* possibility?"

"If so, wouldn't you have sensed it? She'd be here on Calanthe, so you'd know. Unless you haven't concentrated and looked for her."

Her mouth firmed in unhappy acknowledgment of my logic. "I've looked."

"Had Tertulyn's behavior changed at all recently?" I asked, feeling my way carefully. This tentative agreement and conversational territory held hidden vurgsten charges that could explode in my face.

"You mean, since we heard that the terrible Slave King and his marauding armies had razed the city of her birth and were on the way to do the same to Calanthe?" She deliberately employed a tone of cool amusement, her gaze dagger-sharp.

"We didn't raze Keiost. The rumors of my brutality have been exaggerated." I caressed her foot in demonstration, drawing a quirk of a smile from her.

"My point is, we didn't know that. Everyone was upset and feared the worst. So no, she didn't do anything different than . . ." She trailed off, a rare line forming between her brows.

"Something?" I prompted.

"Maybe nothing."

"But . . ."

"But I'd had her watching Syr Leuthar, Anure's emissary, that day I had you, Sondra, and then Ambrose brought to Me for private audiences. She fell asleep and failed to warn Me in time—and Leuthar saw Ambrose with Me when I'd hoped to keep him hidden."

I didn't say anything. If one of my own people had failed in such a critical assignment, I would not have been forgiving.

"She was exhausted," Lia said, as if I'd argued aloud. "I was annoyed with her, yes, and surprised at the lapse, but we'd been under pressure and I'd been asking a great deal of her."

I nodded. Lia's brows forked down in a true frown. "Ejarat take you, Con. I know what you're thinking."

"That taking a nap sounds like a flimsy excuse to fail you in a way that served Anure's purposes?"

She looked away, her mouth tight.

"How about this?" I decided to push, since we'd gotten this far. "That letter from Anure quotes what I said at our wedding toast. I called him an upstart emperor of a false empire."

"Without clearing it with Me."

"And I never will. I don't expect you to, either. Neither of us has to get permission from the other. We can fight it out in private after."

She gave me an arch look and one of her eloquent silences, but I caught the amusement in her eyes. "My point is," I continued, "someone who was there told Anure what I said. Odds are, that same person also mentioned what you wore."

"It could've been anyone."

"It could've been Tertulyn." I returned her frustrated gaze with even calm, willing her to consider the truth. "I'm sure it's painful to contemplate, but you're too intelligent to let emotion interfere with reason."

She pulled her feet out of my grasp and pivoted. I braced for the backlash, but she only blew out a long breath, putting her hands to her lower back and arching into a stretch. "What happened to My man of few words?" she muttered, almost to herself.

"Well, Jeaneth has been healing my lungs and throat," I volunteered. "It's easier to talk now."

She threw me a mirthless glance. "All right, let's suppose your wild speculations are correct: Tertulyn was a spy and she disappeared because she went to Anure. If so, we face utter disaster. She knows *everything* about Me, as you so astutely pointed out. I can only imagine how Anure would exploit that knowledge." She straightened, practically layering steel into her spine. "I need to consult My advisers."

"And you'll convene the Defense Council. We can plan this war." Not a question.

"Yes. But *I* make the final decisions. I won't let you jeopardize Calanthe, Con. No matter what." She reached for her shoes, the stiff corset making her lean awkwardly.

"Let me." I snagged the delicate heels and slipped them onto her slender feet, then eyed her. "Calanthe is already in jeopardy," I pointed out.

"I know that. But it's My duty to do my utmost to protect Her, whatever the cost."

"I know that," I echoed mildly. "But we're better off in some ways. Tertulyn revealing your nature to the Imperial Toad could play into our favor."

"Enlighten Me." She had a dry way of saying that, and I figured she demolished impetuous courtiers with that tone. Not me. Not much, anyway.

"We can make strategic choices because we know what Anure wants now."

"Haven't we always known that?" she asked in a patient tone that wasn't patient in the least. "He wants Me and Calanthe."

I shook my head. "No, he wants *you*. He promised to destroy everything *but* you. This is good."

Her lovely mouth dropped open in astonishment. "Good? How can this possibly be *good*?"

I wasn't explaining myself well. "Lia, you are a beautiful woman, but there are other beautiful women in the world."

She pursed her glossy black lips. "Why, darling Conrí,

you'll turn my head with such lavish compliments. Do go on."

I gave her a narrow look for her sarcasm. "Let me walk you through the logic as I see it. Why do you work so hard to keep your nature a secret?"

She started to snap out a reply, but paused. After a moment of consideration, she said, "My father taught Me to. He said that if Anure ever found out, he'd stop at nothing to have Me."

"And yet he betrothed you to Anure."

"As a deception. Make him think he had what he wanted without actually giving it to him."

"Why didn't Anure insist on taking you with him?"

"I was only twelve."

"We're talking about Anure—he's done far worse than marry a twelve-year-old girl."

She stared through me, her canny mind clicking through a history she'd known so well she hadn't examined it closely. "Because I was not yet Queen of Calanthe."

"And?"

"I didn't have the orchid ring."

I nodded. "The Abiding Ring."

"I remember you and Ambrose calling it that before, when you first arrived on Calanthe."

"Because it's mentioned in the prophecy." When she raised her elegant brows in patent scorn, I added, feeling more than a little defensive. "We talked about it, when we discussed getting married."

"You mean, when you invaded My private chambers and held Me captive until I agreed to marry you?"

"I didn't exactly hold a knife to your throat," I muttered, though she had a point.

"Whatever." She waved that off. "I didn't pay attention

to your talk of prophecies because I dismissed it as another ploy."

I'd thought the same about Ambrose, more than once. "I'm not much for prophecies myself. But it's come true." I cleared my throat and recited.

"Take the Tower of the Sun,
"Claim the hand that wears the Abiding Ring,
"And the empire falls."

She gazed at me, her face a mask of perfect calm, but her eyes betrayed her turbulent thoughts. "Ah. Now I discern the reason for your determination to marry Me."

Shit. "It wasn't—"

She stopped me with an upraised hand, black and white nails flashing with lethal grace, all hint of emotion skillfully hidden under her icy calm. "No, Con. You need not explain. I never deluded Myself that you harbored any but the most mercenary intentions toward Me."

I set my teeth, wanting to chew my own tongue off. But I couldn't deny the truth of that. Besides, she and I were the same that way. We'd entered into this marriage with open eyes, closed hearts, and a common goal. Still, I needed to say *something* . . . "Lia, I—"

"So"—she spoke over me with crisp speed—"it's salient strategically that Anure wants to capture Me, and we can assume he wants to exploit My nature and the orchid ring for some purpose of his own."

"Yes." I allowed the diversion. Really, what more was there to say? "Do you have any idea for what?"

She shook her head slightly, but her gaze remained opaque, hiding something. "Why didn't Anure force the issue once I ascended to the throne and had the ring?"

"I don't know. Because you've cleverly held him at bay?"

"Ha! Nice try." A bitterness laced the edge of her voice, making me want to kick myself for carelessly shattering the fragile trust we'd built. She might've shuttered her gaze, but the line of her jaw, clear and sharp, showed her tension, the fear she'd nearly set aside for a while.

"Anure wants *you*. Intact. That's important."

"Is it?" She raised a dubious brow.

"Yes. And it's useful to know that he wants you frightened and off balance."

"Forgive Me if I'm not reassured."

"He doesn't know you," I told her, reaching for words. I couldn't explain my complicated feelings about her and our marriage, but I could give her this. "You're no fragile flower. He might bluster, but you're stronger than he is."

"I'm well aware of My strengths, and My limitations."

"You have me," I said, wishing I could vow something more. "I have ideas, and this letter helped refine them. When I promised we'd be stronger together, I meant it."

"I know you meant it." She seemed about to say more—probably something biting about how my meaning something didn't make it true—but she didn't. Instead, she moved to stand. I got to my feet, offering her a hand in assistance. After a slight hesitation, she took it. Then I did my best to adjust the back of her skirt, fluffing the useless bit of ruff at her rear end so it looked more or less like it had before. She watched me all the while with that cool bemusement.

I took up the letter and made to give it to her, catching the slight moment of revulsion as she flinched from it. "Any reason to keep this?" I asked, pulling it back.

Her eyes flew up to mine. I glimpsed the fear in them again that she'd buried beneath the icy calm, and something else. Sorrow? Defeat? "No. We know what it says. Destroy it."

"As my lady commands." This was something I could do for her.

I felt like a boy again in that moment, back in Oriel when the bits of vurgsten we carried in our pockets were for sparkle and show, all to impress the girls. I pulled out a striker, clicking it to impact the embedded vurgsten and holding the letter against it. It exploded with a flash and a *bang!* that made Lia jump and exclaim, then press her hand to her heart as a startled laugh escaped her. I grinned back at her. The paper leapt into flame, bright heat and sulfurous fumes billowing. I held it as long as I could, then released it to the sea breeze, watching as the small comet of it wafted away and dissolved into ash.

She watched it go with a look of satisfaction, some of her tension burned away with it. "Thank you. That feels better."

"Worked for me, too." I pocketed the striker, shaking the burn away. "Lia, about the prophecy and our getting married, I—"

"Did you burn your hand?" Her gaze had gone to my flicking fingers.

"It's nothing."

But she took my hand in hers, turning it over. I nearly pulled away, embarrassed for her to see. The skin of my hands in particular is forever stained with the ash of Vurgmun. Black soot is ground into the cracks, the skin gnarled and rough as the rock embedded in my pores.

"Thick-skinned," she noted, repeating what I'd said earlier. Her gaze lifted to mine, the blue-gray of her eyes softer in that stark black-and-white frame.

"Yes. The trouble with thick skin is it makes me insensitive. I don't notice the burn until the damage is done."

Her perfectly painted lips quirked in wry understanding. Then she dropped my hand and drew on her imperious manner like a cloak. "Walk with Me—and explain these ideas. How are we stronger together?"

Recognizing that as a peace offering, I gave her my arm and she took it, though she might as well have been a whiff of mist against me, and I escorted her back to the palace. "When you married me, you gained access to vurgsten, too. We have powerful weapons to use against Anure. And knowing he wants you intact gives us an advantage."

"You're dancing around your meaning. Explain," she commanded, in her casually imperious way.

Sawehl help me that I found that so . . . enticing about her. And that I admired how she still refused to admit that she'd been as frightened as enraged when she sought me out. She'd come to me, though, and that was something, too, despite everything else.

"Basic war strategy," I told her. "If we know what the enemy wants, we can draw him out of his fortress. Wanting something—particularly if it's obsessive, and Anure is nothing if not obsessive—will make his focus narrow on just that. He tends to forget about everything that's not his target. We'll know what he's aiming for, which means we can lay a trap and destroy him."

"And you'll bait this trap with Me."

"It could be worse."

"How?"

"For the last few days, I've been trying to figure how to keep Anure from simply surrounding Calanthe with battleships and barraging us with vurgsten until we were all dead or too broken to fight when he landed his troops to finish the job."

"No wonder you have such a morose nature," she replied, "with such thoughts."

I flicked a glance at her, unable to tell if she was teasing. I cleared my throat. "My point is that now I know he won't attack us that way, because he wants you intact. That's helpful information."

"I'm so relieved to be useful."

I laughed, and she made a little snarling sound in the back of her throat. I stroked her hand. "The point is, we can plan now. Before we meet with your Defense Council, I need to confer with my commanders. Get their take. If you agree," I added belatedly.

She signaled to another of her ladies-in-waiting, Calla, lingering decoratively on the path ahead. "Lady Calla, inform Conrí's commanders that they should meet us in My private courtyard, please. In a bit, I'll require Dearsley, Brenda, and Percy. Ask them to be ready to enter at My summons."

"Not Agatha, Your Highness?" Lady Calla asked.

Lia raised one brow. "The weaver?"

"Begging Your pardon, Your Highness, but Agatha seemed useful to You at the last . . . session." Calla's eyes slid to me and away again. Huh.

"Very well, give Agatha the option to attend if she's interested."

Calla curtsied and glided off, and we turned at the next fork, Lia guiding.

"Thank you for accommodating me," I offered, feeling stupid about what I was trying to say.

"I can be reasonable," she replied in a tone that was anything but. "*If* you communicate with Me."

Ah. She'd tossed me a treat for behaving well. So be it. "So noted. I'm happier with us *communicating*, too."

She snorted softly at my emphasis. "Does this mean you'll stop pacing My gardens like a caged wolf?"

Had I been pacing like a caged wolf? Probably. I'd felt like one. "I thought it would be better for me to stay away from court. I know I screwed up."

"Hmm. Nevertheless," she said without moving her lips as a group of approaching courtiers bowed to her elaborately—and gave me the side eye. Once they passed, she continued, "Avoiding Me solves nothing. We need to present a united front."

I sighed. First Ambrose nagging me, then Lia. "I'll attend stuff when I can. Unless I'm busy."

"Truly busy," she qualified. "No excuses. No *lies*." She scraped one long nail along the back of my hand as she hissed the word *lies*, underscoring our agreement.

"I don't lie," I said simply. "I don't have it in me."

"Why do you say it that way?" She relaxed her nail and glanced up at me, her gaze penetrating.

"What way?"

She considered. "As if something you once had was lost."

As from the first moment she laid eyes on me, she saw through me, right to the hollow core. But I guess she needed more from me, words to make up for my clumsy remarks earlier.

"I did lose . . . everything. The mines . . ." I had to clear my throat. I focused on the walled garden ahead, one of Lia's palace guards opening the inset wooden door and bowing us in. Once we were inside, I spotted the flowering tree with its elaborately weeping branches, and the bench beneath where Lia had awaited me the first time we'd been alone. It seemed much longer ago than a week. But it hadn't been, so no wonder we were essentially still strangers. A big step up from enemies, anyway.

I took a breath, knowing I needed to get through

this. "Vurgmun killed everything human in us, Lia. You should know that. We look like people, but we're not. We're empty inside."

"Surely there's something." She spoke as fluidly and elegantly as always, but with a slight scratch in her voice, as if bothered by what I'd said.

I searched for words. "Yes: the craving for revenge."

She was quiet, assimilating that. "Nothing else?"

The door opened again, admitting Sondra, Kara, and Ambrose. In Sondra's and Kara's eyes, I saw the reflection of the same hollow core I felt in myself, and that same quality of burning rage that consumed all other thoughts and feelings. When the fire of revenge animating us burned out at last, we'd collapse into ash.

"Conrí?" Lia spoke my name gently. She tapped my hand with her nail, and I realized I hadn't replied to her question. I tried to smile at her and couldn't. Whatever she saw in my face put a faint line between her brows.

"What news?" Sondra asked, the burning in her a bright and needy thing. "Do we have movement?"

I nodded, watching Ambrose, his knowing expression saying everything. The sun hit the faceted emerald on his staff, scattering shards of light against Merle's underbelly, giving him an eerie cast. The prophecy's words echoed in my head, as if by speaking them aloud to Lia, I'd given them even greater power.

Take the Tower of the Sun,
Claim the hand that wears the Abiding Ring,
And the empire falls.

That hand now rested on my arm, with the orchid ring flamboyantly fluttering in an unfelt breeze. The true chill of the prophecy struck a dark foreboding in me, and I finally understood the true import of knowing the extent of Anure's obsession, and why I'd needed Lia. By claiming her hand in marriage, I possessed what Anure would jeopardize his empire to seize.

I'd searched for it all this time, a way to draw Anure out of his fortress, an opening to destroy him and his empire. The price had been irrelevant. I'd long since stopped caring about what happened to me. I'd always been resigned to the truth that, in the end, I'd happily destroy myself in order to take Anure with me.

Now I knew I'd have to risk destroying Lia, too. All my promises to protect her were as empty as my blackened soul. She'd called me a caged wolf, and she was more right than she knew. A trapped animal can never be trusted.

4

Con's people formed a circle around him, listening intently as he related the essence of the vile missive from Anure. I marked the way he neatly summarized our extended conversation—probably the longest one we'd ever had—what he included, what he omitted. Staying silent allowed me to play observer, to note the emotional undercurrents among Con, Lady Sondra and General Kara. Calanthe had received refugees from all over the forgotten empires, and I'd made a study of people from many cultures, but these three posed new riddles.

Focusing on them kept me from dwelling on the jagged emotions that sliced at me from the inside out. And accommodating his request to speak with his commanders first both built goodwill between us and gave me a moment to get myself under control.

Shoving down the tumult of unexpected feelings with ruthless determination, I poured ice over the fear, anger, the gnawing pain of Tertulyn's possible betrayal and my role in the prophecy. Ridiculous to feel stung over that. I'd always known Con only cared about revenge and that marrying me had been another rung on that ladder.

Emotion would get me nowhere. I found myself shamed that Con had seen it necessary to remind me of that. I needed to focus on being rational, analytical. Dispassionate. Now more than ever.

So, we both liked the sex. A perk. And yes, Con's point that we could be good to each other instead of tearing at each other was only practical. I'd be a fool to think the passion and occasional understanding we shared meant anything more than that. I hadn't gone into this wanting more than that.

Con had completed his summary, Kara and Sondra firing questions at him. Ambrose had tipped back his head to watch some lilac songbirds fly over. He remained a cipher to me, in keeping with a wizard's nature. His playful attitude was as much a part of his disguise as the sunny curls, canny green eyes, and youthful face. None of that fooled me, as the glow of his power couldn't be easily hidden from my sight. Even if the orchid ring didn't react to his presence with the floral equivalent of girlish giggles and flirtation, I'd have sensed the ancient being disguised by the wizard's boyish mask. I hadn't encountered anyone with his level of power before. Studying him—and the orchid ring's reactions to him—had given me new insights into magic in general, and my own nature. I wanted to ask the wizard questions, but hesitated to reveal the exact boundaries of what I did and didn't know. Ambrose and I treated each other as allies, but—just as with Con—I reserved suspicion in case things proved otherwise. After all, the wizard had made no secret of his own fascination with the orchid ring, and he owed his loyalty to Con. He might be my court wizard in name, but he belonged to Con. Also, from what Con had revealed about the prophecy, I now knew Ambrose had manipulated me for his own ends. I'd do well to remember that.

Thus far Ambrose and I had executed a careful dance around each other. I felt sure he could see more of my own true nature than the non-magical could, but perhaps not the full extent of it. Likewise, he had to know I saw beyond who he pretended to be, but even I wasn't sure what to make of what my senses told me.

All I had to go on was my father's advice on the subject. *Treat a wizard like a fish with a scorpion's tail and with a jewel in its mouth.* Grasp the fish too tightly and it might drop the jewel to be lost forever. Too loosely and the fish escapes your hold. Annoy it, and face the sting. That was all I knew. How I wished I had someone to give me advice.

Or someone to talk to that I could trust to be on my side. Con wanted me to confide my secrets and inner thoughts, but . . .

I didn't know. I enjoyed his attempts at kindness, rubbing my aching feet—who'd have guessed the rough man had such an intuitive touch?—comforting me in my unreasonable fears. I also found myself wanting to open to that, like Ejarat turning her face to Sawehl's sun, Her soil thawing under His nourishing rays.

But kindness could be a lie. I'd grown up around countless courtiers who employed apparent kindness as a tool in their social arsenal. When I was a girl, I'd been fooled a time or two, and discovered the manipulation too late. My father had simply pointed out the lesson and suggested I learn what he called the Rule of Suspicion. *Be suspicious first, but especially of kindness. People rarely offer anything without wanting something in return,* he'd say. *The trick is learning what they want, then deciding if the trade is worth it.*

I'd discovered that very rarely was I willing to give what they wanted, especially in exchange for a temporary and shallow kindness.

In all truth, I preferred prickly animosity like Lady

Sondra's. She and I had de-escalated from outright hostility, but not much beyond. Still, she was honest and I didn't have to spend effort sorting beneath the surface for her true motivations. I didn't begrudge Lady Sondra her resentment—she thought I didn't have Con's best interests at heart and she'd be correct. I couldn't put my husband before Calanthe.

I thought I'd learned my lesson, learned the Rule of Suspicion well. Except for Tertulyn. I'd accepted her kindness to me at face value. Our friendship had been a clean well I drank from, because I thought she'd never wanted anything more than the affection we'd shared.

Con's insistence that Tertulyn had simply manipulated me as everyone else attempted to do . . . Well, I prided myself on facing truth with unflinching and open eyes. I did not allow myself delusions. I couldn't afford to.

I had to face the possibility that Tertulyn had never been my friend, not if she worked for Anure. All those occasions she'd encouraged me to laugh at the emperor's horrible letters, to rest easy that he'd never make good on his threats to retrieve me—had that all been to lull me into complacency? Her kindness and caring, the small gestures of affection that had meant so much, all could've been designed to manage me, to discover more about my nature. How carefully she'd marked the changes in my body as I matured, the evidence of my elemental nature shifting and evolving. How *interested* she'd been—in me, and in the orchid ring.

For all my icy cynicism, I hadn't seen it.

I suddenly felt as old as the creature that looked out of Ambrose's eyes, and terribly alone. The temporary relief from Con rubbing my feet had faded almost as soon as I donned those shoes again, as fleeting as those few moments in the folly when I'd felt connected to him.

The kindness he'd shown had served his purpose. When would I ever learn?

Con remained in intense conversation with his commanders, arguing about boats and soldiers in a shorthand developed over years of having such conversations. I could have stood there with them, listened in and offered my opinion, but that would have affected only the surface currents. This group of three swam through deep waters together. When Con had tried to explain why he called himself empty inside, he'd looked to these others who'd journeyed with him.

They would always have a stronger bond with him than I ever could. That was only to be expected. It shouldn't make me feel more alone than I had before they arrived uninvited on my island.

Weary of it all—my feet aching fiercely—I left them to thrash out their details. I slipped my arm from Con's and made my way to the bench in the shade. This one had been designed to accommodate my gowns, so I could seat myself unaided. Ridiculous, really, that I was the queen of all I surveyed, with the power to command everyone— with the salient exception of my husband—but I couldn't simply sit down without help whenever I liked.

Ambrose ambled over after a moment, which came as no surprise since Merle hadn't taken his keen eyes off me, indicating I had the wizard's attention even though he seemed engrossed in the conversation. Since I could see through the eyes of the birds of Calanthe, I had no doubt Ambrose could do the same with his familiar. Only he didn't seem to need meditative quiet to do it. The wizard even seemed to be able to carry on a conversation at the same time. An enviable skill I'd love to learn, if I could find a way to ask without revealing my comparative weakness in the art.

The wizard gracefully sank to the ground, then sprawled out on the bit of lawn to lean on one elbow. He laid the staff nearby, Merle hopping off to stalk about in the grass, cocking his head to eye what might lie hidden there. Ambrose's robe—a very expensive one not meant for being rubbed on the ground—hiked up, revealing his bare feet and hairy, somewhat scrawny legs.

"Warriors," he commented cheerfully. "They never tire of talking war."

"Their nature, I suppose."

"True. Whereas our nature leads us to discuss other things."

I raised a brow. "And what shall we discuss until they do tire of it and deliver their conclusions?"

"I'm glad you asked. How about the stricture against blood spilled in violence on Calanthe's soil and water?"

I controlled my shock, giving him a bland look as chastisement for attempting to startle an indiscreet remark from me. "Excuse Me?" I replied, letting my arch tone reflect my disapproval of his tactics.

Ambrose grinned, plucked a blade of grass and pointed it at me. "Come now, Your Highness. We're allies now. Isn't this something your court wizard should know?"

I declined to comment on his casual assumption of our supposed allied status. We shared a common enemy, but that didn't necessarily make us friends. "It seems to Me that magic is more your arena than Mine. How could I possibly explain the arcane to an accomplished wizard? I'm no magic wielder." I enjoyed pretending total ignorance, as he knew it was a lie, and it kept him in the dark about just how much I did know.

"No, because you *are* magic, aren't you? Those who are magic seldom wield it, at least not in the same way, for example, that a wizard might." He was clearly enjoying the game, also.

"I don't know that much about wizards."

"Then we are well matched, as I don't know much about nature magic."

I raised a brow. "Nor do I."

He made a scoffing sound. "Calanthe's magic is yours. Or yours is Calanthe's." He shrugged one shoulder. "Same and same, anyway."

"Calanthe is but an island and I am only a woman," I countered.

He fell onto his back, laughing heartily, bare feet kicking. Con glanced over, giving me a questioning look, and I waved him off. "Stop that," I hissed at Ambrose.

Rolling onto his elbow to face me, he abruptly sobered. "I will if you will. This is a critical question, Your Highness. From what I gather the dread trio is planning, we'll be looking at plenty of violence to come. Plenty of blood to be spilled and islands to be . . . enraged? Will Calanthe lift her spine from the water, perhaps, to rampage through the world like the giant monsters of old?"

I controlled my reaction to that far-too-prescient remark. So far as I knew, that ancient knowledge had never been written down, the stories told only in secret, in the sacred privacy of the temples on Calanthe, as all the other temples to the old gods had been destroyed when Anure shattered the kingdoms. I laughed, a silvery titter worthy of the silliest courtier. "What a story! Where did you hear such a fanciful tale?"

He regarded me very seriously, the deep forest looking out of his eyes. "Rumors. Fragments of ancient tales told by peat fires. Whispers in the dark."

"Such a wild imagination you have. The stricture is

key to life on Calanthe only because that's how we preserve our paradise. We are a peaceful people. Violence is strongly discouraged."

Ambrose shook the blade of grass at me. "'Forces beyond your imagining,' you said of it. I recall quite clearly. And just now you referred to it as arcane knowledge. The injunction goes far beyond custom, Your Highness. What happens when Calanthe becomes aware of blood shed in violence?"

I clearly wasn't in the correct state of mind for verbal fencing, particularly not with this wizard who had his scorpion stinger poised. Needing the infusion of energy, I sat back on my perch just enough to touch my back against the tree, inhaling as if enjoying the serene garden. Calanthe's nurturing essence flowed into me, a sweet relief. I'd once explained to Con that orchids can't live on their own, taking their nourishment from the trees, the rain, the very air.

Of course he hadn't understood that I was much the same. I don't know why I'd even hinted at it.

Ambrose narrowed his eyes, his keen gaze looking through me—or at whatever he saw when he looked at me—and an uncanny prickle of foreign magic wafted over me. Straightening, I broke the connection and subtly deflected the wizard's magic into a nearby bush.

Ambrose gave me a knowing smile. "I could test the theory," he said.

With an effort, I sharpened my thinking. We were having at least two conversations—duels, truly—one verbal, one magical. I wasn't winning either one. The wizard had chosen his moment to ambush me very well.

"You could," I agreed, "though if there is a price to pay—from either Calanthe or Her denizens—then you would be the one to pay it. I've heard said that the cost extracted from an offender of the laws of magic is proportionate to the amount of magical power they possess."

Ambrose looked positively delighted. "Have you heard that? How fascinating." His magic returned, a softer touch, almost delicate, like birdsong heard from far away.

My turn to narrow my gaze. "You purport to have immense ability, Syr Wizard. Have a care, as a price of that size might well send you back to where you came from."

He sat up, crossed his legs and propped his elbows on his knees, fingers folded to a point over his closed-lipped smile. His green eyes sparkled with humor. His magic sharpened into a needle, pricking me. "And where do you imagine I came from, Your Most Perceptive Highness?"

"Oriel," I tossed out, allowing myself a slight smile at his hoot of laughter. I broke the needle, letting it shiver onto the stones beneath my seat.

"A clever deflection, but not enough to divert me." He pressed his fingers to his lips, a calculating glint in his eyes. "Where I come from, we don't have your kind," he finally confided.

"Queens?" I asked in wide-eyed surprise. "Or women?"

"Elementals." He shot the word at me, and in the same moment, a sensation like hot water brushed my skin. "I think you are a woman *and* an island."

I pretended not to notice his magic this time, curious to see what he'd do with it. "The philosophers say that no man is an island," I countered, as if we only exchanged witty repartee. He strengthened the wave of magic, and I drained it down through my feet, letting Calanthe have it. She murmured in her sleep, tasting the odd flavor, then subsiding again.

Ambrose frowned absently as he looked inward; then his brightly curious gaze flicked back to my face. "Ah, but we're speaking of a woman, not a man. What do the philosophers say then?"

"They don't," Con inserted, striding over to us, Lady Sondra and General Kara following like the faithful troops they were. "Because women's minds are unknowable." He gave me a wry look, and I rolled my eyes, making sure he saw my disdain. Quite frankly, I was relieved that he'd broken the unsettling duel between Ambrose and me.

"You say that as if there aren't women philosophers."

Con opened his mouth. Firmly shut it again.

"He used to know better, Your Highness," Lady Sondra explained with a disgusted look at Con, unexpectedly in harmony with me for a moment. "Our Conrí has been too long among men."

"You're not a man," Con growled at her.

Lady Sondra batted her pale lashes, swaying and mincing with a refined grace worthy of any court lady—an odd sight with her sword at her side, and in her black-and-gold fighting gear, even the glamorous set she wore for court. She fluttered her fingers at Con. "Thank you for noticing." She pitched her voice too high, so the coo came out rough, and Sondra dropped all playfulness as if it had burned her. The look she then flashed at me held only bitter malice, the temporary harmony gone as if it had never been. "Much good may it do me."

"We have the beginnings of a plan," Con said, watching me closely, "to run past you for approval."

Kara's face shifted subtly, and Sondra gave Con such an incredulous look that I knew this had been a surprise.

"All right." I gestured at the grass around me. "Care to sit?"

"I prefer to stand," Sondra replied, her gaze flicking

to the grass at my feet with scorn. Kara said nothing, but remained standing also, with military rigidity.

"Excellent. Then you can ask the gate guard to admit My advisers." I smiled serenely at her rebellious frown. She had no good reason to refuse to do my bidding, however, so she stalked away to the gate, stiff-legged, all hint of grace banished.

Con knelt on one knee, propping his forearm on the upraised one. The position put our eyes level, and he gazed at me soberly. "Was Ambrose badgering you?" he asked quietly.

I nearly blinked at him. Ambrose wasn't near enough to hear—with human ears, anyway—but Merle certainly was. Did Con not understand the nature of a familiar like that? "We enjoyed a lively conversation. Why—don't you trust the wizard?"

Ambrose, who'd rolled onto his back again to stare at the sky and chew on another blade of grass, smiled vaguely.

"It's not that. Exactly." Con frowned, searching my face. "I just don't—"

"Your Highness!" Percy practically danced across the stones to my little lawn and bowed extravagantly. "You look leagues beyond gorgeous. As radiant as Sawehl, seductive as Ejarat, and with a positively lethal edge of Yilkay's black teeth." He grinned, showing his own teeth, and snapping them.

Con looked disgusted and I patted his hand, refraining from teasing him about well-executed flattery. Especially since I preferred his earnest, if clumsy words.

"Lord Percy." I offered the hand with the orchid ring for him to kiss. "So good of you to attend Me on short notice."

"Are You kidding?" He waved his hands in the air. "The court is aflutter with the news of the missive from His Imperial Horribleness. Since the messenger was so expeditiously returned to his sloop—" Percy paused to glare balefully at Kara, who might as well have been carved of obsidian for all he seemed to notice. "—no one has been able to extract *any* news."

"We're all keen to hear what the emperor's next move is, Your Highness," Brenda added gravely, coming up beside Percy, bowing in her perfunctory way. A square-built woman with short-cut silvery hair, Brenda had served in the wars in Derten and tended toward cursory manners. Not from lack of respect, but because Brenda preferred efficiency in all things. Really, she and General Kara had been cut from the same cloth.

Agatha arrived on Lord Dearsley's arm. Thin and pale, she always seemed ethereal to me, forever cold and easily startled. Within that deceptive exterior, though, she possessed a spine of steel. I didn't know her whole story, of course, but Agatha had survived where few others had. Strength comes in many forms and isn't always visible. They paused before me, both bowing. Sondra followed behind, carrying two chairs.

"A man your age shouldn't have to be kept standing or forced to sit on the ground," she muttered at Dearsley, throwing me a fierce glance.

"Thank you, Lady Sondra. You are ever so thoughtful," I replied with languid ease. My thoughts must be scattered to the stormy seas that I hadn't thought of it. Tertulyn would have handled that, dammit all. "Agatha, would you care to—" Agatha gracefully sank to the grass beside Brenda, wrapping her colorful shawl around herself. Percy arranged his elaborate tails and settled in the chair beside Lord Dearsley, crossing his legs and folding his hands on his knee to properly display the long jeweled tips, much like my own.

"*This* is your Defense Council?" Con muttered in my ear.

"The core of it. These are the cleverest people in all the realms, refugees of the forgotten empires," I informed him. "They helped me defeat *you*, after all."

"You don't have to keep reminding me," he growled.

"Are you sure? You seem to keep forgetting," I replied sweetly, then gestured for him to take the lead and raised my voice. "Conrí, you may proceed."

He stepped away from me, surveying the gathering, the mantle of easy power settling around him. Here was the wolf in his element: at the head of the pack.

He began with a concise summary of Anure's missive, sticking only to the salient information. "Anure is obsessed with capturing Her Highness the queen. We will—that is," he corrected himself, with a glance at me, "I'm suggesting we lure him into a vulnerable position by making Queen Euthalia seem easily captured."

"Out of the question," Lord Dearsley burst out, long whiskers fluttering with his indignation. "Her Highness cannot be placed at risk. Her safety is of primary importance."

"I agree," Con replied gravely, with more gentleness for the old man than I expected. "Her Highness will never be truly unprotected. She will have layers of protection, including me."

"I feel compelled to point out," I inserted, not pleased at how quickly Con had reverted to assuming he'd have his way, "that I have layers of protection already. Calanthe is well defended."

Con studied me. "And yet you've worked diligently all these years—you and your father before you—to keep Anure away from Calanthe."

"Of course. The first layer of defense was to make Anure believe he couldn't come here."

"Why does he believe he cannot come to Calanthe?" Ambrose asked. He still lay on his back in the grass, the moons and stars of his robe sparkling like a handful of jewels scattered across the ground. With his hands behind his head, he stared up at the cloudless blue sky, a picture of indolence.

"My father enchanted him to believe as much."

"Your father was a wizard?" Con asked.

"No, he was a king," I replied patiently.

"A king married to the land," Ambrose told him, helpfully, which earned him a scowl.

They'd forgotten so much, if Con knew nothing about the ties between the royal families and the lands they governed. It would harm nothing to remind them. "In the old ways, the true kings and queens were bound to the lands they governed."

"As the king does, so does the land," Agatha said, quoting the old song.

I nodded. "Exactly."

Con looked from her to me. "You expect me to believe that? I loathe Anure with every particle of my being, but he proved that it didn't matter to the land who rules. Life goes on no matter whose corpulent ass sits on the throne."

So much bitterness there. I could hardly blame him, but I also wouldn't try to convince him. Wasted breath. "Believe what you like, but yes, My father was married to Calanthe and She understood that. My father didn't want Anure here, so She made him unwelcome. It's quite uncomfortable, to be on an island that doesn't want you there."

"If this is something you can control, why didn't you use this against us?" Con wanted to know, and I didn't like the way he sounded as if he'd caught me in a lie.

"I didn't have to," I retorted. "I didn't plan to keep you here, so there was no need to—" I broke off, deciding against saying I'd considered and discarded that plan in favor of trapping them. And that calling Calanthe's power "under my control" would be a stretch. It would work to my benefit for them to believe that, and it would save me explaining that I more coaxed and cajoled—only without words—than anything. Imagine convincing a sleeping feline to do your bidding without waking it up—that comes close.

"No need to what?" he asked.

"To do more than I did. You've personally encountered some of the enchantments I have at My command," I reminded him.

"How do they work? Show me one."

"They're more subtle than that. Complex, with many *layers*." I cooed the word. How dare he grill me like this? I was about out of patience for it. "It's not like piling up vurgsten, lighting a spark, and bringing the wall down a moment later."

"At least explosions make sense," Con retorted.

"Some of us understand more than bashing things with a rock hammer or blowing them up," I snapped back.

"Yes, well, blowing things up gave Anure total power, and he did it without magic, so I wouldn't underestimate that approach," Con gritted out.

"Are you so sure about that?" I replied coolly, and he frowned.

"Everyone knows Anure doesn't use magic. He says it doesn't exist."

"I'd be wary of falling into the trap of believing what 'everyone knows,'" I said with a gracious smile.

Con glowered and General Kara held up a pacifying hand. "Let's take this discussion in order. These . . . enchantments are all that's kept Anure from sailing into your harbor and taking Your Highness back to Yekpehr?" he asked, sounding skeptical.

"All?" I asked him, raising my brows at the dismissive term. "They've been highly effective. Calanthe survived when the other kingdoms fell." Dearsley nodded along with me.

Kara acknowledged that, an old, depthless grief in his dark gaze that made me sorry I'd plucked that nerve. "Can you rely upon these enchantments to keep the emperor away indefinitely?"

Ah, that was the question. Con had been studying Kara with a look of speculation, one he transferred to me. "No," I admitted. "Not anymore. The enchantments were woven into our betrothal. When I broke that promise by marrying Conrí, it released Anure."

Con stared at me, stricken, a flicker of guilt in his golden eyes.

"It wouldn't have lasted indefinitely anyway," I told him. "I weighed the odds. And other things have changed."

"What *things*?" Con ground out.

I looked to Ambrose, who'd sat up, gazing at me with guileless green eyes. Time to find out what he might be able to tell me, since we were all giving up our secrets. "Not only does the emperor, in fact, believe in magic, he uses it. He has wizards working with him, doesn't he?"

They all started talking at once, with various shouts and exclamations, and I rode it out. Waiting on Ambrose. The wizard pursed his mouth in doubt that slowly curved into a canny smile.

"Silence!" Con thundered, then rounded on Ambrose. "Is it true?"

"Oh yes," Ambrose agreed cheerfully. "At least three or four."

"Four," Agatha said. Quiet and definitive. She didn't look up from the considerable length of ribbon fluttering from her fingers.

"Is there a reason," Con asked Ambrose, spacing his words with elaborate patience, "that you never mentioned Anure having wizards before this?"

"Yes," Ambrose replied. Merle croaked his own confirmation.

When Ambrose said nothing more, Con's fingers twitched, curling as if he'd like to strangle the wizard, so I intervened. Really, Con would have to learn how to ask the right questions. "In many ways, it doesn't matter that Anure has his own wizards," I asserted. "I've suspected it, but knowing that changes nothing. We know that no one has been able to withstand any attack of his, which is why he is now the imperial tyrant. He has broken kingdoms like a child with a toy. Now he's coming after Calanthe, and I don't expect to be the exception."

Con focused on me, frustration simmering palpably. Perversely, it made me want to wind my fingers in his hair and soak in all his intensity. "Other than *enchantments*"—he still said the word with scorn—"you have no defenses?"

"There are layers of physical defenses, too," I bit out, no longer finding his temper so appealing. "Only a foolhardy ruler relies upon one defense."

"Your Highness, assuming the emperor brings over-whelming force capable of scouring Calanthe to bare rock, as he's indicated he intends to do," Kara reasoned, "are your physical defenses capable of withstanding that?"

Dearsley nodded with confidence, but I eyed Kara, considering. I'd been studying everything I could find on vurgsten, how Con and his people had deployed it, how Anure was likely to. "No, I don't think so. We have no way to counter vurgsten if he gets close enough to use it."

Con slammed a fist into his palm as if he'd been vindi-cated. Perhaps he had been. "Then a trap is the way to go. We lure Anure to the right place, play on his obsession with Lia, he brings the bulk of his forces, and we crush him. No more Anure."

Brenda smiled with a bloodthirsty eagerness I rarely saw from her, while Percy examined his nails. Dearsley threw me a desperate look, and I held up a hand to stop his next words.

"Crush," I repeated. "You're talking about a full-scale battle. With bloodshed."

Con set his jaw as he looked at me, but he spoke with remarkable patience. "That's how battles typically work, yes."

"Not here," I said.

"Not possible," Dearsley said at the same time.

Sondra made a sound, but Con lifted a hand to shush her. "Yes. Here. Not only possible, but inevitable. Anure is coming to Calanthe and we have to fight."

Ambrose sat up and watched me with glittering in-tensity. I sighed for the inevitability of bringing this into the open. "Not on Calanthe or in Her waters," I said, and Lord Dearsley nodded in agreement. "I forbid it."

"What?" Sondra exclaimed. Kara closed his eyes,

looking pained. Percy and Brenda exchanged knowing glances. They didn't understand the full import of the stricture, but they'd helped me navigate a similar problem before.

"I cannot condone the spilling of blood in violence on Calanthe's soil or in Her waters," I clarified. Ambrose nodded to himself, Merle hopping over and making clucking sounds as if they conversed. Agatha produced a bit of bread from inside her shawl and offered it to the raven, who took it with a polite flutter of wings.

"No monarch of Calanthe ever has," Dearsley added. "We are a peaceful people."

Sondra threw up her hands, glaring at all of us. "What you are is insane!"

"Welcome to the Flower Court, darling Sondra," Percy drawled.

"What do you think Anure will do if we don't fight?" she demanded. "This isn't some garden party where you can give him the cut direct and he'll slink off in shame. We've established that you can't stop him. He's going to come here and—"

"Enough, Sondra," Con said without rancor, his eyes never leaving my face. "Will you explain?"

Since he was making the effort to listen, I made the attempt to meet him halfway. "Do you understand the nature of blood sacrifice?"

He frowned a little. "You mean, like the old ways, ripping out a guy's living heart and offering it to the gods?"

"So gloriously barbaric," Percy crooned, admiring gaze on Con.

"Or a virgin girl's." I spoke over Percy's flirtation. "Think of the Morning Glories."

"The Glories?" Con frowned. "I thought that was an empty custom, a relic of your father's days."

"Just because our rituals on Calanthe seem meaning-less to *you*," Dearsley put in, unable to restrain himself any longer, "doesn't mean they are." He'd been the one to convince me, in the dark days after my father's death, to continue the tradition of the Morning Glories, though I didn't spill their virgin blood as a king would.

Con looked from him to me. "I still don't get it."

"We don't shed blood in violence because we don't care to wake that which feeds on blood sacrifice."

Percy shuddered dramatically, and Brenda gave him a quelling look.

"If we sit here and do *nothing*," he said slowly, "An-ure will come, take the queen, and scour Calanthe. He'll kill every living being on this island, which will be an ocean of blood shed in violence. If I'd wanted to sit on my ass and let Anure raze the world, I could've stayed in the mines." His volume had climbed as he spoke, and I opened my mouth to retort, but Agatha spoke first, in her eerily quiet way that somehow cut through angry words.

"No, you wouldn't have, Conrí," she said, gazing at him with pale eyes. "Some of us can't be caged."

Con brought himself up short, then gave her a courteous nod that surprised me. "True."

"No one said anything about doing nothing," I said, taking control of the discussion. "We're talking about ways to avoid violence. My sacred duty is to protect Calanthe. There's an option we haven't discussed that would stop the emperor from coming here. If he wants me so badly, I can go to Yekpehr and turn Myself over to him." After all, I'd once thought that would be the logical end to my long détente with Anure. I'd seen a future where I'd have to marry him—which would at least give me the opportunity to kill him when he tried to take me to bed. I still could.

An aghast silence fell. Con put a hand on his rock hammer, as if I meant to go right then, and he'd hit me over the head to stop me. "Would it?" he ground out with quiet violence.

"No," Kara said in his grave-dark voice. "Anure will destroy Calanthe anyway. If there's a chance to win this, we need You here, Your Highness, with us and with Calanthe."

Kara held my gaze. Con visibly seethed and Sondra gave him an uncertain glance, then looked to me. Pleadingly? No, I could see that, even if I could muster the courage to do it, Con would never hand me over to Anure. And Kara was right: Anure would destroy Calanthe anyway as punishment, and I'd sacrifice myself for nothing. The time for that gambit had passed.

"We have to fight," Con said to me, adding to the argument, "but a trap gives us greater control of the situation. It will let me do everything in my power to minimize the blood shed in violence. If we do it right, then it will be less than what Anure would do otherwise. *If* Her Highness agrees to this much. Do you agree that we'll fight?" He looked at me expectantly, the others following suit.

I wished I could see a way out of the looming disaster, but I couldn't. They were right: Blood would be shed on Calanthe no matter what. All I could do was mitigate the damage.

The only wild card in all of this was Con. He'd been the unexpected element all along. I understood better now why the dreams of the manacled wolf breaking his chains had felt so pivotal to me. Con's escape and revolution had changed everything. We had no choice now but to travel through the fire and either perish or emerge on the other side. If anyone could change the outcome of this conflict, perhaps my wild wolf could. If he couldn't, well, doom was doom. I feared that I could do nothing to save Calanthe, no matter what choice I made. I conceded with a reluctant nod, and Con's eyes narrowed as he perceived my unwilling capitulation. So I spoke to avoid another argument that would only lead us to the same dead end. "So you'll draw Anure to the palace and trap him how?"

"I haven't figured out that part yet," Con replied, then looked to Kara.

General Kara glanced to Con for permission, then continued. "We need advice on that. Your Highness knows this island better than any of us."

I restrained a sarcastic reply. So good of them to notice. "Do tell." Oops, my sarcasm slipped out anyway.

Kara hesitated, having caught the bite in my tone. Con still stood back in all his caged-wolf wariness.

"When Anure comes here," Kara continued, "if he's determined to retrieve Your Highness, would he come to the palace?"

"That's where I live," I explained patiently, and Percy laughed.

"Lia." Con's voice held reproach, and I threw up my hands in exasperation.

"Yes. The palace is where the emperor would expect Me to be."

"Her Highness is always in residence," Dearsley put in. "As is right and good."

"*Always?*" Con asked me, ignoring Dearsley. "You've *never once* left the palace? How do you even know what other parts of the island are like?"

"I saw them all on my initial tour of Calanthe when I ascended to the throne, and I have—"

"So you're not *always* here," he interrupted, pouncing on the point.

Only by locking down my eyeballs did I manage not to roll them—and then only because we had an audience. "For the last ten years, I've been on the palace grounds. As these people can confirm, it's safest here."

"And comfy," Percy put in.

"Safest why?" Con pursued the topic like a hound on the hunt.

I sighed mentally. I'd have to show them Calanthe's strengths—and Her weaknesses. Her weaknesses were mine, and it went against the grain to put those vulnerabilities on display.

Con blew out a breath in exasperation just as I opened my mouth. "Look, Lia," he burst out in his wolf's snarl, "we face overwhelming odds. The emperor has at least a hundred times more ships than we do, maybe a thousand. Tens of thousands of fighters. If they land on Calanthe, even knowing their objective is extracting you intact, we'll still have to find a way to keep from being overrun. We need a place that will be an effective, and immediate, trap. We can't just lounge around in the gardens and wait for them to feel sleepy or whatever."

"Don't you dare condescend to Me," I said softly. I regretted now, breaking down like that in the folly. I knew better. Never reveal weakness before wolves. They don't forget, and—when it suits their purpose—they exploit it.

Con visibly dragged his snapping temper back and tried for a more rational tone of voice. "We're in this fight together—and we can't win if you won't trust us with the knowledge we need to plan strategy. You agreed to this plan. Help me to help you."

"Oh, are we trusting each other again? I lost track when you were accusing Me of lying and lecturing Me on the defense of Calanthe."

He opened his mouth. Shut it again.

"Better. Now I had been *about* to explain why the palace is the safest place on Calanthe. I can and will show you. Come with Me."

5

"Where are we going?" Sondra asked in her hoarse whisper. I slid her a quelling look in reply. Lia glided up the winding stairs, back ramrod-straight, coolly paying no attention to any of us. We couldn't even follow too closely, because the train of her gown trailed several steps behind her. Not daring to step on it, we became ducklings following in their mama's wake.

Knowing perfectly well that Lia never did anything by accident, I resigned myself to being put in my place—firmly behind the Queen of Calanthe. I'd challenged her in front of my commanders and, worse, *her* advisers. I'd pushed her into admitting she'd have to face bloodshed on the precious soil of her island, so I'd do my penance. At least she'd agreed to a plan and was giving us something useful to work with. I hoped.

"We are climbing to the top of a tower," Ambrose replied to Sondra in my stead. He gestured to the staircase that wound in a graceful spiral up the inside of a tower, a solid wall of stone beside us and open-air windows on the outside, showing the palace grounds spread out below.

"Thank you," Sondra replied sourly.

"Of course, child," Ambrose answered with every appearance of sincerity. "My knowledge is yours."

Sondra growled deep in her throat, but everyone ignored her. I kept my eyes on Lia's slim back, enjoying the sway of her hips, and pondering how such a small frame could contain so much stubborn pride. And how I could burn to pull her into my arms and kiss her senseless in the middle of an argument. Our truces flared into battles with so little warning, I couldn't seem to stick to a solid strategy with her.

The others hadn't come along, though Dearsley had watched me with overt disapproval as he conducted a whispered consultation with Lia. She'd dismissed him, along with Brenda, Percy, and Agatha, cryptically observing that where we were going was nothing new to anyone else.

Sunlight poured in from above and Lia rose through an unguarded opening in the ceiling. I followed behind as fast as I could. She might complain about my hypervigilance, but she went too far in the opposite direction. Everyone on Calanthe seemed to be that way. They claimed they understood the dangers of the world beyond, admitted that their previous defenses no longer worked, and yet they wandered around their isolated paradise as if nothing could ever arrive to give them trouble.

Edging past Lia and quickly scanning the room—one big circle at the top of the tower, open to the air, no furniture, and only a dome of a ceiling—I saw no movement, no immediate threat. A balustrade of the same white stone they built everything from here circled a balcony outside the arches. I stepped out, verifying that no one lurked there, either. The tower enjoyed a view in every direction of Calanthe, with nothing obstructing the line of sight, so I could see how that could be useful. But, by the time we spotted Anure's navy approaching, we'd be already fucked.

Lia didn't come out to the balcony, though, so it must not be the view she wanted to show me. Still, I made the full circuit before I stepped back inside, Lia giving me a cool and remote look that nevertheless communicated her disdain for my precautions. Or her general displeasure with me, hard to say which. *It can be both.* Her words echoed in my head, but she'd said them on such a sensual gasp, her lithe body hot against me, that I had to look away, making a business of hitching my bagiroca back onto my belt. "Pretty view. Why are we here?"

Wordlessly she pointed down. I realized that Kara and Sondra stood at different corners of the room, staring at the floor while Merle hopped around on it. Ambrose had gone out to the railing, looking into the distance. Willing to play along, I also studied the glittering mosaic tiles laid in intricate patterns. The floor was pretty, too. Lots of shades of blue where I stood, then a central mass of browns and greens, studded in places with white shapes. I refocused my eyes. Not just a fancy pattern, but a map—one so large it spanned the entire room.

A map of Calanthe, rendered in precise and exquisite detail. Excitement pricked at me. I strode from the ocean I stood in to the cluster of white buildings that must be the palace. Orienting myself, I sighted out an open arch to a series of hills in the distance. Sure enough, they were on the map. I followed that line, walking out to the balcony again, and discovered an arrow etched into the flat stone rail. Words were also carved there, but in Calanthean, which I couldn't read at all.

Moving next to the view of the harbor below the palace, I sighted it, then worked backward to the map. Not satisfied with what I could see from that angle, I got down on hands and knees, peering at the detail in the harbor, then scrutinizing the patterns of blues in the water, tracing them with my finger outward. Jumping up again, I ran to the rail, surveying the patterns of waves and currents, then went back to the floor map.

It had been made perfectly to scale. I knelt again in the deep-water harbor, then traced the wavy lines outward. "This is a barrier reef," I declared in wonder, stabbing at it with my finger and looking around for Lia. "A huge one."

To my surprise, she stood close nearby, a slight smile on her mouth. Something amused her. Probably my being slow on the uptake. I didn't care. At least she'd let go of some of her anger at me, and the wealth of information in this map had my head spinning with possibilities.

"Why, yes it is," she replied, her voice far less icy.

I sat back on my heels, taking it in. "This was created by a master. It shows everything, doesn't it? The currents, the altitude of those hills, and it's exactly to scale."

"A team of masters," Lia corrected, but her smile had deepened. She loved this place, and she revealed that in a warmth she rarely showed. "There's a guild of artists whose sole focus is this map. They keep it constantly updated, and yes—it contains many *layers* of information."

"Should we be walking on it?" Sondra asked, sounding uncharacteristically uncertain.

Lia gave her a smile, too. A real one that had Sondra glancing behind her. "It's meant to be walked on. The glaze is very tough, and regularly renewed. It always surprises Me how many people who come here stand in the sea on the map, not the land, as if they don't trod on Calanthe as soon as they leave the tower."

"The floor is a major work of art, Your Highness." Sondra had a sound of awe in her voice.

"Thank you," Lia replied. "It's a great source of pride, besides being useful for knowing all about My island." She slid a narrow look at me.

Kara grunted, eyeing the ocean. "A barrier reef, you say, Your Highness?"

"Yes. It protects the harbor and, depending on the tides, makes entrance to it impossible, which is part of why the palace is the safest place on Calanthe."

Kara frowned at her. "We encountered no issues when we sailed our ships in."

Lia spread her hands with a mischievous look in her eyes. "You had help."

"You don't say." He considered her. "Can your defensive enchantments make the tides uncooperative?"

I hadn't thought that far yet, and waited with Kara for the answer.

"To an extent, yes. Calanthe's influence reaches out all around Her, and that includes how the seas move, how the storms pass by."

And she was part of that. I began to get a glimmer of what being an elemental truly meant. No wonder Lia's palace didn't need walls, if she could keep the worst storms away. "You control the weather and the tides?" My turn to sound awed, and Sondra snorted.

Lia waved that away. "Yes and no. And I'd rather not discuss it in detail." She raised her brows, reminding me of our agreement that she could decline to explain rather than misdirect. Fine. I'd get more out of her later. That wasn't against the rules.

"That's how you drew the ship in." Kara smacked his fist against his palm. "I *knew* that wasn't natural." He strode out to the balustrade. Sondra, clearly still uncomfortable walking on the mosaicked floor, followed him out. They stared out at where the reef lay hidden underwater, finding the markers on the balustrade as I had, discussing both. Ambrose moved over to join them, pointing his staff at something.

"Thank you, Lia," I said, hearing the gruffness of my own awkwardness. "This map is amazingly useful."

Lia crouched beside me, her beaded skirts tinkling on the glassy surface. "This place is open to all citizens of Calanthe, of which you are now one. I have to remember that I granted you and your people asylum here, the same as for Percy and the others." She trailed her black-tipped nails over a section of coastline rendered in sparkling silver. A beach, with calm light-green water, probably good for swimming. "Teachers bring the schoolchildren here, and sometimes I come to talk with them. The children, they crawl on their hands and knees, like you are, putting their eyes up as close as they can, and talking to Her, like you were."

I had a habit of muttering to myself when I was thinking. Sondra liked to tease me about it. Lia likely thought me crazed and undignified, ill mannered as a child—and she wouldn't be wrong. "Sorry."

"Don't be." She met my gaze, our faces close. Something shimmered between us, like heat rising off the sands outside Keiost. "I like it. I love seeing the children roll around on this map of their home, the land that gave them birth or sanctuary, finding their villages and favorite places. It's a . . . celebration, and I always feel Calanthe loves the attention. I wish everyone would do it."

"I've never seen anything like this," I admitted, turning my attention back to the mosaic, and firmly away from the sudden and savage fantasy of kissing those glossy black lips, of dragging her down and having her on this map. Some celebration *that* would be. I cleared my throat. "I've been in a lot of palaces, estates, castles, fancy houses with fancy things. Of course, most of them were in ruins, stripped of anything valuable. But I never saw anything like this, even in the ones the Imperial Toad spared and gave to his cronies and the cowards who caved instead of fighting—" I broke off, realizing what I'd said.

"Like Calanthe did," Lia filled in. Her nails clicked over the tiles, and then she stood with a sigh. "I know how little you think of us, Conrí. Of My people, and of Me. It's disingenuous of you to mince words now."

She walked out to join the others on the balcony, beaded skirts hissing across the floor, her steps quiet—and I realized that, despite her earlier statement and her aching feet, she walked up on her toes so her sharp heels wouldn't touch the tiles. I wasn't sure how I'd gone so fast from trying to show her appreciation to pissing her off again, except that it seemed to be my particular talent and failing.

I returned my scrutiny to the map—something I could handle—learning how they depicted the depths of water and the landscape beneath. Lia could show Kara and Sondra where the actual barrier reef lay. The critical information about it had been woven into these intricate tiles. And not in words, but in images that even I, a barely educated ex-prisoner from a foreign land, could understand. Did the makers intend that? What a thing it would be if they could make a map of all the world. I didn't know what kind of room could hold it, but it would be something to see. On a map like that, Oriel could still exist—and persist for all time, instead of growing tattered and faded in my memories and Sondra's.

Yes, in the past, we'd called King Gul and the kingdom of Calanthe weak-willed puppets of the emperor, but I'd learned better. Gul, and Lia after him, had preserved things like this and like all that art in the portrait gallery. And all those people Lia had drawn to her court, people like Brenda, a poet and warrior, Agatha, a brilliant weaver, and Percy—whatever he did—with knowledge and skills saved from oblivion because Calanthe existed.

For the first time, I understood something of how Lia saw the world. I lived for revenge, to destroy Anure utterly and forever. Lia . . . she lived to preserve all this. I bet she stayed in the palace not only because she felt safe, but because all the most precious things were here.

Precious things Anure would destroy without taking a second breath. Standing, I looked out to sea again. Lia was right: Vurgsten changed everything. Even if we held off Anure's forces beyond the reef, vurgsten could be lobbed from that far, and would take out this tower and its treasure in a moment.

I needed to think. Anure would come after Lia, and he'd expect her to be here, in the palace. Where she lives, as she so sardonically pointed out. She had her layers of enchantments. Anure had wizards to break them. I could throttle Ambrose for not telling us that.

Focus. Lia had relied upon the reef to protect them, but that could be exploded, too. That's what I'd do faced with this scenario: Sail a few ships up to the reef, maybe at night. Blow the reef and the harbor wide open. Then have the rest of the navy ready to sweep in, maybe as the tide came in, to add velocity.

Then I'd send in a crack team, maybe several teams, to take Lia prisoner. If Tertulyn was a spy and had gone to him—who was I kidding? No "ifs" about it. Lia's doubts had infected me—then he'd know Lia's habits, where to find her and when.

Once he had her, maybe back on his flagship in the harbor so he could make her watch, he could pound the city and palace with vurgsten.

Though, if it were me and I wanted to hedge my bets,

I'd sneak in first—same approach with several small, highly specialized teams. Take the queen hostage, get her out of the palace to a place well away and safe, *then* blow the reef and bring in the ships. He'd still want her in a place where she'd have to watch the destruction, I bet, knowing Anure's methods, but the harbor still made sense. Most of the resistance—as much as the Calantheans could muster any kind of fight—would be centered here. And with its exposure to the sea on three sides, we couldn't possibly defend it.

But what if Lia *wasn't* in the palace?

We had an entire island to consider. I crawled over it, marking the larger towns, the roads between them. Rural, very rural, with most of the population centers all along the coast and then again in the hills. What were these shapes? I went back to the palace complex, found the tower we'd been imprisoned in, which Ambrose had taken for his own, and the tower I was in at that moment.

The artists had rendered the land and sea flat, as if a bird looked down on them, but the towers and buildings were depicted at an angle. I supposed otherwise they'd look like squares and circles, seen from above. The map tower had been foreshortened, but the design faithfully depicted the open arches, a glint of the map within. With an odd sensation of being two places at once, I almost expected to see a tiny version of myself, crouched on the floor.

I traced the garden path Lia and I had walked . . . Oh, look at that: Lia's private courtyard wasn't there. So some things were secret from the big map. Near as I could tell, every other building in the palace complex and the city beyond was accurately included. Counting under my breath, I crawled from town to town, keeping a mental tally of buildings, not sure what I was looking for, but certain I'd know it when I saw it.

"You might as well leave Conrí and send food, Your Highness," I became aware of Sondra saying. "He'll be like that for hours until he's satisfied."

Her use of my name and Lia's title had penetrated. I put a mental finger on my running tally and sat back on my heels. The four of them stood nearby, watching me—all standing in the ocean, as it were. Lia saw me take note of it and we shared a knowing glance. Odd, to have a shared thought with her the others wouldn't follow. Kind of nice, too. "These towns." I gestured to one near my knee. "The numbers of buildings are accurate?"

Lia dipped her chin. "Everything is as accurate and current as the map guild can make it."

"Not absolutely everything," I noted.

A secret smile ghosted over her lips. "Everything I allow," she corrected.

"And Anure knows about the reef," I continued.

"If he didn't know everything before, we must assume he does now," Lia conceded.

Kara folded his hands behind his back, standing at attention, old habits from the days he'd served as commander of Soensen's navy, the finest in all the scattered kingdoms, and not a ragtag fleet of fishing boats sailed by ex-convicts and starving refugees. "Her Highness has promised me charts of the tides and channels. I'd like to take out a boat and see it for myself, too."

I nodded permission, somewhat absently, surprised that Kara hadn't seen what I had—that the map contained everything he'd need to know. But we all had our own ways of doing things, and I'd learned early on to respect that in my commanders. They might call me Conrí, but we had no true hierarchy. We were all on our own personal crusades, which just happened to be pointed in the same direction.

"Learn everything you can," I agreed, "but we're not letting Anure come to this harbor."

"'Let'?" Lia echoed in a mocking tone. She clicked over to me, not picking up her heels this time, until she stood squarely in the harbor, hands planted on her hips so the long nails arrowed down. "You've been going on about Anure's unstoppable forces and vast supplies of vurgsten."

"It's true," Sondra agreed, following with more tentative steps. "The emperor began stockpiling vurgsten before we were ever sentenced to the mines. Ejarat only knows how much of it he has at his citadel at Yekpehr—except that we can be sure it will be several factors more than what we have. And I'll remind you that we don't even have all of ours with us. We left a lot of it back at Keiost, and that's not including what the supply trains from Vurgmun will have been delivering during our absence."

"You have an active supply train from the mines at Vurgmun?" Lia asked, betraying her surprise.

"Yes," I told her, getting to my feet so I wouldn't be tempted to slide a hand under her shimmering skirt, to touch her beneath as the constant craving for her whispered I should. "Vurgmun is ours. I executed anyone not loyal to our cause, and the mines are worked by free people, sending vurgsten to us so we can take Anure down. The vengeance of many more people than you see fuels our efforts."

"That's why we need ships, Your Highness," Sondra said, clearly continuing an earlier conversation. "The fastest your people have, to ferry vurgsten here."

Lia considered that, thoughts opaque behind eyes

more gray than blue now. "The Lady Sondra says that Anure could use vurgsten to destroy the barrier reef in a moment, then sail into the harbor and destroy the city and palace without setting foot on shore."

I met Sondra's eyes, nodded to confirm that had been my assessment, too. We'd always seen strategy much the same way. Of course, we were both terribly familiar with Anure and his tactics, far more than we'd ever cared to be. "He could. Would, if we let him. Though he'd make sure to extract the queen first."

Sondra followed the thought. "Stealth team to infiltrate and abduct?"

"That's what I figure."

Lia's sharp gaze flicked between us. "I'm not so easy to abduct," she reminded me, "nor is Calanthe easy to infiltrate."

"Even with wizards?" I asked pointedly.

Her eyes glittered. "Wizards are not infallible."

"We are ineffable, though," Ambrose noted cheerfully.

"See?" She nodded at the wizard. "You had one and I defeated you."

"I know a few things now I didn't then," Ambrose pointed out.

"Yes, Anure might have the information he needs to work around those obstacles," I added, regretting my words when she averted her gaze to look out the open arches. She wouldn't betray her wounded heart by flinching, but this thing with Tertulyn had definitely gotten to her.

"Let's assume he does," she confirmed quietly.

Sondra raised a brow, but I shook my head slightly. I'd explain later, when Lia didn't have to listen. "We can't stop Anure from coming to Calanthe," I said, working the problem aloud, pacing along the coastline away from the palace. "But we *can* keep him from approaching the harbor and palace. There's too much here to risk that kind of barrage. Too much exposure. Too much potential bloodshed." I glanced at Lia to find her watching me again, with arrested attention. At least I could give her that.

"How will you turn him away?" Kara wanted to know, brow furrowed as he, too, studied the map.

"Lead," I corrected. "Not push, but pull. We'll lure him away from here and to a battleground of our choosing. Into an ideal trap. Elsewhere."

"No," Lia said with clear certainty. "I'm not going anywhere."

I paced over to her, close enough that she had to raise her chin to keep her basilisk glare fixed on me. "If he knows your secrets," I said quietly, "knows everything Tertulyn knows, then you play into their hands by remaining here."

"Nevertheless," she persisted, "I am the queen. I can't rule if I'm not at court."

"Can't you?" I let the challenge dangle between us. "Even if it means reducing blood shed in violence?"

She narrowed her eyes at me, fully aware of my manipulation and yet without a ready reply.

"Calanthe is more than the palace," I offered, appealing to her reason. "What kind of queen needs a building to govern her realm?"

With a wry twist of her lips, she sighed. "I'll think about it."

Good enough. I'd win this particular battle between us. When we needed her to move, I'd make sure she did. I might be using her as bait, but I'd do everything in my power to avoid destroying her in the process. Except jeopardize the final goal.

If it came down to that, I'd have to make sure that I'd have the backbone to sacrifice Lia, too. The trick in dealing with Anure lay in not caring about anything. He'd have no power over me as long as I cared about nothing more than destroying him. Sondra was watching me with a concerned expression, as if she knew my doubts.

"We just need to find the right place," I mused aloud ignoring Sondra and focusing on the problem, "and, yes, use Lia's presence to draw him there."

"There's a major weakness to your plan, Conrí," Sondra said, then turned to Lia. "Are you certain you're up to being bait, *Your Highness*? It sounds easy in theory, but that kind of thing takes a lot of fortitude and you won't be able to change your mind like you change your gowns."

"I won't change my mind," Lia replied with enough chill that I figured most courtiers would have detected the warning and backed down. Not Sondra.

She looked Lia up and down, lip curling. "You haven't had to suffer at all, or learn to endure much, living here. If you break under the pressure, it could destroy us all." Sondra looked to me in appeal, that doubt still in her eyes. "She's a weak link, Conrí."

"Lia is the cornerstone of this plan because she is the one Anure will compromise his strategy for. We don't have a choice here. I'll protect Lia. She won't be in a position to break."

"But if she—"

"I can protect Myself." Lia interrupted Sondra's argument with cold precision. "My people will be My bulwark. If My pretending to be bait plays into a workable strategy to protect Calanthe from the emperor without undue bloodshed, then I'll play My part. As Conrí notes, I have no choice." She fixed Lady Sondra with an unflinching stare, then flicked a glance at me. "I've endured more than you know. Either of you. It's not in Me to break."

"Enough arguing," I said, my eyes going to the map. "It's all guesswork until we find the right place."

"But where?" Kara asked, pacing alongside me, carefully still in the ocean. "These are small fishing villages. They'd be even more quickly decimated and invaded by Anure's might. I've seen what he does to places like this." His voice had gone even rougher as old ghosts swam up to haunt him. "Conrí, we can't—"

I put a hand on his shoulder. I needed him in the present—and for Lia not to be frightened any more than she already was. She'd heard, of course, given her keen attention on our conversation and on where in her realm I walked. Lia would know every detail about those fishing villages, and likely every person, plant, and animal in them—and in the waters, too. I'd like to ask her to identify what I sought, but she'd be too close, too connected to see what I needed.

I'd discovered this over and over when dealing with locals sympathetic to our cause. As much as they tried to be objective, they loved their homes—or some aspect of them—too much to sacrifice what they needed to in order to win. And Anure had an uncanny knack for knowing what people cared about, ruthlessly using that against them. Maybe the emptiness in his soul made him sensitive to what lay at the center of other people, I didn't know, but we'd won as much as we had so far in part by outsmarting him in this. He predicted what we'd try to protect; we stopped the locals from saving it, and circled behind Anure's forces.

I, of course, had nothing left I cared about, so that made it easy for me to throw tasty morsels into Anure's maw to chew and hopefully choke on while I cut his throat from behind. Lia's problem was that she cared too much about all of it. If I asked her what part of Calanthe she'd serve up to occupy Anure, she'd refuse any piece of it.

So, I'd do it for her. She'd asked for my brutality and ruthlessness in service of her realm. I'd give her exactly that. Still, I found I couldn't quite meet her eyes.

Kneeling down again, I followed the lines of currents with a fingertip. "I need more time to study the map," I told them. "You all have things to do—go do them."

Sondra sighed gustily. "Every time. Told you so."

"I'll have food sent up," Lia said.

I ignored them both and focused on solving the problem. That kept me from thinking about anything else.

6

The excruciatingly long day over at last, and even later than usual, I nearly dragged myself to my chambers. After leaving Con in the tower, I'd made countless decisions, been in one meeting after another, placing ships under Kara's command, cajoling shipmasters into giving up their charts, and soothing anxious courtiers who caught wind of the discussions. Being queen isn't all issuing commands and expecting obedience. I only wished.

Every moment of the extremes of the day radiated up from my blazing feet through my aching spine to lodge in a fireball at the base of my neck. As soon as Nahua—most junior of my ladies and therefore last in my escort—shut the doors, I collapsed onto a chair. The gown and its accoutrements could go hang now. I was ready to be divested of my armor. I might have lost Tertulyn, but Calla and my other ladies had been serving me for long enough to be familiar with the evening routine.

Orvyki unpinned the crown without a word, setting it in its niche. Zariah steadied the wig, then worked to detach the glue that held it in place on my scalp. Nahua snipped the major laces holding the gown in place, relieving some of the constriction. Calla pulled the shoes from my feet, and the stockings with them, while Ibolya removed the silk sheaths on my arms and all of my jewelry, but for the orchid ring, of course. They worked rapidly and with quiet efficiency—and without any of the ritual or chatter of the morning dressing.

They lifted me gently to my feet to remove the gown, and it seemed we all let out a long breath when they cut the laces of my corset. It would be some time yet before my ladies could divest themselves of their own formal gear—unfair, as they dressed before I did and so stayed in theirs longer. A colder woman than I would be unsympathetic and say it was their own fault, that they needn't dress as formally as I did, but I knew their positions and reputations at court depended heavily on their keeping up proper appearances. As their queen did, so must they do.

Calla slipped the dressing gown over my naked body, easing me to sit again, and Ibolya pressed a glass of brandy into my hand. I sipped, savoring the burn as it hit my jangling bloodstream, soothing my nerves and relieving some of the pressure at the base of my skull. Removing the wig and crown had helped with that, too, and the cool evening breezes on my bare scalp felt delicious after my sweltering costume. Zariah and Nahua worked on each side of me, using cotton soaked in solvent to remove the glue, then following with a honeysuckle-scented salve. Calla soaked off the jewels from my face, and the fake eyelashes, while Ibolya and Orvyki did the same with my nails.

The other three worked efficiently tidying my discarded gown, putting away the jewels and wig while Calla and Ibolya removed the last dregs of makeup from my face and exposed skin. The alcohol in their tinctures cooled my skin even more, and the pleasingly redolent lotion followed with luscious salving. They'd already set out the letter of thanks I'd give the Glory in the morning, so I signed that. Everything else could wait until the following day.

I was beyond ready to be done with this one.

"Will there be anything else, Your Highness?" Calla asked, and I opened my eyes to see the five of them in formation before me, Calla at the point of their triangle. Since I'd accepted that Tertulyn had gone forever, I supposed I should add another lady to ease their burden and bring their complement back up to six, but that could go on the list for tomorrow, also. Perhaps the day after.

"No. Thank you, all, for your exacting care," I replied. "You may be excused."

They smiled, still deferential, but their relieved delight at imminent freedom showed through. Some would retire, some would visit the Night Court, some would indulge in other recreations. They all curtsied—except Ibolya, who hesitated. "Would You like one of us to stay and keep You company, Your Highness?"

She asked because Tertulyn would have stayed, I realized. To discuss the day, or to offer me relaxation before I slept. It hadn't been a question since my wedding to Con, because he'd been there when I retired, ready to resume our exploration of the aspect of our marriage that actually worked.

It was a mark of my exhaustion and distraction that I hadn't made note of his absence. But he wasn't near, I realized. True, I couldn't sense Con specifically, but he made such a dense impact on the environment—everyone else noticed *him*—that I could usually find him fairly quickly. Not this time. "Where is Conrí?" I asked.

Calla threw Ibolya a look, a reprimand for calling my attention to Con's absence. As if I wouldn't have noticed my empty bed.

He hadn't attended court when I convened it again—no surprise there—nor had he shown his face for my various meetings and appearances, nor for formal dinner or the meetings after. None of that had been unusual. Still, he'd been so determined to talk battle strategy, I'd expected him to confront me at any moment with more demands and questions. I'd found myself a little disappointed not to be able to use some of the tart remarks I'd prepared, and then I'd gotten caught up in the whirl of all the pressing matters that needed my attention.

Still, he'd promised to attend me if he didn't have more important things to do, and I'd believed him. Besides, he'd insisted from the beginning on sharing my bed and chambers, and no matter how things stood between us politically, he'd been prompt and enthusiastic about those marital duties.

What could be absorbing his attention? Surely not the map still.

I cast about with my mind, finding a passing bat. It flew closer to the map tower for me, confirming that it blazed with torchlight, and the large, dark form of a man crawled on the floor within. "He's *still* in the map tower?"

Good Sawehl—Con had been at his task for more than half the cycle of day and night. No wonder Sondra had commented so drily on Con's tenacity when invested in study.

"We've kept Conrí supplied with food and drink, Your Highness, as ordered," Calla said in a soothing tone. "And he has attendants to see to his needs. You can rest easy."

I should let it go. Confirm to my ladies that they were dismissed, leave Con to his obsessions, and get the sleep I needed. I knew, however, that I wouldn't rest easy without him there. Such a short time for me to become accustomed to his presence—and to the passionate release I found in his arms. Until that moment, I hadn't realized how much I'd been looking forward to burning away the accumulated tension of the day in the fires of sexual abandon.

I didn't want it from any of my ladies. I wanted him. And I wanted the sweet release of being myself, the way I could be when we were naked and alone together. I'd come to depend on it, and I'd never sleep now.

Ibolya watched me with alert readiness, Calla with wary exhaustion of her own. She'd taken on Tertulyn's duties on top of her own and deserved the time off.

If only I'd realized before they undressed me, I could have visited Con in the tower and coaxed—or commanded—him to come back with me. Too late for that.

"Your Highness," Ibolya said, stepping forward and breaking the precise line of their formation, "I'd be happy to stay and keep You company. Or if You prefer to visit Conrí, I will help You dress again."

The other ladies, even Calla, painted on bright and accommodating smiles, nodding and murmuring their agreement. They served me well, making the effort at enthusiasm. It would take at least an hour to dress me to my usual level, and then they'd have to wait up to undo it all yet again. Ibolya was good to offer herself, but it would take even longer for her to get me dressed without help.

This was simply ridiculous. I'd lived all my life with these strictures, and I hadn't thought they chafed, but for the second time that day I keenly felt the absurdity of wielding the power of the crown, and yet also unable to go on a simple errand without five people to help me do it.

"I'm going to the map tower," I declared, standing and swallowing the remnants of my brandy before setting the glass aside. All but Ibolya deflated slightly before rallying their smiles and moving to take up their tasks. "But I'm not dressing," I clarified.

It was almost comical, how they turned and stared at me, the shock dissolving their carefully cheerful masks. "But . . . Your Highness . . ." Calla stammered.

"Oh, bright Ejarat!" I tried not to laugh, then couldn't help myself, which surprised them even further. Had I laughed out loud much, even with only my ladies? Likely not. I'd only unbent that much with Tertulyn, and she'd betrayed and abandoned me. *Don't dwell.*

"I'm wearing something more than *this*, just not—" I waved a hand at the massive closet that held the entirety of the public image of the queen of Calanthe. "Not *that*. Ibolya can assist Me and the rest of you may go."

Calla, no longer relieved, curtsied, bowing her head. "Your Highness, I did not mean to offend. If—"

"You didn't," I said, cutting off the groveling. "Your rank is intact. Ibolya offered and I only need one person for this. Go, Lady Calla," I added more gently. "You've been taking on many extra duties for Me and I appreciate your hard work. Go play or rest or whatever you do to keep looking as lovely as the dawn," I added wryly. "The same goes for the rest of you. Tell no one, however, that I am out and about. As far as the rest of the world is concerned, I am in My chambers for the night."

Once they'd left, I turned to Ibolya. "You were clever with coming up with a wedding gown and less formal wig for the celebration ball—can you dress Me enough to be circumspect and not obviously who I am?"

She smiled with cheeky mischief. "I believe I can, Your Highness."

A miraculously short time later, Ibolya accompanied me out of my chambers again. I waved at my guards to remain posted there, as they would if I were still within. Mindful of Con's dire warnings about the possibility of stealthy abductors—an eventuality Sondra had also instantly grasped, I'd noted—I asked Ibolya to walk with me. Between the two of us we ought to be able to hold off even a group of attackers long enough to shout an alarm. We were in the midst of my palace, after all, and possessed our thorns.

I wore a simple silk cloak of deep blue, a deeply cowled hood drawn low around my face, and long, draping cuffs to cover the orchid ring, which I never removed. I didn't think I could if I tried, until Calanthe approved of an heir, and the necessity of my passing the ring to them. Even then, it probably wouldn't come off until I was dying. Or dead. That's how it had been with my father, and he'd known death was coming for him. He'd only passed me the ring with his final breath.

Or, rather, it had passed itself.

Despite the dramatically incognito outfit, Ibolya assured me I wouldn't stand out, as that sort of thing was often used by noble ladies traveling to assignations they wished to keep private. I had much to learn about how everyone who wasn't me conducted their sexual affairs. The flat silk slippers felt like heaven on my throbbing feet, and my body moved with such easy grace, so cool and light without the structure of my heavy garments. I'd even left the crown behind.

My father would be aghast, though I had no doubt—I'd heard plenty of stories—that he'd left his own crown behind on *his* various nocturnal escapades.

I could, I supposed, turn down the hall we passed and follow it to the Night Court, at last observe and even sample its many delights for myself. Alas, the idea held little appeal. Perhaps I'd too strongly inured myself to that particular temptation over all the years I guarded my virginal reputation.

Also, it wasn't the untasted delights of the Night Court that had chased me from my rooms, but the desire to find Con. I could tell myself that he owed me this much: physical pleasure in exchange for the many irritations he caused. But following my rule of being honest with myself, I could admit that I craved him, and him alone. One of the many unsettling puzzles surrounding my baffling and difficult husband. I'd been fascinated by him from the moment he strode into my court, arrogant and unlike any man I'd ever known. If he wouldn't come to me, then I would go to him.

If nothing else, I'd have the advantage of taking him by surprise.

The palace is a different place at night—particularly once the queen had retired—its atmosphere both quieter and wilder. None of us had adjusted to my changed status. I'd gone from virgin queen whose closed doors allowed licentiousness to spill through the halls unchecked, to a married woman closeted with her new lover. My formal withdrawal still signaled the end of the business of the realm for the day, so all the folk not interested in nocturnal excesses retired to the privacy of their homes and chambers also. The people that remained were fewer in number, but made up for that in revelry, the sounds of which echoed from the gardens and various salons, as well as the music, laughter, and erotic noises coming from the Night Court itself.

The few people we passed in the main halls—most of them in states of undress and some engaged in sensual games—ignored us completely. Ibolya wore a cloak like mine and, as she'd promised, the signaled desire for anonymity meant no one bothered us, or even looked closely.

They had no reason to recognize me as their queen, but I suspected that even if they did, they'd pretend not to.

Such is the camaraderie of sensuality in the Court of Flowers. No one is shamed or judged for their proclivities. Everyone is granted whatever anonymity they seek.

I found the sensation so liberating, so exhilarating, that I wondered why it had never occurred to me to go about as someone other than my formal self. My elaborate costumes disguised my true nature and created the image of myself that it had been ever so useful to perpetuate, but I hadn't realized that, by establishing the queen of Calanthe so firmly in everyone's minds, I'd also created an avenue for Euthalia—for Lia, the woman I was only with Con—to exist beyond that, outside of the queen's tightly governed roles. If not for the ring, I might not even be recognized, a stimulating thought.

This would be useful, I felt sure, in the battles to come—though exactly how remained to be seen. For the moment, it felt good to be someone else. I could be myself from that other world, that other time line. During the first private meeting with Con in my courtyard, I'd glimpsed the life that might have been if Anure hadn't crushed the world in his brutal fist. If I'd grown up not having to conceal my nature, instead celebrating it, and being courted in a garden by people who saw *me* and not the mask I'd been forced to don . . .

No. No sense indulging in wishful thinking. That was a dangerously close cousin to denial, the enemy of honesty. For the moment I could enjoy the shrouding cloak of night. Bright morning and its stark truths would come soon enough.

Ibolya accompanied me up the long spiral of stairs to the summit of the tower. As Calla had reported, Con was indeed occupied exactly as before, inching his way along the coast of Calanthe, nose practically to the tiles as he pushed a lantern along ahead of him. At some point he'd shed the rock hammer and bagiroca, along with his cloak, boots, and all but a sleeveless vest in concession to the lamp-warmed heat captured in the dome by the breeze-less night. They sat in an ungainly pile not far away. Perhaps he trusted for once that he'd perceive an attack long before it reached him.

He'd tied back his hair, though several curling black strands escaped the tie, slipping down around his face and trailing on the floor. With his strong profile highlighted by the lamp, his expression intently focused, he looked un-bearably enticing. He, however, didn't even glance up at our arrival. "I'm not hungry," he growled. "Go away."

Indeed, the food and drink arrayed on a table off to the side appeared untouched, and whatever attendants Calla had assigned to tend Con clearly had been chased off by his surly orders. That made things easier. Slipping my cowl back, I nodded at Ibolya to excuse her.

"I'll wait at the foot of the tower, Your Highness," she murmured.

"You don't have to. Go to your bed. Or someone else's."

"I'll wait. It's my honor and privilege." She slipped down the stairs again, moving soundlessly.

I turned back to find Con sitting on his heels, hands splayed on his muscular thighs, studying me with a look between astonishment and concern.

"Lia?" he asked. Then scrubbed his hands over his face, blinking at me as if to refocus his eyes. "What time is it?"

"Nearly midnight," I informed him.

"Hmm." He glanced out the windows as if to verify that it was indeed night, then back at me. "Why are you out . . . like that?"

"I went in search of My husband, who has failed to attend My bed as promised."

"Yes, but you're . . . you."

"Aren't I always?" I arched a brow, enjoying myself.

He frowned. "Not outside your chambers, you're not. Is something wrong?" Full alert returning, he leapt to his feet and had his rock hammer in his hands, ready to bash whatever threatened me. Silly me for thinking an attack could take him unawares.

"I'm fine, Conrí darling," I purred, further aroused by the sight of muscled shoulders, ridged forearms, and strong body coiled to fight. I could channel that power into something far more interesting. Undoing the ties at my throat, I dropped the cloak, letting it puddle at my feet. Con's gaze followed the fall of it, then roamed over my bare skin, the tense readiness in his body converting to another sort entirely.

"You're naked," he said, voice hoarse, and he cleared his throat, gaze darting to the arches open to the night sky. "What if someone sees you?"

I laughed. Laughter felt so good. I wanted to laugh and love and enjoy the scent of night-blooming jasmine on the humid air, and not think about anything. The nightmares would come soon enough. For the moment, I was free. I strolled toward him. "No one but bats are about to gaze into this tower."

He narrowed his eyes as I laid my hands next to his on the shaft of the rock hammer, the wood polished smooth and silky from all the years he'd wielded it, in the mines and in war. "You watched me through bats' eyes," he ventured, sounding bemused.

I leaned in so my naked breasts brushed the backs of his hands. "Maybe," I breathed, letting my lips fall open enticingly. I hadn't put on my usual makeup, but Ibolya had added a gloss of color to my mouth, highlighted my eyes. I wasn't without my vanity, a personal flaw but likely the least of mine. "Do you need this?" I asked, starting to lift the rock hammer out of his hands.

"It's heavy," he cautioned, letting me take its weight but keeping his grip to support it.

As the density of it sank into my arms and shoulders, I marveled that he could lift and swing it so easily. "How strong you must be."

His mouth quirked, not quite a smile, and he took the weight of the hammer back, carrying it to the pile and setting it down. The arrangement wasn't as haphazard as I'd assumed, but strategically laid out in order of importance, with the haft of the rock hammer angled so as to be quickly seized. Con walked back toward me, his bare feet making no sound on the tiles. Tentative with me in a way he wasn't with his weapon, he laid his big, rough hands on my arms, stroking down as he studied my face.

"I thought you were mad at me."

"Yes, well, if we only had sex on days you hadn't annoyed Me . . ." I ran my hands over the bulging muscles of his arms, savoring the softness of his skin, even the tangle of scars that marked him, and the iron strength beneath.

"Are you here to seduce me?" he asked in his painfully blunt manner.

Surely that was obvious? Tempted to toy with him, I made a conscious effort to dispense with games. Queen Euthalia might enjoy needling him for his uncertainty, but his lover Lia knew more about the inexperienced boy inside the intimidating warrior.

"Yes. If you're amenable?" I added, my tone making it into a question. How interesting—a bit of insecurity of my own. Though it was possible that he'd tired of me.

We'd been thrust together by politics and expedience. Besides, I knew better than anyone that I was hardly the normal woman a man would hope to marry.

He chuckled, a low coughing sound without music in it. "I seem to be constantly 'amenable' when you're near." He glanced down at himself ruefully, the thrust of his erection prominent in the leather pants. "I wanted you in the garden, even with hundreds of people watching. I wanted you in that useless building by the sea. I even thought about having you on this map, spread out naked on it."

My mouth had gone dry with wanting. "What about when you're angry at Me?"

"Especially then," he answered on a growl, his mouth swooping down to seize mine in a fierce kiss. A cry of longing escaped me and I clung to him, the leather vest unexpectedly erotic on bare skin, my sensitive nipple scraping on some buckle with stinging delight. His rough beard scraped my cheeks and tender mouth, the kiss an avid feeding. I felt as if I'd been thirsty all day and finally drank, my body aching for the hands that wandered over me, hard and rough one moment, then softly stroking the next as he remembered to gentle his grip.

I loved both.

I strained on tiptoes to reach him, my hands behind his neck, undoing the tie that held his hair. He passed a hand between my legs, cupping my sex, groaning into my mouth. "So hot," he muttered, stroking a finger into my folds. "So wet."

The climax ripped through me, stunningly fast, my humming body responding with startling immediacy to his touch. But then, the wanting had been building all day. Dropping my head back, I arched into his hand. I'd wanted him all day, too, all those times he'd described and more. "More," I urged, and he picked me up, carrying me easily to the center of the map and laying me down over the Sapphire Mountains.

I had to sit up a little, to move aside the long hair of the wig so I wouldn't accidentally drag it off. I hadn't wanted Ibolya to spend the time to glue it down properly. Con paused in the act of unbuckling his vest, watching me. "Do you have to wear the wig?"

Pausing, I fingered the long black hair, the same I'd worn for our celebration ball, wedding night, and every night with him since. I'd thought he accepted it as the natural me. Or, at least, as close to that as I ever got. Having him say something about it disconcerted me in a strange way. "Don't you like this one?"

"It's fine. Pretty, as all your finery is. But I like you best without all that."

Still, I hesitated, painfully unsure. Con had seen me without the wigs, but only in passing moments. The longest had been the morning after our wedding, and that had been difficult enough—and I'd been braced for it as something that had to happen. I wasn't ready for it this time, and the prospect of taking off my wig for sex seemed like a dauntingly new level of nakedness. I didn't really understand why he'd even want to see me that way.

"You don't have to," he said, resuming taking off his vest. His dark-skinned chest flexed with his movements, the lighter scars crisscrossing his impressive physique catching the light, the strains and puckers oddly enhancing his beauty. I realized I'd frozen there, hands gripping my wig as if it might be stripped from me.

"I don't want to be ugly," I whispered, and it felt like a shameful confession.

"Oh no. No, my Lia." He crawled over to me, face creased with compassion. Such a hard man and such a tender heart inside that scarred chest. "You are celebrated as the most beautiful woman in the world."

"The queen is," I replied, my voice still quiet, as if we could be overheard. But we were as alone as I'd assured him, the tower room silent but for the song of chirping insects below, the spit of flame from the torches, and the distant murmur of my seas. "And that's mostly makeup. *She* is the one who—"

"*You* are." He knelt beside me, framing my face in his hands, kissing me softly now, almost reverently. "That's the reason I ask. I like seeing *you*."

I gazed back, deeply unnerved. The question was, did I want to be seen?

"Don't you trust me, Lia," he asked, "at least with this small thing?"

I nearly said it wasn't a matter of trust, and it was far from small for me. But I also refused to hide without reason. It would be a concession to doubts and fear.

"All right." I shivered, though I wasn't cold, and held still as he slid his hands up to gently pull off the wig. Tossing it aside, he returned his palms to caress my bare skull, the skin there soft and sensitive, his hands feeling nearly hot in comparison. I watched his face as he looked at me, touched me, and saw none of the revulsion I'd dreaded, and gradually I relaxed a little.

"I see the patterns," he said, wonder in his voice. "Like you get sometimes on other parts, like on the back of your thigh. Flower petals here." He traced the skin lightly, then bent and touched his lips to my scalp, kissing that tender skin so I trembled. "Green leaves here. Only it feels like smooth skin."

"My ladies shaved My head recently. Give Me a few days and it will feel different." Weird and rough, the stems of hair that wasn't hair pushing through, reaching for the sun.

"All right," he agreed softly, echoing me. "Let it grow."

"I can't." Stricken, I stared at him, wrapping my arms around myself, as if I could hide. But something in me had been irrevocably laid open, and I couldn't seem to cover it again.

"Shh," he murmured. "Don't be afraid, my flower." He lay down, easing me down with him and draping me over him, arms securely around me. "You're safe with me."

Strangely enough, I did feel safe in that moment, cradled in the bulwark of his big body. Just as I had in the folly that morning. I refused to fool myself that sex with Con, or our marriage, meant anything more than what it did, but I did believe he'd protect me to the end of his strength. Never mind his reasons for it. His goals and mine coincided at least there, and I could trust in that, if nothing else. I didn't have to be suspicious of the kindness Con showed me, because I'd known from the beginning what he wanted from me.

What we wanted from each other. What I wanted more of.

I wiggled loose of his hold and slid up his firm chest, laying my lips lightly on his. At first sipping, then deepening, I stoked the fires between us, letting my thigh drape between his legs against the long, hot, and urgent length of his cock. Indulging myself, I caressed his chest, savoring the iron hardness of the muscles beneath soft skin and silky hair. Tasting him, I trailed kisses along his jaw and corded throat, undulating against him so my taut nipples teased us both.

"Lia," he groaned. "I can't . . ." His body shuddered with need, so I left off tormenting him. I sat up and straddled him, scooting back to undo his leather pants, freeing his cock and taking it in my hands, his heated girth a delightful reward as always. Unable to resist, despite my resolve not to tease him, I licked the head, swirling my tongue to taste the steaming salt like the sea. Here he was all soft, sweetly tender and sensitive. His hips bucked, nearly unseating me, and he cursed, fingers digging into my hips as he lifted me, then lay me on my back again. "Like this," he grunted, arranging me with firm touches, spreading my thighs wide, so I was all the more naked and exposed. *I like seeing you.* It felt good. Strange, but also . . . arousing. Freeing.

"Yes?" Con asked. His gaze flicked up to mine and I nodded, breathless with the intensity of his eyes, gone molten gold as late-afternoon sunlight. Face contorted with desire and concentration, wild hair hanging in a tumult, he was the wolf of my dreams. But instead of rending me, he lifted my hips, gathering me to him as he lowered himself between my thighs, and eased his cock carefully into my entrance. Such a study he made of it, determined to perfect this skill.

As he sheathed himself in me, he released some of his straining control, bracing one hand beside my head, the other behind my hips cushioning me. "Does this hurt?"

I shook my head, rolling it on the glassy tiles of Calanthe, aware of their cool kiss against my bare scalp. I was full of him. For the moment not empty and alone. "Take me, Con," I whispered.

He began to move, and I gave myself over to the delicious, surging tides of it. Yielding myself utterly, if only for this brief moment, another time, another world.

7

The crash of release made me cross-eyed, diamond stars wrenching my brains out the back of my skull. Though I tried to keep myself leashed, I knew I thrust too hard into Lia's deliciously welcoming heat. She thrashed beneath me, a wild thing moaning encouragement I didn't need, our skin slicking against the other, a contact I'd been too ignorant to miss before and now knew I'd crave the rest of my benighted life.

As the brutal fist of the climax relaxed, I at least had the presence of mind to slip a hand under her head, cushioning that fragile-seeming skull from the cold tiles, propping my weight on my elbow, uncaring how painful the hard floor made it. Better my battered body than her delicate one. Dizzy, I dropped my face to my forearm, dragging in breath after breath. You'd think I'd been battling hours instead of making love to a woman. My wife. The Queen of Flowers.

How unreal was that?

Her hands trailed down my back, like she thought I needed soothing. Maybe I did. The comforting caress of her fingertips, bare of the wicked nails she usually affected—or I'd be sporting furrows of blood from them—touched some ragged part deep inside me. I throttled the tender feeling before I did something horribly weak, or confessed something unwise. Lia brought out a side of me I'd thought long since dead, buried under mounds of stinking rock and despair. Lying there on her supple skin, a blossom of a woman, in the warm night with torchlight and some sweet flower filling the still air . . . In another world, another lifetime, I might have called it romantic.

"Mmm," she purred, pressing a kiss to my shoulder. "On second thought I'm not at all annoyed that you didn't come to bed."

I lifted my head to check her face to see if she was teasing me. She smiled, all soft and glowing. Without the wig her eyes looked huge in her small-boned face, glinting with light, like otherworldly, radiant jewels. Lovely eyes, deep blue now, almost purple. No, a rich emerald. I cocked my head, studying one eye then the other. One blue. One green. Glowing, as if lit from within. "Are your eyes different colors?"

For a moment she looked startled and vulnerable, those gorgeous eyes widening, a tremor running through her body, just as when I'd pulled the wig away. I caressed her scalp, sliding my hand down to massage the tight tendons at the base of her neck. The woman was way too tense for someone who wasn't a warrior. Though I supposed she fought her battles every day just the same.

"It's me," I told her, not sure if that made any sense. But there I was, her husband, my life sworn to hers, my body still sheathed inside her. "I won't tell. I won't hurt you," I added, just in case that helped.

"I know." She blew out a breath, her body relaxing beneath mine, though she'd lost her previous languor. "Let Me up."

I hadn't thought I was preventing her, but I heard the

return of the regal tone to her voice and obliged. Obeyed, perhaps. A fine line there. I settled back, watching as she sat up, tucked her legs demurely to one side, and ran her hands over her bare skull, then glanced at where I'd tossed her wig, well out of easy reach. She felt naked without it, I could tell, and she'd love to put it on again—but I bet myself she wouldn't reveal that insecurity by going to get it. That would betray too much.

When she returned her gaze to mine, she'd assumed her invisible cloak of cool poise—and her eyes were once again gray-blue, the same on both sides. "Better?" she asked.

"If you mean, are your eyes the same as each other again, and more . . . not as colorful, then yes. But not better."

She paused, that stillness to her, like a forest animal freezing when a predator passes. It made me want to kiss her, so I took the chance, going to her on hands and knees and hovering my mouth near hers until she tipped her chin up to meet my lips. I kissed her as tenderly as I knew how, aware of how often I didn't. The lust for her raged in me, and I was not a civilized man by any stretch. Fortunately she seemed to understand and accept that. Maybe the wildness in her recognized the same in me.

I pulled back just enough to speak, hoping the words would come out right. "I liked the different colors. Beautiful and magical, like you."

She searched my face, a tentativeness in her eyes, though she'd definitely done something to change and mute them. "What colors did you see?"

It seemed wrong to say just blue and green, but I wasn't much for poetic words. "Don't you know?"

She shrugged a little, then gave me a quick kiss before scrambling away with lithe grace. Not quite fleeing, but not far from it, either. Catching up the wig, she pulled it on, then walked casually over to the robe she'd discarded. I took note of the order—and how she didn't mind at all bending over so I saw all of her pink sex between her legs, but she'd covered her bald head as soon as she could. She turned back to face me, tying the sash of her robe, watching me pull up my pants. I didn't have anything to clean myself with, but oh well.

"I haven't let My eyes show in . . . forever," she said. "It's been so long I can't even remember what they look like. I'm rather astonished at My lapse." She cocked her head slightly, and I didn't miss the hint of accusation.

I very nearly said something about how I'd fucked her senseless, but that was a crude joke I'd heard and I doubted it would come out as funny. Instead I got to my feet and pulled on my shirt, buckling on the vest and belt again, thinking hard. "Deep blue," I said, "like the sky gets after sunset but before it's really night. On the left. On the right . . ." I frowned, considering. "Like that jewel of Ambrose's—you know how it gets really green when the sun hits it just right? Bright, but still rich-looking. Like that."

She smiled slightly, a closed-mouthed pursing of her lips, a quirk to her brows. They were different without the makeup—not etched and elegant, but light and almost feathery. If her real hair grew in, she'd told me, it would be like fine vines with leaves and flowers. It had been hard for me to picture before, but I could see it in my head now, having glimpsed her true eyes.

I frowned, tugging at an elusive memory. Trying to remember stuff from before the mines could be like hooking a fish—I had to lay in wait when the shadow of a memory flitted by, then move slowly, steadily, to draw it in. Make my move too fast and I'd spook it.

Ah, there was a piece of it . . . a book, with illustrations. A very old memory because I was in the nursery, and my sister was there, the book on her lap. She pointed at the picture of a naked girl in a jungle of flowers, her hair and the background weaving together. Her eyes, one blue and one green, shimmered like jewels. Like Lia.

I tried to see the cover of that book. We'd loved it, I remembered that much. And our nurse had read us stories from it, of old gods and . . . elementals. Yes, that illustration had to have been of a being like Lia in some way. If only I could remember the stories themselves, they might give me insight.

"What?" she asked, breaking into my thoughts.

Mentally, I set the hook for the memory, hoping to snag the whole thing. But I thought she wouldn't like it if I told her I'd been trying to figure her out. "If you can change your eye color just by thinking about it, why use the makeup and stuff?"

She didn't cock her head—even without the crown and wig, she held her chin firm and spine straight, like she never lost awareness of that balance—as she considered the question. "It's more than just 'thinking' about it," she said slowly. "It takes concentration. I had to practice it for a long time when I was a girl. Mostly it's habit now, and the minor drain is something I'm used to. If I had another way to disguise My eyes, I'd do it."

"Only now maybe you don't have to. There's no reason to keep secrets about yourself anymore," I added, gentling my voice as I said the words, seeing how she withdrew as I spoke.

"You're wrong," she replied with flat determination. "There's every reason."

"Tell me one." I held her muted gaze in direct challenge, not letting her off easily.

"It's how I survive," she replied quietly. "You have your revenge. I have . . . endurance."

I waited for her to say more, but she didn't. "I don't understand."

"I know." She hesitated, then added, almost reluctantly. "In some ways, I don't understand, either. I've survived this long by hiding. At night, I hear the howls of those who suffer, the ones who didn't stay safe. Their obvious pain is a good reason to keep doing what I've been doing."

I turned that over in my head, still not sure what she was saying. "What do you mean, that you hear . . . these things?"

"Never mind." Firmly changing the subject, she swept her hand at the map. "So, what have you discovered? You spent all day studying My island."

I'd pushed her enough—especially considering what I had to say next. "This place," I said, walking barefoot to a part of the coastline I'd been studying. I'd been over the whole thing countless times, and I kept coming back to that one.

She drifted over to me, looking down, then up at me, that fine pucker between her brows. I bet it didn't show when she had the heavy makeup on and I nearly lifted a finger to trace it, but that would be giving away that I'd picked up on one of her tells. She had so few that I'd better hoard the ones I discovered.

"Cradysica?"

"What does that name mean?" I countered. The word tickled some of that old, same memory.

She shrugged, but she picked at the band of the orchid ring with her thumbnail. Another tell—one that made me wonder if the thing itched or something. "Nothing special—just a place-name, for a village like any other."

"I want to go there."

"Then go. You're a free man. Do as you like."

"I want you to come with me."

With a tightening jaw, she jammed her hands to her hips. "That's what this is," she hissed. "A trick to get Me out of the palace. You want to bring Anure's wrath down on Cradysica. It's a beautiful place with an innocent population. I won't let you sacrifice them to—"

"No?" I stood up, leaned over her. Even so much shorter without her fancy heels, she burned with imposing presence. "Which part of Calanthe *will* you sacrifice, Lia?" I swept a hand at the detailed map, glittering more sullenly now as the torches guttered. "Go ahead and pick it out. I'll wait."

She glared at me, gaze full of fury that could cut a man to ribbons. "You are loathsome."

"Tell me something I don't know," I bit out. There was no reasoning with this woman.

"You have no idea what this is like for Me," she gritted through clenched teeth.

"Then tell me." The near shout strained my throat, painfully grating as it hadn't in a while.

Her eyes briefly glimmered, her face losing its smooth impassivity for a blink. Then she had it back and I wondered if I'd imagined the tears. "You don't have the ability to understand."

The cool words, lethally sharp in their dismissive arrogance—those were a new weapon. I ignored the hit, taking the reveal for the opening it was.

"Not if you don't explain." I returned the words hard. "You said you trusted me."

A flare of impact as that hit home in turn. She closed her lips tight, assessing me. "That was sex."

"It's all the same thing, Lia."

"Oh, Con." She spoke in a pitying tone, lifting a hand to pet me into calm—eyes widening in surprise when I batted it away. Chilling, she stepped back. "The first lesson of the Court of Flowers is that sex is sex. I promised to be your wife, and that gives you access to My body, but I don't owe you anything else."

I pushed through the pain in my throat, and the weary awareness that she didn't share the tumult of emotions that plagued me. What a pitiful piece of shit I was, thinking of making love to her, that the joining of our bodies meant something, when it clearly meant nothing to her. "What about your willing alliance and assistance, which you promised only this morning? I can't win this fight, do the job you married me to do, unless you work with me."

She stared hard, chin lifted in defiance. Then she sagged, almost imperceptibly, gaze going to the village of Cradysica. "Why there?"

"I need to see it first, for real. Then I'll know if it's the right place."

When she glanced back at me, nodding in resignation, I knew I'd won. "But I want to convene everyone again. If Cradysica is the place, we'll need to have plans ready, weapons prepared."

"Shall I have our advisers dragged from their beds, or is morning soon enough?"

"Morning is fine." I ignored her scathing tone, figuring she deserved her anger. "But first thing—not after hours squandered in formal court, spending time on inane meetings about . . . other stuff." I amended what I'd been about to say when she pierced me with a fulminous stare that just dared me to minimize the business of running Calanthe.

We descended the long stairs in silence, but when we met Ibolya patiently waiting at the foot of the tower, Lia instructed her to send messages to everyone to meet first thing in the morning. Far too early, to my mind, given the very late hour, but I could hardly argue now. Still, how did the woman get by on so little sleep?

"Happy now?" Lia asked, and I nodded, though, as usual, victory tasted like ash. I imagined the final triumph would be the same. When I struck down Anure and destroyed his empire, I didn't expect to feel good. I only hoped the ravenous ghosts that clamored for vengeance would at last be satisfied.

As I accompanied Lia back to our rooms, it occurred to me that the only time I had felt anything that resembled happiness was in those moments skin-to-skin with her, buried in her, with her scent around me and her unguarded cries in my ear. Only then did the voices of the past fall into silence.

Like Lia's eyes, however, neither of us stayed unarmored for long—and the voices of the dead renewed their demands all too soon.

Though Lia fell asleep the moment we lay down, her back turned to me in cold dismissal, I remained awake, eyes stubbornly popping open, brain still chewing away at the problem. Cradysica had the perfect landscape for a trap—if I read the map right, and if the currents were what I thought. The name . . . instinct plucked at me. Something there.

It had to be the place. If so, the strategy had to be perfect. It should be simple: dangle Lia as bait, draw in Anure personally, along with his forces, fold the trap around him. We needed a lot of vurgsten, true, but we'd overcome similar odds. Avoiding blood shed in violence would be nearly impossible, but I'd promised Lia I'd try.

As for protecting her . . . Getting her out of the palace was the first step. Keeping her out of Anure's reach should be reasonably straightforward. *If* she obeyed orders, which—let's face it—she wouldn't do.

She made a sound of protest in her sleep, and for a moment, I thought she responded to my thought. Then she whined, piteous, like a small creature in pain. "Lia?"

Another cry, louder, more agonized. It scraped along my nerves, dredging up memories of the mines and hearing sounds like that in the night. Clenching my jaw, I put a hand on her shoulder. Did she have nightmares like we did? *I've endured more than you know.* "Lia, sweet. Wake up."

She did. Abruptly and fully. The moonlight reflected on the shining seas just beyond the nearly full circle of open windows that ringed the bedchamber, lighting the room and her pale face, her eyes luminous. Terror and grief in them. "Is it morning?" she asked, her voice clear, no hint of sleep fogging it.

And I realized I'd spoken as her ladies would to wake her for the day, like setting spark to vurgsten and exploding her from sleep. "No. You were dreaming. Go back to sleep."

Her face smoothed, eyes unfocusing. "Dawn isn't long away, though."

"How do you know?"

"I feel it. Calanthe is waking. Listen."

Sure enough, a bird called, followed by more. A soft knock on the door, and Ibolya called through it. "Conrí?"

"You were right," I said. Maybe I'd slept without knowing it. Giving her a kiss—because she still looked lost—I found her lips cool, nearly waxy. "Are you well?"

She gazed back at me, lips still parted as if she might speak, then she pressed them closed. "I'm fine. I'll see you in a bit."

Still, I hesitated. "Maybe you should sleep longer."

She rolled over, turning her back to me again. "I'll sleep when I'm dead."

Not exactly reassuring. I lifted a hand to touch her shoulder again, but another knock came, louder. "Conrí?"

Getting out of bed, I pulled on the soft robe they'd given me and went out to meet Ibolya. The rooms lay in quiet dimness still, no candles lit, and I realized the bright moonlight mingled with coming dawn. Ibolya smiled, looking untouched as dew, wearing a different gown and wig than a few hours before, fresh flowers gleaming in the soft light. "Good morning, Conrí. Did you rest well?"

"No," I replied bluntly, and she blinked at me in surprise. "Did you rest at all?"

She laughed, a practiced sound like bells. "No. I used the time to refresh myself and change clothes. But I did nap while Her Highness visited you in the map tower." She led me to the adjoining rooms that had been converted for me to bathe and dress in, so I wouldn't be in the way of Lia and her rituals. Ibolya showed me the bath full of steaming water, as if I hadn't been doing this every day since the wedding. This room was brightly lit with glass-paned lanterns. "Do you need anything else, Conrí?" she asked.

"No, I'm good." Maybe I'd catch a nap in the tub.

"General Kara requests an audience. Shall I ask him to wait?"

I snorted at the image of Kara "requesting" anything. Always an early riser, he doubtless kicked his heels in impatience at being blockaded. "I'll see him now."

She curtsied, turning politely away as I dropped the robe and got in the tub. "Shall I bring tea?"

"Coffee," I said. They grew the stuff here on Calanthe, one of its many delights. Plus I could use its stimulating kick today. "And get Kara to bring it. He can make himself useful."

Ibolya giggled lightly. "Yes, Conrí."

"Ibolya?"

She turned, hand on the door latch, brows raised politely. "Have you known Lia—Her Highness—for a long time?"

Her face smoothed into a polite mask. "I've served Her Highness for five years. Not as long as other of Her ladies."

I nodded. "Does she have nightmares?"

"I couldn't say, Conrí."

Nice, specific phrasing. Not confirming or denying. "Thanks. Send Kara in."

"As soon as I load up the coffee tray, Conrí," she replied with an impish smile. An apology of sorts, for not replying, I decided.

I did fall asleep in the tub, because Kara woke me by kicking the side of it. I squinted at the grim specter of his disapproving scowl, glaring at me over a tray laden with a silver coffee service. "Must be nice," he commented.

"Don't they offer you hot baths?" I replied, taking the mug he handed me while expertly balancing the tray on one hand. "Remind me to talk to the staff for you."

"Funny," he grunted. Putting the tray on the table, he added several spoonfuls of sugar to his own mug before offering the sweetener to me. I shook my head and tasted mine, savoring the roasted bitter richness. Kara pulled up a chair, holding his solid mug in his scarred hands.

"What?" I asked.

"I'm concerned."

"Yeah?" I'd met Kara in the mines and we'd fought

together for a long time. He almost never hesitated to speak his mind. Seeking me out when he knew we'd be in private . . .

"There's no way to battle Anure's forces without shedding blood. Plenty of it. The violence goes without saying."

"I know." Of course we all knew that. Everyone but Lia, and the rest of Calanthe.

"And yet you promised Her Highness."

"I said I'd *try*." I drained the cup and set to scrubbing myself.

"Then you don't intend to keep your promise?"

I shrugged, soaping my hair and closing my eyes against the stinging suds. "I'll *try*. Lia doesn't understand war, and right now I need Lia compliant." Did I just say that? What a hypocrite I was, promising one thing to her face, conspiring to keep her ignorant and pliable behind her back. Guess it wasn't the most monstrous thing about me, though.

"What of the consequences?"

I ducked my head and wiped water from my face, getting a look at Kara's. "You don't believe this magic stuff has any real-world impact, do you?"

His eyes got a faraway look. "There are old stories."

"Yeah. About unicorns and dragons, too. There's magic here, I'll admit, and Lia has it. But really, what's the worst that can happen? We've already survived the end of the world. I don't see how anything else could be all that bad."

Kara focused on me again, giving me an unamused smile. "Did you ask Ambrose?"

"He never gives me a straight answer," I grumbled, standing and wringing out my hair before reaching for a drying cloth.

"Are you sure you're not just ignoring anything that interferes with your vengeance?"

"I'm ignoring this conversation. I found a potential location. Cradysica. In case you want to check it out before we meet."

He nodded, his gaze dark. "This plan . . . you're talking endgame here, Conrí."

I pulled on the pants that efficient Ibolya had left for me. "You just figured that out?"

Standing, he refilled my cup, thrusting it at me. "Have more, because your brain clearly isn't working."

Though I didn't want it, I drank, waiting for the lecture. "Spit it out, man."

"I did some calculations. Even getting all the ships, all the vurgsten here for this trap—we're greatly outmatched."

"Not news, Kara."

"If we fail, then there won't be any coming back. This is an all-or-nothing gambit."

"Then we'd better win." I pulled on my shirt, then fastened my belt and bagiroca. Kara waited in silence. "Do you have another suggestion?"

"We could go after him at the citadel, like we always planned."

"Go up against the impregnable fortress? Last I heard, you thought we'd dash ourselves brainless and end up as beach trash."

"True," he admitted.

"This plan can work, Kara. I feel it in my bones. We've never had an advantage over Anure like this. It's what the wizard's prophecy meant."

"Did Ambrose say that?"

"I didn't ask," I bit out, shouldering my rock hammer.

"Why are you bugging me about asking Ambrose every damn thing?"

"I have a bad feeling about this plan."

"You don't even know what it is yet."

"Yeah." He nodded, distant gaze going through me. "Details will help. Cradysica, huh?"

"Cradysica."

We convened in the map tower, so we could look at the geography around Cradysica and the approaches. It helped to have a strategy meeting around a map, but the Calantheans still managed to make it look like a garden party.

Lia's ladies circulated with trays of pastries, fruit, hot floral tea, and cool lemon-mint ices, serving everyone themselves rather than bringing servants in. Setting the tone, Lia wore a gown that seemed to be made of flower petals, all shades of red and pink, like that fountain of roses in her garden. She should have looked soft and gentle in it, but something—maybe the wig of unnatural red that set off the blue jewels of her crown, or the sharp lines of her makeup that put me in mind of thorns—made her look hard and dangerous. Not for the first time she reminded me of the carnivorous flowers we'd encountered in the steaming Mazos jungle.

"Was breakfast really necessary?" I asked when she wafted past. Yeah, I'd never been able to resist poking those Mazos blossoms, either.

"People need to eat, Conrí," she replied with cool disinterest, no sign of the vulnerable woman I'd kissed only a short while before, or the passionate one who'd spread herself open for me an arm's length from where we stood. "I'd think you'd know that, being such a brilliant commander and all. You'll have plenty of time to talk about war. Ah, Lord Dearsley, thank you for indulging Me with such an early morning, come and sit."

Without another glance at me, Lia took the old man's arm and led him to a chair. With him she was all sweet smiles and charm.

"Tea and crumpet, syr?" Sondra inquired in a posh accent, handing me a plate and a fragile-looking cup decorated with more roses.

"Don't start with me," I growled, very glad I'd at least already had coffee.

She snorted. "Teach me to be nice to you."

While she retrieved her own plate, I chewed the pastry savagely. It was flaky and buttery, and more delicious than I wanted it to be. Good thing Lia had agreed to leave for Cradysica the next day. I'd grow fat as Anure eating like this and lounging about, forever talking and never taking action.

"Why so cranky, Conrí?" Sondra asked with fake sympathy. "Didn't get enough sleep?"

"Were you on watch last night?"

"Ayup." She crooked her fingers as she sipped her tea, giving me a malicious smile. Like mine, her hands weren't the sort that normally held pretty dishes. Not anymore. With permanently stained skin, thickened nails, and gnarled knuckles, she made a mockery of the cup just by pretending to hold it like a proper lady. "You two were sure 'studying' that map for a long time."

I didn't rise to her bait. Instead I scanned the gathering. "Where is Ambrose?"

She shrugged. "In his tower. Last night he said he had things to do and wouldn't make the meeting, but that he'll be ready to go to Cradysica in the morning."

"He said that last night? But we hadn't decided yet

that . . ." I didn't bother to finish the sentence, especially with Sondra's caustic expression. "Why do I even bother working out problems if he already knows everything?"

"I'm sure Ambrose would say that magic doesn't work that way."

I grunted a humorless laugh, because she was right. At some unseen signal, Lia's ladies converged to her, flanking their queen as she sat, helping her to arrange her gown. Once Lia nodded, everyone else seated themselves. Except for us. Kara moved over to Sondra and me, and we all remained standing. Lia gave me an opaque glance, then addressed the gathering.

"Thank you, all, for attending Me this morning. Conrí?"

8

Con coughed, clearing his throat and brushing pastry crumbs from his fingers. He passed his plate and cup to Kara, who looked like he'd been handed a wailing infant. Petty of me, perhaps, to take Con by surprise, but I hadn't quite recalibrated my temperament. What little sleep I'd gotten had been spent in nightmares, and Con had nearly caught me in that vulnerable state. Tonight I would have to do better to hide their effects. Not an easy proposition, the way the nightmares seemed to be intensifying.

The dream images had taken on a new clarity, too. A wolf, gnawing off my hand as I tried to help it. Calanthe, thrashing beneath my feet. Waking. The temple above Cradysica falling into the sea. Cradysica it would be. I couldn't fight this. It had been all I could do to drag myself to this meeting. Thank Ejarat—and my clever ladies—for makeup.

"Your Highness." Con bowed deeply to me, then turned to the others. "An update since yesterday. My people are bringing in all the vurgsten supplies we can in preparation. General Kara?"

Kara had relieved himself of Con's dishes, and stood with hands folded behind his back in military style. "Thanks to Her Highness's assistance," he intoned in his harsh voice, nodding to me, "we've sent ships to establish a relay that will expedite bringing as much vurgsten to the island as possible before the emperor's fleet can interfere. We'll keep as much aboard local vessels as possible, so the maximum amount of vurgsten can be relayed to the chosen site quickly."

"I ran some numbers," Brenda put in. "Even guessing at most of them, to spring the kind of trap you're thinking of, we're going to need a fuck-all huge amount of vurgsten."

"And at least that many ships," the flamboyant Percy added, examining his nails as he lounged sideways in his chair. "Preferably two times fuck-all."

Agatha, wrapped in her shawl, though the morning was far from cool, gave him a look. "This is a serious situation, Percy."

"Agatha, darling, until I'm dead, nothing is so serious that I won't poke at Brenda's colorful language," he drawled. "*Seriously*, however, I ran some numbers, too. How do you propose to mount any kind of credible defense when we are outmatched in every way? Your reputation precedes you, of course, Conrí, but these odds are sadly stacked against us. We're looking at staggering losses, even without certain . . . strictures." He glanced at me, but I kept cool and showed no reaction. Perhaps they only now realized that Con and his people had truly conquered Calanthe after all. I certainly seemed to have lost the power to affect events.

"We're looking at staggering losses no matter what we do," Con replied with temper. "Would you rather die fighting or sitting here dithering?"

"You're talking to a room full of people who've gone to great trouble not to die, Conrí," I reminded him. "Including yourself."

He wheeled on me, golden eyes flaring with heat, but

brought himself up short at a hail from below. Nahua, who'd remained near the stairwell, turned at the sound. She took something, then brought it to me, offering it with a curtsy. A small letter, brought by bird. I sliced it open with the sharp side of my nail, scarlet in honor of my bleeding heart.

"Lia! Let me—" Con started forward, reaching for it, and I shook my head slightly.

"It's not him," I said.

He relaxed, chagrined, but I gave him a smile, strangely warmed that he'd remembered and sought to protect me—even in the midst of his impatient raging.

"I've been expecting this," I said for the group at large. "Reports on the number of ships mustering at the emperor's naval yards and harbors in Yekpehr." I passed the letter to Calla, who understood the code, which allowed me to observe everyone as she read aloud the numbers of each type of ship and estimated troop load. As everyone processed the information, the room grew silent enough that I could hear the sound of waves on the rocks.

"Can I see that?" Con asked after a moment. Calla glanced to me for permission, and I was small enough to enjoy Con's irritation at that. Now he knew how it felt. At my nod, Calla took it to him, and he plucked it from her fingers without ceremony or thanks, then handed it to Sondra to read. Charming.

"This is about a party, the guests, and what they wore," Sondra said, a puzzled frown drawing her brows together.

"It's a code, Lady Sondra," I informed her with exaggerated patience.

"One that Lady Calla understands," Con said to me, with some significance.

"Yes? I trust my ladies to—" The force of his suspicion hit me.

"Does Tertulyn know the code?" he asked, though he knew the answer, and he sounded compassionate enough, though I felt like a blithering idiot. I hadn't fully processed the ramifications of this betrayal. It made my head ache.

I held out my hand for the letter, and Sondra gave it to me, with far less courtesy than Nahua had. "The information is good, though," I said, scanning it. "The handwriting belongs to My informant, and the correct cues are present to ensure authenticity."

When Con looked surprised, I added, "I'm not an utter fool, Conrí."

To his credit, he didn't touch that remark. He simply nodded. "Then the worst we can assume is that Anure will be aware that we know this information. As he's unlikely to lower the numbers, we'll figure he might change them up, or increase them. Given this, I estimate we have—at best and with luck—a tenth of the might Anure can, and no doubt will, bring to bear. Probably we'll have considerably less than that. We can't win with might."

"Which," I put in, "I believe has been My point all along."

Con gave me an unamused look. "I never claimed we'd win by fielding greater forces."

"No, you think we can win at all, which is patently beyond us. All of this planning is wishful thinking. Everyone here agrees that the odds are impossible. We cannot win, Conrí."

"Begging your pardon, Your Highness," he said with exaggerated courtesy that only highlighted his anger, "but you don't know what you're talking about."

"See here, young man," Dearsley burst out. "I'll not have—"

I waved him silent. "Thank you, Lord Dearsley, but

I can handle this. You were explaining My stupidity, Conrí?"

He didn't miss my slicing tone, the grooves around his mouth deepening, resignation in the set of his mouth, but he forged on. "Ignorance is not the same as stupidity, Your Highness, or I'd be the stupidest man on Calanthe with all I don't know. What I *do* know is fighting Anure. Have *any* of you accomplished what we have? Have you taken cities back from Anure's grip, stolen his ships, taken his fiancée for your own?"

Oh, he did not say that. Heat flooded my face, and I only hoped the white makeup covered it. That was another reason I didn't depend on my will to alter my appearance—I couldn't always depend on myself to keep the deception in place. Obviously, or I wouldn't have slipped so mortifyingly, allowing Con to see my true eyes. And because of sex. I couldn't believe myself.

Like a man knowing he'd dug himself deeper and had no way to back out of the grave he'd made, Con continued with grim determination. "This is what I know. Arguably, it is my one skill, but I do know Anure's weaknesses and how to play on them. This is a good plan. I'm asking you all to invest in it."

"You're asking us to commit everything to it," I corrected, not bothering to disguise my vehemence.

He met my gaze. "Yes. Yes, I am. Because everything is what it will take."

"That is not how I was raised to rule, Conrí."

"No, you were raised to take the side of caution, to play along, to hide in plain sight pretending to be something you're not."

"It worked," I pointed out with cool asperity.

"Until it didn't," he shot back. "You knew all along that it was a staying tactic, Lia. You always knew that someday enduring wouldn't be enough, and you had your plan for that, didn't you?"

I didn't reply to that. Couldn't. Con had seen right through me, divining from the start that I'd been resigned to being eventually forced into marriage with Anure—and that I'd hoped to kill him in the throes of passion. To at least rid the world of the Imperial Toad, sacrificing myself for that end.

"Well, Lia?" he asked softly, as if it were only the two of us arguing, instead of in front of our rather large, entirely rapt audience.

"I don't like it."

"But will You do it?" He'd become aware of our audience again, too, using the honorific he so often forgot in the heat of argument.

"I have no choice, do I?" I bit out.

He shook his head. "None of us do."

"Then set your trap. May Sawehl and Ejarat have mercy on us all."

"Guile it is then." Percy spoke up, fluttering his sparkling nails in the air as if celebrating. "But that means your trap must be perfectly set."

"It will be." Sondra grinned toothily, sliding a look at me. "As Conrí pointed out, this is *our* area of expertise."

A subtle jibe in there, but I had no idea why she aimed it at me. Con flashed her a quelling frown. Clearing his throat, he continued. "For the trap, we've settled on a potential location. Her Highness and I will travel to Cradysica in the morning and—"

"Cradysica!" Lord Dearsley exploded, dropping his teacup, which shattered on the glazed tiles of the western ocean. Orvyki looked to me and, when I nodded, scurried over to help clean up the pieces. I tried not to look, unwilling to see what the spilt tea leaves foretold. As if I needed more omens of the terrible future. "Your Highness," Dearsley said over Orvyki's bowed head, "You cannot think to go to Cradysica at this time."

I raised a brow at Con, who returned my cool look with an obstinate one of his own. No help there. "I must, Lord Dearsley. I ask you to hold the throne in My absence. I trust you to do as I would, as My father would."

"Your Highness." His faded blue eyes beseeched me. "There are things I cannot do. Without the orchid ring, I can't, that is, no one can—"

"It won't come to that, Lord Dearsley," I interrupted. Con narrowed his eyes with interest, but I ignored him. I'd agreed to share relevant knowledge with him, but this wouldn't affect his battle and damned if I would give him everything of myself. He had enough hold on me already. "We will go to Cradysica. If the battle does occur there, and we—by some miracle—prevail, then I'll return to the palace and there will be no interruption."

"And if You are defeated?" Dearsley demanded.

"We plan to—" Con started, but I held up a hand to cut him off.

"In that likely eventuality," I said to Dearsley as gently as I could, "then you will have worse problems than the line of succession. Calanthe will become one of the many conquered kingdoms. I'll be counting on you to do what's needed."

Looking as defeated as his worst fears made us, Dearsley nodded. He took the fresh cup of tea Orvyki handed him but didn't drink, only stared at it in his lap. I knew how he felt, and I couldn't help him. "Continue, Conrí," I said.

He didn't speak immediately, looking at me with a frown, but when I only gazed at him impassively, he took up the thread again. "I'd like for you all to study

Cradysica or, if you're already familiar, pass along notes. General Kara will provide a relay to bring him information. Anything you can tell us about the topography, the seas, predictions on Anure's likely plan of attack once he knows Li—Her Highness is there. Everything you can think of. We need every advantage."

Brenda had risen while Con spoke, walking along the coastline on the map—staying in the ocean, I noted— until she reached Cradysica. Kara quietly pointed out some features to her. She said something and Kara shook his head. I'd have liked to hear their conversation. I had no doubt, however, that she would pass along her observations.

Agatha raised a hand. "When do you intend to make it clear Her Highness is traveling?"

Con glanced at me. I had no answer. This was his game now. I was but a pawn. Bait in his trap. The queen who'd travel to Cradysica under false pretenses, to drown them in blood. I'd escaped Anure's plans for me only to become Con's game piece. I didn't know whether to laugh or cry at the cosmic joke.

"Immediately," he said, his voice hoarse. Regret? Surely not. "If Cradysica isn't the place, I have a second and third option in mind. Her Highness will not be back before the battle is won."

And if it's lost, She won't be back at all! I nearly said. Lack of sleep and the strain of events had made me punchy.

Agatha nodded thoughtfully, then stood, her shawl falling around her in shimmering waves of shifting color. "With Your permission, Your Highness, I will make sure word of Your journeying reaches the right ears. How shall I frame it?"

I'd been thinking about that.

"We'll travel by ship along the coast," Con announced before I could speak. "Under cover of night, preferably. Anure can learn of Her Highness's presence in Cradysica when we reach it."

"No," I said. Only long training kept me from cracking a smile at the glare of consternation Con turned on me. *Oh no, sweetheart. I might be going along with your doomed and impetuous plan, but I'm not ceding all control to you.* I focused on Agatha, gesturing to my lady, Zariah, to go with her. "Let it be known far and wide that I'll be escorting Conrí on a tour of Calanthe. My ladies, Conrí's companions, and any of the court who'd like to come along are invited to join the entourage. We'll leave by carriage in the morning. The people of Calanthe are welcome to observe the parade, and may expect largesse. Our first overnight stop will be Cradysica, so Lady Zariah, please send the appropriate messages to the head family so they may prepare, and assist Agatha however she needs."

Zariah curtsied. Agatha bowed her head. They both moved toward the stairwell.

"Wait," Con said, not a shout, but quite loudly. They paused and he turned on me, the gold of his eyes boiling over in the pitted cauldron of his face. "Overland? A parade? You have got to be fucking kidding me, Lia."

Someone laughed, a shocked sound, I didn't catch who. Dearsley looked apoplectic, Percy patting his arm solicitously as he nodded at Orvyki to bring more tea. There might not be enough tea in all of Calanthe to soothe Dearsley's offended sensibilities.

I will not laugh. I will not laugh.

"Ah, Conrí." General Kara cleared his throat and approached Con, who looked like he might have a fit of his own. "In all truth, we could put the ships to better use transporting vurgsten and our troops, if you and Her Highness find traveling overland a viable option."

"Oh, it is," I put in gaily. "Such lovely views, and the perfect weather for an excursion. We'll have such fun!" My ladies, well accustomed to me, made happy sounds of approval.

A vein throbbed in Con's temple so visibly I wondered if it would pop, and I swore I heard a low growl from him. I met his furious gaze evenly, letting him see the challenge in my eyes—and that I would not yield this point. I knew my people and I would at least give them this spectacle if I must travel. No need to panic everyone unnecessarily.

"Fine," Con muttered with ill grace. I nearly rolled my eyes at him.

Brenda had followed Kara back over to the group. "Your Highness?" she asked.

I nodded for her to speak, even as I kept an eye on Con.

"The geography looks promising at first pass," Brenda said, tipping a small salute at Con. "I need to spend some time studying the place more, but it's a big area. If those numbers on Anure are correct, or an underestimation, the vurgsten Kara here says they can bring is going to be spread mighty thin. Now, I haven't worked with the stuff, not in combat, anyway, but I have some ideas."

"Good," Con said, sounding reasonably human again. "I was hoping you all would have ideas. We need you to develop the best ways to extend our vurgsten supplies as far as possible."

"The most advantage for the smallest amount," Brenda mused. "What form will the vurgsten be in, what materials do we need to explode it, and are there any minimum values?"

"And are there substances that sensitize the triggers or

amplify their effects?" Percy asked, dropping his façade of languid indifference.

"Sondra can fill you in on those details." He pointed at her with a blunt finger, and she smiled with a cruel anticipation, clearly in her element.

"Oh, love," Percy drawled, "come sit by me and let's talk explosions."

I left them to their discussions. Con might not think much of my approach to ruling Calanthe, but I did know how to delegate to the experts. No one person could handle every damn thing, and at least I understood that.

You were raised to take the side of caution, to play along, to hide in plain sight pretending to be something you're not.

Con's words rattled around in my head, the truth of them cutting me in places I never exposed to anyone. This. This is what came of closeness to another person. They saw things in you that really no one needed to see. You exposed to their examination that which couldn't bear to be scrutinized.

Having no one close to me set me apart, yes. Made me alone in many things. But I was accustomed to that. I could see now, having been so blind to Tertulyn's true motives, that I'd only imagined our rapport. Our intimacy had been physical, and I'd conflated that with emotional intimacy. And hadn't I done the same thing with Con?

Lowering, to realize that opening my body to him, that sharing in the sizzling passion and unraveling release with him had eroded my careful defenses. I'd let an imagined sense of loneliness weaken me, something a queen could not afford.

There was a difference between aloneness and loneliness. Something I must remember. Having someone to confide in, to talk over problems with, that could be comforting, but it was a luxury I couldn't afford. I had to keep firmly in mind that Con was no more my true friend than Tertulyn had been. He might not intend to betray me, but he also wanted his revenge far more than he wanted the best for me.

That was all right, because I belonged to Calanthe, wedded to Her with a bond that went far deeper than any relationship I might have with another person. I paused a moment on the crushed-shell path that led through the lily gardens and back to the palace proper. My ladies paused also, staying back when I raised a hand to stop them. Closing my eyes, I invited the dreamthink in, to cleanse my mind and spirit. The scent of flowers and distant rain filled my head. The music of honeybees, birdsong, and ocean waves played in enduring harmonies. A light breeze brushed over my face.

Calanthe greeted me, Her love warming my heart. And through Her, all the people, the plants and the animals—birds, fish, insects, mammals great and tiny—fed me bits of life, all they felt and sensed.

I was never alone. Not while Calanthe lived.

"Your Highness!" Dearsley's voice broke into the dreamthink, and I reluctantly relinquished it. I had too much to do to be daydreaming in the garden. I heard Calla trying to shush him, but I turned, signaling that it was fine.

"Walk with Me, Lord Dearsley."

"Your Highness, I'm most concerned. How can You allow this Slave King free rein to—"

"Don't call him that. His title is Conrí."

"I apologize, Your Highness. Conrí."

I nodded my acceptance. "I understand your concerns,

but I'm no doormat, Lord Dearsley. Not even for My esteemed husband."

"Begging Your pardon, Your Highness, but I feel I must tell You that I don't agree."

"Oh?" I asked with icy warning that he bravely ignored.

"I don't mean to displease You, but I would not be a good adviser to Your Highness if I did not mention that I see You being soft where Conrí is concerned. There is obvious affection between You, and I fear—"

"You fear that I will lose My head and heart like a ninny and agree, swooning with passion, to whatever Conrí wishes?"

"Well, n . . . no, Your Highness," he stammered at my cutting reply. "I never meant that."

"I assure you: There is no love lost between Conrí and Me. We are attempting to work as a team, when possible, but that's all."

"Still, Your Highness," he continued doggedly. "Your father wouldn't—"

"My father is dead. And he lived in a different world. As his shade doesn't speak to Me, I can only make the best decisions I can."

"You have me to advise You," he replied with stiff dignity. "If You will only listen."

"And I value your advice, Lord Dearsley. I have listened. What I hear is that there are no optimal outcomes from the present situation. If you have a solution you have not yet mentioned, I'd love to hear it."

"Perhaps His Imperial Majesty could be reasoned with. King Gul managed that. We haven't tried diplomacy and . . ." He trailed off as I stopped walking and raised my brows at him.

"You honestly believe we can repeat My father's

surrender? That we can sell ourselves to Anure over and over, refuse to fight, and continue to bleed Calanthe dry to appease an appetite that only grows?"

Dearsley opened and closed his mouth in the face of my sharp words, his own voice failing to make it past his lips.

"Calanthe couldn't have continued as we were, even before Conrí and his people arrived," I said more gently. "You told Me that yourself. The increasing tithes, Anure's spiraling instability. That's why I married Conrí. Because in him I saw the only way out. I won't give him free rein, as you fear. I will always do My utmost to preserve Calanthe and Her people, but I see no other paths. I wish I did."

He hesitated, nodded glumly, then bowed. "If Your Highness is determined to depart tomorrow, then we have a great deal of business to conduct."

"Indeed, Lord Dearsley. Let's see to it."

Con returned to our rooms just as my ladies withdrew. It was far from early, and yet not as late as I'd been making it to bed recently. I wore a nightgown and the head wrap I'd always worn before our wedding. Since marrying Con, I'd been vain enough to wear a wig to bed—not comfortable—and donned my head scarf only for the Glories' benefit. They kept them as souvenirs, something I'd always regarded as silly at best, and mildly revolting at worst. But tradition was tradition, and even our silliest customs were rooted in magic ritual.

So, for this last night, this last Morning Glory, I superstitiously wanted the head scarf to be as it had been—something I wore all night as I slept. There might not be true magic in the old ritual, but I couldn't be sure there wasn't. For all I knew, I might never return to my palace, and it seemed we could use all the good luck imaginable.

It also gave me something of a shield, helping to protect those parts of me Con had laid bare with his words. *You were raised to take the side of caution, to play along, to hide in plain sight pretending to be something you're not.* Some of that might be true, but I was also raised to stand on my own. I couldn't afford to be so vulnerable to Con again.

Con looked me up and down, wariness in his posture, though I'd greeted his arrival mildly enough. "Am I late?" he asked.

"Not at all. I'm early. And I'm exhausted. I thought to get more sleep tonight, before our departure in the morning."

"Sleep," he repeated, following me into the bedchamber and watching me slide into the turned-back covers. He began undressing, dropping his clothes on the floor.

"It's a habit of Mine," I replied drily. "Greatly restorative, I'm told."

"Are you still pissed at me?" he asked. Naked, he got under the sheet on the side of the bed he'd co-opted, snuffing the last candle as he did. For a big man, rough in so many ways, he moved with quiet grace.

"No more than usual," I replied, and rolled onto my side, turning my back to him. "I need to sleep is all." An excuse, sure, but one that let me reestablish some barriers between us. And that gave me room to brace myself to face the nightmares. Soon enough they'd be my reality.

"Lia." He put a tentative hand on my shoulder, the heat burning through my thin gown, the roughness of his calluses just perceptible. "I'm not good at this. I don't know what I'm supposed to do."

No, neither of us did, did we? Both fumbling at this

forced partnership, coming from vastly different arenas of ignorance. Casually wounding each other with sharp words. "You're supposed to sleep. Or go pace, if you can't."

He withdrew his hand. I missed the warmth, the contact immediately. But I had to stay firm.

"We'll talk in the morning," he said.

I didn't reply.

~ 9 ~

We left in the morning, to great fanfare, of course. The queen's chariot led the parade, pulled by four perfectly matched horses with the best lines I'd ever seen. They also seemed to need no driver. I decided not to ask about that. Probably more of Lia's magic that she'd only be cagey about. Along with everything else she was barely speaking to me beyond what formal courtesy required.

I still wasn't sure what had happened the night before. We'd never not had sex, and the lack of it put me in a surprisingly foul mood, especially considering I'd spent my entire life until Lia without it. Now it seemed I couldn't fall asleep without the release I found in her arms. Her cool rejection had put me oddly off balance.

Like a lovesick fool, I'd ended up sidling as close to her naked body as possible without waking her, breathing in her fragrance, feeling her sweet warmth. When I'd finally fallen asleep, I'd slept like the dead—and Ibolya had to shake me awake. Lia hadn't moved, but I felt sure she feigned sleep. I'd have liked to ask her why, but I sat on that question, too, uncertain how to navigate this terrain.

Instead, I rode in the carriage with my wife, the Queen of Flowers, wearing my crown and playing king. I felt

like a Sawehl-cursed fool, even more out of place than I'd
been in the gardens. But I went along with the best graces
I could dredge up. I could tell by Lia's sideways glances
that my efforts fell short of her standards. At least she
seemed vastly entertained by making me as miserable as
possible.

She'd dressed in some fantasy ideal of rural splendor,
abandoning the sharp edges of her usual court appearance
for something like a cross between a country milkmaid
and a hothouse flower. The wig was sunshine blond, with
dangling ringlets, her dress another confection of pink,
light blue, and white lace. Even her eyelashes and eyebrows were pink—the same light shade as her lips, permanently curved in a merry smile that didn't touch her keen
gaze. I didn't think I imagined that she'd made her eyes
be even more gray than before, extra compensation for her
slip in the tower. She looked beautiful, as always, and this
costume should've made her seem soft and approachable,
but she'd coated herself with a layer of forbidding ice.

Her ladies followed in a carriage immediately behind
us, all dressed in flouncy, flowery gowns, too. Their laughter and chatter billowed up occasionally. Ambrose rode
with them, wearing his rainbow wizard robes and apparently regaling the ladies with outrageous stories and
sometimes sending up fountains of sparkling colors to the
applause of the crowds. Sondra had been pressed to ride
with them, but refused so firmly that Lia had crooked a
pinkie and summoned a horse for her instead. When I
suggested I could ride a horse also, the look Lia gave me
was so cold it might have given my balls frostbite.

So I sat like a lump in the carriage, rock hammer at
my feet and bagiroca on the seat beside me, riding backward, while Lia smiled and waved at the people gathered

to see us off. Pelting us with flowers. Of course. At least I'd held firm and wasn't wearing the light-blue ruffled silk monstrosity of an outfit her ladies had brought me. I was more than half certain she'd had them dig it out entirely in a vengeful attempt to knock me down a notch. She probably watched through a spider's eyes or something to enjoy her joke. Zariah and Nahua had taken it away so fast, and brought me garb in my usual black so immediately, that I knew Lia had to be behind it, though she hadn't said a word about it.

Hopefully she'd get over being so royally pissed at me. I'd made a mess of that meeting, though she had, too. *Two bulls in a small pen*. It made me wonder if she was right, that she and I would never be able to work well together. And then I'd remember that we only had to make it a few more days and it wouldn't matter, because all of this would end. One way or another.

"Are you going to brood for the entire journey to Cradysica?" Lia inquired with a pretty smile that no doubt looked good from a distance. She lifted the hand with the orchid ring, waving gracefully to a knot of cheering subjects.

Oh, are we talking now? "Actually I thought I'd brood for an hour or so, then take a nap."

"Funny."

"I thought so."

We fell silent awhile. She smiled and waved. I watched the crowd for signs of danger. Finally she huffed out a sharp sigh. "You could make an effort to acknowledge the people, maybe look like you *want* to be doing this."

"I *don't* want to be doing this."

Her smile chilled into place. "You wanted to go to Cradysica."

"Go, yes. To plan a battle. Not . . . make a party of it."

"We've been through this. You do understand, Conrí, that this is My realm and I know how to do things here."

"You do understand, Euthalia," I growled back, "that we are at war."

"I don't want my people alarmed."

"They're sure as hell going to be alarmed when Anure bombards them with vurgsten."

Her smile fell away entirely. "Can we call a truce, at least for the duration of this ride? Otherwise it's going to be a miserable journey."

"You're the one who's pissed at me."

She gave me an astonished look. "And you weren't at all angry at Me, Conrí?"

"Not any more than usual. We've been pissed at each other before and we still had sex." I fumbled to a halt, feeling I could say something more, but not sure what it would be. I'd hurt her somehow, and I had no idea how to deal with that. Sex was the one thing we had that worked, and if I'd screwed up even that . . .

She lowered her gaze, but I still caught a flash of real surprise in her eyes before she did. "I was exhausted."

And she was lying. I knew it in my bones. Something else was going on with her—besides all the ways her life had been gutted. I supposed I could cut her some slack. "I'm glad you got some sleep then," I said, meaning it sincerely. "You look well rested."

Pink crystals glittered as she glanced up. Then she smiled, something both sad and sincere in it. "Thank you. Though I—"

Just then, a group of children ran shrieking up to the carriage. One climbed the side, quick as a monkey, and flung something at Lia. I had only a moment, but it was enough. I swung my bagiroca without thought.

In slowed time, I saw the weapon on target, the wide, terrified eyes in a panicked face, Lia's horrified expression beyond, the flowers in the kid's fist. Before I could pull the strike—if I even could have—my arm went numb and I found myself reeling back against the lavishly soft pillowed seat. Staring up at the cloudless blue sky.

Only when a flock of birds with red, yellow, and purple wings flew over, did I realize I'd been staring at it a while. With effort, I lifted my head. Lia sat across from me as before, only now she held the bouquet of flowers. Ribbons that tied it together trailed colorfully over her skirt, her trim ankles crossed neatly below all the white lace. My skull pounded in a way I remembered from the one and only hangover I'd ever had. Maybe Lia had cracked my skull because only a head injury would explain my imagining that she looked contrite.

"How do you feel?" she asked, sounding almost as if she cared.

I rolled my head on my neck and realized we'd gone some distance, winding up out of the basin of the harbor and the low cliffs the palace sat on, and into the steep streets beyond, still lined with pretty cottages and cheering people. Narrowing my eyes at her, I rubbed the back of my skull. "Like I did when your ladies put that punch of a hex on me when I first tried to talk to you."

She arched one brow, expression cool again, the pink line crisp and bordered with tiny sky-colored jewels that matched the ones in her crown. "When you tried to attack Me on My throne, you mean."

"I was provoked," I grumbled. I tried shaking my head, but that only increased the pounding.

"Here." She held out a hand, huffing in exasperation when I eyed it dubiously. "Trust Me," she added with a malicious smile. "Truce, yes?"

Right. But I took her small hand—amazing how delicate she felt to me when she was anything but—and the ache in my head subsided, a feeling of well-being replacing it. "Thank you," I said, bemused, still holding her hand. "What did you do?"

She tugged her hand away with a secretive smile. "I couldn't let you harm that child. Your crown is there beside you, and your bagiroca, too, though you might reconsider using it to bash the innocent children of Calanthe."

I snatched up the bagiroca from the rocking floor of the carriage, testing its weight. Satisfied, I set it on the seat next to me. Only then did I put the crown back on, wishing I could skip that. Lia watched it all with a gaze as alert and interested as a cat.

"What were you checking?" she asked. "With your bagiroca."

"How did you knock me out?" I returned the question with the one she still hadn't answered.

"Those are hardly equivalent levels of information."

I shrugged as if it didn't matter to me. "We don't have to talk. There's always brooding for me."

She very nearly smiled at that, mastering the twitch of her glossy pink lips with a stern stare.

"I get used to a particular weight," I explained, figuring I might as well share. If that's what she wanted to talk about, then fine, we could start there. "If you took any of my rocks out, I'd have to replace that one or practice to learn the new heft of the whole thing."

"Why would I steal one of your rocks?" She seemed genuinely perplexed, even a bit indignant.

Habit, I realized, just assuming that stuff would get stolen when I wasn't watching. "In the mines, we—" I coughed to clear my throat. Not something I liked to talk about, but maybe this would prime the pump with her. I untied the knot on the bag and poured its contents onto the seat, laying out the stones. "They fed us because they had to, or we couldn't work, and they had to give us the tools we needed, but they didn't have to be generous about it. You know. Desperate people stop being human and get to be more like animals. You didn't watch your stuff, it got stolen. I forget sometimes, that I'm not in that world anymore, not on Vurgmun."

I glanced up to find an arrested look on Lia's face, her lower lip caught in her teeth. She realized it the moment I looked at her, and deliberately relaxed, closing her lips again in a serene smile. I guess she never did smile showing her teeth. Must be something else she hid—though from what I'd seen of her teeth they looked like regular ones.

"Didn't you have guards to keep order?" She sounded partly like the queen annoyed at someone's incompetence, and also dismayed for me.

I laughed at that, a harsh sound I shook off. "Oh yeah. We had guards, all right. Bored and angry ones. Vurgmun was hardly a prime posting, so the lazy and disobedient got sent there. They'd get bored. Fucking with our heads was pretty much the only entertainment in that barren place. They liked to pit us against one another, bet on the outcomes."

"Con . . ."

To stop whatever pitying thing she'd been working up to say, I held up a rock. "This one is from Vurgmun. The first stone I collected." I laid it in her palm, the egg-shaped gleaming black stone filling it.

"It's . . . pretty," she ventured, stroking it with her other hand, the orchid on her ring billowing and fluttering.

"Yeah, there's lots of that stuff on Vurgmun. Something to do with the volcanoes. I found that one and wrapped it in a piece of shirt." My father's shirt, but I knew I'd never get through saying that out loud. "I kept adding more rocks to the bag, reinforcing the cloth, until it had a heft that worked for me. After we escaped, I picked up this rock, from the beach where we landed on the Shwem coast." I handed her a plain gray stone, washed smooth by the tides. "And left one behind. To keep the weight right."

She stroked that one with a fingertip, crystal-blue nails flashing, then glanced at the pile beside me. "Do you know where all of them are from?"

"Yep." I took the two back from her and replaced them in the leather sack, selected another and handed it to her. "I picked up this one at Keiost when Anure's ships docked to retake the city." I grinned at her. "That didn't go as the Imperial Toad planned."

"You mentioned on our wedding night that the rocks are from places you conquered—do you have one from every battle you've won?"

"That would be too many. Just from key places I wanted to remember."

"Is that one from My palace?"

I should've known her sharp eyes would pick out the faceted purple stone. With chagrin, I handed it to her. "Sorry. I pried it out of the decorations on the window in the prison tower. I'll put it back."

"No." She tried to hand it back. "Keep it. You have a stone from every other place you conquered."

I wouldn't take it. "We didn't conquer Calanthe," I reminded her.

"Didn't you?"

"You won that battle, took us prisoner."

"Sometimes I wonder," she murmured.

"I'm not your captor, Lia. I'm your husband. You can

talk to me about stuff. I thought we'd gotten past some of this."

She studied me. "I'm not good at this, either," she finally said, and I realized that she was thinking of what I'd said the night before. "I want you to have this. Call it a gift." She held out the purple stone.

Taking it from her, I brushed her fingers, watching her eyes for a glimmer of color. "I'll keep it always," I said.

10

At least Con had stopped brooding and started talking—though I supposed if anyone could do both at once, he could. He held the flat and faceted amethyst oval I'd immediately recognized from a familiar floral relief in the palace, remembering how when he'd stormed my chambers he'd carried a bag made from the pink silk of the Lady Sondra's borrowed gown. Con must have pried many stones from the window border to make a bagiroca hefty enough to replace the one my guards had confiscated. When he regained his leather one, and kept only the amethyst, he would've had many left over.

"What did you do with the other stones?" I asked.

Busy gathering the rocks he'd dumped out and putting them back in the worn leather bag, he cast me a questioning look.

"You would have pried out a number of them to make a weapon of any weight for escaping the prison tower," I clarified. "But you only retained that one. Where are the others?"

I'd never have predicted Con could look sheepish, but he eyed me, brushing the bits of dirt and sand off the plush seat, residue of his rock collection. "Sorry about the dirt," he said.

I waved an impatient hand. "Leave it. That's hardly important. You're ducking the question."

He puffed out a breath, started to scrub a hand through his hair and stopped himself, remembering he wore the crown. Zariah and Nahua had done a sterling job of grooming him, though even their best efforts created only a sheen of polish over the restless predator. I rather enjoyed the contrast.

"I was going to mortar the stones back into place, but Ambrose took over the tower and won't let anyone in there."

"I know." I let my own exasperation show. "Not even the servants to clean. Though I'd think the wizard would make an exception for you."

"Nope." He grinned at me, a different smile than that feral grimace when he mentioned Keiost, and far better than the haunted look his face had gotten when he spoke of the mines. With this smile, a dimple showed in one cheek just above his beard, a glimpse of genuine amusement. "He likes you much better."

Hmm. I didn't think that was true. Ambrose had attached himself to Con for a reason that went beyond anything as prosaic as affection. Con was at the center of whatever the wizard's deep agenda included. "So . . . the stones?" I prompted, morbidly curious now.

"I tossed them in that fishpond."

I restrained a groan. "You threw a small fortune in jewels into a fishpond."

He searched my face, suspecting a joke. "Jewels?"

"Every one."

"The pond had pretty rocks in the bottom already."

"Not precious gems, however."

"Why would you put jewels around a window in the first place?" he burst out, waving a hand at nothing. Several young women, thinking he waved at them, squealed and tossed flowers. One swooned dramatically, her friends catching her with laughter. Con seemed to be completely oblivious to his effect on them, as he had been with all the ladies—and plenty of lads—who gazed at his impressive bulk and seething sexuality with overt longing. My wolf of a husband stood out, yes, but not the way he thought.

"In point of fact, *I* didn't put them there," I replied as drily as I could since I truly wanted to laugh. "But consider this—if you're essentially an occupied kingdom, one that already tithes heavily to a greedy overlord who plagues you with emissaries and spies, and you'd like to retain *some* wealth, just in case, what's a good way to hide precious gems in plain sight?"

"Window decorations." He considered that. "Your father was a clever man."

"Yes, well, cowardice and stupidity don't always go hand in hand."

"I suspect he wasn't a coward, either," Con said slowly, gaze on me.

"There's a reversal," I said lightly, to cover my surprise. "Not what you implied yesterday."

Con tilted his head, adjusted the crown. The black stones in it were from Vurgmun, I realized. He'd crowned himself with the stones he'd once mined. "Maybe I'm learning there's all kinds of ways to fight, and not all of them include bashing things," he added, with a twist of a smile.

"Fortunate, as My palace would be denuded of decorations if everyone decided to make bagiroca with precious gems."

"When we get back, I'll wade into the pond and retrieve them," he answered with rueful grit.

When we got back. A lovely fiction to believe we might

return. "There's no need. The fish probably ate them all anyway."

"I doubt that, and this clearly bothers you. I'll make it right."

"Conrí." At my stern tone, he met my gaze. "Now is a time that I'm teasing you," I told him gravely.

He narrowed his eyes. Thought a moment. "What about the blue outfit?"

I inclined my chin in gracious acknowledgment. "That too."

With a look of consternation, he stared at me a moment longer. "You have a truly wicked sense of humor," he said, dawning realization in his voice.

Did I? What an interesting idea to consider. I'd been so annoyed with him after that meeting, and frustrated with myself that I couldn't indulge in sex with him and keep up my guard enough to hold him at arm's length. Messing with him by sending that ridiculous outfit had been an entertaining distraction from . . . well, everything.

I supposed if I did have a sense of humor, I'd had little opportunity before this to exercise it. Mostly I amused myself, in the discretion of my own thoughts, having learned long ago not to reveal how truly ridiculous I found most of the court posturing. In the pitch and gravity of recent events, I'd lost some of that satirical internal voice.

Or perhaps I'd discovered an outlet for it in my unlikely husband.

"I'll try to restrain Myself," I offered.

"Oh, don't change the game now that I'm catching up."

"Is that what this is—a game?" Absurdly, it pleased me that he didn't want me to change.

He regarded me with alert interest. "Sometimes I think everything is a game with you."

"Except when it's deadly serious."

"True." His gaze wandered over my face. "I like it, that a lot of what you do is part of your little joke on the world. It makes you more human."

I caught my breath at the unexpected sting. Oh, how he had the power to pierce my armor. I must have looked stricken because he reached over, putting his hands around mine where I clutched the nosegay. "I didn't mean it that way," he said. "Not . . . the real you stuff. I meant that you're always so regal and remote . . ." He paused, searching for words. "Poised," he declared with some triumph.

"I see."

"I mean, knowing that you're laughing inside at your little jokes helps me understand you."

Oh. That warmed my heart in another unexpected way, salved the sting. "I see. All right."

He didn't move immediately. "You're sure?"

Con looked so earnest, eyes soft with concern in that roughly handsome face, that I couldn't resist. And I'd missed touching him. I leaned in, tilting my head just enough to meet his lips and keep the crown balanced. The crowd roared jubilation at the kiss, showering us with flowers and delighted cries. Con slipped a hand behind my neck, holding me there a moment longer, deepening the kiss, which turned quickly hot. Laughing breathlessly, I broke off, straightening. His gaze held mine, molten gold. *I wanted you in the garden, even with hundreds of people watching*, his voice echoed in my head, hoarse with desire, and I trembled, the need hitting me hard and fast. Worse than ever for the one night of denial.

"A crowd-pleaser," I managed to say, waving out both sides of the carriage to roaring approval. A fountain of magical flowers bloomed above, jetting from Ambrose's staff and raining down on us with soft sparkles. "I wish Ambrose wouldn't do that," I commented, jumping at the distraction, working to keep the pleased smile on my lips instead of letting them firm with disapproval.

"Why not?"

"Magic work attracts attention. I'd think the wizard would know as much."

Con shrugged. "Probably. But if it's the Imperial Toad's attention you mean, I'd guess that Ambrose knows this journey is partly designed to make sure we draw Anure's eye."

I supposed he had a point. "How can he know? He wasn't at the meeting where we discussed it."

"Apparently he told Sondra he'd be ready to travel to Cradysica before you even came to visit me in the map tower and I asked you about the place."

I tried to focus on that extraordinary information, not on what we'd done on that visit. How Con had spread me out naked on the representation of my island, sending me mindless with erotic release. Still, I had to search for words. "You're saying Cradysica was . . . inevitable."

Con nodded, then shrugged. "I don't know how this stuff works."

"When did you know that the wizard said this?"

"Right before the meeting started. Sondra told me about a minute before you convened it."

I considered that with some surprise. "But you didn't use that in your arguments."

He met my gaze, a raw honesty in his eyes. "I never wanted to bully you, Lia. I know I can be an ass, and I'm always sure I'm right, but I wanted to convince you we can win. I believe we can. I didn't want to . . ."

"Use predestination to push Me into capitulation?"

Smiling slightly, he shook his head. "You're about as easy to push around as I am."

I found myself smiling back, the unexpected understanding humming between us. Another shower of showy magical fireworks went up and I glared in the wizard's direction, much good as it did.

"I'd say you should order him not to, but we both know that Ambrose does as he likes." Con sat back, folding his arms, muscles bulging in his shoulders beneath the closely tailored black silk and leather. He'd been so annoyed about the pastel-blue outfit my ladies had pranked him with—and so relieved to see the real one—that he'd simply put it on without comment. He looked good in those clothes, though. Deadly, physically powerful, as always, and also regal. More like the king of Oriel as he'd been destined, instead of the Slave King. "If you can figure out how to govern the wizard, you will truly be a ruler to fear."

He'd meant it as a joke, of course, but there was truth in that. "How did you meet the wizard?" I asked.

Con cocked his head with a slight smile. "By my count, it's your turn to tell me something."

Ah. "Is that why you told Me about the stones in your bagiroca?" And about the mines. That glimpse of horror remained in my mind, like spoiled grease I couldn't quite cleanse from my mouth.

"I thought, yeah, I should tell you something about me, if I'm going to ask about you." He glanced around as the road wound higher up the hills, leaving the last of the crowds behind, the forest too dense on either side for anyone to gather. We'd have quiet until we reached the next village, and privacy. "Seems like we have time," he noted, echoing my thoughts. "And you owe me two an-swers, by the way. Pay up, sweetheart."

I squirmed internally, wishing now that I'd let him ride a horse. Regrettable that I'd allowed a foolish mo-ment of jealousy stop me, but I hadn't been able to dredge up the generosity to be pleasant about Con riding with Lady Sondra. I knew they weren't lovers, or even thought about each other as anything but comrades in arms. In some ways, that made it even worse. I possessed plenty of weapons to fight a sexual attraction. Their deep friend-ship . . . well, it was clearly nothing I understood, since Tertulyn had so thoroughly fooled me. It annoyed me that Con preferred Lady Sondra's company and conducted easy conversations with her when I found extracting words from him akin to pulling teeth.

Of course, I didn't think I'd had an easy conversation with anyone in my entire life. I'd been assiduously trained never to speak of anything I hadn't precisely determined to reveal. From my earliest utterances, my father had taught me to weigh every word before I spoke it.

As I was doing at that very moment, Con observing me with that mocking challenge glinting in his eyes, and I wondered if he found the same difficulty conversing with me. Very likely so. All right then, he had a point that this ride was as good an opportunity as any, and that I owed him. It would be a delicate line to walk, revealing some of my abilities while keeping enough hidden to use against him, should he turn out to be my enemy, as Tertulyn had.

"The two questions are, I believe, how I incapacitated you and how I made you feel better, yes?"

He smiled slightly, a glimmer of admiration in it. "I love how you can do that—keep track of a conversation that way. I bet you never forget anything."

"You've spent a great deal of time learning the weight of your bagiroca and how to effectively swing that rock hammer. I've spent a great deal of time learning to pay attention to what people say—and what they don't say."

"Heh." He huffed out a laugh. "A warrior of words."

Unexpectedly flattered, I smiled at him, then set the posy on the seat next to me. "I didn't 'punch you with a hex'—I don't even know what that would be—but I did reverse the flow of your life energy." I paused, letting him absorb that. That particular ability wasn't unique to me, so it was relatively easy to discuss.

He frowned, reflexively rubbing the back of his skull again. "I understood the individual words, but they're not stringing together into anything that makes sense," he complained.

I laughed, and tried again. "Everything alive has energy. That's how plants grow, how we move around, and so forth."

"I got that."

"Intelligent beings focus the flow of life energy into intention." I picked up the bouquet and handed it to him. Bemused, he took it, the flowers a delicate spray of color in his darkly scarred hands. "I formed the intention to hand you the posy, then directed My body to hand it to you. More than that, My intention communicated itself to you so that you understood I wanted you to take it."

He studied the flowers. "That seems like a complicated way to explain a simple thing."

"True, but bear with Me. When you formed the intention to hit that child with your bagiroca, I—"

"You were in danger," he interrupted on a growl, "and I didn't form an intention—I acted."

"I know that. And while I appreciate your readiness to

defend My person, I couldn't allow a defenseless child to be harmed. You would have felt terrible about it."

He gave me a humorless smile, making me wonder if he would have spent a moment on regret. Perhaps not. The mines—and the war—had honed him into a remorseless killer. Something to bear in mind, no matter how charming he might be, or how hard he might endeavor to be a gentle lover as well as a passionate one. "I think you give me more credit than I'm due," he said slowly. "I wouldn't have given the kid a second thought if it came to a choice between your safety or theirs."

"I don't believe you." I studied him and he gazed back, face a remorseless mask. "What if you'd hurt the child then discovered the truth, that I was never in danger?"

He shrugged, the restlessly pacing wolf in the gesture. "I've learned not to dwell overlong on mistakes like that. People get hurt in war, the good and bad, the young and old. What happens to people has nothing to do with their innocence or evil deeds. We might want to believe people are rewarded for doing good and punished for doing wrong, but it's not the way of the world we live in. None of us actually get what we deserve. Which works out well for me, or I'd be dead long since."

I didn't have a reply to that, uncertain what I believed—or if he was even telling me what he truly believed. I wouldn't put it past him to take a stance to see how I'd react. "You've saved many people," I said.

"I've killed more. Destroyed lives and terrorized others."

"Are you certain? It seems to Me the exact math would be difficult to determine without an objective survey."

"Don't romanticize me, Lia," he replied after a long pause. "You're smarter to be suspicious of me. I'm not a good man."

I wanted to argue that—then wondered how I'd ended up on the side of defending his actions, or of losing my resolve to observe the Rule of Suspicion with him. Certainly I didn't romanticize anything, least of all this dangerous warrior I'd married for expediency and nothing else.

"Besides," he added, "we can't save everyone."

"That doesn't mean we don't try."

He stared back at me, some thought moving behind those golden eyes, but he didn't speak it. Instead, he inclined his head as if granting me a point in the game he claimed we played.

"Back to the subject at hand," I said crisply, aware of the irony that I was changing the conversational topic back to one I'd previously avoided. "You acted, yes, but not without forming the intention first. You've simply trained yourself to act on your intention so fast that you aren't aware of a . . . process of deliberation, as other, less proficient fighters might have been."

He grunted at that, thinking it through. "And you can sense that."

Not a question. "Depending on the intention, yes. In this case, you formed the violent intention and initiated your attack. I simply reversed it, so that the power of your life energy you'd poured into doing that thing instead slammed back into you."

"Huh." He studied me. "Violence again."

"Excuse Me?"

He laughed, a voiceless huff of breath. "Your whole thing about how blood can't be spilled in violence on Calanthe. By the way, you still haven't explained what exactly would happen." When I only stared back, lips pressed firmly together, Con shrugged. "I didn't figure it would be that easy. But it's interesting that your defensive magic hinges off violent intent—and maybe so does Calanthe's."

When I still didn't reply—it took all my effort to conceal my reaction and not reveal how very close he'd come to the truth—he smiled in grim resignation. "On to the answer you currently owe me, then. When you made me feel better—was that my life energy, or yours?"

Clever man. "Mine. I gave you some of My well-being to ease the ache." And salve my guilt for having to hurt him, even if I had tempered the lash of power and he'd recovered quickly.

"You do that during sex, too, don't you?"

The question took me by surprise, particularly since I didn't have an answer. I made a show of considering, however, while I thought about it. He burst out laughing, a rare full-voiced belly laugh from him. He shook a finger at me. "I got you on that one. You didn't cover your reaction in time. You didn't know you do that."

"I'm not convinced I do," I replied coolly, though it came out on the prim side. How could I know? My only other sexual experience was with my ladies, and they were chosen for my retinue in part because they shared this ability and thus could serve as bodyguards. Though I had always found their sensual touches soothing and rejuvenating in a certain way. All except Tertulyn, who'd enjoyed pride of place without having this ability. We'd had another sort of closeness—or I'd thought we had—so I'd never really considered that difference.

"You do," Con confirmed, sitting back again in satisfaction. "I wondered why I always feel so good when we have sex. That explains a lot."

That disconcerted me even more. I couldn't decide how I felt about it, either. "Perhaps it's more that fucking in general feels good? There's a reason it's the favored pastime of so many."

"Yeah, well, Calanthe is different that way. You all have sex on the brain. Not everyone is that easily distracted by it."

"No? Weren't you the one being mean and broody because we didn't have sex last night?"

He frowned. "That's because you weren't talking to me and I thought you were upset with me. Not because I have sex on the brain."

The man should know better than to give me a challenge. As we remained unobserved and well screened by the high sides of the carriage, I slowly raised the ruffled hem of my gown, easing it up my stocking-clad legs. His gaze followed the movement. With the lacy underskirts lifted away, I uncrossed my ankles and gave Con a good look at what I wore beneath—and what I didn't. His golden eyes riveted to the view, he swore under his breath.

"I'm sorry, Conrí," I said sweetly, "were you explaining about how you're not easily distracted by sex?"

His gaze rose to mine. "It's different with you, Lia," he said, voice so husky that I wanted to suggest he get on his knees and put that mouth to good use.

Tempting . . . but we weren't quite alone enough for that. I dropped my skirts, arranging them and crossing my ankles again. It surprised me how much I wanted it to be true, that I was different, but believing it would be kidding myself. I did believe, though, that he'd been worried about me shutting him out. I hadn't liked it, either. I just didn't know how else to handle the terrible vulnerability he evoked in me. Could I afford to be weak in front of this wolf?

"You can't know if it's different with Me," I pointed out. "I'm the only lover you've ever had."

He regarded me thoughtfully. "True. I don't have much basis for comparison."

"Do you want to?" I surprised myself by asking. A serious lapse in my much-vaunted skills at carefully selecting what I planned to say.

"Do I want to . . . what?" he asked slowly, keen eyes on my face.

"Explore with other partners to form some comparisons. You could take other lovers. All the Night Court has been in anticipation of when you'll indulge." I couldn't seem to stop myself, a relentless sort of self-flagellation.

He frowned, the expression black. "I thought you were certain we travel to our doom and final defeat and that you won't return to the palace."

"Theoretically then," I said, unable to stop myself, not at all sure what I wanted to hear from him, what lonely, frightened part of my heart drove me.

"We're married."

"That doesn't mean monogamy."

"I'm pretty sure it *does* mean that."

Interesting. "Why do you think that?"

He shrugged, a bit restless. "My parents had a good marriage. Loving. Monogamous."

"We could always indulge together," I suggested, aware that I was in part needling him and part testing the boundaries of this supposed loving monogamy.

"What are we talking about here—bringing another woman into bed with us, or another man?"

"Either. Both, if you like. Though until you got Me with a legitimate heir for Calanthe, I personally would abstain from intercourse with another man, but you could."

I'd shocked him. Then he considered that I might be teasing him. I saw the moment he decided to treat the suggestion seriously, just in case. "Is that what you want?"

It shouldn't have surprised me that he asked, but it did. I supposed I didn't expect him to be genuinely interested in what I wanted. I also hadn't expected him to be . . . hurt. Yes, he'd been hurt by my rejection the night before. "I want many things," I temporized.

He laughed, a harsh bark without music or humor. "Now you sound like the wizard. Tell me the truth, Lia. Remember? No lies."

Ugh. That agreement had been easier when I'd been thinking of it in terms of how to dance around the secrets I needed to keep, rather than my own feelings. *You're not entitled to personal emotions*, my father's voice whispered. *Everything You feel is about the throne.*

"It doesn't matter to me," I replied coolly. "I'm pleased to accommodate you in this, if only in this." I arched my brows to make a joke of it, but he didn't bite.

"I don't believe you," he said echoing my accent and phrasing with uncanny mimicry. He leaned forward. "Doesn't it mean anything to you, Lia, how it feels when we're together?"

It did, and I didn't want it to. It unsettled me deeply that I'd unraveled in his embrace so far that my eyes had reverted to their natural state. I'd missed him the night before with such a physical ache that I'd nearly gone back on my resolve—and I never do that. It also made me terribly uncomfortable that we'd somehow ended up in this particular conversation. I glanced behind me to make sure no one was eavesdropping.

"Just us," Con said, somewhat grimly, when I turned back. "And no easy escape."

I gave him a hard look for that one. He'd deliberately pinned me with this conversation when he knew I'd normally endeavor to brush him off. Sighing, I gazed off over his shoulder. The branches of the trees formed a lacy arch above us, making a tunnel of green, the wood as artistically twisted as if carved that way. Orchids trailed their way all along the trunks and branches, blooming in the cooler shadows, dependent on the strength of those trees, unable to survive on their own. "I didn't marry you to indulge my feelings. I did it for Calanthe."

"The only thing that matters to you," he filled in.

"Yes." I met his gaze unflinchingly. "As your vengeance is the only thing that matters to you."

"True enough." The wolf stared back at me. "You're still ducking the question."

"I enjoy sex with you," I replied evenly, "but I think it would be unwise to allow Myself to become emotionally involved with you." There. That amounted to ripping my heart out and throwing it as his feet, didn't it?

"Because you don't trust me."

"Conrí." I said his name with considerable exasperation. "We both just agreed that for each of us, our highest priorities could well be in conflict at some point in time."

"Is that what we agreed? I don't follow you."

"Oh, don't play the dumb oaf. I know better. If your vengeance requires sacrificing Calanthe, you'd do it in a heartbeat. I know you well enough to see you think that's a likely outcome of this battle you plan at Cradysica."

He didn't deny that, only watched me, expression stern. "And you'd deprive me of my vengeance, you'd sacrifice your own life and happiness, if it meant protecting Calanthe."

"In a heartbeat," I replied crisply. "I tried once already and nearly succeeded. Then I failed. I'm now on My backup plan."

"What all is entailed in your backup plan?" he asked, almost conversationally, for him, anyway.

"At the moment? You've successfully convinced Me

that if we have a slim chance of winning, it's because of what you plan. That, at least this far, our objectives align. I'm waiting to see if that continues to be true."

"And if you come to believe our objectives don't align?"

I didn't allow myself to hesitate. "I'll do what I have to in order to protect Calanthe."

"Even if it means going against me, your husband and lover."

"Yes."

"So cold."

"Yes," I said again. And I felt cold inside. Better that, though, than the melting need for him that steadily grew in me.

To my surprise, he actually smiled. "You fascinate me, Lia. That's saying something, since not much has occupied my thoughts except destroying Anure."

For Con, that amounted to an impassioned declaration of affection of his own. What a pair we were.

I allowed myself to unbend enough to reply. "I find you compelling also, Con. Which is saying something as I've always known I only cared about Calanthe."

"I have an idea." His smile faded and he regarded me with smoldering intensity. "Perhaps we could each agree to giving the other second place."

My lonely heart tripped like I was that ninny I'd told Dearsley I wasn't. Because I couldn't entirely disguise that reaction, I did the next best thing and used it. Fluttering my elaborate lashes and pursing my lips into a bow—an expression the jewels perfectly accommodated—I blew him a kiss. "Why, Conrí, what a saucy offer. I don't know what to say."

He gave me an impatient scowl, not at all amused. "It's a sincere suggestion, Lia. We're married. I'm trying to tell you that means something where I come from. It means something to me."

I sobered. "Good Ejarat, you're serious."

"Of course I am. We already made the vows. We shouldn't even need to have this conversation."

"What about your loyalty to your friends?"

He cocked his head frowning. "You're my wife. That makes you the most important person in my life."

Such a strange perspective he came from—but my foolish, surprisingly idealistic heart wanted that, leaping at the idea of mattering to him. And if we only had a few days left to live . . . well, I could hardly refuse the offer. "All right, I can agree to being second place only to your need for vengeance."

He nodded. "Can you say the same—or do you need to think about it?"

I laughed, hearing the bitter edge in it. "Oh, Con, there's nothing for Me to think about. I have no one else in My life. You have second place by default, and all the places below, as well."

An odd look crossed his face, and I thought I glimpsed pity in his eyes. Fortunately I also sensed people ahead. "Look sharp, Conrí. A new village of admirers awaits their first sight of you."

"Oh joy," he commented wryly.

11

We didn't get to talk much after that, as there always seemed to be people lining the road, crowding onto rooftops—even hanging from the trees, like more of Lia's exotic orchids. I tried to wave now and again, especially when Lia gave me a pointed stare and I realized I'd sunk into my thoughts again. So many questions she hadn't answered fully. Though even if we had a lifetime together—not likely, the way things looked—I'd probably never fully understand her.

At least trying to be nice to the crowds gave me something to focus on, so I didn't fall into staring at Lia's temptingly displayed figure—and imagining the parts that didn't show. Did other men's wives do that teasing shit, like lifting their dress and showing them all the naked bits beneath? I doubted it, because I was sure I'd have heard guys brag about it. Lia wasn't quite naked under there—she'd had on some kind of pink ribbons holding up her stockings and a scrap of lacy silk that showed off her sex instead of hiding it—and she'd been clearly as aroused as I was.

I couldn't stop thinking about that vision, or about having her. Probably one of the crafty little games she played to amuse herself. Teasing me seemed to be her new favorite pastime, and she no doubt enjoyed making me stew in my thwarted desires the whole way. To pass the time, I plotted a bit of retaliation of my own. I'd already gone over and over in my head what I needed to see at Cradysica, in what order—and it would have to wait for morning light, regardless. We'd have time tonight and I didn't intend to waste another with her.

Calanthe was big as islands went, but that wasn't saying a lot, so we arrived at the "village" just before sunset. More like a city. As I'd figured from the depiction on the map, the settlement was quite a bit bigger than Lia had made it out to be. A temple crowned the hill—its dome reflecting the light with near-blinding gold that had to be real—a narrow road winding up to it. Little houses bordered most of the road, except at the last third or so, which looked too steep for building on. Mostly moss-covered rock up there, by the look of the terrain where we came in along the coastal road. From the lower two-thirds down, the village spread out along a hilly ravine, then cupped the harbor below.

Squinting against the angled light of the setting sun, I saw no rocks or reefs, only deceptively calm water between two arms of the island, the high and narrow ridges spurring out into the water above and below this reach of coast.

Perfect.

"Is this the only road in and out?" I asked Lia, just to be sure, though I'd seen that on the map.

"Yes." She raised a brow at me. "Planning your escape already?"

Sondra, who'd ridden up beside us now that the road allowed for it, made a snorting sound. "We plan for all possibilities, Your Highness. You've clearly never had to think about exit strategies."

"No, indeed." Lia made a show of yawning into her pink, sparkly nails, demonstrating a boredom I knew she didn't feel. "That's why I married this one." She flicked a careless gesture at me. "My father taught Me early on to delegate mundane tasks to others."

"To your inferiors, you mean?" Sondra's anger flared as she took Lia's bait, swallowed it whole, and fought the line. I shook my head. Sondra still underestimated Lia. She looked at the Queen of Flowers and saw a younger woman, of similar station—but who hadn't been tested by the same fires of hell—and made the critical mistake of thinking Lia wasn't a warrior, too. Sondra never even saw the blade coming. "Conrí exceeds you in every way. *Your Highness.*"

Lia had turned her lazy gaze onto me, making a show of assessing me with a dubious quirk of one elegant brow. "Yes, but thickness of skull only counts for so much. Now, there is the matter of his masculine endow—"

"Sondra," I interrupted. "Why don't you go see if General Kara has sent any messages ahead?"

She flashed me a wounded look. "Conrí, I—"

"That's an order."

Pressing her lips into a hard line and leveling a glare worthy of a fistful of daggers at Lia, she galloped off. "Protecting your lieutenant from Me?" Lia asked, greatly amused.

"The bite you had of her was enough—I didn't want you to spoil your supper."

She laughed, a real one that made her eyes sparkle. "The Lady Sondra has a point that your wit is unexpected."

"Sondra is also making a potentially fatal error by falling for your tricks. She doesn't understand who you are."

"And you do?"

"I'm getting there." I paused, thinking how to ask it. Then decided there was no good way. "I'm wondering if you would make an effort to befriend her, as a favor to me."

Lia made an O of her mouth that didn't quite conceal her very real surprise. Yeah, I was getting better at reading her. The exaggerated expressions showed how she truly felt, but stretched to the point of comedy so the observer would think she was being sarcastic. The one that bore watching was the perfectly calm face she could put on like a blank mask. Then she had complete control, her poisonous thorns at the ready.

"Are you claiming I've been unkind to the Lady Sondra?" she asked archly, a hint of that venom beneath.

"No, you've been nicer than I'd have expected. Giving her a place at court, clothes that makes her happy, introducing her to like minds. I'm saying Sondra could . . . use a friend."

"I believe she's become friends with the Lady Brenda. Perhaps lovers."

I shook my head sharply enough to have Lia raising a brow at the abruptness. "That won't happen. The lovers thing. Friends maybe, but . . . Sondra could use someone with your insight. You understand how people tick. She needs that."

"I don't know what to say," Lia replied after a significant pause. "I think I'm flattered by your good opinion."

"Not flattery. I know something about people, too. You could help Sondra."

"And why would I bother?" She drawled the question, lazy and bored queen again.

"Because I'm asking it."

"Hmm." The look she gave me wasn't persuaded.

"You never gave me a wedding gift."

"And here I thought I gave you an island paradise and a free pass to fuck the most beautiful woman in the known world," she shot back.

I laughed and, though her disdainful expression didn't alter, her eyes sparkled with that wicked humor. "Thank you," I said.

"Save your gratitude. I may not grant your petition," she replied airily.

"True." I grinned at her, thinking of what I planned to do to her. Soon, very soon. "But you'll do it, for me."

She sniffed. "Maybe."

"You will," I insisted. "Because you can't resist my masculine endowments."

Rolling her eyes, she managed not to smile. "Such arrogance."

"We'll see."

We pulled up in the circular drive of the leading family's "bungalow" not long after that. It was, of course, a palace by most standards, with a cheering crowd of people turned out to receive their queen. Anure likely had no idea how much Lia's people loved her. I doubted Anure could get to her, all things being equal, which of course they weren't. Anure always had the advantage, Lia was right about that much. And Lia's people could only protect her if she let them die for her, which she wouldn't. She didn't know it, but that's why she had me.

She might worry about blood shed in violence, but I'd seen so much of that it barely registered anymore. Lia needed me to be ruthless where she couldn't be. If I could extract Lia from this doomed enterprise without destroying her, I would. Calanthe and its people were another matter—and not my responsibility.

The head family of Cradysica greeted us lavishly—

including me in their rituals, offering the intricately woven wreaths of flowers, as Lia's people had done when I'd first landed with Sondra and Ambrose—and this time I accepted them, though I felt like an idiot. I was doing my best to be a decent consort for Lia. If that meant being draped in flowers, fine. The sideways speculative glances she slid me provided some reward. She wasn't sure what I was up to, which I figured worked to my benefit.

If I kept her guessing, she couldn't outmaneuver me. Not as easily, anyway.

Ambrose and Merle were received with delight, especially when Merle apparently laid an egg in the hands of one of the leading family's daughters, which then hatched into a small fluffy birdling. He repeated the trick for each child present. Lia kept a polite smile pasted to her perfectly painted lips, but the glimmer in her eye revealed her disapproval. She worried about Ambrose being noticed.

That discussion about Anure having wizards of his own—which went against what I'd always been told and what the world believed—would explain a great deal about the Imperial Toad's uncanny luck in war. Would Ambrose be a match for *four* wizards, if Agatha was accurate on that number? The wizard had seemed unconcerned, but I needed to talk with him about it, no matter how frustrating that conversation might be.

The lady of the house personally led us to the rooms set aside for the queen. We formed another parade, leading while Lia's ladies followed, and servants brought up the rear with the many trunks Lia couldn't travel without. I would've preferred to do a security sweep first, but I didn't even suggest it, easily able to predict her reaction on that one. Who said I was a slow learner?

Besides, I figured I could rely on our move to travel to Cradysica being fast enough that Anure wouldn't have been able to anticipate it. Even if the false emperor had been close enough to attack—and according to the letter from Lia's spy he wasn't yet, assuming the information really wasn't compromised—then it would take Anure at least a full day to adjust. And even if the spies he had in Lia's court sent a bird as soon as we left, we should have until the next day for him to change his own plans. I doubted Agatha and Zariah could have spread the news any faster than that, either. I calculated that that gave us all of the following day and night, at a minimum, to set our trap. I wouldn't hope for more than that.

I was also counting on Lia's arcane abilities to suss out any local danger. At least, I assumed she'd be alert for that. So far everyone treated this excursion like a big party, so I'd go along with it. I had to admit, Lia's strategy for that had worked well enough so far. No one seemed to suspect our real motives for being there.

Still, I couldn't help scanning the shadows—*so* many open windows that anything could come in—though I made myself take my hand off the bagiroca at my belt at Lia's sideways glare. Ambrose elected to stay outside to play with the kids, saying he didn't need to change for dinner. Neither did I, for that matter—though Lia might have other ideas—but I knew she would want to, and that fit well with what I had in mind.

The hostess showed Lia through the extensive spread of rooms, the ladies-in-waiting marshaling the servants to deposit trunks and goods in various places. Would Her Highness like to bathe and change clothes before supper? Oh yes, she certainly would.

I smiled to myself—and checked all the alcoves

and balconies under the guise of appreciating the fine curtains and balmy night air. It had grown full dark— Calanthe sat near the equator, which made the days as stable as the weather, the sun always rising and setting at the same times—but the exterior of the house was well lit with torches and bonfires. No one could sneak by in shadows anyway.

No apparent danger, so I relaxed a little, finding Lia in conversation with her ladies on the dress she planned to wear, the hostess and servants having left.

"Dare we relax our guard now?" Lia asked with an arched eyebrow.

Of course I hadn't fooled her. I gave her an easy grin, letting her see the wolf in it. "I can, but *you* might keep your guard up." I flicked a glance at the ladies. "Leave us."

"Excuse Me—" Lia began, but I ignored her, speaking over her to Lady Calla, the operational first lady-in-waiting now that Tertulyn was gone, if not the titular one.

"Her Highness will summon you when she's ready," I said as I'd order my soldiers, and I pointed at the door.

The ladies hustled out with gratifying speed—enough that I didn't mind that they checked for Lia's impatient nod first—and I followed, locking the door behind them.

"Conrí, if you wanted to speak privately with Me, then—" Her eyes got big in a real reaction, not a manufactured one, as I advanced on her, and her indignant reprimand ended on a squeak when I picked her up by the waist and sat her on one of the pretty couches. Pulling up a chair, I sat across from her.

"Do it again," I instructed.

She gaped at me, and I might've enjoyed taking her so thoroughly off guard if the painful need hadn't been riding me so hard. So far, my plan was going exactly as I'd plotted all that long day.

"Con," Lia said in a coolly placating tone. "I don't know what—"

"Do. It. Again." I spaced out the words so I wouldn't growl them too much, but it didn't work. And repeating myself hadn't made her understand. "What you did in the carriage." I gestured at her skirts, motioning for her to lift them.

Her lips parted, eyes softening from snapping anger, arousal taking its place. "Why should I?" she sniffed haughtily, not fooling me for a moment.

"Because if you don't, I'll do it for you," I promised darkly. Oh yeah, that wiped the superior smirk off her pink lips.

Her breasts rose with the breath she caught. Keeping her gaze on me, she reached down and lifted the shifting mass of lace and ruffles, spreading her thighs as she did. The way she looked, her swelling sex so carnal in that frame of pretty feminine floof . . . My cock shouldn't have been able to get any harder, but it sure felt like it. I flexed my hands, finding that I was the one floundering, no longer sure I could control myself.

"Well, Conrí?" she purred, widening her thighs, her pointed heels lifting her knees. She had her face composed again, all pink and blue and winking jewels, the crown perched daintily on her elegant head. "What are you going to do about it?"

With a snarl, I launched myself at her, loving the way she gasped, a mewling sound of surrender as I tore away that bit of lace and silk and put my mouth on her. She tasted of flowers and the way broken leaves smell, somehow sweet and green at once, and I lifted her slim hips, holding her there while I fed on her.

She shuddered into a climax, sobbing my name and other words, but I didn't pause. Thrusting fingers inside her hot passage, I stroked those quivering muscles as I nipped at her bud of pleasure, then licked in long strokes, driving her up and shredding her composure again and again. Her nails dug into the back of my neck, holding me in a cage of them, and I fought back by biting the soft flesh of the inside of her thigh. She let me go and I rewarded her with a kiss there, and then on her slick woman's folds again, but softly, easing off, teasing and titillating her sensitive flesh until she begged me with little inarticulate cries, thrashing in my grip. As much as I'd let her.

When she was desperate to climax again, I let her go. But only long enough to release my cock. She watched me with hot eyes, and with great satisfaction I saw they'd reverted. Sapphire and emerald. A sure sign I'd stripped away her icy reserve and clever masks. I wanted to tell her not to wall me out again, but if this was the only way I could reach her, then so be it. I picked her up and she fastened her mouth on mine, wrapping arms and legs around me like a wild thing, her dress bunching between us. "You wear too many clothes," I muttered in frustration.

"True," she panted, writhing. "Let's change that."

"Just let me—"

"In Me, now," she ordered and bit my lip, hard.

All those plans I'd made fled my brain. "The dress . . ."

"Fuck the dress," she growled, grinding her hips against me as best she could.

I set her on a table, fighting my way through the floof. With a savage curse, I pulled my knife and started slicing. She laughed hysterically, then threw her head back on a strangled scream when I found my way to her, slamming myself home. It staggered me for a moment, how right that felt. Home. A feeling I thought I'd lost forever.

"Con, My wolf, please . . ." she moaned, bringing me back to my senses.

Bracing myself, I thrust into her, losing all thoughts, all sense of anything else, only needing her, being in her. She urged me on, those bicolored eyes glowing as if with their own light.

When the orgasm crashed over me, my vision went black, stars sparking through me and draining all of myself into her. In its place, her essence, vital and magical, flowed into my being. And I gave myself into her keeping.

Sometime later, she laughed in my ear, husky and amused. I realized I'd collapsed on her, still standing with my pants around my ankles—and surrounded by shreds of her ruined gown. With effort, I levered up, but she held on, pressing a kiss to my ear and then biting it so I hissed.

When she released me, draping her arms over her head, she watched me from slitted eyes as I pulled up my pants. She stayed as she was, legs splayed in wanton disarray, languid, smiling, her makeup such a smudged mess I knew I must have it all over me. Wiping my mouth with the back of my hand, I noted a big smear of pink, a jewel sticking to it.

"What brought that on?" she inquired, sitting up and surveying the damage. It looked like we'd had a brawl.

"You shouldn't tease me."

"Oh, warrior man of Mine," she replied in a sultry voice, "if that demonstration was meant to dissuade Me from teasing you in the future, you're going about it all wrong."

In the future. That phrase arrested me in the midst of

helping her down from the table. Would there be much of that? This journey to Cradysica had set events into motion. When we left this place—if we both left it alive—we were unlikely to leave it together. Had that driven some of my desperate hunger for her, the clawing need to bury myself in her?

"What's wrong?" She sharpened, losing all the languid sultriness. "Why do you look like that?"

I gestured at the shambles of her gown. "Sorry about your dress."

She regarded me a moment longer, assessing. Then held up her arms. "You might as well finish cutting Me out of it. Then you can summon My ladies to commence repairs to My appearance."

Taking up the blade I'd dropped, I motioned for her to turn, then sliced the fabric at her back. I'd had some idea of having my way with her under all those skirts without disrupting the rest of her. No such luck there. When she faced me again, standing naked in a pile of foaming cloth, still in the wig and crown, her eyes showed her wild self still and a spray of flowers gleamed through her skin over one shoulder. Marks from my rough hands showed on her, too.

"I should get dressed for dinner," she said gently, like you might talk to a wild animal you were afraid of spooking.

"What will your ladies think?" I gestured at the mess I'd made of her, the gown, hell—the room. With the grinding need backed off, I wondered what the hell I'd been thinking.

"I'm pretty sure they know we have sex," she replied with an arch expression.

"Your eyes are two colors," I said.

She narrowed those eyes, then lowered her lids and opened them again. They were back to their covert shades.

"That did it," I told her, and went to summon her ladies. Then I turned back. "Lia?"

She was unpinning her crown, still unselfconsciously naked in the ruin of it all, and she paused, giving me her full attention, a question in the line of her body.

"What you asked me about in the carriage? In case I didn't make it clear: I don't want anyone else in our bed," I said.

Smiling a little, she nodded in acknowledgment.

"Or anywhere else," I thought I should add, since we hadn't made it to a bed the last couple of times. "I don't want anyone but you."

"You could have just said," she pointed out coolly, but her smile was warm.

"Yeah. Me and words, you know. Not so much."

"You're eloquent enough in your own way," she corrected, setting the crown aside. "Anything else?"

Might as well say it. Who knew how much time we had, but . . . "Would you promise me the same?" It came out more gruff than I'd expected.

She strolled over to me, still in the wig, but nothing else, besides the orchid ring that swayed with the same silky grace that she did. Laying her palms on my chest, she rose on tiptoes to kiss me. I slid my hands down her back and over that tiny, gorgeous ass, marveling that I had the gift of a woman like this. Some kind of reward I didn't deserve to savor before I died.

Or something for the gods to rip away as a last torture before they killed me.

"Yes," she whispered. For a moment I thought she agreed with my thoughts; then I realized she'd answered my question.

"Good," I said, which felt inadequate. I searched for something else to say, something to express the wild voices in my heart, but a smile bloomed on her face like I'd said the most romantic thing ever. Maybe I *was* getting better at this wooing thing.

12

"Bright Ejarat," Calla sighed, fanning herself dramatically once Con left the room. Nahua was finishing removing the last of the jewels that hadn't come off during that mind-blowing sex with Con, while Zariah combed through the cushions to retrieve the rest of them. "When You release that man on the Night Court, he's going to cause *such* a stir."

Ibolya, gathering up the remains of the gown, threw Calla a sharp look, then raised a brow at me. "Orvyki should have Your bath ready, Your Highness."

"Thank you." I'd asked her to heat the water a bit more, to help keep me from stiffening up too much at dinner. "And I'm not releasing Con on the Night Court, Calla, so you might as well direct your fantasies elsewhere." My tone came out a little too terse, but Ibolya smiled knowingly. I wondered sometimes about how some of my ladies, though privy to more knowledge than most, still seemed to regard Anure's attack as unlikely, if not impossible. They helped me create the elaborate theater that all was well, but surely they must understand the gravity of our situation. It irritated me at times, how carefree their preoccupations—and then I realized I'd been spending too much time with Con. I'd begun to adopt his gloomy outlook.

I groaned as I sank into the water, the skin on my inner thigh stinging where Con had bit—actually *bit*—me. Ibolya handed me a soaped cloth. "What comes of taking a wolf to one's bed," she murmured for my ears alone.

Deciding I had no good answer for that, I simply smiled. Calla held up a gown for my approval, and I waved a hand without looking. I didn't care what I wore. More precisely, I'd rather stay naked and loll about with Con, seeing how far I could push him and what delightful responses I could elicit. We'd been more or less polite in bed with each other until now, wary of the tentative status of our marriage and fragile political alliance. Con had been rough with me before this, yes, but inadvertently, and quickly regretting his clumsiness. Tonight . . . well, something had burned through his reserve and he'd been at me like a wolf, indeed.

I wanted more. I wanted more right then, but I had to go sit through a feast. Oh joy.

Sighing, I set myself to washing with more determination. "What news?" I asked Ibolya, ignoring the pang that it would've been Tertulyn who carried the information to me before.

She told me the local gossip, already gleaned while my ladies took advantage of the delay in tending me to freshen themselves, and to chat with the other women of the household. "Many people here are wondering why You stopped in Cradysica first," Ibolya related. "Of course, they're very proud to be the first to receive Conrí, but also puzzled—though they won't say so right out. Other villages around Calanthe are discreetly inquiring about the next leg of Your journey, and word is that many are planning special festivals, on the chance that they'll be privileged to host You after this. It looks to become quite competitive."

"Your Highness might consider announcing which You will visit next," Calla added. "If only to reduce some of the arguments already breaking out over which village most deserves Your attention. Some have sent outright invitations."

I should have anticipated this. It had been years since I'd traveled around Calanthe—since I ascended to the throne after my father's death. I hadn't felt comfortable leaving the palace, not with Anure's spies watching my every move and Syr Leuthar, the now deceased imperial emissary, poised to undermine me. And I didn't really need to physically travel. Every part of Calanthe spoke to me in its way. But that wasn't the same as me visiting my people. Naturally they vied to be the next to host us.

I'd have to make some excuse, as I had little doubt Con would find whatever it was he sought in Cradysica. The certainty had sung from his skin, and the wizard had known before we did. I'd considered pressing Con for details, but in this I indulged in a bit of denial. I didn't want to know what dire fate he planned for this lovely place. On some level, I didn't trust myself not to stop him. He'd pinned me perfectly when he asked which part of Calanthe I would choose to put in jeopardy. We both knew I couldn't. It would be like asking me which hand I'd rather cut off.

"Let Me see the invitations," I said on a long sigh.

At Ibolya's signal, Nahua brought the missives that had followed me from court, and a few that had apparently come straight to Cradysica—Zariah and Agatha had done their jobs well—and I sifted through them while

Zariah cleaned and oiled my scalp. "Your hair is growing in again already, Your Highness," she noted.

That was faster than ever before, additional evidence of my eroding control over myself. It was tempting just to let it grow and—as Con had startled me by suggesting—to let my eyes show. If Con was right and Tertulyn had gone to Anure, I had nothing to hide anymore. Though if Con was right about Tertulyn, then any of the ladies now tending me and giggling over Con's prowess and the marks he left on me—any of them might be spies ready to betray me. At least with Con . . . well, I knew all of his motivations, didn't I? No wondering there what his priorities would be.

Handing the letters back, I resolved to deal with the matter in the morning. I stood, ready to begin dressing for dinner, where at least I'd see Con. How bitterly ironic that the ruthless invader I'd imprisoned and considered executing had turned out to be the one person I could trust. If only because I knew exactly what he'd betray me for.

I stood in the temple at Cradysica. The distinctive dome of the temple was a rare one that celebrated the joining of Sawehl and Ejarat, rather than one god or the other. It arced above me, as silver on the underside as it was gold on the other. It was all one piece, made from long-ago magic, the two metals fused together, and so finely wrought that the sun filtered through at high noon, filling the temple with translucent light.

The dome had been added to the original temple, a shrine that celebrated something much older, wild and ancient magic that predated the gentler gods of modern day. It was a graceful, peaceful place.

Then the image shifted, crumbling and then shattering. Stinking smoke filled the air, crowding out the golden light, suffocating it. Fire raged over the hillsides, turning them crimson red as the blood ran in rivers downhill to the sea. A cannon from a ship in the harbor boomed, and vurgsten landed on an unscathed patch of forest nearby. Birds, screaming, shot into the air, their feathers on fire, and I clamped my hands over my ears, though nothing could silence the shrieking of Calanthe and Her creatures, wounded and dying, crying out in her madness for the blood spilled in violence. The wind caught me up and I rose, up in the air, out over the sea, my feathers burning and skin bubbling, blistering. Calanthe cried for me, but I flew—was dragged?—onward.

Helplessly pulled toward Yekpehr.

"No," I sobbed. "Please, no. Please stop, I'll do anything. Please."

A wolf came for me and I reached for him, hoping he'd help me get back to Calanthe. He leapt at me, snarling, blood dripping from his jaws. I threw up my hands to stop him. His fangs closed over my left hand. They snapped down, severing my hand at the wrist, the wolf swallowing the orchid ring. I'd lost it. Lost what I'd sworn to protect. As if that action had snapped my last tether, I hurtled through the vast, uncaring sky. Falling, falling, down a long, dark tunnel. To my death.

"No!" I screamed. "No no no!"

"Lia!"

"No, please, no."

"Wake up."

"No, please don't. You don't know. You can't know. No no no . . ."

Con was there in the temple, taking me into his arms and holding me while I sobbed, weeping bitter tears against his warm and naked chest. I tried to show him that my hand was gone, but he couldn't seem to see it. "There now, Lia love," he murmured. "Shh. I'm here and you're safe."

"The birds . . ."

"Singing sweetly. Listen. It's nearly dawn and they're calling out good morning."

"No," I hurled the denial at him, pounding his chest with my fists. My fists. Two hands. "Why are you doing this, Con? Why? You have to stop it."

"Lia. Nothing is wrong. Open your eyes."

My eyes were open, the burning smoke stinging them, the birds shrieking in their terrible agony. Or . . . singing? And my eyes were closed. I forced them open, water spilling out, and blinked to clear them of the blur. The sky outside the open window held no smoke or clouds, only a deep gray that contained a hint of the blue to come. Sunrise rode on the fresh breeze, and birdsong chorused, crashing through the sound of surf as the tide changed below.

Oh no. *No no no.* The nightmare protests echoed in my mind, repeated by my waking humiliation.

Con held me by the wrists—no doubt to keep me from pummeling him—leaning over me with concern on his face in the dim light.

"I'm all right," I said. "Go back to sleep. Let Me go."

He let out a long breath and released my wrists along with it, lying down and gathering me against him. I didn't resist, but I also didn't relax, rigid in my mortification. Maybe he would go back to sleep and I'd be able to find the dreamthink, to rally myself. Maybe he hadn't fully woken and would forget that—

"That was a hell of a nightmare," he said, shattering that futile hope. "What were you trying to stop?"

"Nothing." With my hands freed, I wiped my face with the covering sheet, finding it already damp, from my tears or sweat, I didn't know. Maybe both. My nose was running from the tears. I'd been bawling like an infant, like a weak-willed child. I wished I could crawl under the bed and curl up into a ball. "Go back to sleep."

"I have to get up anyway. They'll be bringing in the Glory soon."

"No Glories, not here." I gave in and sniffed, making it quiet so maybe he wouldn't notice. Better that than having snot run out of my nose.

"No Glories? That's good news." He ran a hand down my back, then reached a long arm to the side of the bed and found one of the cloths my ladies had thoughtfully left for us. For sex cleanup, not wiping away the embarrassing dregs of an emotional outburst, but there it was. He handed it to me and I pressed it to my face, dearly wishing I could blow my nose. "What was the nightmare?" He pulled the blankets around us and cuddled me closer.

"Go back to sleep. I'm sorry I woke you."

He shifted, putting a finger under my chin to tip my face up from where I had it buried. I really didn't want him looking at me, but fighting it would only make him more determined. He'd proved that amply.

"Lia. Look at me." He waited for me to open my eyes and look at him, his face close in the early-morning light. "Don't apologize for something you can't control. It was a bad dream. I get them, too."

"Not like these, you don't," I blurted out, still too distraught to be discreet.

"What do you mean?"

"Nothing. I just—" For some stupid reason, my eyes filled with tears again, and they spilled down my face, another sob breaking out of me. Ejarat take me, what a mess I was.

"Here now, it's all right. I didn't mean to make you cry."

"I'm not," I insisted, my voice watery.

"Oh, right. My mistake. The Queen of Flowers isn't a real woman at all who has bad dreams and whose nose runs when she cries."

"Dammit." I pulled away from him and sat up, wiping the treacherous tears away and blowing my nose. Con lay on his back, one arm behind his head, the white sheet stark against his darker skin. He calmly handed me another cloth. I threw the soggy one to the floor and took the dry one. Taking my time, I wrestled myself under control. Not easy without some time in the dreamthink. I'd never had to overcome the effects of the dreams with someone watching me, which was a very good reason I should never have agreed to share a bed with Con. Sex, yes, but this exposure of my frightened, weak self . . . I couldn't bear it.

"Ready to talk about it?" he asked gently.

"No." And I never would be.

"Do you have nightmares often?"

Only every night.

"Lia. Talk to me."

"Yes."

"Who do you usually talk about them with—your ladies?"

"I don't. I don't *want* to talk about them." I had to control the involuntary shudder at the thought of verbalizing those horrible feelings.

"You'll be less upset if you do. The dream images lose their power if you describe them."

Was that true? I didn't have any idea. I'd truly never spoken to anyone of the prophetic dreams that plagued my nights, and the present and past voices of the crying, dying lands. Even when I consulted with Castor, I'd framed my questions generally—and well after the dream images had loosened their claws.

"Lia, you really can talk to me." He smoothed a finger down the line of my spine, his skin rough, his touch comforting and warm. "I promise it will help. It does for me."

"Who do you tell your nightmares to?" I asked instead, not looking at him. I couldn't imagine the tough warrior explaining a bad dream.

He shrugged against the sheets. "Sondra. Kara sometimes. My father . . ." He cleared his throat. "Before he died."

Surprised by that admission, I looked at him. He returned my gaze solemnly. "I thought you didn't want to talk about your family. We agreed we don't owe each other our stories." Though he had mentioned his parents and their marriage before. *Loving. Monogamous.*

"We were strangers then." He flattened his palm on my back, caressing me with firm strokes. "Since then, we've agreed to share secrets, yes?"

True. At least some secrets, though I managed to be wise enough not to add that qualifier. "What do you dream?"

"Are we trading dream for dream?"

I hadn't meant it that way, instead hoping to divert him, but he watched me cannily.

"I'm willing," he continued. "Lie down and I'll tell you." He unfolded his arm invitingly and raised a crooked brow when I hesitated. "It's too early for you to get up. Think how frantic your ladies would be that they weren't dressed and ready to greet you."

A week of marriage and he knew exactly how to get to me. With a resigned sigh, I lay down and snugged against his warmth, because the predawn air was cool and it would be rude not to accept his offer. A good pair of excuses, those. In the aftermath of that nightmare, though, I allowed myself that small bit of denial. I didn't want to need Con's comfort, but I did.

"My nightmares are what you'd expect," he said, staring up at the ceiling. "I'm trapped in a mine and can't breathe. *That* one's a favorite," he added with wry disgust. "Or I'm in battle and naked, trying to fight with something stupid like a child's sweet tree-finger."

"A what?"

"You didn't have those? We did in Oriel. The court wizards made them for special festivals."

"Never heard of them." I wondered if he might be playing a joke of his own on me.

"I'll see if Ambrose can make one for you. Suffice to say, they make terrible weapons. That's the thing about *that* dream."

Armed only with something from his childhood, sweet, transient, and easily broken. It made my heart hurt for him. "If Ambrose is able to make them, you should have one, too."

He chuckled, his dimple briefly showing. "It's a deal."

"I can understand why those would be terrible dreams to have," I said softly.

"Heh. And that's not even the worst one."

I tipped my head back. "Tell me."

He watched me, solemn now, gaze haunted. "The worst dream is . . . my father is dying in some horrible way and I can't get to him." He blew out a long breath. "I hate that one. And you know what the worst part of it is?"

"What?" I asked softly, my cheek against his skin, his scent anchoring. This was real. Not the stinking smoke and fires.

"When I wake up, I'm confused, and I think he's still alive. That I need to get to him, help him." His voice had gone choked. "Then I remember the truth, that he's . . . dead. And I get the grief all over again, but fresh, like it just happened."

"I'm so sorry," I whispered.

"Thanks." He pressed a kiss to my forehead. "I've never told anyone else about that one."

"Why me?"

He shrugged, his muscles rippling under my cheek. "You're wife. And you're a good listener." He fell silent a moment, then blew out a long breath. "What I hate most about the nightmares is the helplessness, that I can't control anything in them."

"Yes. I keep trying to get better at controlling mine."

"I don't know—you have enough control over everything else. You probably need the outlet." When I didn't say anything, he added more softly, "You were weeping in your sleep. Even before you woke. Like your heart would break."

It had felt like that. My wrist still burned, though the orchid ring shimmered on my finger of that hand, reminding me of its presence. I shifted and his arm tightened around me. I'd have to tell him something. Should I tell him the truth?

"Your turn, Lia," he reminded me. "What was the dream?"

"I don't know how to describe it. It was images. No story to it."

"Then describe the images."

I'd tell him about this dream, as a test. Then we'd see

about the others, how I felt about disclosing that greater truth. "I was here, in Cradysica, standing under the dome of the temple on the hill."

I described it as it had occurred, my words halting at first, hating to give voice to the horror of it all. To my surprise, however, it did get easier as I talked, the terrible pressure in my chest at last giving way. When I finished, Con brought his hand down to stroke over my bare scalp—I hadn't worn a head scarf or wig to bed, indulging Con's request—then he simply cupped my head, holding me secure. That felt good, too—like he wanted to shield me from the terrible visions. If only he could. Instead, he would be the one to make them reality.

"No surprise, really," he said when I finished. "I know it's hard on you, to imagine the emperor attacking this place."

I needed to tell him the truth. To at least try. I shook my head and leaned up on my elbow. "It's not imagination. Those are visions. That's the future."

He didn't argue immediately, just considered me from beneath lowered lids. "You don't know that," he finally said.

"I do know that."

"How?"

"Because this wasn't My first nightmare, Con. I have them all the time, every night."

"That doesn't mean they predict the future." He sounded entirely obstinate.

"This from a man who follows a prophecy."

"I don't like it. Ambrose cornered me into it." He scowled at the ceiling. "Besides, that's different. It's magic. How can a dream be of the future, when the future hasn't happened yet? It doesn't exist."

"That's what I used to think," I agreed glumly.

"What changed your mind?"

"One came true," I said, then wished I hadn't.

"What was it about?" He asked the question carefully, as if some part of him already knew.

"You!" I caught myself, moving to get up, but his arm around me tightened, keeping me against him.

"What about me?"

I pressed my lips together, unwilling to say, wishing to Ejarat I'd kept my mouth shut.

"Lia . . ." He sighed heavily, dropping his head back on the pillow, hard, like he'd rather bang it against a wall. "Just tell me. Enough with these secrets."

"I dreamed about a wolf in chains," I told him. "Howling, begging Me to help him. I'd try to take the chains off him and he'd bite Me, savaging my hands." I flexed my fingers in memory of the blood and pain. I hadn't told him the part about the wolf biting off my hand and swallowing the orchid ring. It had to be Con—but . . . "There's more. Explosions. My palace falling into the sea. Blood and death. A stink in the air, like something rotting."

He tensed under me. "What kind of rotting stink?"

"Like eggs left too long."

He made a pained sound deep in his throat.

"What is it?"

"Vurgsten," he told me. "That's what it smells like. Did you notice it, the other day, when I set Anure's missive on fire?"

"No." I thought back to that moment, how it had meant something to me that Con had understood to burn the letter. "But there was a breeze blowing away from Me."

"Did you smell it in the dream you had just now?"

"Yes."

He lay still for a long moment. "I guess we already knew this would be the place. I thought I'd be happier when I confirmed it."

"I want to send My people away." And the animals. The birds. I could coax them into leaving.

Con was shaking his head. "Not yet. No, wait, listen to me." He rolled onto his side, draping a heavy thigh over mine. "We know he has spies. We can't give away the game too soon. Once the trap is set and he's committed, he won't be able to change course. I'll tell you when, and then you can send them away."

"Do you swear?" I searched his face, clearer now, almost stark in the brightening morning light.

"I promise that I will tell you when the toad is so committed he can't retreat. Then you can act however you like to protect your people."

I didn't miss what he hadn't promised. It could be that the point of no return for Anure would be beyond the point of catastrophe for Cradysica and all its denizens. Con watched me with a knowing expression. "Now *you* swear, Lia, that you won't take any actions without telling me."

I hesitated, considering how to modify the promise as he'd done, but he squeezed me, getting my attention. "You could easily undermine everything. We won't get a second chance."

"You're asking Me to do nothing. To stand by and let My people be endangered." Hadn't he railed at me for that very thing? *You take the side of caution, play along, pretend to be something you're not.*

"Yes," he replied with due gravity. "To risk a few, to save the many. It's a hard choice, so I'm making it for you. You asked for my ruthlessness. Here it is."

With his naked body against mine, hair tousled from sleep, he didn't seem all that ruthless. I sighed out my dread. "I don't like it, but all right. I won't act without discussing with you first. But, Con—I won't be here much longer."

He tensed. "You're leaving?"

"The dream. I'm going to be taken away from Calanthe."

His arm tightened around me, as if he could hold me there. "No. I will protect you. Anure will never get close enough. I promise you that."

"You can't promise that. You don't know what—"

"I *can* promise it," he bit out savagely. "The dreams are symbolic. I refuse to believe that a future that hasn't yet occurred can't be changed. Besides—" He paused, taking a breath. "—I won't let him have you. I'd die first."

My obstinate wolf. He believed he could change the world. That's probably why he'd succeeded as far as he had. "Thank you, Con. I believe you." At least, I believed he meant it, but I didn't add that last.

He smiled, as if I'd given him a gift, then sobered. "Any other visions of the future I should know about?"

"Not of the future, no."

Picking up on my prevarication, he put a finger under my chin again, tipping up my face. He kissed me, soft and achingly tender, and I melted into him, then he murmured against my lips, "What are the other nightmares about, then?"

I huffed out an exasperated laugh. "Now you're bribing Me with kisses to pry out information?"

He grinned, that dimple winking into existence, like the first star of evening. Faint, but there. "Whatever works."

Rubbing my hardening nipples against his chest, I slipped a hand between us, to where his cock pressed hot and urgent against my thigh. "This works," I purred, stroking his shaft, watching his eyes blur with pleasure.

"Works for me, too," he replied in a sensual growl. His head dipped, hot mouth trailing kisses down my throat. No ferocity this time. He lavished my skin with gentle caresses, licking and soothing. Hands roved over me, petting, arousing and comforting. Murmuring sweet words, he described my beauty in the morning light, the scent and taste of my skin. He cupped my breasts and showered them with kisses, lightly drawing on my nipples, the sensation rolling through me. Not like lightning and thunder, but a soft rain, nourishing, tender.

I found myself rising to meet his touch, taking in what he offered like a flower turns her face to the sun. He was making love to me. And so help me, I unraveled. Languid with the exquisite sensations, I drew him into my body, our moans twining together like vines, blooming with brighter bursts of pleasure as he moved in me.

I was the ocean, the earth, Ejarat, and he came into me with golden light, powerful, vibrant, exuberantly illuminating my depths.

The orgasm shattered me in a whole new way, pieces of brittle fear spinning into the abyss, my walls crumbling into nothingness. But instead of being cold and naked, brutally exposed to a critical light, I was bathed in warmth. In gentle compassion. Cherished.

If I wept a little, I could put that down to the intensity of the pleasure he brought me.

In the melting core of my heart, however, I knew that I'd fallen for this man—so far that I could no longer apply the Rule of Suspicion to him. I knew what he wanted, yes. The problem was, I wanted to give it to him. I wanted to give him everything, and I didn't know what I'd have left if I did.

Sometime later, I opened my eyes as he shifted. The room had filled with light, the sun truly rising. "It grows late," I observed with chagrin. "I should get up."

But he stopped me. "Uh-uh. Tell me about the other nightmares."

I laughed. A mistake, as it sounded a little forced. Already I was losing that sense of being protected, the chill wind of the dread future dispersing the golden light like withered petals on a spent blossom. "Do you forget *nothing*?"

"Not important things," he replied somberly, holding me against him. "You distracted me with sex—and yeah, I'll admit you can, probably whenever you want—and you needed that breather. Now you can tell me the rest."

"Managing Me with sex?" He'd done that at the folly, too. What really annoyed me was that it worked.

He grinned, that dimple winking in his delight. "Whatever works, sweetheart. Tell me, Lia. You promised."

"I don't know that it matters," I said. "And it's difficult to explain."

"All right." He waited.

I closed my eyes, thinking how to phrase it. "When I'm asleep, it . . . opens up My mind in a way that's different from when I'm awake. And in My dreams, I hear the crying lands. All the lost kingdoms, calling to Me of their suffering, showing Me what they've endured." Begging for help, just as Con had in my dreams, holding out his hand to me, long hair tangling in a storm wind.

He was quiet. I opened my eyes to find him studying my face thoughtfully. "How can a piece of dirt speak to you?" he asked slowly, and I knew he'd been thinking how to ask it.

"I told you it was difficult to explain."

"I know. Don't get huffy." He cupped my bottom with a big hand, nestling me back against him. "I'm just trying to understand. Are you saying the land is . . . alive?"

"Of course it is."

"Don't say it like that. I've never heard anyone say that before."

I sighed, pressed my forehead against his chest. "I apologize. It used to be that everyone knew. The royal bloodlines, they weren't only hereditary rulers, but born of the land itself. The true kings and queens share blood ties to the land."

"What does that mean?"

"They are intertwined on a deep level. The rulers give their lives for the land, and the land gives them life."

"This is like that thing you were saying in the carriage, about everything having life force."

I nodded. "All life is connected."

"And before that—about blood sacrifice."

"Yes."

"Hmm." His thoughtful hum rumbled through his chest beneath my cheek. "What happens when you take the royal bloodline from the land?"

And there, he'd gone straight to the heart of it. "The land only answers to its bloodline. Bereft of that, it's orphaned. It dies or goes wild."

"So Anure knew what he was doing, killing off the royal families."

I tipped my head back to look at him. "Or enslaving them."

He gazed back with dawning understanding. "If he owns the royal, he owns the land. Because he can't on his own."

I nodded. "Anure is not from any royal bloodline. He stole the rule of the land by taking prisoner the people connected to it."

"All those former rulers he keeps with him at Yekpehr."

"Yes."

"So why do the lands cry to you?"

I shrugged a little. "I don't know, exactly. Maybe it's just that I can hear them."

"Maybe they're calling for their rulers. But if those people are alive, isn't the connection there?"

"They're not *on* the land, Con. It's not the same."

"Blood ties," he murmured.

I felt it in him when he realized the implication, his entire body thrumming with it. "Oriel," he breathed.

13

Oriel wasn't dust, but it *was* dying. Or dead. Because I had never gone back. I looked down at Lia, her eyes bright with the knowledge she'd woken in me, as surely as if she'd taken a stick and stirred the banked coals of old despair in my heart. "Why didn't you tell me?" I demanded.

She gave me an impatient look, then wriggled away. This time I let her go, watching her glide naked to the washbasin, petite ass twitching in her irritation. A new vine twined over her skin, thick with budding leaves, so lifelike, it seemed they might burst into being at any moment. I wanted to trace it with my tongue, to taste and feel her skin. How I could be pissed at her and crave her at the same time escaped me. It made no rational sense. Except that it seemed to be the story of our relationship.

"When should I have told you?" she asked in the same tone, fastening a pretty scarf over her bald scalp. "Should I have told you when you failed to tell Me you were the crown prince of Oriel, even though the knowledge would have improved your marriage proposal? Or when you told Me that who you were didn't matter because Oriel was lost to dust and ash and you didn't owe any allegiance to the land?"

I sat up in the soft bed, rubbed my hands over my face, willing myself to *think*. "I didn't know," I said into my hands, but then . . . Some things my father had said to me over the years rumbled in the back of my brain. Always in the mines he'd protected me, given me a share of his food, shielded me from the worst cruelties of the guards. For Oriel, he'd said. And Sondra . . . did she know? *I ask only to hold the torch.*

Lia's hand touched my shoulder, light as one of her butterflies. "Hey," she said softly, gentle with unexpected compassion now. "You *didn't* know." She blew out a breath, then retrieved her silk dressing robe and shrugged it on. "I wasn't sure you wanted to; you seemed so determined to leave Oriel in the past. I'm still not sure it changes anything."

I understood better now, how someone like Lia would view a man like me, a crown prince who turned his back on the land he'd been born to. And she was the one who had to hear its piteous, lonely cries. Maybe that's part of why Lia walled herself off with ice. If I had to listen to that shit every night, it would drive me crazy.

Oriel, calling to me. My father tossing and turning, asking about my nightmares. Saying he had them, too. Had I heard the land in my dreams, too? All this time I thought it had been the ghosts of my family, my dead and imprisoned people, howling for vengeance. All this time, it might have been Oriel demanding blood. *Conrí.*

"Conrí?"

For a confused moment, I thought Lia's voice was Oriel's calling me by my title.

"I think maybe my father tried to tell me," I said, thinking back over things my father had said, things I'd refused to hear. I'd been so angry, so full of hopeless despair.

She sat on the bed, her slight weight moving it no

more than the breeze from the window, her green essence soothing. "He would have been very careful. No one has ever been sure how much Anure knows and how much he's guessed, or blundered into via blind luck. This is sacred knowledge, passed from kings and queens to their heirs. I had My father longer than most, and he died before telling Me everything I needed to know. He was secretive, cagey like that."

"I guess you come by it naturally then."

She didn't immediately reply, and I thought maybe I'd annoyed her. But I looked up to find her watching me with concern, that line between her brows that the makeup normally covered. "What happened to your family?"

The question seemed out of context. Not something I wanted to talk about any more. "I told you—my father died in the mines with me." My voice came out hoarse, grinding with the grief, and I glared at her for making me say it again.

"You implied as much, though you'd never said exactly," she replied, though without rancor. "What of your mother and sister?"

I flinched, and I knew she felt it. "Dead," I said shortly— and with enough finality to get her to drop the subject.

"All right. I'm not asking you to say more now. But I am asking you to give this thought—lest you come back to Me at some point and demand to know why I didn't tell you this sooner." She smiled slightly, without any humor. "Why did Anure send you and your father to Vurgmun?"

"To mine his rock for him," I spat back.

She raised her brows at my tone, but spoke patiently. "Oriel was the first to fall and—"

"I know that part."

"Don't get huffy." She threw my words back at me with some satisfaction, pleased when I winced. "Arguably,

Anure didn't have his system worked out yet, but if he figured out how to control the lands by keeping royals captive at his citadel in Yekpehr, why didn't he at least retrieve you, a crown prince of the Oriel bloodline he already had in chains?"

"Because I escaped before he could?"

"Maybe." She inclined her head at the possibility.

A light knock came on the door. "Your Highness?" Ibolya called through it.

"A few moments, please," she called back.

I caught her wrist as she rose. "What are you thinking, Lia?"

She laid her hand over mine. "Are you sure you want the truth? It might hurt." Her eyes looked silvery framed by the shimmering scarf, and they weren't hard, but full of sympathy.

"I can take the truth. Spit it out."

"I think the toad had plenty of time before you escaped to bring you to join his stable of captive royals. In fact, My best guess is that Anure doesn't know that Conrí, crown prince of Oriel, is the Slave King who's plagued him. If he'd put that together, he wouldn't have been so lackadaisical in suppressing your rebellion."

Offended, I frowned at her. "A great many people fought hard and died in those battles."

"That's beside the point. Strategically speaking, you were lucky," she replied evenly. "You were smart, too, sure. I've studied the reports. You took advantage of Anure's inattention and arrogance. He'd sent the dregs of his forces to the fringes of his empire, and he grew fat and lazy. It was clever of you to exploit that, but we both know that if the emperor had taken your rebellion seriously early on, he could've crushed you. If he'd known who you are, he would have moved swiftly and decisively."

I couldn't argue with her assessment. Lia saw things with a cool dispassion, dissecting events with clear logic. She'd easily grasped exactly how I'd seen it. It surprised me, though, that she'd studied our battles. "What *reports* did you review?" It wasn't like we'd had a gaggle of academics following us around.

"Ambrose has been keeping a diary, didn't you know?" Her lips quirked at my astonishment. "He intends to write a history someday. I asked to know more about you and your conquests, and he gave me the relevant pages to read."

"When?" I demanded. I couldn't imagine when she'd read this stuff that I hadn't seen.

"In the days after our marriage. I don't squander *all* of My time in formal court, or spend it on inane meetings." She raised a brow at me. "But you wouldn't know that, would you?"

"I already apologized for that," I replied stiffly. "Doesn't seem fair for you to continually bring it up."

She regarded me with a hint of consternation, then inclined her head. "You're right. I suppose that's a good marriage rule to observe: argument, resolution, then it's done and we don't resurrect it unless there's a recurrence of the problem. Fair?"

"I can live with that." I grinned, awfully amused by how she tried to run our relationship like she did Calanthe. "You didn't use that knowledge against me," I pointed out, "in the strategy meeting when I said I knew what I was doing."

"No, I didn't." She examined her nails, picking at something. "I thought about it. But I didn't want to undermine your authority in front of our people. And while I don't like this plan, I don't have a better idea. Besides, despite all odds, you did succeed where no one else has.

I only hope you can pull off the same when faced with Anure's full might and attention."

"I can," I told her. "I know we can win."

"I believe in your confidence," she replied.

"Your Highness," Ibolya called again, knocking. "I'm sorry to interrupt, but should we tell Your hosts that You won't be at the breaking of the fast?"

"I'm coming," she called back, then looked at me.

I held out my hand and she took it, smiling when I kissed her palm. Green leaves, sunshine, and a sweet taste of the sea. "Thank you for believing in me."

She started to say something, then closed her mouth and squeezed my hand, before starting to let go.

I held on, remembering our conversation before I got distracted. "Wait. You never said why, according to your theory, the toad didn't drag me to Yekpehr when he had me?"

She met my gaze, regret in her eyes. She'd hoped to distract me, to avoid telling me this, I realized. "I think he didn't need you because he had someone from Oriel's royal family already."

"No, that can't be it." That was a relief. I'd been braced for something terrible to contemplate. "My mother died. Early on. I saw her corpse."

"And your sister?"

The breath caught choking hard in my chest. "She—" I couldn't say it.

"Did you see *her* body, Con?" Lia asked, her voice and posture compassionate, but with insistence, as if she knew I couldn't stand to think of her.

"I—" I couldn't think. The memories crowded up, fierce, ugly, and stinking. Blood and screams. I wiped my free hand over my face and found it clammy with cold sweat.

"Your Highness?" Ibolya said through the door. "I'm so sorry, but if You're to be on time, we must begin dressing You."

Lia looked at me in question. "Should I stay or would you rather be alone?"

"No." I glanced at the light-filled sky out the window. I'd meant to be gone by now. I had things to be doing. Important decisions to make about the present instead of dragging through the ashes of the past. "Sondra will be waiting for me."

She nodded then called out, "I'm coming now." She let go of my hand. Moving to open the door, she paused there. "I could be wrong. Just give it some thought."

I would be thinking of nothing else.

Still, she hesitated. "Will you be all right if I go?"

I nearly laughed at her, except that I did feel so raw. All the shit I'd been through, and here I was tempted to ask this woman I'd somehow married to come and hold me. "I'll be fine," I said. "I have things to do." With my voice so rough with emotion, my words came out terse enough that she smoothed her expression into her usual cool poise.

"Very well. Have a productive day, Conrí."

The door snicked shut behind her with a quiet finality. Exhausted with the day not yet begun, I made myself get out of bed and find my clothes, resolutely pulling them on. I did have things to do. A fucking war to fight. All the rest didn't matter. Focus on the here and now and I'd be fine.

I didn't even believe myself.

Sondra met me at the stables with horses saddled and ready to go. She cast a glance at the sun, well into the sky, then arched a pale brow at me. "Good morning, Conrí.

I thought you wanted to be out at the point earlier than this."

"We have time," I said, mounting the gelding. Nicely arched neck, fine, intelligent eyes, and an alert mien. Excellent steed. So was Sondra's, the mare she'd ridden the day before. Beautifully refined, like everything on Calanthe.

"An hour until high tide," Sondra agreed as we set off. "I verified with the locals. Did you sleep well—or not at all?" She smirked.

"Shut up, Sondra."

She cast me a second glance. "You look a little rough this morning. The hellcat take her claws to you?"

"And lay off Lia. She's not your enemy."

"Nor would she thank you for protecting her, I bet," Sondra retorted. "Certainly not from little ol' me who's so far beneath her."

"Jealous?" As soon as I said it, I regretted it. Not for Sondra's sake, but because I really wasn't up for a conversation. I wanted peace and quiet, to think over Lia's revelations and their implications. But time and tides wait for no man, as some philosopher said.

"Me? Jealous of Her I-Smell-Like-Flowers Fancy Ass Highness?" Sondra made a rude noise. "Not hardly. It's just not like you to be distracted from the cause is all I'm saying."

"I'm not distracted." Except by sex. That happened all too easily. "Lia and I were discussing important things."

"'Discussing important things,'" Sondra mimicked in a whiny burr. "Listen to you. I never thought I'd hear you talk like that."

"Like what?" If Sondra was spoiling for an argument, she'd get one.

"All soft and misty-eyed over a woman."

"You're the one who pushed me to marry Lia. You even gave me advice on how to woo her," I reminded her.

"Yes, for the cause! Because the prophecy demanded it, because our vengeance required it. Or have you forgotten that part?" Sondra wrinkled her nose. "No one needs you to fall in love with her."

I coughed, choking on my own spit, and swallowed hard. "Who said anything about *that*?"

Sondra gave me a pitying look. "You're soft on her. And getting softer by the day."

"Fuck you," I replied, but without much heat.

"Well, not me, because I wouldn't have you, but yeah, maybe you should."

"What?" I wasn't even following her.

"You should have sex with someone else. Someone not Her Highness," she clarified, tossing her hair over her shoulder.

I threw Sondra a black glare. One that would have instantly cowed anyone else. Not Sondra, though. "What do you know of it?" I growled at her. "Suddenly you're an expert on sex."

She made a disparaging sound. "Absolutely not. But I do know she was your first sex, and that has power over a person."

I scrubbed a hand over my face, wishing I'd taken time to bathe. Or grab some food. But it had been later than I thought when I got my shit together, and we wouldn't have many chances to check these currents. Today, *maybe* tomorrow. Then we'd have to trust to luck, and mine had always been bad, no matter what Lia said.

"If Anure finds us here before we're ready, stuff like sex won't matter," I pointed out, sounding reasonably calm.

"If you say so," she replied. "If you can keep your head straight."

"Spit it out already."

Sondra gave me a long look. "Come on, I know you've thought of it. Using the Queen of Flowers as bait—and don't get me wrong, it's a good plan, so far as that goes— but you can't forget the critical component of fighting Anure. You can't care about what he expects you to care about."

I knew that. Hell, I'd figured that out and taught it to Sondra, along with the others. "I know."

"Do you?" She stared out at the sea as we followed the path out to the point of rocks. "Because it seems to me like you're starting to care about her."

"She's my wife," I ground out.

"A marriage of convenience in every sense," Sondra retorted. "Last week she would have seen you executed. That bitch has a cold heart, Conrí. Just because her pussy is hot doesn't—"

"Enough!" I cut her words off with a shout of iron, sur- prising us both. I looked away from Sondra's shocked— and knowing—stare. "I made vows. The marriage is real, in every sense. You will respect that."

"Fine by me." She shrugged, chirping the words non- chalantly. Then she gave me a hard look. "But when it comes down to it—and we both know it will, Conrí—will you be able to sacrifice her?"

I didn't reply.

"Because if you're going to falter on us, if you're going to put your *wife* before what we need to do to bring down Anure, now is a really good time to tell me. He'll expect you to care about her—because he does—and if you actually do, he'll use that against you. You know it and I know it."

"If we plan right, it won't come to that."

"And if it does? *If it does*, Conrí, what will you decide?"

The sun had risen high enough to bring color to the
water, the surface glassy with the tide so high, the water
full and calm between the two spurs of land. I reined up
and dismounted, looked for a good place to observe.

"Conrí?" Sondra followed me, voice harsh as Merle's.
"I need an answer from you."

I looked over at her, hair whipping like a pale banner
in the coastal breeze, eyes hard in her lined face. "I never
asked you to call me king." When she opened her mouth
to snarl a reply, I held up a hand to stop her. "But you
were the first to give me loyalty, and I haven't forgotten
that." *I ask only to hold the torch.* "I also haven't forgotten
why we're here, or what claiming Lia's hand meant. Still
means. Nothing will prevent our vengeance. I won't fail
you, or the cause."

She pressed her lips together, then nodded. "Thank
you." Turning, she followed the line of my sight, studying
the water. "Are you going to tell me what we're looking
for?"

"Watch the water." I glanced at the sun. "Tide should
be at high point now, then will start reversing. It might
take a while, but that's when it will happen. I think when
we see it, we'll know. Unless I'm wrong."

Making a snorting sound, she shook her head, even offering me a smile. A peace offering, I supposed. "You're
never wrong, Conrí."

I didn't know about that. Lia's words plagued me, rolling in my head. Had I been wrong about my sister? I
hunkered down, picking up a rock and weighing it in my
hand. Untying the bagiroca from my belt, I added it to
the rest. Then I took out one from Vurgmun and set it on

Cradysica's bones. I didn't have any stones from Oriel, of course. My habit of collecting rocks from every place I visited had begun long after Anure's guards dragged us away. Weighing the bagiroca in my hand, I thought about what Lia had said about the lands calling for their rulers. If I carried this bagiroca to the citadel at Yekpehr, would the captive royals know the fragments of their own lands?

Strange thoughts. Sondra squatted beside me, studying the water. Still full and calm, deceptively peaceful. The perfect trap.

"Can I ask you something?" I had to cough to clear my throat.

Sondra glanced at me askance. "Since when do you ask permission?"

"It's about . . . before Vurgmun."

Her eyes darkened and she looked away. "Is this punishment for what I said earlier?"

"No. But it is part of what Lia and I were talking about, why I was late."

When she looked at me again, her gaze held remorse. "Shit. I'm sorry, Conrí. I'm an idiot. No wonder you looked rough, if you were talking about . . . that."

"Yeah." I nodded, and we both fell silent for a bit. None of us asked the others about their time before the mines. It had always been an unspoken agreement, an allowance of privacy for people who'd lost everything in the worst ways. Even my broaching the topic felt like a violation. "Never mind. I—"

"Ask." Her once pretty profile looked sharp, even haggard against the bluing sky. She turned her head and pierced me with her defiant stare. "Ask."

If only I knew how. "You were . . . with Rhéiane, that

day." I said it fast, proud that I'd gotten my sister's name past the constriction in my chest.

Only the stillness of her face betrayed Sondra's shock. Slowly, she nodded.

"Did she—" I had to clear my throat yet again. "Did you see—" Sawehl take me, but I'd get through this. "Did you see her body?"

Sondra's throat worked as she swallowed. "She's dead, Con," she replied, soft and grating. "Don't go there."

I nodded, but I had to press. "Did you see?"

She sighed and gazed at the water, hands clenched between her knees, fingertips red and knuckles white. "It was bad," she said finally, still not looking at me. "You know that. The things they—" Pressing her knotted fists against her mouth, she stopped the words. "No one could live through what they did to her. I nearly died. I should have died."

"Don't say that." I put a hand on her shoulder.

Silent tears rolled down her pitted cheeks. It had been a morning for women who rarely shed tears to openly weep. I'd never imagined I'd see Lia cry like that. An omen, maybe. Sondra shook her head, but didn't shake me off. "They took her away," she said. "And she looked dead to me."

"But you don't know for sure."

"Until this moment, I'd have sworn to that truth."

"And now?"

She moved her shoulders restlessly. "I hope she's dead," she said flatly. "Because the alternative doesn't bear contemplating."

That was the worst part of Lia's theory. Unbearable to consider.

So I set it aside. Sondra gradually relaxed as I said

nothing more. Our silence became almost companionable as we made ourselves comfortable on the rocks, the rising sun warm, flocks of shorebirds in brilliant shades of greens and purples, whistling and calling as they made complex patterns in the sky. The boats in the harbor were safely docked and none came into it, which only confirmed for me that the local fishermen knew of the dangers beneath the lovely waters.

"It's a pretty place," Sondra commented.

I grunted. "Everything about Calanthe is pretty."

"Yeah." She picked at some mud on her boot. "Doesn't seem fair, somehow."

My turn to give her a sidelong look. "You say that—after your lecture on me getting soft?"

She scowled. "I'm just saying I understand the temptation. It would be . . . nice, you know, if we could have this. If you could adore your beautiful wife and we could live in paradise and, I don't know, I could find some strapping islander to treat *me* like a queen. But this isn't for the likes of us. We lost that chance a long time ago."

"I know." And I did. Her reminder had been timely. I'd allowed Lia to believe I'd tell her in time to save at least the people, but I wouldn't. Nothing could tip Anure off to the trap we'd lay for him. Lia's chance of making it through this depended on that, too. I'd make the hard decisions for her, and she could hate me afterward. If we both survived. I seriously doubted I would. She could always curse my memory.

We fell back into silence, staring at the water. I don't know if I saw it before Sondra did or if she simply waited to be sure before she said anything. "Holy fucking Sawehl," she breathed. "Is that . . . ?"

"A whirlpool," I confirmed with great satisfaction. The water, no longer calm and peaceful, swirled in a great circle that spanned the reach between the two spurs of land. The currents spun outward, generating considerable surf that roared against the rocks. Anything caught on the outer reaches would be smashed to bits. In the center, a deep hole formed, a darker blue like Lia's sapphire eye. I almost imagined a monster gazed back from it, perhaps even the baleful stare of Calanthe Herself. Following the whimsy, I saluted Her.

No disrespect intended, Lady Calanthe, but I hope You're ready to drink the blood of Your enemies, because I fully intend to be feeding them to You soon.

Except for Anure. The eater of realms would be mine to crush, and Sondra's to burn.

14

The orchid ring had been tugging at my attention all day. Not in a useful way, but like an insect buzzing at my ear that disappeared when I turned to look for it. I'd spent the morning hearing petitions and accepting tributes, listening to concerns about the rumors that had made it to Cradysica about Con declaring war on the emperor, and the defense we might mount.

I trotted out all sorts of well-crafted platitudes to calm their fears. As the people felt, so did Calanthe, and I didn't need Her growing more restless than She already was. The orchid ring murmured unhappily, a muted echo of the worry on the faces of the people who came to speak with me. Con was nowhere to be found, of course, as I spoke the lies he'd forced onto me.

"Your Highness." The head priest of the Temple of Cradysica made my title into a plea. He'd donned a fine robe for the audience, but came before me barefoot in his humility. "Should we perhaps consider evacuating the innocent citizens of Calanthe? If His Imperial Majesty takes offense at the rumors, then—"

"Where would we send our people? Even if we had enough boats to carry them all, where could they go? No. Calanthe is still the safest place in all the empire."

I hoped. Though I firmly believed no other place would be safer.

"Keiost isn't that far," the governor of Cradysica put in. "And I understand that it's being well run and fortified since the Slave King captured—"

"Conrí." I added a frown to the correction. "The next person to voice that vile epithet rather than My consort's correct title will risk My displeasure."

"My apologies, Your Highness." The governor bowed, and his wife beside him gave him an angry look. Ambrose, standing nearby and keeping me company, seemed uninterested, but Merle bobbed his beak at me in approval.

"If, by some great stretch of the imagination," I said, managing to sound dismissive of a remote possibility, "His Imperial Majesty should take it into his head to chastise Me for My marriage to Conrí, he would never attack the jewel of his empire. What would that serve him? The emperor cherishes Calanthe." *Cherish.* I wished I hadn't used that word. I'd felt cherished by Con, but the dreams promised he'd destroy me, just as Anure would destroy Calanthe.

"But if he does send his ships, we cannot possibly match his forces," the governor protested. "What will we do then, Your Highness?"

"In that eventuality, I shall deal with His Imperial Majesty Myself." I allowed a cool smile to show, hoping it looked as it should. I wore a gown of aqua blues and greens to celebrate Cradysica's famed harbor, and nail sheaths cleverly wrought in similar shades with gold tracery that created the feel of branching coral reefs. It was a perfectly appropriate gown, but it failed to fit my mood. One of the many reasons not to travel: How could I know days ahead of time what my mood would be when it came to dress?

Although what kind of gown *would* fit my mood, I didn't know. Something hanging in ragged folds of ash, rent with blood and fire. I felt all out of sorts, control slipping through my fingers. *Trouble*, the ring whispered in an irritating buzz. Ambrose and Merle both looked at the ring then, making me wonder if the wizard could sense it, too.

"I am not without My own resources," I reminded all of them. "I am queen of Calanthe, of the old blood, and I shall do what is necessary to protect My realm."

At least that worked to quell their anxiety, if not my own. Ambrose went back to smiling vaguely at the assembly. Merle eyed me with speculation, ticking his claws on the faceted emerald topping the wizard's staff.

"We greatly appreciate Your assurances, Your Highness." Sawehl's priest bowed in deep respect. "We are but a provincial people here in Cradysica, unused to royal visits and rumors of war."

"I understand. I am always happy to reassure My people." I attempted to look maternally beneficent, but that expression escaped me. What I needed was time in the dreamthink. It wouldn't be easy to find a place quiet enough, but it couldn't hurt to make the attempt. My schedule here wasn't as tightly crowded as at the palace.

"Will You attend the sunset service at the temple, Your Highness?" the priest inquired.

"That is My plan at the moment." I inclined my head graciously. The gown had been intended for that ceremony, so at least I wouldn't have to change. And with Con nowhere about, I didn't have to be concerned about him shredding this one in his lust. I couldn't decide if I was pleased about that or not. I'd already had him multiple times—when we arrived, when we retired for the night,

that meltingly intimate coming together before dawn—
and still I craved more.

"We are hoping that Your Highness and Conrí will
appear together, to enact the ritual of Blessed Ejarat and
Bright Sawehl," the priest continued smoothly, bringing
me back from my carnal fantasies, "to bring the bless-
ings of the god and goddess to Calanthe in these times of
uncertainty."

I managed not to show my consternation at being out-
foxed, and by this peacefully beaming priest, no less.
With a framing like that, I could hardly refuse. And yet
how could I possibly guarantee Con would appear by
then, much less that he'd cooperate with the appropriate theater such rituals required? Probably I should not
have shared my speculations about his sister with him.
I'd known he'd be upset. Now he'd be channeling all that
caged-wolf aggression into laying his trap for Anure, with
no charm left for playing Sawehl as bridegroom.

And already I'd paused too long.

"We shall be delighted to oblige," I declared, smiling at
the spontaneous applause and delighted cries of pleasure.
The people of Cradysica were so much more demonstrative
than my own wily courtiers. Calla, seated a step below me,
bent to adjust her skirts and caught my eye with a questioning brow where our audience couldn't see. I gave her a
slight nod. Con would have to be found. I glanced, too, at
Ambrose, who regarded me with a sharply amused smile.
Fine then—he could assist with the corralling and har-
nessing of our wayward wolf.

"And now I believe I shall take a rest and enjoy the
sculpture gardens of My hosts." I gave the head family
a gracious nod, observing how they sent several young
servants running ahead of me to be sure all was in order.

While some time in dreamthink might not happen, I could at least set some precautions in place. "Ambrose, would you care to accompany Me? You might enjoy seeing this."

Ambrose smiled with sweet grace, he and Merle bobbing their heads with enthusiasm. I didn't look beneath his illusory surface, as I had no wish to rattle my composure further, but I sensed his keen interest in the bargain he no doubt anticipated I'd be offering.

With Calla off to locate Con—surely he hadn't gone far—my other ladies trailed us at a discreet distance. My hosts had indeed cleared the sculpture gardens for us, so we were otherwise alone. Ambrose leaned heavily on his staff, the tip grinding through the crushed shells of the path. The orchid ring fluttered, as if vying for his attention, making my finger tingle, and I scratched at the itching underside with my thumbnail, picking at the spot where the band indelibly clasped my skin.

We paused before a sculpture of a butterfly. Several times life size, it perched on a pedestal, translucent wings shimmering gold and blue. Then the wings flexed, slow as a gentle sigh, the creature's antennae uncurling to taste the currents of magic wafting off the wizard. With a delighted grin, he extended a finger toward the butterfly—pausing to tsk at Merle, who looked at it a little too hungrily—then giggled when the creature brushed his finger. It changed to a deep ruby red, then burst into a cloud of swirling rose petals. When it re-formed, it had become a blue-and-gold rose, its petals slowing unfurling like butterfly wings.

"What sort of magic is this?" he asked me.

"Don't you know?" I countered, curious.

He straightened and pursed his lips as if chastising a student. "Now, now, Your Highness. We discussed this.

I think you know perfectly well that there's all sorts of magic in the world, far more than any one wizard could possibly learn, even in a very long lifetime."

"And how long has yours been?" I inquired politely. Merle flapped his wings and cawed.

"Besides," Ambrose said, as if I hadn't asked. "This is my first visit to Calanthe, which has long been at the heart of the strangest magics of all."

Not an encouraging answer from the wizard I hoped could perhaps contain the worst disaster, should I fail to.

"Before I answer, let Me show you another," I said. He followed my lead around a bend, to a square meditation garden with a waist-high wall around it. Shifting sand filled the basin, rolling in regular waves like the tides. Above that, granite boulders floated, bobbing gently with the currents of air.

"Miraculous," Ambrose breathed in delight. Merle took wing, flying to the nearest and perching on it, then pecking with his beak. "It's stone," the wizard announced, astonished. "How amaz—"

He broke off and I winced as the boulders all suddenly fell to the sand with a resounding boom, the resulting waves of sand crashing up in amplified waves. I grimaced ruefully and Merle circled them, cawing his annoyance.

"They don't all work correctly anymore," I told him.

"Then Merle didn't break it?"

"No. See?" I waved a hand to the settling waves of sand, and to the boulders that sat less heavily, a few smaller ones beginning to float again. "When I was a girl, you could run about in the sand and bounce the boulders against one another, even hang on to them and drift." Tertulyn had been there with me, playing those same games. At least the pain of that particular betrayal had begun to fade into a dull ache, easier to set aside. "Now they come crashing down unexpectedly, so we had to put a wall around it, so no one gets hurt."

"Fascinating," Ambrose commented, and I could see he'd dearly love to climb over the wall and inspect it for himself. He eyed the wall, however, and very likely could see that more than its inconvenient height would repel any attempts. "How is a floating boulder like a butterfly?" he asked rhetorically, a thoughtful frown on his boyish face.

"One more," I said, and led him to a wide pond. Beneath the crystal surface, instead of fish, jewel-bright birds flew through a depthless sky. Ambrose gasped at the sight, turning astonished eyes to me. "It's slippery, but this one you can walk on," I encouraged him.

"Or dance!" he declared, passing off his staff and Merle to Orvyki, who hastened up with a charming blush. He held out a hand to me. "Your Highness?"

Surprised—and in truth, pleased by the offer of whimsy when my mood had been so very dark—I laid my hand, the one with orchid ring, in his, and curtsied in response to his flamboyant bow. We stepped onto the bright surface, chilled water splashing around us, and music swelled from nowhere. Ambrose whirled me into a gliding dance with the tempestuous music, grinning when I laughed. Beneath our feet, the magic birds flocked to follow our movements, swirling in patterns that mimicked the rise and fall of the music Ambrose had evoked.

The music came to a crashing crescendo as we swept to a halt, out of breath and laughing. I stepped back and tested that my crown and wig had stayed in place, while Ambrose walked in a circle, showing no more sign of lameness now than he had while dancing. Experimentally he kicked at the water with his bare foot, watching the spray of droplets hover in the air before they floated down, light as downy feathers. The droplets continued to descend, sinking through the crystalline surface, and the birds surged to snap them up, feeding greedily.

Ambrose raised his gaze to me, canny wisdom in it. "Elemental magic, yes? Somehow the essential natures of these creatures are inverted, and turned in a different direction. Water becomes air. Crystal is wet, but dampens nothing. The butterfly . . ."

"Made of color," I supplied. "The ancient wizard artists of Calanthe made these as entertainments, but also as student exercises, to perfect the craft of creating one thing from something unlike."

He gazed about, still rapt, but something of sorrow in it. "Then the skills have been lost?"

"Unfortunately so. We have the artifacts, but since the departure of all the wizards, no one to explain them. Or to repair the ones that have broken, like the rock garden."

"I wonder if I could fix that?" he mused. He held out a hand, and water formed in a small spout beneath it, flowing up to meet his palm. "I know something of magic that works this way, but not a lot."

"Just as you know a wall is different from a door," I replied, recalling how he'd magically locked the door to my chambers but hadn't been able to ward the wall. Con hadn't understood why the wizard couldn't treat them as the same thing, but I'd wondered if intention lay under the wizard's use of magic, too. A doorway can be made to reverse itself to refuse passage, but a wall built for other reasons—such as for privacy or to hold up a ceiling— couldn't be made to admit passage.

Ambrose nodded absently, digging a toe into the pond surface. "This is how You did it," he commented.

"Excuse Me?"

He laughed at my arch reply and wagged a finger. "I told Con that the way You'd broken my invisibility spell on the sailing ship was as if You'd picked up a river and set it down again so it ran in the opposite direction."

Ah, that. "Some things are within My nature," I conceded. "Others are artifacts created by those long gone that are more difficult for Me to understand. Man's magic—wizardry—is not the same as what comes from the elements of life." I held out my hand with the orchid ring, which of course fluttered and silently cooed at the wizard.

"The flower that cannot die," he said somberly. "The Abiding Ring that clings to the hand of the true ruler of Calanthe, and only releases them upon their death, when it goes on to the next true heir."

"If there is one." *There must be one*, the ring insisted, pricking my skin so that I dug at it with my thumbnail.

"What happens if there isn't a true heir?"

I returned his serious gaze. "I don't know. It's never happened. Maybe . . . with the right magic, someone could take it and coax the orchid into bonding with them. It likes wizards."

Ambrose held out his palms. "May I?"

I laid my hand in his and he turned it over, examining not the gorgeous bloom as everyone else did, but the band that encircled my finger. Made of neither metal nor living wood, but something that flowed between the two elements, in much the way the rose and the butterfly did, the band hugged my skin tightly. Ambrose poked at it, digging a fingernail beneath the band—or trying to—and then using a delicate probe of magic. Both prickled uncomfortably.

"Is it grown into your skin?" he asked. "Oh no—I see. It's another of these elemental mergings. Interesting. You and it are one and the same at the intersection." He muttered to himself, Merle flying over to land on his shoulder and peer at the ring also, making his own soft raven mutters.

It amused me the way the two conferred, and I waited patiently as they analyzed the ring's properties. So interesting that Ambrose focused on the band, not the blossom, as everyone else did. Of course everyone else who'd looked at the ring had been looking at the top of my hand, likely distracted by the orchid's extravagant loveliness. I'd never really had an objective assessment of my own impressions of how the ring functioned. The scholars I'd collected could advise me on all manner of inventions and our growing scientific understanding of the world. Magic, however, defied that rational analysis. In many ways, it embodied the reversal of scientific process, just as we'd been discussing. I would have to consider that further.

Ambrose looked up at me from his bent position, the forest green of his eyes deep, ancient, and full of quiet power, and I saw him more clearly than ever. Not bent over, but far shorter than he normally appeared. "Shall we trade answer for answer?" he asked, his voice clear and resonant as a deep bell ringing. "Three for three, as is the old way. Truth for truth."

Feeling slightly out of body, I nodded. It could be a treacherous bargain, but I'd been waiting all these years for a true wizard to consult, and I needed his help. I'd best choose and phrase my questions wisely, in case the price was one I couldn't afford again. Though if the dreams were to be believed—and I did believe them—I wouldn't live much longer, regardless.

"I'll ask two, to give you time to think," Ambrose said with a canny smile, "and save my third for last." He'd stopped using my title, I realized, and it signified that we spoke as equals for the moment. Or, rather, as our most essential selves, without the rank and trappings of the outer world we occupied. Standing in the midst of that frozen pond that was neither of those things, we were not Queen and Wizard, but two creatures of magic, washed ashore on the beach of a world we no longer quite belonged to.

"I'm first asking for the story of the ring's transference, from your father to you." Ambrose still held my hand, part of his focus on the band of the ring. Both it and his magical attention tickled, the vague itch spreading through my hand to my heart. He'd know if I lied to him. Not that I intended to, but he'd without a doubt sense it. "I could ask this as a series of questions," he added, "but I don't think you'd want to owe me so many in return."

A fair point. I closed my eyes, recalling that day. My father had sickened, so quickly the court murmured of poison. It had been an ugly, humiliating death, as painful as it was relentless, and it had resisted the efforts of all the healers. The day he died, however, he found enough peace and clarity to ask to be transferred to a ship and carried out to sea. He'd become a wraith of himself, skin nearly translucent, and with no fluids left in his papery body, he'd been spared the endless diarrhea and vomiting that had consumed his last days.

When he asked me to come with him, I'd known what was coming.

Clean, purged in every way, he took my hand as he lay on the bier of orchids, the deck of the ship swaying softly beneath us. "This is sooner than I hoped, Euthalia," he said, "but you are a true queen of Calanthe. Your mother accepted me and made me king, but *you* are true-born. Trust in that, in what you know without knowing."

The orchid ring on his left hand looked wilted, the colors oddly muted. I'd have known that this heralded the king's death, regardless of all the other signs. My father interlaced the fingers of my left hand with his, then gazed at the sky and let out a long, rattling breath—but his hand tightened on mine. Though our people ringed us in somber observance, he and I were alone in the circle.

Except for the song of Calanthe, which filled my very blood, chiming in the air. Seabirds and land birds flew in dense swirls in the sky, and the water around the ship teemed with porpoises, fish, and whales, making more circles. My father smiled, radiant with joy. "My love," he murmured.

I felt Her embrace, too, one that had been around me every day of my life, but stronger in that moment. So very present. My father's eyes blurred, the blue fading into mist, and the orchid ring crawled from his hand to mine. It felt like a spider, the sticky hairs of its tendrils viscerally alarming, and I might have yanked my hand away if he hadn't held it so tightly.

The blossom settled itself on my hand, the vines twining around my finger and sinking into my flesh, my bones. They continued, digging deeper, into the marrow of my bones, crawling up my arm and throughout my skeleton, finding root in the soil of my body. I sank to my knees and wept from the deep pain and for my father's ignominious, too-sudden death.

On my finger, the orchid blossom unfurled, taking on greater life and color, drawing nourishment from me.

My father's hand slipped from mine, and the solemn circle of his closest advisers closed on us. Lord Dearsley helped me to my feet, and held me in a firm grip as the others tipped my father's bier into the sea. The water boiled, swirled, and he sank into Calanthe's final embrace.

"The king is dead," they intoned. And all the beings on Calanthe echoed the mourning, sending up howls and scents, the land shivering in mourning. "Long live the queen." The sounds turned to celebration, even as I tasted the salt on my lips from the tears.

Long live the queen. I heard the orchid ring's voice for the first time.

"Thank you," Ambrose said. I realized I'd forgotten to speak aloud, I'd been so rapt in the memory. He smiled cheerfully, however. "No worries. I got it all. I understand now, why the ring cannot be removed while you live, and how you must have a true heir to pass it to."

I felt my wits sharpen as the haze of memory departed, and I focused on him, certain he'd used magic to coerce all the details of that from me. Willing or not, I hadn't planned to give him so much. He smiled angelically.

"You promised me that if I married Conrí, I could bear a true heir of his seed. Were you lying to—"

"Ah ah." He gave me a piercing look. "I'm going to stop you because our bargain is still in effect and I don't think you want to waste one of your three questions on something we already discussed." He raised one brow until I nodded. "My second question is simpler. How did your father impregnate your mother?"

"I don't know exactly," I replied in all honesty. "I know a ritual was involved. The previous queen was aged and had no true heir, so young men traveled to the temple to answer the call. They presented themselves to the island, and Gul was selected by Her. He lay with many virgins, island maidens—as many as wished to offer their bodies as surrogates—and I was born, the only true daughter of Calanthe born in that year." And although he had sired countless babes after me, none of my myriad half siblings were true heirs. Calanthe would've told me.

"Ah. I still have questions, but I'll bide on my third. Ask your three."

More than anything I wanted to ask him about the orchid ring, how its magic worked and if I should be using it, but from comments he'd dropped and the questions he'd asked me just now, I thought he didn't know the answers I sought. I wouldn't want to waste this opportunity to get honest answers only to find out he knew little more than I did. Instead I asked what I'd been pondering for some time, deliberating on how to pose it in such a way that it would give me the widest array of the information I needed.

"Why did you seek out Conrí to act in your schemes?"

Ambrose laughed gaily and shook a finger at me. "Aha. Clever girl, combining several assumptions into one question so I have to either correct your misapprehensions or risk telling an untruth. I understand why your mother chose your father for her champion, if you get your wily intelligence from him."

I kept my counsel, thinking it best not to tell him more about Calanthe's intelligence than necessary. Though as far as human politics went, then I likely did inherit those skills from my father. Certainly he's the one who taught me. Calanthe doesn't concern Herself much with words.

"So," Ambrose said, tapping a finger on his chin, "you're speculating that I sought out our Conrí, rather than the reverse—or maybe he told you as much—and you further suppose that I have a scheme we follow, and that I have a reason to have recruited him to act in service of some deep agenda of my own."

I assumed my best politely interested expression. If the wizard hoped to feel his way through by assessing my reactions, he'd have little luck. His smile widened at my placid mask, and he cocked his head, Merle doing the same.

"I'm going to answer your question honestly, though

it may not sound like it. Being a wizard is like having a special sailing ship that can navigate the stormiest of seas. I cannot be drowned, and I can harness the power of the ocean to my own ends, to some extent, but I do not control the ocean I sail upon. I bring skills and tools to charting my course, but ultimately where the currents take me is the ocean's decision. The prophecy I follow is like constellations that guide us. Why Conrí, you ask? Because he's the island where I ran aground."

Hmm. I believed in the truth of that answer, especially given what I suspected might end up being critically important about Con's blood ties to Oriel. If Ambrose's ocean of magic was akin to the power of the lands craving their true caretakers, then that particular running aground might have been inevitable.

At least, as inevitable as such capricious things as fate can be.

"Since you stuck to the letter of My question, what is your scheme then—what do you seek to achieve by guiding Con, and Myself, via this prophecy?"

He became very serious. "Anure is a false ruler, as I believe you understand. He is not at the root of all that's gone wrong in our world. Magic had been thinned and soured by sloth and greed. Rulers forgot that they served the land and treated the land and its children as theirs to use and exploit. Anure is, however, a parasitic blossom that flowered on that diseased body. My scheme, my agenda, my heart's desire and self-determined destiny is to change that. I have an old debt to repay, restitution to make for unforgivable crimes, and labor of deepest love before me."

"You want Anure dead more than any of us," I replied to that astounding speech with some awe.

"Is that your third question?" he asked, eyes flashing gimlet green.

"No—no more than that was *your* third question. That was a statement."

"In the spirit of generosity then, I'll confirm that I certainly want Anure removed from his self-bestowed office, but he is only one blossom among many. I mean to kill the parasite and revive the body."

I eyed him with considerable interest, plagued with curiosity and a desire to know much more. Did Con know that Ambrose was thinking about a much larger-scale mission than simply defeating Anure? *Simply defeating.* Who would've ever guessed I'd have such a thought? I would have to wait to find out more, however, because my last question would be not for myself, but in service to Calanthe.

"What is your third question?" Ambrose asked, almost gently, as if aware of my intense longing to know more of what he planned. How much of my destiny he'd foreseen.

"We're two for two," I replied. "It's your turn." If he asked what I expected he would, then that would lead neatly into what I would ask of him.

"Your Highness, Queen Euthalia," he asked quite solemnly. "What happens when blood is shed in violence on the soil or waters of Calanthe?"

I had my answer ready, as that was exactly what I'd expected. I folded my hands together, the orchid ring chortling softly to itself. "I'm going to answer your question honestly, though it may not sound like it."

He bowed with a wry smile, acknowledging the point.

"She will wake," I said. "Blood spilled in violence is like blood given in sacrifice, as in the old ways. How much or how little it will take, I don't know. But we on

Calanthe have erred on the side of none at all, because
we've been taught that Her waking would mean the end
of our piece of paradise. She would come to life, fully
and completely, which has not happened since the time of
monsters. What that means for us, precisely, we can only
suppose. Suffice to say that humans and monsters don't
coexist well."

He eyed me speculatively. "I want to ask if you would
be able to control Her."

Not exactly a question. "I don't know. I've never had to
do it. No one in memory has." I looked at the orchid ring,
the Abiding Ring, the symbol of eternal life and endurance through every storm. "If I'm here on Calanthe, if
and when She wakes, I'll do my utmost. Which leads to
what I will ask of you, wizard."

He straightened, Merle giving me his utmost attention.
Yes, they'd both caught my phrasing, and Ambrose had
wit enough to be concerned about what I would ask. I was
changing up the rules, but a queen makes the rules. She
doesn't blindly follow them. "If, for some reason, I am
not here and Calanthe wakes, will you do your utmost to
control Her in my stead?"

I'd surprised him, to the core, I suspected. He hadn't
seen that eventuality. Merle leaned in, seeming to whisper in his ear, and the wizard nodded. "Cleverly done.
I could simply say no and leave the question as asked
and answered. Your Highness, however, has seen clearly
to my heart and You will know I cannot refuse—both
as Your court wizard, and as myself." Merle spread his
wings and chatted several soft caws. "Merle agrees for
himself also. We accept Your challenge—with the caveat
that neither of us has experience in such an effort."

I smiled, letting him see my relief. "All I ask is that
you try. It's no more than I could do."

"I suspect You could do far more," he said, with a wry flourish and bow. "But in Your absence, I agree that Merle and I are Your next best option."

I studied him a moment. "I notice you haven't argued with Me about whether I will be on Calanthe."

He raised a brow. "Should I?"

"Con did. He's vowed to protect Me and says he'll never let Anure have Me."

Ambrose sighed. Merle dug something out of one talon and spit it aside. "Conrí is a true hero," Ambrose explained. "He believes he can conquer all, and that belief allows him to accomplish the impossible. But You and I . . . and Merle, yes," he added when Merle protested. "Sorry, habit. I forget I don't have to pretend that you're only a raven with Queen Euthalia. We understand that the seas of destiny hold terrible storms, currents that can't be avoided, monsters waiting to devour us. Conrí has the courage and determination to set sail, the willingness to take the chances that You and I flinch from, because we can see all too well how difficult the journey will be."

I considered that. "Is that why you don't guide him more than you do?"

Ambrose broke into a wide smile. "Conrí might have his blind spots—and he has lessons yet to learn—but he is the captain that will sail our ship to where we need to be. If You'll allow me to extend the metaphor."

"I'll remember that when the storm surge sweeps Me overboard," I replied drily.

He beamed and offered me his arm. "Yes, Your Highness. Please do remember that."

~ 15 ~

"This is a waste of precious time," I groused to Lia.

She paid no more attention to my complaint than she had any of my previous gripes—which meant that instead of studying the currents of the Bay of Cradysica as the evening tide turned, or fine-tuning the battle plans, I was riding up a hill, dressed in bright-gold cloth, playing Sawehl to Ejarat.

Serenely riding beside me on a bay mare through the golden light of the sinking sun, Lia managed to resemble a painting of Ejarat as maiden. The blue dress she wore cascaded over the horse's rump, overlaid with an elaborate lace veil in golds and browns. She looked mind-numbingly gorgeous, as she always did, whereas I looked like a court jester.

I understood why folk always wanted to dress up Sawehl's chosen to look like the sun, but the shining silks made me feel like I had a big target on my back. Nothing like being the brightest person in a crowd to make a guy easy to pick out. It wasn't my first stint playing Sawehl for the priests. Whatever it took to make them happy and get them behind the cause, but the god knew better than I did what a blackened, corrupt spirit occupied my scarred body. No one who truly knew what kind of man I was would pick me to represent Sawehl. Sure, I'd gone along with various—very short—rituals, but this one felt too serious, too important. I didn't expect Sawehl to strike me down for sacrilege—He hadn't so far—but even I had limits to my presumption.

"You could've asked me first," I pointed out.

Lia gave me a sidelong glance, her eyes bluer than usual with the framing of the dark lashes and the wig in the colors of the sea, just like her sparkling crown. "I likely would have, if you had been anywhere to be found."

"I was busy," I muttered.

"So you mentioned," she replied smoothly. "Any number of times."

"We're here for a specific reason. You know that. Anure's fleet is on its way and I need to be preparing the trap, not participating in a costume drama."

"Zsst," she hissed, eyes flashing. "Lower your voice. Show some respect for what the people believe, even if you don't. This won't take long, then you can go back to staring at the water like you've been doing all day."

"Aha." I nudged my horse closer to hers, so our knees bumped. She gave me a glorious smile, but her gaze spat the warning of a snake ready to strike. "So you *did* know where I was."

"Yes. And I gave orders that you shouldn't be troubled until the timing made it absolutely necessary. You're welcome."

"And you decided this was absolutely necessary."

She fixed me with that granite gaze. "Yes."

I put a hand on her knee, not able to feel much through all the layers of her skirts, but liking the tremor that went through her. Lia might control her face with the artistry of a master, but her body gave her away. I let my own gaze show my desire, and then dropped it to her bosom, remembering the taste of her naked breasts. It hit me with sudden force that tonight might be our last night together. Kara had sent word that Anure's fleet had departed Yekpehr. I'd been watching for the second bird with more details on that fleet's size, composition, and heading when Lady Calla had retrieved me at Her Highness's insistence, and with the oblique threat to drag me back unconscious, if necessary.

Having no desire to be put out for the night and wake up past the morning tide with a skull-cracking headache, I'd gone with her. For this.

Also, I knew I should tell Lia the news, but she would want to move her people and it was too soon for that. So yeah, I'd delayed going back to face her because I knew I was a shitty liar and she'd see right through me. Unless I could distract her with sex or arguments. Either worked.

"Conrí, darling?" Lia murmured through lips curved in an adoring smile.

"Yes, sweetheart?" I murmured back in the same tone.

"Get through this ceremony, treat it with appropriate reverence, and I won't cut off your balls in your sleep." She lifted a hand to caress my cheek, the orchid ring fluttering and glass-sharp nails trailing along the skin over my beard, murder in her eyes.

I burst out laughing—not a pretty sound, more like a dog's pained howl than anything—and turned my face to kiss her palm. "You'd do it, too, wouldn't you?"

Her eyes glittered with a hint of real amusement. "In a heartbeat."

"I won't be getting heirs on you in that case."

With a careless shrug, she tapped my lower lip with a pointed nail, then nudged our horses enough apart that I lost my grip on her. "Heirs are for the future."

The finality, the sorrow in her voice, as she spoke of the future as an impossibility hit me like a blow to the head. Suddenly I didn't want to think about war or the battle the next day would surely bring. Here I was, in the brilliant gloaming of a tropical paradise, married to the most beautiful and fascinating woman in the world. I should savor that. "Do you suppose Ejarat and Sawehl fight like we do?" I asked her.

She raised a brow. "Why do you suppose He works so hard to appease Her with His golden light? Sawehl spends all His time circling Ejarat, lavishing Her with warmth so She can be rich and fertile."

"I never thought of it that way."

"See? You should take a lesson from Sawehl's wisdom." Her smile remained lovely and closed-lipped, but her laughter rippled beneath.

We reached the peak of the hill, crowned by the truly impressive temple, and surrounded by a solemn crowd holding unlit candles. To my surprise, Ambrose waited within, standing with several priests. I dismounted, then went to Lia to lift her off her horse. I could nearly span her waist with my hands, and with her bracing her hands on my shoulders, she seemed to weigh no more than a spray of orchids—and that was probably mostly her gown. As I set her on her feet, she squeezed my arm muscles, lips curving in a sensual smile just for me.

Tempted to kiss her senseless, I kept my head and offered her my arm, escorting her sedately up the steps to the temple. It was a simple space, as Sawehl's temples and shrines tended to be, with smoothly polished pillars

holding up the curved roof. That dome, though, was unlike anything I'd ever seen. The underside was silver—a
surprise with the top being gold—and seemed to radi-
ate light. I frowned at it thoughtfully. I'd been up here a
couple of times already, but my attention had been on the
surrounding countryside, my thoughts all on the trap we
were laying, piece by piece. I hadn't noticed how truly
unusual the dome was until this moment.

"The metal bilayer is so thin the sunlight shines
through," Lia murmured under her breath.

Ah. Bilayer, though—gold and silver melded together?
I hadn't known that was possible. I lowered my gaze to
find Ambrose's delighted and dancing one observing me.
He probably knew all about how this thing was made.
Alchemy and magic, no doubt.

Besides the magnificent dome and plain pillars, the
temple stood open to the environment, as everything on
Calanthe seemed to be. Smooth tiles glittered on the floor,
a mosaicked pattern as in the map tower. Colored arcs
denoted the range where Sawehl's sun rose and set,
bounded by darker arrows at the solstice points, and a
glittering star of gold at the summer equinox, a silver one
for winter.

Was the weather any different between the two? I
supposed I'd never find out.

Frowning at it, I noticed something else I hadn't before. The central pattern, which I'd taken for an abstract
of spiraling colors, resolved into a replica of what I'd been
looking at all day. A vast spinning whirlpool. In the sunset
light, another form seemed to emerge from the pattern. As
soon as I tried to focus on it, I'd lose it.

Was it . . . a monster? The memory welled up again of
that book from my childhood. Rhéiane holding it on her
lap and pointing to the images. The woman like Lia, with

her bicolored eyes. And on the next page . . . shrines? Temples to the old gods overlooking the sea . . .

"This is no Temple of Sawehl," I muttered to Lia, as the priests intoned a chant, the people outside taking it up in low tones, the rhythm of Sawehl's journey, even and reliable.

"This place is sacred to both Sawehl and Ejarat anyway," she replied in a low voice, eyes gleaming, deep as the sea. "And the ceremony is all Theirs. Shh."

The long rays of sunlight dipped below the dome and streamed straight at us. A shiver of something ran down my spine. A touch not of this world.

I'd never been much for religion. I hadn't had any interest in it as a boy, and in the mines nobody worshipped anything but survival and revenge. I supposed I'd made Vengeance my personal goddess, though there was no such being in the pantheon I knew of. She'd have sharp, bloodied teeth and claws, a cavern of a chest with a burning coal of a heart within. Kind of like that monster I'd glimpsed in the tiles beneath our feet. An image that had disappeared again.

Though I'd never seen this particular ceremony, the steps were easy enough, and I circled Lia slowly to the beat. She pivoted in place, her face always to me. The face of Ejarat, beautiful, wild, serene, and ruthless as all life is. I'd chosen the wrong goddess to worship, perhaps, but that choice had been made long ago.

As I completed the first circle, higher voices chimed in, overlaying the deep rhythmic chant of Sawehl. Ejarat's song filled the gloaming, a sweet and sorrowful farewell to Sawehl for the night. She would sleep, the voices sang, until He kissed Her awake.

Lia held out her hands to me, facing the setting sun, her expression an image of longing. Drawing me to her, she lifted her face for my kiss. It was meant to be a ritual kiss of parting, but as I touched my lips to hers, the scent and flavor of her, soft as a flower petal, fierce as the jungle, full of the grace of a life that might have been, it all drew me in and I groaned, gathering her close.

She didn't resist. Far from it. Her arms tightened on me, her lithe body pressed so close to mine that I could feel every line of her taut thighs and hardened nipples, the bones of her corset and framework holding out her skirts like an extension of her skeleton. I drowned in her, drinking from her and feeding her in turn. The emotions rose to choke me. Maybe Sawehl did exist and somehow gave me a glimpse of His all-encompassing love for Ejarat. Inside my chest, that burnt coal of my heart flickered with something like living flame.

I understood something profound in that moment: Without the world, the sun would continue to shine, but there would be nothing to receive its rays. Only the cold, vast darkness. Somehow, somewhere along the way, I'd lost the thread of vengeance. My focus had slipped and Lia had become the center.

The music rose to a swirling crescendo of joy as we kissed, and it felt as if the temple, the world spun around us. The hot light of the setting sun vanished, my back cooling, and I imagined the quiet hiss of the sun as He whispered, *Fare well, My son.*

We broke the kiss, reluctantly. Lia stared up at me wide-eyed, and startled—like when I woke her from the nightmare. One blue eye, one green, a flush of flower petals fluttering over her high cheekbones, bright enough to show through her makeup. I kissed her once more, lightly. "Your eyes," I murmured, knowing she'd want me to, though I hated for her to change them.

The priests intoned the final blessing, and the crowd sent up a joyous cheer, pelting us with flowers. Of course.

For once, I didn't mind.

I remained at the temple while Lia rode down, leading the parade of dancing, singing people. That's part of the ritual, too, that Ejarat departs and Sawehl remains. Ideally the man playing the part of Sawehl holds vigil all night until just before dawn, when he slips into the bed of the woman playing Ejarat and wakes her in the most delightful of ways.

Lia had told me straight off she'd spare me the all-night vigil—as a nod to more pressing needs, and as sneaking into the queen's bed was a great way to get killed by guards. I'd accepted that for the concession it was earlier. Now I nearly regretted it. That touch of the numinous, the voice that had sounded like Sawehl's blessing . . . If I held vigil, awake and fasting all the night, would the god speak to me again?

Though what useful advice He could give, I didn't know.

"That was lovely," Ambrose said to me, standing by my side as we watched Lia ride down the winding trail, the sky full of sunset light and evening birdsong. Merle croaked an unlovely agreement, and I grunted an acknowledgment, sounding much the same. "Well?" Ambrose asked, expectantly.

"Don't you know already?" I replied, though without rancor. The solace of the ritual made me feel well disposed even to the wizard. When he pointedly didn't reply, I answered him anyway. "Kara says Anure's fleet has departed. The trap is being laid, but we need the fleet to arrive at the right time. The timing needs to be exact. Can you help with that?"

He shook his head. "That's not how magic works."

"Of course not."

"It is, however, how an elemental works," he offered, thoughtfully. "Have you asked Her Highness?"

No. It hadn't occurred to me, but the stuff about the weather, reversing currents . . . I guessed I should. "I don't want her involved in this," I said. "Not more than necessary," I amended.

"Ah." He was silent a moment, the song of Ejarat floating up to us. It reminded me of something to do with Rhéiane. Maybe only because I'd finally spoken her name aloud again, maybe from that memory of the book and the stories in it. I suddenly and viciously wished I'd made myself look at her face in the painting. I might never make it back there, which meant I'd lost my chance forever.

"It's a dangerous game you play with Her Highness," Ambrose observed.

For a moment I thought he meant the teasing and ferocious sex, then I realized he meant using Lia as bait. "We won't let him have her," I vowed. "She'll be protected."

"Then you'll stay with Her? Stand staunchly by her side to defend the Queen of Flowers from the one who might pluck Her?"

I laughed, a hoarse chuckle. "You know as well as I do that our rose has the sharpest of thorns, and plenty of protection."

"Then you won't stay with Her?"

"I can't. I have to lead our forces."

"Hmm."

I rounded on him. "What aren't you telling me? Don't play enigmatic wizard."

"My dear boy." He patted my cheek. "I *am* an enigmatic wizard. I don't have to play at it." He held up a hand to stop my retort. "I simply think your place is by your wife's side, holding the hand you claimed." He sighed. "Though I also know you won't."

"How am I to direct the battle if I'm hiding in my wife's chambers?" I demanded.

Ambrose laughed, Merle flapping his wings and cawing. "How do you plan to force Queen Euthalia to hide in Her chambers? You have such grandiose ideas of your ability to affect the forces of nature in the world around us."

I barely managed to avoid snarling at him. "She's a woman, not a force of nature."

"Are you sure?" Ambrose sobered instantly. "Seems to me that She could be both. You'd do well to respect the forces of nature in your life, Conrí."

Turning to look down the hill path again, I caught a last glimpse of her shining horse and sparkling crown, before they disappeared beneath the canopy of hand-sized, waxy green leaves. Orchids, pale as Lia's flesh, gleamed in the last of the light, studded the darker foliage like stars.

"Why don't you help us more, Ambrose?" I asked.

"More than what? One needs a metric—"

"No." I rounded on him, unexpectedly angry, full of dread, as if I stumbled blindly in the dark toward some terrible . . . monster. "None of your riddles. Anure has four wizards helping him. I'm sure they don't mock him and refuse to give straight answers."

Ambrose didn't smile. He and Merle regarded me with stern expressions. "I wouldn't be so sure of that, Conrí," the wizard replied, and his voice had a resonance that made me want to bow and apologize. "The king who believes he controls a wizard finds his belief is exactly what the wizard wants him to have. *That* is how magic works, my dear Conrí."

I stared at him, unable to muster a reply.

"I am helping you, Con," he said, much more gentle and human sounding. "More than you can realize at this point. I'm simply . . . keeping a light hand on the rudder." He broke into a smile, amused at himself, and Merle cawed in apparent appreciation.

"I'm not a ship to be sailed, wizard," I growled, doubting its truth as I said it.

"Aren't you?"

I didn't have a good answer. "Why didn't you at least tell me that Anure had wizards? That would've been helpful to know."

"How so? You, yourself, can vouch that wizards are unpredictable assets."

True. The absurdity of picturing Anure arguing with intractable wizards hit me, and I nearly laughed aloud. "You still could've mentioned it."

"Would you have come this far if I had?"

Good question.

"A storm?" Lia gave me a sidelong look when I asked the question. Her ladies had undressed her for the night, and she wore only her sheer silk robe, the pretty scarf from this morning knotted around her head. "Though your confidence in Me is flattering, I cannot control the weather."

"Oh, come on, Lia," I said with considerable exasperation. "I understand your need to keep secrets from me. No, wait—I don't understand that, but I accept it." Sort of. "But we're on the same side of this battle. I need to keep Anure's fleet from reaching the mouth of Cradysica's harbor until tomorrow morning. Can you do that? Ambrose thinks you can."

"Does he? Hmm." She poured two glasses of the fantastically excellent brandy her people kept her supplied with. Easily the best liquor I'd ever tasted. Handing me one, she clinked her glass against mine. "I can hold them off once they reach Calanthe's waters, yes."

I sipped, the delicious zing of the brandy filling my head like the subtly floral fragrance of her skin. "With a storm?"

She laughed, the amusement lighting her gorgeous eyes. "Nothing so dramatic. I can simply ask the waters to slow their progress, flow in the opposite direction, as it were."

"If you can do that, why not hold him off indefinitely?"

"Because Calanthe's seas are connected to the oceans of the larger world. I can only work against the greater forces of nature for a short time, in small ways. We are, all of us, subject to the vast flows of the world." She looked saddened by that. Before I could ask, though, she shook off the thought. "But yes, I can slow them that much. You can tell Me when you want them to arrive."

I frowned, thinking. "We could set a time. Or I can send a message."

"A message?"

"Maybe a signal of some sort."

"I'll be right beside you, so you can just tell Me."

Uh-oh. "No, you won't be with me. I've made arrangements for you to stay in a . . ." I trailed off at the incandescent anger flooding her face. ". . . a bunker, of sorts."

"Conrí. I will not cower in some windowless room while My people die for Me." With that final pronouncement, Lia turned her back on me and strode into the bedchamber. Even with no crown or elaborate makeup, she still managed to be intimidatingly regal, wearing the scarf like it crowned her Queen of All the Damn World.

"We discussed this," I ground out, determined not to give her the last word on this argument.

She whirled on me, that flower-petal pattern I'd

glimpsed in Sawehl's temple brightening on her cheek-bone like a blush. "Did we?" she asked in a cool, arch tone. "Oh no, my dear Conrí, we did *not*."

I set my teeth. "I thought you understood that Anure's objective will be to seize you and hold you captive so he can destroy Calanthe while you watch. And my objective is to protect you from that."

"I understand that."

"Then fucking *listen* to me." I came close to shouting at her.

Far from flinching at the volume, she leaned in. "I have no wish to be seized, but I cannot shirk My duties to Calanthe and My people. A queen leads. That's non-negotiable."

I could throttle the woman, I really could. "They'll have a plan," I explained as clearly as I could. "They know about your abilities, how your ladies can and cannot defend you. I brought you with me so I could keep you safe, not leave you out in the open, vulnerable to abduction."

"Oh? And here I thought I brought *you* with Me, and that the point of Me being here is to be the bait in your trap."

"None of that matters." Even as I said the words, I knew I was wrong. As Sondra had caustically accused me, I was losing my ruthless edge where Lia was concerned. I didn't want her to be the bait. I only wanted her safe.

"If I'm in plain sight, it will be all the more difficult to spirit Me away, and I'll be more visible bait," she countered with infuriatingly cool logic.

I threw up my hands, no longer caring if I shouted. "Don't you understand? You could be hit by an explosion. A misguided arrow could kill you by mistake. This won't be some garden-party game. You could *die*, Lia!"

"So could you," she replied quietly. "So could any or all of My people."

"Well, I will not allow you to put yourself in danger." As soon as the words left my mouth, I wanted to haul them back. She didn't jump on them, however, didn't coolly remind me that I had no power to command her movements and decisions.

Instead she smiled at me, closed-lipped, that sorrow back in it. "I've always been in danger, Con. All My life. I appreciate that you care to try to stop that—I don't think anyone else ever has, at least not for Me, rather than to safeguard the throne—but you simply can't. I was born to be queen of Calanthe, and that has always meant that Calanthe's welfare, and that of all Her denizens, are more important than Mine. I cannot hide while we are attacked. It's simply not possible."

All the anger drained out of me, replaced by quiet despair. "Please listen to me on this," I said, sounding ragged and desperate, not at all the forceful warrior I'd been in my head when I planned this argument.

She came to me, threading silken arms around my waist. I'd stripped down for the night, too, and wore only the pants I'd leave next to the bed, where my rock hammer and bagiroca already waited, in case I needed them in the night. In case Anure tried to abduct Lia.

"What if I asked you to stay back with Me?" she asked. She tilted her head, eyes gleaming in the light of the few candles, her body heat burning through the thin silk, fingertips soft and bare of their wicked tips caressing my back. "Would you give up being at the forefront of springing this trap, to stay by My side?"

I dropped my head to hers, encircling her in my arms, wishing I could keep her there like that forever. I'd even given it thought, staying back by Lia's side, after Ambrose suggested it. But Kara's messages affirmed that it was near certain Anure had left his citadel to voyage to

Calanthe, so he could lay personal claim to Lia. At last we'd found something to pry him out of his fortifications, and he would be within reach. I'd bet on this, and I'd won.

My area of greatest expertise: I understood exactly how the need for revenge gnawed at the heart and mind, how it led a man to make crazed decisions and finally expose himself. Anure and I . . . we were alike in too many ways now. Including the insatiable desire for the woman I held in my arms. But even for her, I couldn't give up being there to gut Anure myself. Too much could go wrong. I had to be there. If something went wrong because I was hiding . . .

"I can't," I admitted, realizing that Lia and I shared that need to be at the front.

"I know," she whispered back. "This is what you need to do. I've always understood that. It might have been the first thing I understood about you, before I even met you in the flesh. I'm asking you to understand that I must do what I need to do, also."

Unfortunately, I did.

"Lia." I said her name on a groan of longing that had nothing and everything to do with the sensual glide of skin through silk against mine. With the raging need for her, the way my heart flamed in her presence. She lifted her mouth, fitting her lips easily against mine, the kiss long and languid and painfully sweet.

"I know," she said again.

"I never thought I'd feel this way about anyone," I told her, driven by some need to confess. Something about the emotion in the ritual at the temple, Sawehl's undying love for Ejarat filling me, that tender flame that flared in the burnt coal of my heart burning only for her. My Lia. "I—" I broke off, unable to say the words.

"Shh. Enough words." She led me to the bed.

As I sank into the yielding succor of her body, as that elemental, essential well-being Lia brought suffused me, I wondered at this strange pass I'd come to. I should never have fallen in love with the Queen of Flowers.

But I had.

A final joke from the gods who'd abandoned me. It changed nothing that my heart had come to life. It only meant I'd bleed more when I died.

16

When the nightmares chased me from sleep, Con had already gone. I should've been relieved at his absence while I examined my hands, seeing that I still had them both, but I missed his comforting presence. With a sigh of regret—tempted to go look for him and knowing it to be futile—I reached for the dreamthink instead.

Lying in the sheets that smelled of my husband and sex, I let my mind wander out to Calanthe. The birds showed me the rising sun. The fish swam through crystal waters, fat and pleased. Unease rippled through the people in some sharp bursts, but for the most part they rose lazily from their beds, or worked at their morning tasks, with their usual songs and greetings.

No foreign fleet in Calanthe's waters. Not yet.

It lay out there, though, like one of the tropical storms still far beyond the horizon, spinning its way toward Calanthe. And this one I would not be able to send gently around us. I could only hold it for Con's ideal arrival time. Trust him to take it from there. The manacled wolf, now free of his chains, and at the helm of the vessel I rode on. I had no choice now but to travel through the fire with him, and either perish or emerge on the other side.

By tomorrow, I'd know which it was. There was a restfulness to that, a fierce resolve in enduring the fury of the storm unleashed. No more hiding. No more waiting and dreading.

Because I had the time—no Morning Glory waiting for me to wake—and because it might be the last time, I cast my mind all over the length and breadth of Calanthe. I visited every part of the land and water and air of my realm, drawing succor from the vitality and innate joy of my home and mother, touching all those lives and sending my love. I wanted them to know that, if I was forced to leave them, I didn't want to go.

I found nothing to answer the questions in my heart, however. Whatever Con had been about to confess, I'd been relieved that he hadn't. We'd made vows to each other, tied our lives and fates together. We didn't need emotional declarations to muddy the waters. Any more than they already were.

I stretched, deliberately making noise, and Ibolya peeked through the barely cracked door. Seeing me awake, she came in, gorgeously dressed for the day ahead, and curtsied. "Arise, Your Highness," she said with a smile. "The realm awaits the sun of Your presence."

And so it began.

Con took one look at my gown and swore viciously under his breath. Striding across the courtyard to me, he took me by the arm and guided me away from my entourage of ladies and anxious Cradysicans.

"Did you have to announce we'd be facing battle to the entire world?" he hissed in my ear.

"Yes," I replied. "To present Myself otherwise would be a lie, and I won't lie to My people." Besides, the gown made me feel better. Not exactly armor, but the finely wrought overlapping leaves in shades of gold and silver gave that look. Without underskirts or my usual framework, the skirt flowed light and loose, allowing me to step quickly on flat-heeled golden boots. I wore no flowers today, only the jeweled designs of bloody roses interspersed among the metal leaves. Matching gauntlets covered my arms, finishing with points at my hands, and rising to frame my throat with curling thorns. No elaborate wig for me today, I wore one I'd asked Nahua to modify—a sleek black cap of hair that lay close against my scalp, just enough for my crown to be pinned to.

"You're wearing armor," I added. He looked intimidating, dangerous, and ferally sexual, too. With his hair loose, the black armor of leather, metal pins, and the cloak of stitched skins, he could've stepped out of my dreams. We'd come some distance together that I found him fatally attractive instead of terrifying. In those scarred hands, I'd placed the salvation of my realm, and possibly of myself. Not that I expected to be saved.

"Yes," he said, "but people expect it of me and my people. You know perfectly well what kind of message you're sending."

"True." I gave him a cool, unrepentant smile, letting him see that I wouldn't back down. Nor would I hide. "I brought it with Me all this way, expressly for this purpose. I can't *not* wear it," I finished in an aghast voice, mimicking one of the fashionable ladies of court.

With a shake of his head, suppressing a smile, Con picked up my hand, examining the scarlet sheaths of my nails. "In the mood to kill, then?"

"Let them come at Me," I replied. Our gazes caught and held, and we shared for a moment that same bloody determination to fight. He acknowledged it with a hint of ruefulness. "I have a gift for you," I said.

"Now?" He seemed taken aback, even embarrassed, making me wonder what he thought I intended.

"Yes. Because this might be my last opportunity."

"Don't say that." His hand tightened on mine.

"Of peace and quiet," I clarified. "Soon we'll be consumed in activity."

"Oh." He relaxed, but barely.

I signaled to Zariah, who came forward, the wolfhound at her side. She curtsied, and the hound sat at my heel, looking Con over as Zariah withdrew.

"That's the biggest dog I've ever seen in my life," Con commented with some awe.

I laid a hand on the wolfhound's head. "This is Vesno. He wishes to be your companion."

The wolfhound's jaws opened, tongue lolling out in a canine grin, and he woofed softly at Con.

"My . . . companion?" Con seemed unduly stunned. "The . . . dog wishes?"

"I can touch his mind, Con," I explained, stroking Vesno's silky head. "I asked and he affirmed. He is one of Mine, so I will be able to see through his eyes, hear through his ears. He will defend you."

"And report on me to you," Con finished wryly.

"Not like that," I protested, before his stern expression melted into a grin, the dimple of real happiness flashing into life.

Con crouched, holding out a hand to Vesno—the correct way, offering the back of his hand, fingers safely tucked in, just in case—and waiting for the wolfhound to come to him. Vesno sniffed, then licked Con's hand. Con stroked the dog's head, glancing up at me, emotion in his eyes. "This is the finest gift anyone has ever given me."

"Good," I replied, having to steady my own voice against the surge of unexpected feeling. "Every wolf should have a pack," I added, managing to make that sound lighter.

"Thank you." Con stood and touched my cheek. "Even your makeup looks like armor," he noted. "The warrior queen. Lia, I want to—" His eyes flicked past me. "Ah, and here comes Ambrose, with *my* gift for you."

Feeling like Con must have, I turned in surprise—with a sense of giddy pleasure. My subjects and emissaries gave me gifts all the time, naturally. Tokens to curry favor. Rare items to grace the Court of Flowers. Carefully preserved relics painstakingly smuggled to Calanthe for safekeeping. None of them were truly for me, for the woman. All were meant for Calanthe, and I dealt with them accordingly.

With a broad smile and a flourish, Ambrose presented me with a stick. Made of gleaming knobs of violet and pink, it looked like a finger from a giant. Con grinned at me, his dimple deep and delighted, and I remembered. A sweet tree-finger, he'd called it. I accepted it, scenting its candy perfume now, and raised a brow at Con. "Where's yours?"

"I thought we could share," he said, with an intimate smile. "Taste it."

I examined the thing, uncertain. It looked too hard to bite.

"You lick it," Con said, a laugh in his voice, and took the thing from me. Holding my gaze, he put the tip to his mouth, tongue swirling over it suggestively. I narrowed my eyes at the sensual challenge. Taking it back, I put it to my own mouth—painted scarlet like my nails—and mimicked Con. It was sugary and rich, with a flavor unlike anything I'd ever tasted. Full of the effervescence of magic. A little moan of pleasure escaped me, and Con threw his head back in a full belly laugh, hoarse, but uninhibited.

Ambrose only looked genially pleased. "It's been a long time since I made one of these. I'm so glad You like it."

"I do. Thank you." I waited for Con to look at me, his golden eyes sparkling with a hint of the verve of that long-ago boy in the painting. "Thank you for this gift, Conrí. It may be the most thoughtful gift I've ever received."

His big hand settled on Vesno's head. Already attuned to Con, the wolfhound lifted his nose in affection, nuzzling Con's wrist. "It's not a lasting gift," Con said. "Not like Vesno, or jewels, or—"

"I have no need of more jewels, nor more lives to be responsible for," I interrupted, giving Vesno a mock scowl. The wolfhound grinned at me, undaunted, tongue lolling. "This is all the sweeter for being transient." And because it was a token of the childhood I missed having, since I'd always been treated like a small queen, never a child. I suspected Con knew that, which was why he'd gone to the trouble.

He cleared his throat. "Since we're more or less private, anything yet?"

Indeed, though people had thronged in the courtyard, either because of my presence, or because they sensed the imminence of some important event, they gave our trio a wide berth. Even Lady Sondra, wearing full battle armor like Con, I noted, remained at a discreet distance. When she saw me studying her, she looked quickly away, her mouth slanting down.

"Not yet," I replied.

"Ambrose?" he asked.

Ambrose was slowly turning his staff, the emerald catching the sun and scattering prisms of light as Merle danced atop it, muttering. With a sharp nod, Ambrose's eyes focused on it. "Anure has followed the bread crumbs. Even now the sea carries his ships to Cradysica."

"Can he alter his course?"

"He is committed." Ambrose's gaze settled on me, and he gave me an apologetic smile. "I tied a magical suggestion to his obsession with Your Highness. He will not be swayed at this point."

"When will he reach Calanthe's waters?" Con demanded. "Soon."

Con squinted at the sun, calculating. "Lia, can you keep them from entering the mouth of the harbor until high tide, later this afternoon?"

"Yes."

He nodded, mind going to the next steps.

"And then what?" I asked. When Con hesitated, I let my nature shine through my skin, in warning and declaration of my intent. "Tell Me now, Conrí, and I will work with you. Keep Me in ignorance and I may foil your strategy." *Accidentally or on purpose*, I left unsaid.

"We let him sail into the harbor and box him in with our ships," he said. "They'll be trapped in there, and we can blow them apart, one by one."

"While they lob vurgsten at the shore," I clarified, "and also blow your ships apart."

Con nodded. "But not for long. If we time it perfectly, they won't have much time before the tide turns, and Cradysica's monster chews them from the bottom." He said it quietly, and in a code, as if still concerned about Anure's spies.

The understanding hit me with such force that I wanted

to kick myself for not realizing his plan before this. "Clever," I acknowledged. "It just might work."

"It better work," Con replied with a snarl in his voice. "The trick will be isolating which ship Anure is on. I want to make absolutely sure he's dead. The sea can't have him, not until I'm done with him. Well, and to minimize the blood shed in violence, of course."

He didn't fool me for a moment. Con gave lip service to that promise—and he'd make what he thought was a reasonable effort—but that wasn't why Con wanted to kill Anure personally. Arrested by the glimpse of darkness in him, a level of obsession I hadn't quite grasped before, I caught Con's eye. "Does it matter?" I asked him, levelly, but with insistence. "As long as Anure dies, it doesn't matter how it happens."

"Maybe not to you," he snapped. "I vowed to see him dead by my own hand. Nothing else will silence the voices of those who cry for justice." He paused, looking unsettled, as if he hadn't meant to say that last aloud.

Madness. "Be careful, Conrí," I gave him the warning as potently as I knew how. "Don't let how Anure dies become more important than that he does."

"Don't presume to lecture me, Lia," he growled back. "We have something else to sort out, too."

"Yes, we do. What is your backup plan?"

"Excuse me?"

Bright Ejarat, Con sounded just like me, arch and regal. "What happens if you commit all your ships and vurgsten to this trap and he escapes—what then?"

"He won't escape. That's why we've done all this planning."

"Then you should also plan for the poss—"

"Plan for what, Lia?" he nearly barked. "Plan to fail?

That's a great way to lose. I plan to win." He signaled for Sondra to approach, clearly done with that conversation.

"Yes, Conrí." Sondra saluted. He updated her, and her face took on the same taut excitement, her gaze the same mad gleam. The pair of them, so excited to wage war.

"Today," she breathed. "I'll gather my team."

"See you on the battlefield."

She saluted again and jogged off, blond hair waving like a banner when the sea breeze caught it.

Ambrose met my gaze, knowledge in it, and Merle dug at his wing. He plucked a feather, black as the polished rocks from Vurgmun, and I watched as it drifted lazily to the ground in the still, warm air of the courtyard. The vague dread that had lingered from the nightmares intensified. Ambrose studied the feather's fall as if it communicated something. For all I knew it might. Fortune-tellers, before Anure killed them all, had once claimed to read the future in all sorts of things. The dropped feather of a wizard's familiar made more sense than a rabbit's entrails or a collection of tea leaves.

From Ambrose's uncharacteristically sober and resigned expression, the die had been cast. Con had set our path and whatever lay ahead, it would be terrible, indeed.

Con met my gaze, his face neutral and grimly controlled, the face of the hero who never flinched from the portents, forging ahead with bold determination. Nothing of my dimpled, passionate lover remained. He'd become all snarling wolf. "Will you wish me well?"

"Do I have your leave to clear out My people now?" I returned smoothly, then realized I stupidly still held the sweet tree-finger. Motioning to Ibolya, who hovered within easy distance, I handed it to her, then took the lemon-scented damp cloth she proffered, wiping my hands clean of the sticky candy.

"Yes," Con said, watching me with an odd expression.

I spun on my heel, calling out orders for my ladies, for the priest of Sawehl, for the governor and head family. I would set evacuation of the human noncombatants in motion, then find a place quiet enough for dreamthink so I could send the animal populations on their way. The animals could move faster than the people anyway.

"Lia!" Con shouted, and I paused, looking back at him. "No kiss for luck?" He tried to add a cocky grin, but it failed to find traction on his harsh face.

"If you're lucky, I'll kiss you when you come back to Me," I answered, and turned away from his disappointment. Never had I been more pressed to contain my true feelings. I wanted to hold on to him and never let him go. I felt hollow inside, afraid and full of dread. If I kissed him now, if I touched Con, I'd likely end up clinging to him, weeping and pleading. They'd have to drag me off him, and what a sight that would be.

Not behavior befitting a queen leading her people in a battle for their homeland. We would fight for Cradysica, even knowing what it meant to spill that blood on Her soil and waters. A paradox of the worst sort, dooming our homeland by trying to save Her, but intention matters. We could hardly stand back and do nothing to protect Her.

I took a step and gasped, my stomach clenching, head spinning. The sensation of looming dread intensified to a sharp peak. With a wrenching pain, I felt Anure enter My waters.

"Lia?" Con had his hands on my shoulders, and I realized I'd hunched over, clutching my belly, the orchid ring a firebrand burning through my blood.

"He's in Calanthe waters," I said, watching the black and bitter lust for murder flood his countenance, completely replacing that lingering hope for a farewell kiss.

Would Con's hatred forever eclipse whatever tender feelings he might nurture for me, for Calanthe, his new home?

"Where?" he demanded.

"Close. Two hours' sail for the lead ship to the mouth of the harbor," I replied crisply, feeling like one of his soldiers more than ever.

"Can you hold him for eight hours?"

"You won't be here to tell Me when?"

"In case I'm not."

"Yes, I can."

This time, he strode away from me, Vesno at his side. I watched him go, regretting that I hadn't kissed him goodbye.

17

My team had set up on the point, hiding in the lush, tropical foliage. Across the water, on the rocks forming the other side of the harbor, Sondra waited with her team. Kara, along with our entire navy, hid in some nearby bay, ready to sail in behind Anure's fleet. Over the last few days, Kara had landed people and equipment in surreptitious batches on the nearby beaches. Lia's map had come in extraordinarily useful for finding good hiding places, and they'd used the intervening time to set up installations at well-camouflaged points all around the bay. I knew—trusted—that they were all in place, though I couldn't detect any sign of them.

Then we all waited. That was the thing about war—long stretches of tense boredom while you waited and waited, punctuated by the utter raging blur of battle.

Not that the waiting seemed to bother the wizard. Ambrose sat on the branch of a large tree nearby, Merle on the branch just above. The wizard kicked his heels idly as he stared out to sea, working his will in some invisible way, the raven busily preening, sending the occasional black feather wafting down.

I'd passed into that surreal state of alert awareness that came from not sleeping. I often didn't sleep the night before a battle, and last night had been no exception. After I'd nearly told Lia I loved her—which would've been a huge mistake, awkward for her and humiliating for me—I'd lain awake all night.

Sleep simply hadn't been possible. I understood why Lia had said she'd sleep when she was dead. With my death—or, worse, hers—looming so close, I wanted to savor every moment, not waste it in sleep. With Lia's lithe form against me, I'd studied her face by the light of the single candle until it guttered out. She looked somehow even wilder and lovelier in sleep. She'd discarded the scarf and the fuzzy vines had showed on her scalp, some curling, a few sporting tiny new leaves. Even what might be flower buds.

That book that Rhéiane and I had loved . . . I wished I could remember more about it. I couldn't stop thinking about Rhéiane, too. Something about the stark honesty of night, and all the ghosts it brings, had me revisiting old memories. I'd been so sure she was dead. Had she been Anure's prisoner all this time, waiting for me to rescue her? Sondra's words had circled round and round my brain, bruising and leaving open sores behind.

I hope she's dead, because the alternative doesn't bear contemplating.

Rhéiane. Now that I'd spoken her name, it wouldn't leave me alone. *Rhéiane.* And Sondra was right: The alternative didn't bear contemplating.

But if I killed Anure, and Rhéiane was his prisoner at Yekpehr—such a big *if*—then would I be losing my only chance to save her? Surely not. Anure's death would liberate them all.

Regardless, I definitely couldn't contemplate Anure laying hands on Lia. I couldn't stay back with her and guard her myself. Not because I had to be sure to capture the toad in my own net—I wanted that, I did—but because I didn't dare let him get so close to Lia. The thought of him even touching her sensitive skin, inhaling that green living essence of her. Of how she'd suffer at his hands. Her delicate skin bruised. Her generous heart shattered. It drove me mad to think about it.

No. I'd stop him on the water. At first opportunity, I'd kill him.

Nothing mattered more than keeping him away from Lia. *I'm so sorry, Rhéiane.*

I could set all that aside now that the ships were arriving on schedule. Our scouts had spotted them. Lia had known the moment they'd touched Calanthe waters, and she'd been uncannily accurate. I wouldn't be sitting here with my thoughts much longer. Merle dug at his breast, plucked out a feather, then cocked his head to watch as it drifted to the soil below.

"Why is he doing that?" I asked.

Merle gave me a sharp look, but Ambrose took a while to respond. "Hmm? Oh, the feathers? Seeding."

"Seeding?" I repeated, unsure if I'd heard the word correctly.

"Yes. Exactly." Merle clacked his beak and Ambrose looked away again, attention far away.

I decided trying again would do me no good. Instead, I studied the landscape, making myself be patient. The tide was high, the water smooth and glassy. Alluringly lovely. The town peaceful and quiet at the far end of the bay. Only the fighters remained—those the Calantheans had in Cradysica—and they'd hidden themselves. Fighters, and Lia and her ladies. Hopefully she'd be smart about exposing herself to danger.

I didn't delude myself that she would be that circumspect. You'd think a woman who'd lived this long—and ruled the last remaining intact kingdom—and had done it by keeping a low profile, would be willing to hide. But no, not Lia. Something had changed in her. She'd grown fatalistic in some way. So certain of doom that, though she said she believed we could win this, she ultimately didn't. I could see it in her eyes.

I would prove her wrong.

Today Anure would die and Lia would be free. Even if I died doing it, I could give her that last gift. I only wished I'd kissed her goodbye.

No sense thinking about regrets. Focus on what I could control. I surveyed the area. There wasn't much to see because our people had done an exceptional job of hiding themselves in the verdant foliage. Any moment now . . .

Right on schedule, the lead ship of the emperor's fleet nosed around the rocks, Anure's flag high. Black jagged rocks on a field of gray, the citadel worked in a red dark as liver blood. Another ship followed. And another, then five more. A dozen more. Excitement and triumph sparked through me. It had begun. I idly weighed my bagiroca, as if I could smite them from here.

More ships glided into the big tranquil bay, then still more. Anure had brought the best of his fleet, and the bulk of it. All to capture and punish one woman. The man was mad.

One of my lieutenants made a sound. "So many. We're outnumbered ten to one."

"Probably worse than that. But we'll destroy them anyway. We have a few tricks on our side."

I went to Ambrose. Reached up and shook his foot when he didn't respond to his name. "Which ship has

Anure on it?" I asked when his unfocused gaze turned in my direction.

"I'll tell you when I know."

I bet Lia would be able to point it out. Vesno paced beside me, a faithful companion indeed. Studying his brown eyes, I wondered if Lia looked through them even now. "Which ship is Anure on, boy?" I asked. Vesno woofed a reply. Possibly the correct answer, too.

A cannon belched fire, the boom following after, echoing off the water and curve of the hills. It landed in the water of the bay, near the harbor docks and pretty fishing boats anchored there, but falling short. Not for much longer. Their range was even better than the last time I'd seen them. The familiar stench of vurgsten rose through the air, crowding out the floral fragrance of Calanthe, making my throat tighten and my lungs ache. Fucking foul stuff.

Two more cannons boomed, the vurgsten bundles exploding midair, making a show of fire. It rained down, almost floating, and I crawled to the edge of the rocks, staying down behind the scrub vegetation and straining my eyes to see. The fire whirled, then drifted. I'd have said by an errant breeze, but it went too deliberately to the docked Calanthean boats, settling on them and setting them instantly ablaze.

Had to be magic. Anure's wizards at work. I threw an annoyed glance at Ambrose, who seemed to be doing nothing to assist us that way. He never even noticed.

A roar of fury echoed across the water. People, fighters and others supporters, poured out of hiding, bearing buckets of water and creating a chain to pass them down and douse the fires. They might as well spit on a bonfire, but you could never persuade the locals not to try to defend their own. They never did understand how much of Anure's tactics were designed to create surface damage initially, to soften them with fear and despair. He had an uncanny knack—or his wizards did—of pinpointing what they couldn't bear to lose, then destroying it.

As if triggered by my thought, a tongue of flame and smoke shot out from the leading ship. The golden domed temple on the hill exploded in a fiery burst of fury. Oily smoke billowed into the sky, followed by the wail of people. I felt a momentary pang for the beautiful temple, where I'd held and kissed Lia, feeling that divine love and light.

Sawehl, though, was a powerless god against the might of vurgsten. Or whatever old spirit the people thought they worshipped here. A sad reality that the people of Calanthe would have to face along with the rest of the world. And temples could be rebuilt, if only we could get free of Anure.

Anure's fleet wouldn't cause too much other damage yet. He wanted Cradysica broken and afraid. To teach them that their gods had no power and their monuments could be swept away. Then he'd land—or land his people, but I was betting he'd do it himself—and pluck Lia from their unresisting arms. *Then* he'd level the place.

But I intended to stop him well before that point.

Another boom, from cannons on several ships. The explosions landed square in the chain of water carriers, sending bodies flying, obscured by smoke and flame. Regret stabbed me like a knife to the gut. I'd brought the fleet here, knowing they'd destroy this beautiful place. A deliberate sacrifice. Not even the worst in a long career of terrible acts. But I felt the worst about it. Probably because I cared about Lia, and through some transference had developed affection for what she loved.

That wouldn't stop me. I would do it all again, I told myself. The end justified the means. It was worth whatever it took to trap Anure exactly this way, and finally remove his blight from the world. One little town on a small island was nothing compared with all that Anure had decimated.

Turning my back on the bombardment of the town, I studied the ships, speculating on which carried the emperor. Would he sail straight up to the dock? Maybe. Depended on how confident he felt. Or how his obsession drove him.

"Conrí." Bert, once Kara's squire, acting as runner for this battle, came up, out of breath. "Should we fire on the ships?"

"Not yet. Hold all fire until my command."

"Yes, Conrí."

More ships entered the bay, a seemingly unending chain of them. How many had he really brought? All the while, the ships at the front bombarded the vulnerable village along the bay, the docks falling into the water, the houses on their stilts crumbling into flame and ash. For a while, some of the broken dome of the temple shone on the hilltop, but smoke eventually obscured it.

We did nothing as Cradysica shuddered under the relentless barrage—maintaining the illusion that the peaceful place had no defenses to mount—and still Anure's ships entered the bay. We had to get them all in before we could attack. At least they so crowded the bay now that they'd have trouble maneuvering. With anticipation, I watched the tide. It would be turning soon and then we'd have to act regardless. If some of Anure's fleet escaped the trap, we'd run them down.

A flare shot up. Finally. Kara signaling that the last ship was in—and blowing our cover. They'd know we were here now. I ran for Ambrose, hidden in the foliage of the tree. "Which ship is Anure's?" I demanded.

He was frowning, Merle now on his shoulder. "He's being obscured."

"His wizards?"

Ambrose shrugged, then held up a hand. "Feel that?"

The ground shuddered beneath us, a great groan going up. I turned to see what could be doing that, but spotted nothing beyond the ordinary. If you counted the fires of hell raining down on a peaceful village ordinary. In my benighted life, it pretty much was.

"Calanthe," Ambrose supplied. "Blood spilled in violence is waking Her. Just as Her Highness predicted."

"What does that mean for us?" It still seemed like the least immediate of our problems. And yet . . . rattled, I put a hand on Vesno's head, at the level of my hip. A big hound, steadfast and faithfully sticking to my side, just as Lia had promised he would. Hopefully he'd let me know if Lia was in trouble.

"I don't know." Ambrose swung his bare feet like a boy climbing a tree for fun, not a man part of an army in hiding. "It will be very interesting to witness."

I had no time for this conversation. As if confirming it, a massive boom hit the rocks we stood on.

"We've been spotted!" one of my people yelled.

More likely the ships were just peppering the surrounding countryside, to add to the general confusion—and the smoke clouding the sky. They'd been keeping clear of the fancier houses uphill, Anure presuming that's where Lia would be. He might have better intel now that he'd arrived in the area, pinpointing Lia's exact location. At least he hadn't been able to have a stealth team kidnap her before his ships arrived.

Another reason I'd lain awake all night, just in case

they tried to grab her. Adrenaline surged through me now, banishing all thoughts of anything like lack of sleep. *I'll sleep when I'm dead.*

"Fire on the fleet," I yelled. "At will. Maximum chaos." At least Lia's healer had repaired my lungs and throat enough that I could pour volume to the orders without the agonizing pain. My people fired the cannons we'd hidden under the vegetation. They concentrated on the imperial fleet ships near the mouth of the channel, discouraging escape in that direction, taking advantage of the opportunity to barrage them for the short time our own ships weren't at risk.

The imperial fleet's orderly formation dissolved quickly under unexpected return fire from unknown directions. *Surprise, fuckers.*

Several of the faster-thinking captains had their ships wheeling about to refocus their cannons on the unexpected attack from their flanks and behind, but they couldn't move fast enough. My people were good. We rarely had the luxury of battlefield communication, so each group acted as an independent unit, making decisions more or less autonomously. Pretty much what you'd expect from a bunch of rebels, ex-slaves, and escaped prisoners. What we lacked in military training and cohesiveness, we made up for with sheer inventiveness, tenacity, and bullheaded independence.

It made us nearly impossible to predict, a quality we'd learned to use to best advantage. Vurgsten—the old-fashioned method of flaming rocks hurled at the ships to explode on impact—barraged some ships while others sailed unmolested. I studied the overall effect. We were doing well, keeping them bunched and confused. Like one of Lia's clocks, ticking right on schedule, a well-oiled plan springing the trap.

Bert appeared again. "Conrí—that's the first of ours." He pointed at the battleship—one of Anure's that we'd stolen back at Keiost—coming into sight, also flying Anure's flag. We'd saved the things with meticulous care, finding it ever so useful to pretend to be part of the empire we loathed. Until we stabbed them in the back. That would be Kara's flagship.

Right on schedule, it belched fire.

The smoke looked different, the boom that followed quieter. Had to be whatever refinements Brenda, Agatha, and Percy had made. I frowned, not seeing much effect.

Ah, there it was. The nearest ships began to founder, as if they'd lost their rudders, then sinking lower in the water. Not big explosions but pinpoint strikes.

Others of Anure's fleet tried to react to this new attack from their unguarded rear. Sailors swarmed the rigging, working the sails, trying to come about and fire back.

Too late. A boom rattled our installation, off target and causing us no damage, revealing their panic. I studied the water and the sky. Perfect timing. The final piece of the trap was about to spring, everything falling into place, piece by piece. Not there yet, but so close I could taste it. Soon Anure would be dead at my feet, at long last.

Which ship are you on, you loathsome toad?

There. The currents began to change. "Bert! Pass the signal to our ships. Stay back from the bay. Ambrose! Time to move."

Bert saluted, sending up the signal flare for our fleet. The wizard leapt lightly out of the tree, then leaned heavily on his staff, dragging the bad leg as if it pained him. Merle rode on his shoulder, bright-eyed and cawing.

"Which ship?" I demanded.

Ambrose shook his head. "He's here and he's not. I can't pinpoint him."

"Then we'll get closer. The slippery bastard won't get away. Second stage!" I roared.

At my command, my team began pulling their cannons. Groups carried them down the rocks on the side of the ridge away from the Bay of Cradysica. On the beach below, more of our people pulled rowboats from cover, others loading cannons and people into them.

I lingered on the point a moment longer, watching as the tide turned.

"This is going to work," I told the wizard with savage glee. With the turn of the tide, Anure's ships began veer off course. Their vurgsten missiles went awry, landing in the trees and water.

Sailors scrambled to get their ships into position to fire back at the attacks from our installations that remained under cover all around the bay, or to attack our ships beyond the mouth of the harbor, now drawing back to safety, sails rigged to ride out the tide.

The changing tide was in full swing, the currents moving into a circular pattern that began spinning the ships in Anure's fleet. Already wheeling about to fire back on Kara and the selective barrage from our landside installations, Anure's ships found themselves continuing the spin too far. One battleship fully rammed into another, panicked orders and shouts of wounded men ringing across the water. Some frantic idiot sent cannon shot into the ship next to them. The close impact cracked both ships, pieces of wood and sailors flying, setting both ships ablaze.

Would shedding the enemy's blood so violently into Cradysica's bay count? Probably. Nothing to be done for it now. Besides, we were winning. Lia could do all the rituals to placate Calanthe that she liked in the coming days.

The spinning accelerated, ships lurching into one another or being flung out from the center to founder on the rocks of the bay's embracing arms. Waiting for them, more of my people would take them prisoner where possible. A concession to Lia's stricture on shedding blood. I'd rather have them cut down. I no longer needed to build an army for revenge. Vengeance was mine. After winning this final battle, the Slave King would no longer exist, and his army would disperse.

At least Cradysica was taking the biggest bite today, Her massive whirlpool spinning and savaging Anure's fleet. Violence, sure—but of nature's forces. Surely blood spilled by Calanthe Herself didn't count.

It was a glorious sight to behold, and I would've liked to stay longer and watch the fleet shatter with the immense spin of Cradysica's whirlpool. Time for me to board my own rowboat, however, and join Kara for the final phase of the battle. Sondra would be on her way, too, so we could all be together for the killing blow. This was going so cleanly, the trap sprung so neatly, that we might be victorious by sunset. I might even survive. Then I'd take Anure's head and lay it at Lia's feet. I could just picture it. She'd been so fucking stunning in her warrior queen garb.

She might even love me a little, if I could deliver the death of her enemy.

Full of that vision, on fire with victory, I started down the slope, Vesno bounding ahead. Ambrose, however, didn't follow.

"Can you make it down the hill?" I called to him. He seemed weary, as he never did.

"I'm not going with you," he said. "I promised Her Highness I'd help to keep an eye on Calanthe. That's a lot of blood you're feeding Her." He gestured with his staff at the frenzy below.

One of Anure's ships managed to fire back on our position, and leaves shattered around us. "You're not safe here, wizard."

"Oh, I'm as safe here as anywhere." The ground groaned under us. Merle hopped down, rearranging a feather on the soil, and the shuddering receded. "See?" He waggled his eyebrows. "We're needed here."

"*I* need you—to show me which ship is Anure's."

"I can't." Ambrose shrugged, which became a weary shake of his head. "He's here and not. Sometimes you can't fight wizardry with wizardry."

"Then I will hunt him down myself," I snarled. So far as I could tell, wizardry fought nothing at all.

Ambrose gave me a placid look. "As ever has been your destiny. Remember: Claim the hand that wears the Abiding Ring."

"I did. Today the empire falls." I took one last look at the chaos in the bay, savoring the triumph. It did feel good. Not like ash at all. But of a future filled with promise. Ambrose had guided us to this victory, and I owed him for that. "Be careful, wizard. Keep an eye on Lia for me."

"Conrí," Ambrose said as I turned to go. "The empire *will* fall."

"I know," I replied impatiently. "I know the prophecy. Anure will die today, and his foul empire with him."

"Just remember my words," Ambrose called after me.

I waved a hand, skipping the path to leap from boulder to boulder, Vesno bounding before me, the last rowboat of soldiers waiting. The battle rage filled me with heat and boundless energy, and I couldn't wait to engage. *At last at last at last*, the vengeful voices of the past chanted in my brain. Like me, they felt the glory of this moment, their voices finally joyful.

We had won.

18

We rowed around the point, joining our small fleet of ships waiting outside the mouth of the bay for the tide to finish and the whirlpool to calm. We might be small in comparison, but our fleet was entirely intact. Like vultures and wild dogs, we'd sail into the wreckage of Anure's fleet and pick them apart.

It began to look like we might emerge from this battle not only victorious, but with minor losses. This upset would go down in history.

We reached Kara's flagship, climbing the battleship's steep side via the rope ladder. Kara's rough hand gripped mine, hauling me up the last bit over the gunwale and onto the deck. He hauled me into an embrace, pounding my back.

"All hail, Conrí!" he bellowed, releasing me. The sailors and soldiers aboard echoed the cheer, pumping their fists in the air. Kara grinned broadly at me, an expression I'd never seen on his sere and sorrowful face.

"It's working!" he shouted to more cheers. "Did you see it?"

I nodded, taking the long glass he handed me. I would've loved to have it on the hill, but Kara had needed it more. The view wasn't as good from down here, but the chaos was obvious. "I saw. The whirlpool has shredded them. We did it."

"You did it, Conrí." He saluted, then gazed at the turmoil in the bay. "I never thought I'd see this day, when Anure's entire fleet chewed itself to bits on its own teeth. What's this?"

"Vesno." I patted the wolfhound's head. He seemed as unbothered by being lifted onto the ship as he'd been balancing in the rowboat. "A gift from the queen," I added.

"Where's Ambrose?"

"Stayed ashore. He couldn't be sure which ship Anure is on. It's up to us to spook him out."

Sondra came striding up. Spattered in blood, her hair streaming and eyes bright with murderous glee, she looked like an avenging warrior maiden from the old books. Figured she made it to the flagship first and had already seen hand-to-hand fighting. "Are you sure Anure's here?"

"Ambrose said he is. Just being hidden by his wizards. It's up to us regular humans to flush that bastard out of his hiding spot."

She grinned back at me, feral and sharp. "You know how I love a good hunt."

"The tide is about out and half the ships are run aground, none in good condition. Let's go run down our frightened rabbit then," Kara declared, his grin going as vicious as ours. "A banner day for us, my friend, my king."

"Sail on!" I called, inspiring more cheers.

We sailed into the formerly peaceful bay of Cradysica, our perimeter ships clearing the way with vurgsten-powered gravel to cow any of Anure's archers still feeling frisky enough to fire at us.

Some of their cannons fired in our direction. There were so many of them that, even decimated, a few had managed to retain the capacity to fight. Anure was aboard one of those ships, and his fleet would foolishly defend him to the bitter end. We'd see to it that it was bitter indeed.

"Whichever ships fight hardest, that's where Anure will be," I declared. "Focus on those. No reserves. Give them everything we've got!"

My soldiers cheered and obeyed, barraging any ship that dared fire on us, squandering vurgsten in this final push. I only hoped they'd shield the emperor long enough for us to take him alive.

Kara, however, caught my arm. "*No* reserves?"

"This is it, Kara. We've won. We need only execute Anure."

"They haven't surrendered."

"And they won't," I replied impatiently. "Anure is too stubborn."

"Or he knows something we don't." Kara, always so cautious, frowned at the scene.

"What can he know?" I waved an arm at the devastation. "Half his fleet is sunk. Another third on the rocks. This is cleanup. We don't need reserves."

"As you say, Conrí." But he didn't sound convinced.

Vicious and persistent as a pack of jackals, we picked at the remnants of their embattled fleet. Our ragtag collection of fishing boats and pleasure yachts gnawed away at the few foundering ships. Our three battleships hung back, peppering them with light fire, mostly to keep them ducking. I didn't want to accidentally sink Anure's ship. He was mine.

Lia would be so fiercely proud when I brought her his head.

The hunt dragged on. As we sank ships, or captured them, dragging or rowing the derelicts to shore, the knot of the intact fleet grew smaller, reducing the possibilities for Anure's burrow, but not fast enough. The sun was sinking, shadows growing long. We couldn't risk losing him to cover of night. "We need to intensify," I said. "Bring in the remaining battleships."

"We'll need them if Anure somehow slipped away and we have to give chase," Kara countered. "Regardless, we're running low on vurgsten and we've lost a number of the smaller ships."

This shouldn't have taken so long. I gripped the rail, willing Anure to appear. "Show yourself, you fucking bastard," I growled. So close.

"We've won this battle, Conrí," Kara said. "Let's mop up and—"

"It's *not* won until we have Anure."

"Conrí is right," Sondra chimed in with savage frustration. "Even if I have to drag his corpse from the water, I want to see him dead before we claim victory."

"This *is* a decisive victory," Kara argued. "Our greatest victory to date."

"If night falls and we don't have him, we'll have lost him. And we'll have won the battle to lose the war," Sondra said. Smoke grimed her skin, and her expression had gone grim.

"We can't lose him. Not after all this," I agreed.

"If Anure escaped, he's running scared," Kara pointed out. "We drove him away from Calanthe and broke his navy. We can savor winning this battle and have time to plan the final one."

"*This* was meant to be the final one," I nearly shouted.

"It won't be the first time we thought we were closer than we are," Kara fired back. "Either Anure is already dead, which means the empire will unravel, or he's escaped. Let's call this done while we're ahead."

"He's here. I know it," I bit out, beyond frustrated. "This could be our only chance. If he burrows back into that citadel, we might never get him out again. This ends now."

"Night is falling and outpacing us," Kara persisted, grit in his voice. "Our current method isn't fast enough."

"We have to draw him out," Sondra said. "If he's here, then we need to smoke him out and finish this. I agree, Conrí."

If only Ambrose had stuck with me, where he belonged. "Lia might be able to find him," I mused.

"Yes." Sondra nodded, her lusty grin returning. "Seeing her will draw him out."

"I meant we could ask her." I frowned at Sondra.

"She's the bait, remember?" She returned the glare. "Conrí, you promised. She is the final weapon. It's time to wield it. You can't go soft now. This is our chance. You know that. This is why you claimed the hand with the Abiding Ring, remember? This was foretold. The empire *will* fall."

Sondra was right. We couldn't let Anure wiggle free. He'd only come back in greater force and we'd never have a chance against him. Now or never. Lia wouldn't be in danger. Show her to him. Walk her out on the dock, then move her to safety. Easy. "I'll go to her."

"No, Conrí. I will." She gave me a solemn look. "Trust me to do this. You need to be here, ready to grab Anure when he pokes out his head."

It made sense. Why did it feel wrong? It wasn't wrong. This was what the prophecy said. Ambrose had even reminded me of it, just a bit ago. And Lia had agreed to being bait from the beginning. We'd saved her precious island; she could do this for us. "You'll protect her?"

Sondra saluted. "With my life. No harm will come to

the queen. I'll just dangle her in view long enough for him to see. Make it look like he can grab her and escape."

Kara nodded grudgingly. "It's a better plan than picking away at that hornet's nest. We can hold here. Once Anure makes his move, we'll strike."

Vesno pushed his head under my hand, looking up at me with worried eyes. "Tell her it will be all right. One last thing is all I ask, and then she'll be free." Surely Lia would forgive this. In many ways, I was doing this for her. Looking to Sondra, who gave me an odd look for talking to the dog, I said, "I'm trusting you with Lia's life."

"Yes, Conrí. I won't fail you. Or her," she added. "Give me thirty minutes. I'll signal. Once you have Anure, if you can, wait for me to get there?"

"We'll do our best. You'll hold the torch to finish this day."

"All hail, Conrí!" She saluted once more then ran off, calling for a few of her trusted warriors to fall in with her. They went over the side to their boat.

"Give them cover fire!" I ordered. The small boat rowed swiftly away. Sawehl curse me, I should've sent a message with Sondra for Lia. I stroked Vesno's head, the wolfhound faithfully at my side. I didn't need to send her a message. Lia would know.

A boom, and vurgsten fire rained down on Sondra's boat. "Dammit!" I yelled. "Take out that cannon."

"Can't, Conrí! We don't have the range," someone yelled.

"Send battleship two."

Kara didn't argue with the order this time. He relayed it, and battleship two came around, sails billowing to sail at the ship firing on Sondra's boat. Standing beside me, we both leaned out, willing them to escape. "Why are they firing on one rowboat out of so many?" he muttered viciously. "They can't know it's important."

"They can," I corrected grimly. "Wizards."

Realization dawned on his face. "Then we're fucked. Recall!" he roared. "Pull back!"

"What?" I demanded. "No!"

Kara ignored me. "Retreat! All ships—"

A boom cut off Kara's order and my arguments. Battleship two went up in a spectacular conflagration, the heat and force throwing us back. Our ship rocked, masts creaking. We got to our feet, staring in disbelief at the ruin of the battleship.

"What did that?" Kara's voice cracked.

"Nothing we've seen before." I raised my voice. "All in! Belay the retreat! Go! Everyone go!"

"Conrí!" Kara gripped both of my arms. "They've outwitted us. They held something in reserve. We have to retreat or we'll lose everything."

"We didn't get this far by retreating. We can still win. They're desperate. All we have to do is hold them until Sondra gets to Lia. Once Anure sees her, he'll make his move."

"*If* we can hold them," Kara said dourly, flames lighting his hard face in the gathering dusk. "*If* he's alive."

"He is." Three more of our midsized ships went down, burning as they sank. More blood for Calanthe. This time ours. "They wouldn't still be fighting like this otherwise. He's been playing dead, waiting for his chance. He's obsessed with Lia. He'll sacrifice everything to have her." I gripped the railing, staring at the remaining fleet, willing my enemy to appear. "Come on, toad. You know you want her."

Kara gave me a sidelong look. "Conrí. I've never doubted you, but—"

Boom! Our other battleship went up in flames. Farther away from us, it didn't knock us down, but we had to duck the blazing pieces of wreckage that flew past. Vesno yelped, and I smothered a burning coal in his fur with my hand. Never felt it. *Thick-skinned.*

"Conrí!" Kara shouted at me.

"Don't start doubting now," I grated out. "We're there. At the finish line. Wait for it. Don't blink."

"We're going down," he snarled back. "Everything. All of our ships."

"Steady. Not much longer." I lifted the long glass. "There she is."

Lia in all her glorious avenging-angel savage beauty strode out to the ragged end of the remaining pier. She carried a white flag. So fucking smart, my Lia. *That's my girl. Make him think you surrender.*

She looked so calm and brave, apparently alone out there. Her crown, her warrior gown of metallic feathers— all caught the last of the dying light and reflected the flames of the blazing harbor, making her bright as a star. Oddly enough, her pale skin reminded me of those orchids in the forest canopy, glowing in the gloaming. I couldn't make out her expression, or see her eyes, but every line of her body was regally composed.

From the knot of the wreckage of Anure's fleet, a small, sleek ship moved. It moved fast and without sails. Propelled by magic, it had to be. "There he is!" I shouted. "After him!"

Sailors called. Ropes snapped. Sails billowed and the flagship wheeled to make chase. I lost sight of Lia as we came about, but I trusted Sondra. She'd have seen what I did. She'd have moved to whisk Lia away.

"Conrí," Kara yelled over the booming of sails and renewed fire. "We're sailing right at the live ship. We can't—"

"Use everything we have! Take them out. We have An-ure now."

A rattle of fire in the rigging. Sailors swarmed to put it out. Kara seized me by both arms.

"We're two battleships down. We'll be their next target. We have to—"

A burning bag wafted gently overhead. Almost lazily, it lowered to land on the deck, as if guided by an invisible hand.

"Abandon ship!" I roared. Grabbing Vesno, I threw him overboard and dove after. Dogs can swim, right? Better than exploding.

The water was fouled with detritus, body parts, and oily residue, the vurgsten stink sliding down my throat as I cast about. Sailors, soldiers landed in the water around me, frantically swimming. Kara, too, not far away. Where was the dog?

There. Vesno paddled valiantly beside me. I struck out, swimming away from the battleship as fast as I could, the wolfhound pacing me.

The battleship went up in flames behind us. The explosion made a wave that swamped us. Brain rattled, ears ringing, I fought for direction. Swam to the surface. Unable to find it. A hard yank my hair and my head popped above water. Vesno, my hair clamped in his jaws.

"Good dog," I panted. Or tried to. A skiff came up to us, and Kara reached down, hauling me in. Other hands grabbed Vesno. "After that ship," I choked out.

Kara looked grim, snapping out orders. A small escort flanked us. Night had truly fallen, lit only by the many fires, showing us the way through the wreckage. At least Anure's remaining live ships couldn't see us to fire upon us.

The oily smoke and heavy night parted, showing Anure's ship at the dock. Triumph cleared my head. We had him. Dead to rights. Probably Sondra was already aboard, holding him for us. We pulled alongside. So did several of our escort.

"Prepare to grapple!" Kara ordered.

They threw the grappling hooks over. I reined in my impatience. *At last at last at last*, the voices howled. Our soldiers flowed over the rail of Anure's personal yacht, all manner of weapons in hand as they cleared the decks of the few Imperial Guards that mustered themselves to fight.

He hadn't surrounded himself with enough, though. My people cut through them like grass.

I went in with the second wave, rock hammer in hand, bagiroca spinning. *Rocks. Hammer. Rocks. Hammer.*

If I had any disappointment, it was that I'd fought so little myself. Naval battles don't lend themselves to up-close-and-personal fights. But that was all right. I would have Anure. That would be more than personal enough.

I would have this final, decisive victory. The battle *and* the war.

"Anure!" I roared. "Show yourself, toad!"

Vesno streaked past me, weaving through the corpses and burning detritus. I ran after, feeling Lia's presence with me, the taste of savage victory in my mouth. We'd triumph and live through this. How sweet that would be.

We ended at a barricaded door—fancily embossed—Vesno snarling at it. We'd beaten Sondra here after all. Nudging Vesno out of the way, I hooked my bagiroca to my belt and swung the rock hammer.

Boom! The wood splintered.

Boom! The door sagged in the frame, coming away from the hinges.

Boom! A final swing and the door imploded. Vesno and I leapt over it into the lavishly appointed cabin.

Empty.

Vesno sniffed along the jumbled interior, whining. With a yelp, Vesno went to a closed door.

I yanked it open, hammer at the ready.

Tertulyn sat within, hands folded serenely. I halted my swing, gaping at her.

"Oh, look," she chirped. "If it isn't Lia's pet dogs. His Imperial Majesty Anure, Emperor of All the Lands, regrets to inform you that he had an urgent engagement elsewhere, with his new prize. I hope you're not too fond of Euthalia." She smiled sweetly. "You lose, Slave King."

I raced out to the deck, flinging myself to the rail. Peering through the smoke and gloom at the dock. Frantically scanning.

No sign of Lia or Sondra.

"Lia!" The scream ripped out of me as I flung an impotent hand to bridge the distance. Beside me, Vesno added his voice, my ragged howl blending with his.

You lose, Slave King.

19

I woke to the foreign sensation of a boat swaying under me. For a moment, I felt sure this was yet another nightmare, the one of my father's death and the consignment of his withered corpse to the sea. I hadn't set foot on a boat since that day. Not that I'd needed to make an issue of it. Calanthe needed me on Her soil, and I'd had no reason to sail anywhere. It had been easy to avoid sailing ships, except in the occasional bad dream.

Con had said he dreamed of his father's death, trying to save him. I hadn't found it in myself to confess I sometimes had that same dream, or similar.

No, this was a living nightmare. I was on a sailing ship, and the waters were rougher than Calanthe's. With the art of long practice, I kept to the pretense of sleep, allowing the dreamthink to settle around me, and reached out. Nothing. For the first time in my entire life, nothing and no one answered my silent call.

I was no longer on or near Calanthe.

This was bad. Very bad. The worst had happened.

"Your Highness?" a hoarse voice whispered. "Lia. Are you awake?"

I cracked my eyes open to see Sondra's, barely a handbreadth away. With distant curiosity, I observed that she'd called me by Con's nickname, and that I didn't mind. "I can't remember anything," I told her quietly.

"Do you remember the battle?" she asked in the same murmur. We lay on a bed together, on our sides, facing each other in the stifling dark of a ship's cabin, the chinks in the wood allowing daylight through. Heavy chains bound my wrists and trailed from a similar collar around my neck. Sondra wore an iron collar, too, with chains running through a ring at the front, so I imagined that's what I had on me.

"I remember that, yes." Every impact of vurgsten, every fire, each death—all had felt like physical blows hammering on me. Worse, Calanthe had felt them, rumbling awake as I'd feared. It had taken everything in me to keep Her subdued, and I'd been shredded to a flimsy, brittle version of myself when Sondra arrived. I'd agreed to the plan with resignation, knowing what would come, praying this last gambit of Con's would work.

I'd carried the surrender flag out to the pier, luring Anure in, and . . .

"Nothing after waving the surrender flag."

She closed her eyes briefly, then opened them, the blue intense. "We were captured. A kind of . . . cloud fell over you. I ran out, but it was nothing I could fight. Then I woke up here. I failed in my duty to you, and to Conrí."

"I appreciate your attempt to defend Me, but it was magic. Nothing even your mighty sword could slay."

Her mouth twisted in a grimace. "If Anure has us . . ."

She didn't finish, didn't have to. "Of course it's him," I said. Oddly, I didn't feel the terror I'd expected. Instead that same fatalism persisted. The worst had finally occurred, so I didn't have to dread it any longer. At least I'd left a wizard on Calanthe, so my realm might yet survive. I'd done my best to hold Her in check all that long, bloody, horrible battle. Now Ambrose would do the same. I hoped. "Are you injured?"

"I don't think so. Just numb. I think we've been lying here awhile. I just woke up, too."

My hands were bound behind my back, but the familiar cool velvet freshness of the orchid ring brushed against my skin. The dreamthink was there, but empty of anything. I tried again, reaching through the ring's connection to Calanthe, looking for Vesno's mind. He greeted me with a leap of gladness, and I took a moment to reassure him, though I had no way to push the message through to Con. I caught a glimpse of Con, back on land, surrounded by smoke and fires, raging. Angry but apparently whole. "Con is alive. Pissed as hell. I don't see Ambrose, but General Kara is with him."

Sondra smiled a little, then frowned. "How do you know?"

"I just do." I adjusted my neck. "Did they take My crown?"

"This is what you're worried about?"

I supposed it didn't matter, and I decided better not to mention that I was glad they'd managed to remove it without taking my wig. Sondra would never understand that. Still, it felt like adding insult to injury. I'd lost my magic. It felt like I'd lost half of my soul, hollowing me out. I'd never in my life been away from Calanthe, so I hadn't known, had never realized how much Her magic suffused my being. I felt like a plucked and wilted flower, dying for lack of water.

I *would* die. This was what the dreams had warned of.

But I had my pride, my resolve, and I wouldn't go without a fight. I'd endured this long and I wouldn't just wither and die because Anure had plucked me. A spark of anger lit in my heart, and I carefully fanned that flame. I would need it to be the venomous blossom, poised to dig my thorns into Anure's flesh. I was back to my original plan, the one I'd crafted all those years before Con arrived on my island. Alone again, I was on my own. But I would do my utmost to take Anure down with me.

The cabin door opened with a startling bang. Sondra flinched, lines of fear bracketing her mouth, all toughness gone from her ravaged face. In that moment, I clearly saw the brutalized girl she'd been. "Pretend to sleep," I murmured, gratified that she obeyed instantly.

I rolled back enough to lift my head to look over her shoulder at the Imperial Guards. "How dare you treat Me so," I addressed them with my most regal disdain, going on the attack, as worked best with subordinates like these. "Unchain Me immediately."

The older guard, clearly ingrained to obey commands, started forward before his younger companion spoke up. "Your Highness," he said. "You are a prisoner of His Imperial Majesty Anure, Emperor of All the Lands. Your Highness will have to request that His Imperial Majesty have the chains removed."

I let out a heavy sigh, as if impossibly bored with their incompetence. "Then take Me to His Imperial Majesty at once."

"Yes, Your Highness." Relieved to be able to obey, the older one moved quickly to unlock my chains from the bed.

The younger guard snorted in disgust. "We follow His Imperial Majesty's orders. He sent us to bring Your Highness to him, so don't be thinking You give the orders here."

I refrained from pointing out that his habitual use of my honorifics showed otherwise. After unbinding my wrists from each other, the older guard solicitously helped me sit up. Though my body protested the movement—apparently

Sondra had correctly assessed that we'd been unconscious and in one position for a long time—I forced myself to move with at least a facsimile of regal grace.

Adjusting my crumpled gown as best the ruined thing could be, I then stretched and used the opportunity to surreptitiously check my wig. Fortunately Ibolya had used extra glue, anticipating the long day of fighting, and it seemed in place. I hoped she and my ladies had survived and escaped capture.

The older guard helped me stand, giving a little bow as he did, eyeing the orchid ring with awe. I let him look, holding up my shackled wrists in question. One long chain connected them, running through the loop of the collar, dragging on my neck. "Apologies, Your Highness," he muttered. Dragging his fascinated gaze from the ring, he locked my wrist manacles together rather than releasing me.

I raised a brow. "I am not to be allowed to freshen up before meeting His Imperial Majesty?" I inquired, as if aghast at the breach of protocol. "Where are My ladies-in-waiting?"

"Listen to that," the younger guard snickered. "All You've got is the warrior bitch there, and You're a prisoner, Queen of Flowers. So start working those royal slippers instead of that mouth." The older guard looked appalled, but the younger—and unfortunately, apparently senior—guard chortled at his own wit. He flung open the door to lead the way. "Bring Her."

"Your Highness." The older guard hovered his hand near my arm, needing to obey and also hesitant to give offense. In the bright light coming through the open door, I could see his lined face. Very likely he remembered life before Anure. I pretended to be slightly dizzy. It didn't take any acting, not with my being unconscious for so long, my stays and the understructure of the gown biting into my flesh, as well as the lingering effects of whatever Anure's wizards had done to me. I swayed, murmuring, "If I might take your arm, kind syr? I don't feel quite well."

"The honor is mine, Your Highness," he breathed with reverence.

I laid my hand, the orchid ring prominent, on his proffered forearm. We stepped out onto the deck of a sleek sailing ship, cannons studding the rails every few feet. I'd seen what those cannons could do, and even with the salty sea breezes blowing, filling the sails taut, I smelled vurgsten. Familiar now from Cradysica as well as my dreams, and I understood full well why Con hated that smell, and found it so impossible to forget.

Con. Raging in his helplessness at having lost Sondra and me. It would be tearing him apart. I couldn't think about that. I needed to set emotion aside and be alert, clear thinking, more than ever in my life. This was the battle my father had trained me to fight. All the intervening years had been practice, my court a dueling ground to refine my skills, for this.

Con hadn't been able to kill Anure, so I would.

I layered cool reserve around my jangling emotions, like an oyster wrapping an irritant in pearl. I would be smooth, radiant, without flaw or cracks for Anure to dig his claws into. My heart hadn't been thawed so much by Con's ardent passion that I couldn't rebuild the icy shield that had protected me all this time. I would not let Anure get to me.

Sailors, soldiers, and guards stepped of the way of our little procession, gawking at me. Lifting my chin in regal disdain, I ignored them all. When we came to the bow of the ship, however, I nearly faltered.

Rearing against the sky—far too close—the emperor's

citadel loomed on the jagged cliffs. We'd nearly arrived at
Yekpehr, which meant I'd been unconscious even longer
than I'd guessed. I'd seen paintings of the place, and of
course the image was embossed on every Ejarat-cursed
thing Anure used, but even the best artists hadn't captured the cruel grandeur of the place.

Nor its size.

The cliffs of Yekpehr rose sheer out of the sea, unrelieved by greenery, gray and striated with blacks and reds.
The surf dashed itself against the base, sending white
spray high into the air, but wetting no more than the lower
quarter of the height. The citadel itself rose from the edge
of the rocks with no discernible demarcation between
land and building. With sharp angles, it sprawled, wing
upon wing of fortress, as far as the eye could see.

And even in daylight, it burned. I couldn't make out
the mechanism—of course, it was wizardry, though what
a scandalous, frivolous use of it—but the walls leapt with
flame, oily black smoke coiling up to pollute the sky. Just
like at Cradysica.

The despair threatened to swamp me, and—my resolve to remain unmoved already faltering—I struggled
to fight it off.

"It's not so bad as it looks, Your Highness," my escort
murmured, not unkindly, urging me forward. I stepped
with smooth alacrity, abashed that I'd allowed the sight
of a castle to trick me into showing fear. I understood using that kind of sleight of hand, the smoke and mirrors of
creating an imposing façade. Though I'd never had magic
of that magnitude to squander that way. Still, I refused to
allow Anure to intimidate me with simple tricks.

We made our way to the helm of the ship, where His
Imperial Majesty, Emperor of All the Known World, stood

with legs braced and hands on the wheel, making a show of how he controlled even this. Con had been right all along: Anure had come for me personally. And the slimy bastard had still managed to slip through the trap.

I devoted all of my attention to the man I'd been all but engaged to, who'd reshaped my entire world and perverted my life path. Whom I hadn't laid eyes on in nearly fifteen years.

I'd hated Anure before he ever set foot on Calanthe, so I'd never found him remotely attractive. That hatred had colored my youthful impressions, but he had been objectively handsome back then. With a fine-boned face and chiseled profile that gave him the veneer of refinement, he'd also had a striking shade of auburn hair and piercing blue eyes. His height had made him an imposing figure, along with broad shoulders and narrow hips. In the early days of his rampages, the women went to him willingly, I'd heard, sighing romantically over his noble mien.

Nothing, however, could make up for the fact that he had no noble blood. The land would never answer to him, no matter how he dressed himself up or what titles he gave himself. Worse, however he'd begun life, his vanity, greed, and consuming need for power had corrupted him beyond redemption.

The years hadn't been kind to Anure, and that inner rot had oozed to the surface. His hair had faded to straw, and the wisps I could see through his gaudy monstrosity of a crown looked thinner. He still towered over me—though many people did, including Con—but Anure's once broad shoulders seemed to have melted, sinking down to sag around his middle. Though he wore a richly brocaded waistcoat, no amount of tailoring could disguise his soft belly and sagging ass. Even his profile had softened, his nose bulbous and big-pored in the way of someone who imbibes far too much, and his complexion had a greasily yellow cast.

His eyes, however, remained the same light blue, full of gleeful malice as he glanced over at me. It wouldn't do to underestimate him. He might be crazed and degenerate, but he'd ever had a sharp mind.

"Your Imperial Majesty." The younger guard bowed and scraped, managing to preen at the same time. "As You requested, Her Highness Queen Eu—"

"I know who she is, worm." Anure turned from his wide-legged stance, carelessly releasing the wheel, oblivious to the hapless sailor who dove to grab it again and steady the ship before the driving wind. "Euthalia." He drew out the syllables, making my name into something ugly. "It's been so long. The bloom has quite worn off the rose, hasn't it? A pity, as you used to be so lovely."

I seriously doubted courtesy would do anything to better my chances with him, but it cost me nothing. "Good morning, Your Imperial Majesty," I said, as I curtsied low, not easy with my hands chained before me, but I managed. "A beautiful day for a sail, isn't it?"

He hesitated, just slightly, but enough that I knew I'd disconcerted him. Had he expected me to fall weeping and pleading at his feet? Probably.

"I'm glad you're coming home with Me at last," he confided. "You have something I need. No more playing the coy virgin, eh?"

"Is that what this is about?" I shook my head as if disappointed. "Surely You can find *someone* to have sex with You short of suffering the losses You did at Cradysica."

He laughed, seeming honestly amused. "Oh, Euthalia. Such ego. Yes, I have innumerable women anxious to satisfy My needs, none with such an unpleasant personality as you have. You know what they call you: the Ice Queen. No, I have no interest in thawing you. Certainly not when you've been chewed up and spat out by another. Where is your loving husband now, hmm?"

"The Slave King?" I made sure to sound carelessly mocking. I didn't want Anure to know Con was a weakness he could use against me. Or for him to turn his attention to Con at all. Con had cautioned me that Anure had a talent for discovering what people cared about, and I believed him. That meant I could never let the toad glimpse how much Con meant to me. He already had Calanthe as a lever on the soft place in my soul. Adding Con to that pressure might be more than I could withstand. "*If* that brute survived the battle, he's likely seized whatever valuables he could scavenge and fled Calanthe."

Anure smiled, not pleasantly. "Such are the wages of sin. But tell me, are you so indifferent to the man? I'd heard that you seemed uncommonly fascinated with him."

Tertulyn. It had to be. I sighed mentally and summoned a cruel laugh. "Men are so easily led about by the cock, don't You think, Your Imperial Majesty? I don't think anyone could blame a girl for using her wiles to make the best of a bad situation."

He studied me, that corrupt and canny mind clicking away. "I don't think much of your supposed cleverness, Euthalia. You should have known you couldn't hide from Me. Note how easily I found you. My 'losses' at that dirtwater fishing village were an acceptable sacrifice. Small price to pay for a much greater treasure."

Me? But he'd said he didn't want me. Worrisome. But I fluttered my lashes, hoping I didn't look like too much of a travesty. "You flatter Me."

He laughed. "Not you. You were a pretty enough girl, but I take no man's leavings. I don't want you, but what

you have." His pale gaze drifted to my hand, lust bright
in his eyes.

The orchid ring. The Abiding Ring. Con had been
right about that, too, that day he told me about the prophecy. Anure had never been obsessed with me—just with
the ring. Con had been the same, though we'd grown to
be something to each other, hadn't we? It didn't matter
now. Funny to be this person in my last days. A queen
without a crown. Stripped of my power and my magic, no
longer the center of any story. None of it had ever been
about me, only about this orchid that attached itself to me
at my father's command.

"What I have?" I asked, making sure to sound confused and curious.

"What *I* have," he corrected. Grasping me by the arm,
he yanked me forward, bruising me with his grip. I pulled
my defensive power around me, ready to fling the violence
back at him, perhaps take us both overboard to feed the
sharks. End this soon and swiftly. But nothing responded
to my call. I was bereft, isolated, and weak. I'd become
what I most feared and loathed.

"Look!" Anure pointed me at the citadel. "It's the larg-
est fortress in all the world. Impregnable. Your new home,
as long as you live. Which," he confided, "will be totally
up to you. You're Mine now. No fighting that. But if you
cooperate, you can have a reasonably comfortable life
with Me."

Gazing up at the imposing edifice, I felt the fight drain
out of me. I'd known from the beginning, from my earliest days, that Anure could not be defeated, that he would
always win. Conrí, with his determination, the way he'd
overcome impossible odds to get as far as he had, had
convinced me that we could triumph.

Daydreams and foolishness.

"Take a good long look at your new home, Princess, for you'll never get this view again."

He would keep me, I realized, just as I'd told Con I suspected Anure had kept his sister. Anure needed us to rule his lands. I had delivered Calanthe into his keeping. And the Abiding Ring. Which would matter more? I didn't know, and my exhausted mind served up no canny solutions. Helpless to change my fate, I watched as we sailed into the shadow cast by the fiery citadel, the stifling stink of vurgsten in my lungs, and despair in my heart.

Somewhere out there, Calanthe wailed Her loss, crying for me to come home. But there was no one left to hear Her, or any of the forgotten, abandoned kingdoms.

I prowled the ruins of Cradysica, as if I might find Lia and Sondra in the rubble, if only I searched long and hard enough. Vesno kept me company and did the best he could to help. He'd found a metallic feather from Lia's extravagant gold dress, but nothing more. Ridiculous of me to search, but I couldn't seem to stop myself. Even though Anure had clearly taken them, somehow spirited them out of the harbor. Wizardry, no doubt.

I would ask Ambrose how it was done, but he'd vanished, too.

Covered in soot, blood, and grime, I'd talked to everyone who'd been nearby when Lia walked out on that pier. No one knew anything useful. By all accounts, Sondra had suddenly charged out, sword drawn. Then the witnesses lost them both in the smoke and darkness. The two of them had vanished. One moment they were there, the next moment not.

A day later, I'd still discovered nothing more than that. I'd interrogated that foul traitor Tertulyn, who remained my captive. Not that it did me any good. She seemed to have lost her mind, simply repeating her same message, over and over. I'd even let Calla and Nahua tend the woman. They'd been her friends once, and they'd petitioned to bathe and feed her. When Calla reported to me, she'd only shaken her head, saying they'd found no evidence of the Tertulyn they'd known. She seemed to be capable of saying nothing but repeating her message for me. Her glassy gaze saw no one. More foul wizardry. It would be incredibly useful to ask Ambrose about all of this, but again, he wasn't to be found.

Gone. And all my fault. I'd take a knife to my own heart, but that wouldn't help Lia and Sondra. I had to get them back, whatever the cost.

So I prowled, telling myself I was searching, knowing it was a lie. *Pacing like a caged wolf.* I'd come up to the ruined temple at the top of the hill, wanting to see its destruction for myself. All rubble. I'd destroyed it as surely as if I'd done it with my own hands, and for what? *You lose, Slave King.*

Vesno shoved his muzzle under my hand, brown eyes full of worry. I hunkered down to scratch his ears, wishing I had comfort to give. Or some way of knowing if Lia could hear me through the dog.

"If you can hear me, Lia, don't despair," I said, cupping Vesno's head and rubbing his brows the way he liked. "I'll come after you, if it's the last thing I do." Somewhere in the muddle of sleeplessness and agony, I'd decided getting Lia back was the most important thing. No other voices plagued me, the cries of the ghosts drowned by the utter sense of wretched loss where Lia had been. "I let you down, I know," I said, looking into Vesno's eyes, "but I'll make it right. I promised to protect you and I—" My throat closed up, and I had to close my eyes against the tears.

"Conrí." Kara's voice dragged me back to sense, and I stood, clearing my throat, using my sleeve to wipe the sweat from my face. At least, I hoped it looked that way. Grime from the pervasive dust and lingering smoke left a smear on my sleeve.

"Is there a report?"

"We've brought in the last of the boats and prisoners, surveyed the wreckage. That's everything and there's no sign of Her Highness, Sondra, or the wizard. Everyone else is accounted for: alive, wounded, and dead."

"People don't just vanish," I bit out savagely. "Anure took them."

Kara scratched his neck. "Knowing Sondra, and the orders you gave her . . ." He hesitated. "She would die before she failed you. She would've stuck, no matter what. Wherever Her Highness is, Sondra is with her."

Sharing her fate. I'd consigned them both to hell. "They're at the citadel. Ejarat only knows where Ambrose has gone, but Anure will have taken Lia and Sondra to the citadel. And I'm going after them."

"How, Conrí?" Kara fixed me with his dark, relentless gaze.

"I'll sail there."

"Even if you had a seaworthy vessel, which you don't, you cannot assail the citadel with our remaining forces. That wasn't a good plan back in Keiost and it's a far worse proposition now, since our losses at Cradysica have been so great."

"I still say stealth can work. I'll go alone. Surely there's *one* ship that—"

"There isn't," Kara interrupted forcefully. "Not that can cross the stretch of sea to Yekpehr. Those are rough waters, and even the most marginal choice of vessels will need days, if not weeks, of repair."

"Lia doesn't have that long," I exploded. "If Anure has her then he could have already—" I cut myself off, unable to speak those words, either.

"I know," Kara said softly, without flinching. His hard gaze held no accusation, only compassion. He gripped my shoulder, a rare gesture from the man who avoided most physical contact. "Conrí, I know, but I can't change reality. We committed everything to that battle, and we have very little left."

"*I* committed everything," I said. "You advised me to hold ships and vurgsten in reserve, just in case, but I was so sure of victory." I should've known. It had felt too good, and if I'd learned anything, it was that winning tasted like ash. We'd won the battle and lost the war. *You lose, Slave King.* Tertulyn's sweet voice mocked me. "Anure played me for a fool. And rightly so. You warned me, back at the palace. So did Lia. I was a stubborn idiot not to listen."

You're hotheaded and reckless. Lia had been so right.

Kara was silent a moment, releasing my shoulder with a last squeeze and turning to stare out over the bay. Some fires still burned, but the smoke had mostly cleared, the scent of flowers mingling with the stench of blood, vurgsten, and death. "You always told us that Anure has a gift for knowing what we care about most, and he uses that to destroy us."

"Sondra warned me," I said, even then not knowing how to handle the problem. "She said if I cared too much about Lia, then Anure would use that to defeat me, and he has."

"Not that." Kara shook his head. "I think you loving your wife might be the saving of you, of us all. That wasn't your mistake, no disrespect, Conrí."

"Just spit it out and tell me."

Kara nodded thoughtfully. "All right then. I wouldn't

agree he played you for a fool, but we—and I include my-self in this error—counted too much on him not under-standing who you are."

"I am nobody," I replied bitterly. *King of Nothing.*

Kara wheeled on me, face grim, eyes hard. "You have to stop that shit," he said, surprising me into nearly biting my tongue. "I understand that feeling, but your conviction that you are no one, a man of no importance—*that* got us here." He swept his hands at the wreckage of the dome and Cradysica, the shattered shards of priceless metal in jagged heaps.

"I am no one import—"

"Listen to me, Conrí!" he thundered, losing all quiet reserve. "Yes, the emperor played on your weakness, but it isn't Her Highness. It's that you put your need for re-venge above all else."

"Don't claim that you don't want vengeance, Kara." I leaned in, my fury snapping at the leash.

"Of course I do," he snarled back. "It's all that keeps me alive. But I. Am. Not. King." He spaced out the words, making it clear he thought I needed them beaten into my head.

"Neither am—"

"Yes you are! You are Conrí. Our king. *My* king. Now these people's king." Again he swept a hand at the devas-tated bay. "You were so determined to kill Anure your-self, no matter the cost, that you lost all perspective. A king can't afford to lose perspective. A good king weighs the costs and protects what's most valuable."

I opened my mouth. Closed it again. Vesno shoved his head under my hand, and I rubbed his silky ears, glad of his comfort, no matter how little I deserved it.

Kara wiped a hand over his face, as sweaty and grimy as mine. "You thought you were setting bait for Anure,

Conrí, but he sacrificed his entire fleet to your trap, just to win the prize."

"We were so close to victory," I said, the bitterness choking me. "I really thought we could win."

"That's the trick," Kara conceded. "You did win that battle. You protected Calanthe. It just turned out that you and Anure strove for different prizes. Letting you think you could win was the bait he set for you."

And I'd swallowed it down, stomaching the hook and dancing on the end of the line while Anure stole what he wanted. I stared at my filth-covered boots, then raised my gaze to Kara's. He met my gaze unflinchingly, a hint of compassion in it. "What is your advice, General Kara?"

"What would Her Highness do?" he returned with a lift of his brow. "What would she want of you, Conrí?"

To lead her people. To protect Calanthe. And, knowing Lia, she would gather all her most clever advisers and get their advice. She would tell me to take the time to think and plan. Vesno's wet nose nuzzled my palm, and I felt calmer in that moment than in days. Starting with Kara, I began giving orders.

20

They carried us through the citadel on grand palanquins, displaying Sondra and I like a macabre combination of visiting royalty and captured slave girls. Displaying us to all as Anure's new acquisitions. We knelt on satin cushions, the chains through our collars attached to large rings in front of us, hands bound behind our backs with chains reaching behind us. All along the docks, across bridges, and into the citadel, curious crowds watched our lurid parade.

The people didn't cheer, however. They simply observed with solemn expressions and tired eyes, as if dutifully attending. Whispers here and there attested to the fact that they knew who I was, and that they assumed Sondra to be one of my ladies-in-waiting. I hadn't been back to the ship's cabin, and only glimpsed Sondra as they wrestled her—screaming and kicking—onto the palanquin behind me. Just as well. From the disgusted glares I did see, I gathered she had only contempt for the fact that I hadn't fought.

I'd learned long ago the value of appearing to roll over and show my belly to the conqueror. The great danger, of course, lay in not paying attention to the moment when pretending to surrender became true capitulation. That was the difference between Sondra and me: She would never stop fighting, and I didn't know how to start.

I only knew how to endure and to wait, so that's what I did, gazing steadfastly ahead, spine straight and chin regally lifted.

Our bearers carried us directly to Anure's ostentatious throne room. I took great pride in the Orchid Throne and my own Court of Flowers, as a place of beauty and a tribute to the highest ideals. The emperor's seat paid tribute to the worst of his impulses. The throne loomed at the top of a long flight of stairs, easily three times higher than my own, and the back of the massive chair stretched up at least two stories.

The Imperial Toad, who'd disappeared when we docked, escorted away by a large entourage and leaving us to follow after, now sat on his throne. He'd changed into a costume as elaborate as any of mine, and which—to my practiced eye—included considerable framework and padding to make the man look bigger. A thickly furred velvet robe swathed him and draped over the throne and down several steps.

The throne itself, I realized as I studied it more closely, wasn't truly that large. It had been designed to trick the eye, to look huge, and also amplify the size of the emperor.

Smoke, mirrors, and sleight of hand.

Anure had also piled the steps with literal treasure, displaying both his wealth and that no one dared touch it. Open chests spilled coins of all denominations, the colors a rainbow of the shattered and forgotten empires he'd pillaged. Jewelry and loose gems fell in piles and draped lavishly over all of it. No artwork, which didn't surprise me, as Anure had only the greed of a dragon and none of the discernment. I spotted my crown, the Crown of Calanthe, in a prominent place on a pile of the other jewels I'd been wearing. I let my gaze pass over it, unseeing and uncaring. Anure would have to do better if he thought to upset me that way. The crown itself wasn't what I cared about most.

Flanking the throne, however, stood wizards—four of them, just as Agatha had said—two on each side of Anure and several levels down, like more treasure on display. I knew them by the glow of their magic, and the orchid ring's tremulous reaction to them. They were the real danger, and I kept a sharp eye on them without making it obvious. Hard to say if anyone else knew who—or what—they were.

The wizards wore plain robes. Nothing like the one I'd gifted Ambrose. It could be they didn't wear better robes because Anure hoarded all the glory. But they each wore a different color—red, blue, purple, black—which could denote rank. The wizard in black stood closest to the throne, so I picked him for the senior of the group.

My bearers set my palanquin down, a thump behind confirming they'd brought Sondra, too. Imperial Guards came forward, disconnecting the chains that bound me to the conveyance, but leaving them to dangle heavily from the collar that dug into my shoulders. They lifted me to my feet and made me walk forward, the chains rattling as they dragged on the polished granite floor.

Lifting my chin, I met Anure's mocking gaze.

"And so," Anure said. His voice hissed through the vast chamber, resonating and amplifying. Tricks with acoustics that anyone could replicate, but the effect was unsettling as it sounded as if he spoke from all around me. "The Queen of Flowers is at last My guest. Look about you, Euthalia, and see what you could have had.

You could have been by My side and now you cower at My feet."

I gazed only at him, composed and neutral, wielding one of my few remaining weapons—silence—and saying nothing.

He shifted irritably on his seat, and I smiled to myself. Never would I have revealed myself to a prisoner in such a way. Anure played at ruling, but he would never be more than a pretender, no matter how much treasure he heaped around himself or how many wizards he leashed to his foul purposes. Small comfort.

"Nothing to say?" Anure demanded. He flicked his fingers and the guard beside me struck me in the small of my back, sending me hard to my knees. It hurt, but I kept my expression cool, my steady gaze trained on Anure.

This is power, in mastery of self.

He flushed with anger, but he couldn't outlast my silent endurance. "You'll want to speak, because I have a bargain to offer you, petal."

Oh, how interesting. A bargain. I waited to hear what it might be. The wizard in blue spoke to the one in purple beside him, both trying to see the ring behind my back, chained out of view along with my hands. The assembled court made very little sound for a large group of people, and I tasted the feeling in the room as I would my own court. Fear and tension. Someone coughed here, muffled by their hands, or scraped a foot. Otherwise they vied not to be noticed. Quite the reverse of my court. The wizard in black stared at me, then climbed the steps to whisper in Anure's ear.

Anure tapped impatient fingers on the arm of his throne, annoyed at whatever the wizard said. "Unchain her hands," he ordered.

The Imperial Guard who'd struck me hauled me to my

feet again and unlinked the manacles at my wrists. I let my arms hang at my sides, resisting the urge to roll my shoulders, as that would reveal my discomfort. The wizard in black glided down the narrow path between the hoarded treasures, picking his way on silent feet, until he stopped before me.

I studied him, looking through his aged appearance as I had with Ambrose's illusions. He seemed to be entirely human, however, and truly elderly. His magic, powerfully warm like Ambrose's, had a stinking edge to the heat, and his eyes were glued to the ring. Ignoring the human being wearing the orchid ring, he seized my wrist in a spidery, too-tight grip. His skin was soft, unblemished, and without a single rough edge, and I suddenly and fiercely missed the work-hardened and stained skin of Con's hands.

The wizard didn't touch the orchid itself. He bent close, sniffing it, and narrowly examining the bloom. The orchid ring responded to his magic, but not with the flirtatious fluttering it did around Ambrose. Instead the petals furled, draining of color. The wizard dropped my hand and nodded, bowing to Anure, and then stood to the side expectantly.

I realized in that moment how badly I'd miscalculated. Anure wanted the ring because this wizard did. And I knew with icy intuition that nothing I could say or do would manipulate this twisted creature.

Anure smiled at me. "I am a generous man and a loving emperor." He looked expectantly around the room and the court applauded, added a few cheers to his health. It came a beat late to my ear. Had my own court attended me so sluggishly, I'd have known in an instant that something had gone very wrong with my rule. "I realize I asked too much of you, Euthalia, in charging you, such a meek and sweet girl, to stand up to the ravages of the

Slave King. I will not hold you at fault for being so cru-
elly and repeatedly raped by that cur."

The assembly gasped, aghast and titillated whispers
bouncing off the walls and worming themselves into
everyone's ears. Sondra growled and I hoped she'd keep
her temper. She would be safer as my supposed lady-in-
waiting than as Con's lieutenant.

"You have suffered much, but you are safe with Me
now." Anure gave me a paternal smile that made me want
to gag. "I am willing to pardon you." He nodded at the astonished and approving murmurs, waiting for that belated
applause again before holding up a hand to stop them.
"I already have your jewels as tribute," he said, pointing
at my crown, no doubt afraid I hadn't noticed it. When I
gave no flicker of reaction, he frowned. "Give Me your
ring, and I will not punish you further. You could have a
good life here, Euthalia. Honored. Feted. In return, I shall
leave Calanthe intact, unharmed. The pearl of My empire
as you shall be the jewel of My court."

I made sure to seem surprised—and to be considering
the offer—as I worked to hide my vast relief that Anure
hadn't realized he could use Con against me. Not that I
could make this bargain, even for Calanthe. I wasn't sure
when I'd become more worried about saving Con than
Calanthe. Maybe because I knew Calanthe was already
lost. All four wizards watched with glittering intent.

"I would give this ring to Your Imperial Majesty if I
could," I finally said, hearing the honest resignation in
my own voice, "but I cannot."

"Lies. I've had enough of your lies," Anure replied,
sounding more like a whiny child than a ruler. "This is
your only chance, Euthalia. Give Me the Abiding Ring or
I'll raze Calanthe."

And there it was, the name by which the wizards knew

my ring. Helpful to me? Likely not. "It's not within my power."

"Take it from her then," Anure cried.

Several Imperial Guards stepped forward, one holding my wrist in a crushing grip, the other digging his nails into my finger to pull at the band. When the ring didn't so much as budge, the jowly man renewed his efforts, pulling painfully at my joints. "Don't crush the blossom, you idiot," the wizard in black said, his voice unexpectedly deep for his skinny frame.

So he didn't know the orchid couldn't be crushed—or rather, that it sprang back luminous and uncreased from any impacts. I doubted they knew much about the ring at all.

"My apologies, Your Eminence." The guard turned my hand over, working at the ring band from the other side. Flicking a revolted look at me, he snatched his hands away, audibly swallowing. "Your Imperial Majesty, Your Eminence, the ring seems to be . . . grown into her skin."

Indeed the twining tendrils of it prickled at the bones of my finger, hand, and entire arm, burning and burying into me, as if sensing its peril. The band itself had nearly disappeared into my skin, as if holding on tighter, hiding itself. The court murmured with more excitement than they'd yet evinced, their voices burbling with speculation.

"Let me see," the wizard in black commanded, stepping close again and peering at my hand as the guards held it out. Not that I fought them. I simply looked past the wizard and spoke directly to Anure.

"It cannot be removed," I repeated, willing him to understand. "Believe Me, with Calanthe at stake—My home and the only thing I care about—I would yield it to You if I could."

"Liar. Such an ugly trait," Anure hissed. "Punish her."

The guard's fist crashed into my face, snapping my head back on my neck, the wig dislodging. Not important, I knew, and yet I fretted even as I tried to process the shock. The pain flooded in belatedly, my eye and cheek rushing with heat, tears wanting to surge up with a sob from my chest. I would not cry in front of these people. Lifting my head, I regarded Anure as coolly as I knew how, even as the wig fell to the floor. The court exploded into shrieks of horror and hysterical laughter at the sight of my bald head. I only hoped no one would look close enough to see the soft crop of vegetation there. Anure convulsed with laughter. "No better than a slave," he commented. "Did *he* do that to you?"

I didn't reply. At least they didn't seem know much about my nature. Maybe Tertulyn hadn't betrayed everything? I didn't see her anywhere, and it seemed certain Anure would want to taunt me with her presence.

Anure lost patience, snapping, "Get *on* with it!"

"Allow me," the wizard in black intoned.

The guard held out my hand palm up for the wizard's inspection. Something dripped from my nose to my throbbing lip, and I figured it for blood. The wizard studied my hand, shook his head at the emperor. "It is as Her Highness claims, Your Imperial Majesty. We cannot simply pull it off."

"Cut off the whole finger then," Anure said.

"No!" Sondra shouted, the sound cut off by a thump and scuffle. *Don't be a hero*, I thought at her, as if she could hear me. She still had a chance to escape, rather than share my doom.

More guards brought over a block and a sharp knife. One of them spread out my fingers on the block, two more holding my wrist in place as the wizard supervised, giving

me a gentle smile. I didn't struggle. It would be undignified, and I couldn't win. I simply ignored the wizard,
pretending I didn't know what he was. I steeled myself
for the pain.

It came, bright and sharp, with nauseating impact. I
hoped my father could forgive me that I couldn't remain
unmoved. I screamed, and a hot faint crawled over me.
Swaying, I remained upright only because my captors
supported me. I really had no practice at withstanding
pain, a grievous lacuna in my education.

The men murmured, one of the guards muttering a
prayer to Sawehl, and I became aware through the agony
throbbing in my hand and shooting up my arm of the living tendrils of the orchid ring. The wizard hummed with
interest, reminding me of Ambrose for the first time. I
managed to look, swallowing my gorge at the sight of my
mutilated hand and the gushing of blood from the stump
of my missing finger—and saw that the orchid ring had
withered and vanished from the severed finger, then re-
bloomed on the next finger over.

Another wizard, the one in red, descended the steps,
conferring with the first. They wondered what would happen if they removed my entire hand. "How is the Abiding
Ring transferred from one ruler to another?" the wizard
in red asked me.

The scene flashed into my mind of standing on the sky
pond with Ambrose, answering that very question, and
overlaying it, the bobbing of the ship under my feet and the
heat of the sun as my father lay dying. Ambrose had read it
in my mind without me speaking it, so I buried both memories deep under thick ice.

"Queen Euthalia," the wizard in red, as aged as the
first, said to me, not unkindly, especially given the

circumstances. "If You don't give us the secret of the transfer, we will have to cut off Your hand. You may not survive."

I straightened my spine, fighting through the dizziness and agony, refusing to beg them not to do it. "There is no secret," I told him. "It cannot be transferred while I live."

"You must realize that means You will have to die. We will have the Abiding Ring, and we will kill You to have it." He frowned. "Surely Your life isn't worth this ring You don't even know how to use."

"It doesn't matter if it's worth My life to Me or not," I informed him, wondering how he knew I didn't know how to use it. "It's not a choice for Me. I'll warn you, however, that My death alone may not do the trick."

The wizard in purple joined them, the one in blue stepping up to remain beside Anure. "What will do the 'trick'?" the purple wizard demanded.

"I don't know."

"You received it, so You do know," the wizard in black pointed out.

"All You need do," the red wizard said, nodding, "is tell us everything that You remember. We can work from there. Comply and I'll see to it that You are returned to Calanthe." He glanced at the other two wizards, who seemed to consider, then nodded agreement and produced thin smiles for me. I didn't miss that Anure was no longer a participant in the debate. He frowned at us from the heights of his throne, unable to hear, unwilling to appear out of control by asking. "You will not only save Calanthe, but go home," the red wizard urged with a warm smile. "You want that, more than anything, don't You, Your Highness?"

Tempting. So tempting. To go home, to feel Calanthe's sweet embrace in my mind and heart. And Con would be there. I'd wrap myself in Con's strong arms. Why hadn't I kissed him goodbye? Yes, I did want that. But not more than anything.

Even if I could bring myself to betray the trust of wearing the ring that was the emblem of my office, I couldn't contemplate what these wizards would do to the world with a magical artifact they wanted so very badly. Anure wasn't so clever. It turned out I cared about all those lands who called to me at night more than even Calanthe.

"I can't," I spat at them. I wanted to weep, and beg, but I managed not to. Clinging to my ice, I hardened myself. "Even if I could, I wouldn't."

The wizard in red shrugged. "Cut off Her hand then."

I managed not to scream as the guards forced me to my knees, shoved the metal cuff higher up, and laid my arm across the block, but I couldn't look. Oh, Con . . .

Then my vision went dark and, my tongue thick in my mouth, I could say nothing. Heat, thick and stomach-roiling, rose up and dragged me under.

Pain and nausea greeted me when I regained consciousness. At least fury, cold and clean, followed quickly after, clearing the miasma from my head. I'd do no one any good if I was a weeping, puking weakhearted mess.

With a feeling of desperate lunging, I reached for the dreamthink, beyond relieved to find I still had that. The familiar state of mental clarity and peace settled my mind further and I pushed out my senses to the world around me, finding the thoughts of a woman nearby, obscure in the way that all non-Calantheans are, with more opaque minds all around past her, and beyond them . . . nothing. Only the burning fires on the walls of Anure's citadel, the oily smoke stinking even in the dreamthink.

How I missed the brilliant purity of life in Calanthe. I would die in this place, and my body would never return to the land that birthed and formed me. In my despair, however, I imagined I scented orchids, and that I felt the petal-soft and florid brush of the orchid ring, and that helped more than I could ever describe.

With a sigh, I opened my eyes, to find myself once again staring into Sondra's intense blue ones. "This is getting to be tiresome," I commented.

To my vast surprise, she grinned at me. "Thank Ejarat. You must be all right if You have the strength to be mean."

My hand throbbed, sending burning fire up my arm, and I lifted it. How odd that I could feel pain there, because my hand was gone. Someone had bandaged the stump of my wrist, and washed the blood away.

And the orchid sat—or, should I say, *abided*—higher up on my wrist. It had become a bracelet, as floridly lovely and fragrant as ever, vines twining decoratively around my forearm almost like one of Con's gauntlets. I breathed a sigh of bone-shivering relief that I still had it, that they hadn't started chopping off the rest of my arm. That Anure and those foul wizards hadn't managed to take the ring for whatever horrible acts they planned. Lowering my arm gently back to my side, I looked to Sondra. "What happened?"

"That question is getting to be tiresome, too," she quipped wryly, then held out a goblet. "Drink some water."

I sat up, aware of my still-woozy head, vaguely surprised that Sondra lent me a steady arm. I needed the support, too, and no amount of pride would change that. Taking the goblet in my remaining hand, I drank, discovering my raging thirst as I did. "Is there more?"

"Yeah. Blood loss and trauma will do that," Sondra replied, refilling the goblet from a pitcher. "And You lost *buckets* of blood before they made up their minds that letting You die would be a bad idea—and likely still wouldn't get them the ring. Um, bracelet. Gauntlet? Whatever."

As she poured, I took a look around the room. Windowless, featureless, lavishly appointed, yet still a prison. Neither of us wore the chains anymore, though we both still had the collars and cuffs locked on. Well, one cuff for me, obviously. Sondra handed me the full goblet and regarded me seriously. "I have to hand it to You, Your Highness. You are one stone-cold bitch." She shook her head with a laugh. "Con said I'd underestimated You and he was right."

"Hardly," I replied once I'd swallowed the water. "I fainted."

"Your Highness, they beat You, cut off Your finger, and then Your whole fucking hand, and then did nothing to stanch the blood loss for a *long* time." Sondra cursed mildly and worked free a lock of hair that had caught in her collar. "I'm impressed. And this is belated, but I'm proud to call You my queen." She inclined her head.

Would wonders never cease. Much good may it do me. "I think you might as well call me Lia. Ejarat knows that Con does and so you probably do, too, behind my back." She gave me a sheepish smile and I nodded to myself. "And since we seem to be stuck in this cell, formalities seem . . . superfluous." I scanned it again as I spoke. How I hated that I would die in this place.

"No windows, one door," Sondra said crisply, reporting to me as she would to Con, I realized. "The stones are tight and the mortar sealed with something. No crumbling. The door is metal, on hinges, at least three locks, but they're well oiled and maintained, so there might be more than I could hear. They cut off Your hand at the wrist, severing the tendons, but—and I couldn't see well, only overhear—but the orchid moved again, to Your arm." She nodded at it. "They debated about cutting off Your arm, too, but those old guys—were they the wizards?"

"Yes."

"Anure really does have wizards," she said reflectively, as if trying to convince herself. "I thought you all were spinning fantasies. Agatha's messed up in a lot of ways, so I thought, You know, *evil wizards* was a metaphor for her. But no. *Four* wizards. We are so fucked. We never could have won this war, could we?"

"I don't see how," I replied, trying to be gentle but firm. Con had even me believing in the possibility for a while, so I could hardly blame her. "So they decided against cutting off My arm—or killing Me outright?"

"Yet," she said grimly. "The wizards disagreed, but ultimately they worried that if they cut off Your arm, the ring would just move to another, more central part of Your body. Then the one in black pointed out that they didn't have the secret of transference from You, and with You all passed out they weren't getting it soon. The fuckers finally decided that if You did die, it could be the orchid would die, too, and then they'd be out of luck."

"Hmm." That could be true. "They discussed all of this in front of Anure's court?"

"No. Several people fainted, even before You did, then one lady puked when Your hand came off, and the toad started screaming for them to clear out."

"You'd think Anure's court would be inured to displays like that. I have to lie down again." I hated to make the admission, but better that than passing out—or vomiting up that water I needed—and my vision was going black at the edges again.

"Of course." Surprisingly gentle, Sondra eased me back on the bed. "Truly, I'm amazed You woke up already."

"You don't have to use the honorific," I said, staring at the low, ugly ceiling.

"I owe You that honor," Sondra replied. "Though I'm surprised You can hear the capitalization."

"I can always hear it," I mused. "I especially hear when it's not there. They gave us water, but did they provide food?"

"Yes. Can You eat?" She sounded dubious.

I rolled my head on the pillow in negation. "I asked only because I wanted to be sure you have nutrition. You'll need it. Do they know who you are?"

She shook her head. "They think I'm one of Your ladies-in-waiting. A charity case." She passed a hand over her scarred face and smiled wryly.

"You were born nobility, Lady Sondra," I said. I held up the stump. "Our physical wounds don't change that."

She regarded me with rare emotion in her quite lovely eyes, and for a moment I glimpsed the vivacious court butterfly she'd been, delighting all with her golden voice and native ebullience.

"Also, giving us food is an indication of their plans. They'll keep us alive, for now."

"We might decide we'd rather die than remain captive," Sondra said gravely, arranging the covers to make me as comfortable as she could.

The pain ground at me, making me feel weak and helpless, but I forced my eyes open. The eye on the side where the guard hit me didn't seem to work very well. "Could you do it—kill Me and then yourself?"

She firmed her lips and nodded. "They took my weapons, but I could find a way. Do You want to do it now?"

"Not yet." Maybe it was a sign of profound cowardice, but I couldn't choose death right then. Maybe soon, when the last of my ability to hope faded away. Though I didn't know what I hoped for. The orchid ring—bracelet—sent a shiver of sweetness through me, and I clung to that. "Is that all right with you?" I asked Sondra. Con had charged her to protect me with her life—she'd said so when she came to me with the plan to draw Anure out. I knew she wouldn't suicide while I lived. "Can you bear to live awhile longer, until I gather the courage? Or," I added, "I might yet perish of this injury and then you'd be free of the onus of My life."

Sondra smiled a little. "Stone-cold bitch with the heart of a lion," she said. "I'm Yours to command, my queen." She dampened a cloth and smoothed it over my temples and forehead, dabbing at the swollen side. It felt lovely and cool, and I sighed with that simple relief, even though a sting indicated they'd broken skin.

"You've got an impressive black eye," Sondra informed me. "And Your cheek is bruised and swollen, but I don't think they broke any bones."

"Small mercies," I commented wryly.

"True enough," Sondra replied cheerfully. "I think You won't die on your own. The wizards did something so You wouldn't get an infection. I heard them tell Anure that. And Your color is remarkably good for someone who should be dead. I've seen a lot of people die, so I know."

I breathed a laugh, beginning to understand why Con loved this woman. She had a bone-deep lack of sentimentality that somehow made the unbearable easier to face. No wonder she'd survived what so few had.

"I didn't know You were bald," Sondra commented, sounding interested and not at all disgusted. She freshened the cloth and wiped it over my scalp, which felt lovely, too. "I mean, obviously You wear wigs, but I thought that was an affectation. Why bother?"

"Because I'm not fully bald, am I? I know My real hair is growing in."

"Is that what that is? I was worried You were getting a skin fungus or mold or something in this creepy place."

I laughed aloud, surprisingly, and it jarred me painfully. "No. That's the real Me. Normally My ladies keep my scalp shaved, but with recent events . . ."

"Yeah. No time for primping during war. But why wigs? If I were You, I'd just wear my crown on my bald head and let the critics go fuck themselves."

"This from the woman who refuses to cut her hair ever again."

"Conrí told You about that, huh?" She tucked a flowing strand of pale hair behind her ear. "I think it's different, because they forced that on me, on all of us. Having shorn heads marked us as slaves. No one forced this on You. I don't think anyone could make You do anything."

"Patently untrue, given our current circumstances," I commented wryly, but she shook her head.

"You stood up to them. Whatever Your reasons for being bald, I'm sure they're good ones. Besides," she added, with a twist of a smile, "You manage to be more gorgeous with no hair than anyone else with a full head of the stuff."

"Con says I have an elegant skull," I said. The memory of his touch came back to me so vividly, and with such aching regret, that it drowned out the physical pain. To my shame, tears pooled in the corners of my eyes and leaked down my temples.

Sondra didn't comment on my tears, simply wiped them away.

"I didn't treat him well," I confessed. "I should've been kinder to Con." It occurred to me in that moment that Sondra was being kind to me, and she had no agenda. I could do nothing for her, and she offered kindness anyway.

She snorted, the rude noise startling me. "Conrí doesn't need kindness," she said matter-of-factly. "He needs a woman to kick him out of his funks and challenge him. And to be the cool head of reason to balance his hot-headedness. And mine. You do that. You've been good for him," she added grudgingly. "I didn't want it to be true, but You are."

I thought about how Con had asked me to befriend Sondra and how I'd resisted. Ironic, in a way, that she might be the last person to see me alive.

"Your real hair is kind of pretty, actually, in a weird way," she said after a bit of silence. "Now that I'm not worried You have brain mold and I'm really looking at it. Like a fuzzy green lawn. It even looks like little leaves and a flower bud or two."

I sighed for the inevitability of that.

"The wizards, while they were debating, they called You an earth witch," she continued on in her practical way. "One of their ideas, if they accidentally killed You, was to plant Your body and see if they could harvest magical orchids from You."

I considered that, and what I knew of my own nature. "That might work. I don't know."

"Don't even think about it." For the first time, she sounded truly appalled.

I lifted my good hand and clasped hers. "I'm not. Even if I'm never brave enough to ask you to kill Me, I'm asking now for you to make sure they can't . . . use My body like that. Find a way to burn My body."

"With my last breath, if necessary," she replied, solemn as the vow. She laughed a little. "Back on Vurgmun, when I helped Conrí burn my former king's corpse, and we said the old prayers for Conrí's father, I told him I'd follow him to the end of my days, and that I asked only to hold the torch. Of course, I *meant* so I could burn Anure's empire down, but I suppose this would come close." She sobered, though still with a crooked smile.

I summoned something of a smile and squeezed her hand. "I suspect 'close' is as good as we can hope for."

She was quiet a moment. "He'll try to come after us. I know Conrí, and while he lives, he'll try."

I let go of her hand and stared at the ceiling. "If he does, we'll only have to watch him die." Would I be able to hold out then? Probably not.

"They'd use it against you," Sondra said, as if reading my thoughts. "They'd torture him to get You to give up the information on the ring. Even without him, they might try using me to get You to crack," she added, after a thought. "You should be prepared for that eventuality."

"It's a good thing we're not friends," I said, "or that might work."

She laughed, that hoarse sound with a hint of old music in it. "See? That was my plan all along."

21

We left Cradysica and traveled back to the palace. It made no sense to stay any longer in Cradysica. They had a great deal to rebuild. The citizens who'd fled returned to bury their dead or nurse the injured back to health. Having me and my people there only added to the burden.

Besides, they all hated me, and I couldn't blame them for it. I'd brought about the destruction of their home as surely as if I'd aimed the cannons myself.

So after doing what little I could—everything I thought Lia would do if she were there—I left behind a group of able-bodied troops to help with rebuilding, and led everyone else back to the palace.

It was a grim march, and I found myself acutely missing the festivity—however false it might've been—of Lia's parade on the way to Cradysica. No small part of that was desperately missing her.

I left the carriages to the ladies and rode the mount that had been Sondra's. Kara had taken our most salvageable oceangoing vessel down the coast, coaxing it along and limping it to the shipyards of Calanthe's best shipbuilders.

As soon as it was ready, I'd sail it, along with a crew of volunteers, to Yekpehr and Anure's citadel. Even though

I had no idea what we'd do there. Even knowing it would be far too late to save Lia and Sondra. I had to try.

I had no one to keep me company on the journey— really, no one wanted to speak to me, whether because they blamed me for the disaster at Cradysica or because I wasn't fit company—and that suited me fine. Vesno ran beside me, ever faithful, and the quiet let me think, turning the knot of the impossible problem over and over in my head.

It said something, however, that I missed even Ambrose's taunts and mind puzzles. Had Anure and his wizards somehow captured Ambrose, too? It seemed that they must have, for he'd disappeared as if he'd never been. Of course, it could be that he'd been killed or injured—if a wizard could be, I didn't know—but surely we'd have found at least his body. Or Merle.

But nothing. People sure had a way of disappearing on Calanthe.

In between casting about for some way to infiltrate the citadel, I thought a lot about the defeat at Cradysica on that long day's journey. For it had been a defeat of crushing magnitude, no matter what anyone said about the battle itself. Lia had been right all along in her assessments that we'd never really had a chance of winning. Looking back to that day in Keiost, when we stood in the golden tower and I'd thought I'd be able to grab some magic ring and use it to smite Anure . . . Well, I seemed like a child in comparison with now. So full of ignorance and hubris.

Now I felt ancient, ground down, and it seemed my punishment would be to live on. Maybe that's how it had always been. I was doomed to continue on with my miserable, worthless life while everyone else around me died.

So I decided I would put Calanthe's business in order as best I could, and leave the throne in Lord Dearsley's hands. He'd been handling things in Lia's absence from the palace and could continue to do so. He wasn't a true heir, but at least he was born of Calanthe, and he knew the realm intimately. That made him a far better ruler than I could ever be, no matter what Kara said. At least the earth tremors had settled, so the fears about Calanthe somehow rising like a monster from the sea wouldn't come to pass.

If I died trying to rescue Lia and Sondra—if they were already dead—then I could at least make one more last attempt to take Anure with me.

"I need a weapon," I told the assembled group of Lia's scholars. "Something I can carry on my person, with enough power to do serious damage."

We met in Lia's private courtyard, which felt both right and agonizingly wrong. Every leaf rustling in the sea breeze, each sweetly wafting fragrance from some exotic bloom, had me expecting to see her. At any moment, my heart whispered, she'll walk into the periphery of my vision, and she'll be there—impossibly lovely, dripping with flowers and sparkling with jewels. She'll give me that long, level look that assesses all of my flaws and failures, then give me a cool smile.

Idiot wolf, she'd say. *Let Me handle this.*

If only. Instead I surveyed the group watching me with confusion and bitterness. I'd lost them their queen. Of course they hated me.

"What kind of weapon and define serious damage," Brenda said.

"A vurgsten device," I clarified, "with enough power that I can kill Anure with it if I get within a reasonable distance."

"Hmm." Percy tapped a long nail against his lip, both

painted dusky violet to match the mourning clothes he wore, eyes sharp on me. "No plan to rescue Her Highness first?"

I decided against pointing out that he was the one dressed as if his queen were already dead. Ibolya had asked if I wanted the violet mourning clothes, but I declined and put on my usual black. She'd smiled, making me think she approved.

I also slept—fitfully and not long—on the couch in my dressing room. I couldn't face the bed I'd shared with Lia. "The weapon would be for after that. If I can get inside the citadel, maybe I can get in the same room with Anure and take him out. But rescuing Lia would be top priority. It's just that . . ." I doubted she or Sondra would be alive. "I have to get to Yekpehr first."

"How do you propose to travel there?" Brenda asked. She sat back, arms crossed, a black scowl etched onto her face.

"Sailing ship, unless you have another suggestion."

"You're still days from having one seaworthy," she replied, not surprising me that she knew.

"The shipbuilders are working as fast as they can," I said, reining in my impatience. She and Percy exchanged a look. Lia probably could've interpreted it, but I couldn't. I ticked off the points of order on my hands. "Once the ship is seaworthy, I can sail to Yekpehr, get into the citadel, attempt to locate Her Highness, and assess—"

"And Lady Sondra," Brenda inserted.

I met her gaze and nodded solemnly, appreciating that she'd said so. I hadn't wanted to rank my friend and lieutenant with their queen. "And Sondra. If they're alive, I'll see if they can be extracted. I don't know how that will go as no one here has ever been inside the citadel and—"

"I have." Agatha's thin voice shouldn't have had the

volume to interrupt me, but her statement acted like a blade, cutting me short, and stunning the gathering.

"I didn't know," Brenda said quietly, stretching a hand toward Agatha, but the slight woman only huddled deeper into the colorful shawl drawn around her shoulders, avoiding the touch.

"All this time, all those boring days with *nothing* to do, you've hoarded a story like *that*?" Percy exclaimed. "I'll never forgive you."

Agatha actually smiled, though it was wobbly, and immediately faded when she looked at me. "I can guide you to the prisoners."

"Good," I said. "You can draw me a map."

"No, I'll go with you."

Brenda muttered something darkly. I had to agree, looking at the enervated slip of a woman. Agatha threw Brenda a defiant glare, then returned her gaze to me. "Her Highness saved my life, and Sondra has become a friend. We don't have any idea where the two of them will be. I have friends there, on the inside, and they will know. No map can substitute for that."

I nodded, unwilling to argue, especially when my own judgment had turned out to be so very bad. I was the last person to turn down help at this point. "If the queen and Sondra are alive, we'll find them and get them out," I said.

"Even if Her Highness is dead, you must bring Her back to Calanthe," Dearsley said, speaking up for the first time. Lia's old adviser sagged in his chair, nearly broken by these events, and peered blearily at me. "Her body cannot remain in Anure's hands."

"Lord Dearsley." I frowned at him, not in small part because the idea of seeing and touching Lia's lifeless corpse was nearly more than I could contemplate. "I can try, but—"

"You must," he insisted. "Even if She's been buried. Dig up Her body and return it to Calanthe. It's critically important. Please, Conrí."

"I will do my best then to see that her body returns to Calanthe, if the queen cannot be saved." I'd hedged my promise there. If Lia was dead, there was no reason for me to return. The surest way to kill Anure would be to detonate the weapon on my body. Maybe my death could be more effective than my worthless life had been.

"So what are you thinking for this weapon?" Brenda leaned forward, capable hands knotted. "A 'reasonable distance' could mean a lot of things, and no one is letting you that close to Anure. You'd need enough to clear a good-sized throne room, and we don't have a lot of vurgsten left. Mostly the small amounts you lot gave us to experiment with."

"He doesn't need much," Percy pointed out, toying thoughtfully with a piece of his costume. "He wouldn't need to annihilate the entire room. All he needs is to get near Anure and have easy access to a trigger—like that device Agatha's been working on—and *boom*!" He fluttered his long nails dramatically.

"It could work," Agatha allowed. "I can refine it on the ship, then set it up with Conrí, once we assess the options. But, Conrí, I don't know that I can add an effective delay. You'd maybe be too close to the device when it went off."

"If Lia is dead, that part won't matter," I said flatly.

They sat in silence, contemplating me. "And if she's alive?" Brenda asked.

"I'll figure something out."

She met my gaze, and finally nodded at whatever she saw there. "I can help you, too," Brenda told Agatha and Percy. "But the ship still won't be ready for days."

"Well . . ." Percy drew out the word, raising his brows at Brenda.

She looked surprised. "Would you?"

Percy shrugged. "Her Highness is our dear queen. How could I not? She saved my life, too," he added, looking at Agatha.

"I'm impressed, Percy," Brenda commented drily. "I thought you were irretrievably selfish."

"I am," Percy snapped. "Don't tell anyone—you'll ruin my reputation."

"Does someone want to tell me what we're talking about?" I asked with considerable patience, considering the drumming of my heart.

"I have a life raft," Percy admitted.

"We'll need something bigger than that."

"A big life raft." He stared me down with a glittering gaze, daring me to make something of it. "The *Last Resort*. A yacht, really. Not huge, but top of the line. She's fully stocked and ready to go. Call it a . . . habit of paranoia. I like knowing it's there."

"So you can run away," Brenda said, though without rancor.

"To live another day and all that, yes, darling." He looked at me again. "Take it. Bring them back."

Agatha stood. "I'll pack my things. We leave today?"

I glanced at Percy, who shrugged. "Leave in an hour if you like. The ship is ready and the tide is good."

Brenda stood, too. "I'll get everything together. Agatha will have to take the pieces with her."

"Conrí?" Ibolya stepped up as I turned to go. She'd come along to serve refreshments, unobtrusively faithful to what Lia would have expected. "May I come with you?" she asked when I raised a brow at her.

"It won't be an easy journey."

"I don't plan to leave the yacht, Conrí," she assured me. "But if you retrieve Her Highness, either way, she'll need tending. It's my duty to be there."

"All right." I nodded as I said it. "Either way, I think Lia would appreciate that."

As they had for the last several days, the Imperial Guards had chained and then carried me to the wizards' work-rooms, leaving Sondra locked in our cell. I loathed those workrooms, and every day, as I weakened more under their determined torture, my terror of them grew. All part of their strategy, of course. But knowing that didn't make me any stronger.

"Your Highness." The wizard who always wore red, and had turned out to be the most senior, greeted me with a bow. The other three hung back in a circle around a polished slab with ominous runnels carved into it, likely for carrying blood to the urns perched under each corner. This was new. So far they'd focused on extracting the secret of the orchid's transfer from me.

"I hope You're feeling recovered from yesterday's experiments?" the wizard asked, his gaze fastened on the orchid at my wrist.

I nearly laughed in his face. The "experiments" had involved them trying to force their way into my mind while they applied various tortures to try to break my mental guards. My father's training had finally served me well, though, and even they hadn't been able to melt the ice I'd walled myself in with. Fortunately, they couldn't afford to torture me *too* much, for fear that, in my weakened state, I'd die on them. That was all that had saved me so far.

They'd given me two days at first, during which I mostly slept, drank water, and then ate what Sondra coaxed me to. We saw no one other than the Imperial Guards who replenished our food and water—both in plentiful amounts. Sondra turned out to be quite the effective combination of martinet and nursemaid. She didn't care if either of us was hungry. Until we made the decision to die, she declared, we would take the opportunity to strengthen ourselves as much as possible.

It had gotten so she pushed food in front of me with such regularity that I finally suggested if we survived this—which of course we wouldn't—and she needed a new job, she could be a walking timepiece.

Not at all bothered by my irritated remark, she'd taken to making ticking noises when she set another plate in front of me.

But no, I was far from recovered, and they knew it, predatory gazes glittering over their false smiles. I was the weakest I'd been, despite Sondra's best efforts—and close to breaking, all a result of the wizards' meticulous assaults.

As I hadn't replied, the red wizard stepped aside, gesturing to the slab and giving me a clear view of it—and of the tray of wicked-looking instruments and other alchemical devices. This would be very bad indeed. I already sagged in the grip of the guards, not strong enough to stand on my own, but it felt as if all my bones went to water.

"Queen Euthalia, You must understand what You face here," the red wizard said. "It would be in Your best interests to cooperate. We cannot be certain You will survive this procedure."

And there it was. The orchid on my wrist sizzled in response to the magic of the four assembled wizards, as it always did. But though I took comfort in its tangible magical presence, I still had no idea how to use it to help myself. Sondra had nagged me to death—ha!—about that, too. Obviously it was a powerful tool, as these wizards wanted it so badly.

I had tried to communicate with the orchid, making wishes and pleading with it until my bones ached from exhaustion and my stump burned with such an itching fire that Sondra had to tie my other hand down while I slept so I wouldn't tear off the bandages and reopen the wound with my furious scratching. My jeweled nails had long since fallen off, but the natural ones on my remaining hand had grown extravagantly quickly in the last few days. Like rose-colored thorns, they curved into wickedly sharp tips. If only I could wish poison into them.

I could wish for many things.

"Does His Imperial Majesty know of what you plan to do to Me?" I inquired haughtily as possible for a woman dangling helplessly in the grip of two Imperial Guards, a last gambit. I would die on that slab, I felt it in my bones, and without putting a scratch on Anure. "I'm still Queen of Calanthe. He needs Me."

The red wizard assumed an expression of regret. "I'm afraid He doesn't, Your Highness. Once His Imperial Majesty understood what the Abiding Ring can give Him . . ." He lifted his hands and gave me a cold, cruel smile. "Between us, He was in quite the rage that He waited so long to claim Your hand in marriage, only to discover it had never been necessary at all. Thus, my colleagues and I have been given full permission to do whatever it takes to recover the Abiding Ring. Give us the secret of transference, and You might live. If You refuse, I guarantee nothing. It would be a terrible waste to destroy a creature of Your particular nature. We appreciate You, even if His Imperial Majesty doesn't. Cooperate and You can stay with us. We'd take excellent care of You."

The other wizards nodded, smiling warmly. The avid

gleam in their eyes made me think they'd keep me captive to explore my "particular nature." Through that lens, living sounded less attractive all the time. "Syr Wizard," I said in my most regal tone, though my voice was as cracked as Sondra's from screaming, "as I've repeatedly explained, the orchid transfers itself."

"Upon the wearer's death, yes. We have some ideas there."

He waved for the guards to put me on the table. The big men lifted my slight and heavily chained self without effort. Hoping desperation would have a galvanizing effect, I made a final attempt to free myself—or at least take some of them with me—and tried reversing their energy. Once second nature for me, that skill had disappeared with my connection to Calanthe. Away from Her, I'd been reduced to nothing. Death would come as a relief, to be honest, a true surcease, and not just from physical pain.

The stone was cold and hard against my barely fuzzed scalp, and chilled my skin through the thin gown they'd given me when they took away everything else. The guards locked me onto the table, then withdrew at the black wizard's command.

I stared up at the ceiling as the four wizards gathered around me. The guards had strapped down my left arm with several bands and the wizards peered at the orchid, greedy curiosity sharpening their faces.

"Our plan, Queen Euthalia," the red wizard informed me, as one of my scholars might discuss an interesting text, "is to bring You as near death as possible, to determine if we can trigger the artifact into transferring itself. I can't promise it will be completely painless, but we have no wish to torture You. Not anymore."

I had to suppress a sarcastic remark at that. Amazing

that I still had the spirit for it. I supposed that was all I had left: my twisted sense of humor, an array of regrets, and the hollow, aching emptiness where Con had been.

The purple wizard fiddled with something outside my peripheral vision, then nodded to the other wizards. The blue and black wizards took up sharp instruments and made quick slices at my good wrist and both ankles. It hurt, but nothing like what I'd already endured. Being punched in the face had been more alarming. That spoke to something about my fears and my instinctive lack of judgment in determining what sort of injury should truly capture my attention. My blood dripped into the urns with a steady cadence, almost musical, and loud in the otherwise quiet room. Then I felt the dread—*far too late*, I chided my instincts—as the blood loss registered. Nausea rose up, thick and oily, and my heart thundered, trying to keep up.

"We're capturing Your blood," the red wizard assured me, his hand grasping my left arm, conveniently near the orchid, "just in case this experiment doesn't work the first time. This apparatus is quite ingenious." He dipped his chin at something I couldn't see, which was just as well. "Using it, we can replace the blood in Your body and bring You back to life again. We realize that finding the exact trigger for the transference might take several trials to get correct."

Stars pricked my vision, blackness overtaking me, a terrible weakness saturating my limbs.

"We're using magic to keep You balanced on the knife-edge of life and death," the wizard continued conversationally. "So You might feel Yourself passing back and forth over that barrier as we attempt to pinpoint the exact condition for transference. Feel free to share Your observations, which might be excitingly unprecedented. We are taking extensive notes. Also, if You talk, we can better assess Your state of mind."

I didn't reply. Even if I could find the strength to speak, it would be to spew obscenities to match these foul men's souls. And as it looked like this would be the end of me and I hadn't broken yet, I needed all of my concentration to keep it that way. I kept thinking of Con, though, of the fire in his golden eyes, and the strength in his scarred body. How he'd held me and learned to be tender . . .

The red wizard tapped me sharply on the forehead. "I'm disappointed, Your Highness. You have such a reputation for sponsoring knowledge and research of all kinds. Your interest in attracting a wizard to Calanthe spread far and wide, within certain discreet circles, of course." He gave me a conspiratorial wink. I could only count myself and Calanthe lucky that this vile magic worker hadn't turned up on Our shores. "Surely You would want to contribute to this grand experiment. It could be Your last contribution to the world. We could name it for You! The Euthalia Method."

I swam in a miasma of darkness and blazing heat. I hadn't expected blood loss would make me so hot. Or perhaps that was the magic. The wizards fell into discussion among themselves, at least leaving me alone. A pinprick in my throat announced that they'd decided to add my own blood back in, a glow of magic accompanying it. The stump of my wrist itched and ached with distracting fury. Absurdly, being unable to scratch at it bothered me almost more than anything.

A convulsion wrenched through me, agonizing to my battered body and alarming the wizards. Good. Maybe I would die. The prospect seemed more restful than frightening now. Sondra would be freed of her vow, and hopefully the orchid would die with me, without transferring. I'd been careful not to think anything that would will it to move, just in case it would respond to my thoughts. I'd failed to take Anure to face Yilkay's judgment with me, but at least I'd kept the artifact out of the hands of these wizards with their terrible scorpion stingers.

At least Con hadn't come after us. It helped to know he, at least, would live.

Smiling at the wizards' voices raised in consternation and accusation, I reached out to Vesno with the last of my life energy. Though I hadn't been able to feel his mind lately—I'd been too weak, and the walls of the citadel too thick and poisonous—I prayed to Ejarat that the wolfhound could still hear me. I gave Vesno all of my love for Con, and for Calanthe, hoping to pass that message along.

If I'd had time to ruminate, I'd have wanted to contemplate why, at the end of my life, my thoughts and feelings went primarily to Con. Odd how, in dying, one didn't dwell much on politics and tasks left undone. All of my regret centered on my love, and what might have been. Too late now. Alas for that.

If nothing else, Con would be amused that I'd finally put him first.

Thinking of him, I let myself fall into the painless ease of death.

~ 22 ~

Vesno raced across the deck to me, wrapping himself around my legs as best as a huge wolfhound can, and pressed himself to me like a shivering puppy. "Vesno—what is it, boy?" I hunkered down, letting the dog lap my face, giving him the reassurance he seemed to suddenly need. The *Last Resort*—truly a pleasure yacht, ostentatious beyond imagining—pitched beneath me, sending my gut lurching, too.

Or was that something else?

My stomach hollowed out, my heart dropping into the hole it opened.

Lia.

"Conrí?" Kara put a hand on my shoulder, shaking me with it, making me realize I'd been crouching there some time, Vesno and I racked with grief. "Are you hurt, Conrí?"

I only had my heart carved out of my body. I wouldn't say aloud what I knew to be true. Lia had died. Though the Calantheans had been able to sense the marriage bond, it hadn't ever felt like much to me. Now I recognized its sudden absence. Across the deck, Ibolya stood by the rail, facing me, tears running down her face. Lia had been alive until this moment. So close. Too late.

I rubbed Vesno's ears, which drooped with the same mourning that wanted to cleave me in two. Maybe Sondra lived. I'd recover Lia's body and send her home, as I'd promised.

After that . . .

I had my suicide weapon. Agatha had shown me how it worked, though she wasn't happy at the short delay from trigger to explosion. Knowing Lia was gone, I had no concerns about that. I would find a way to be in the same room as Anure, kill us both, and perhaps join Lia in Yilkay's domain. Maybe if I died ridding the world of Anure, Yilkay would forgive a few of my more terrible acts and only punish me for a few millennia.

"I'm fine." I stood, Vesno still clinging to my legs, and faced down Kara's dubious frown. "How close are we?"

He turned to look at the sea, measuring the waves and the distant rocks, though I knew he already had an answer. Kara had the great gift of always knowing exactly where he was on the ocean. "With circling out and coming on the citadel from up coast, I'd say we could send you ashore within walking distance in another few hours. A brisk pace would get you there just past midnight. I'd like to get you closer, but . . ."

"Better slow but sure," I agreed, prompting another frown. All along I'd been chewing on Kara to get us there faster. Naturally he'd wonder at my sudden lack of urgency. "Do you mean Agatha's brisk pace or mine?" I asked to distract him.

"I can match any pace you set, Conrí," Agatha informed me in her quietly slicing voice, having sidled up on our conversation in her unobtrusive way. "I'm an excellent runner."

With the shape my lungs were in, she could likely run circles around me. "All right. Agatha and I will row ashore as soon as you give the word, Kara." I could at least row a boat with reasonable power. "We'll get to the citadel, assess, and Agatha, at the very least, will meet you back at the rowboat by dawn."

She opened her mouth to protest, and I stopped her. "Once you get me in and find out what we need to know, I need you to take back that information."

"Getting into the citadel is far less problematic than getting out again," she said, not for the first time, lines deepening on her papery skin.

"Which is why I want you out again as fast as humanly possible. If all goes well, I'll be with you, along with Sondra and—" My voice caught and I had to clear my throat. "I can carry Her Highness, if need be."

They didn't love the plan, but no one had come up with a better one. Though none of us voiced it, the entire mission was truly one of sacrifice. When Kara clasped my shoulder in a goodbye, neither of us could speak the words. He gave me a long look, knowing me well enough to see my grief, that I'd lost hope. Likely he knew I didn't expect to see him again on Ejarat's soil.

Of course, we'd all known this attempt was suicidal, even without the weapon. Even the plans for Agatha to return were born of optimism rather than any of us believing she would. The wraithlike woman never ceased to amaze me: she was clearly terrified of returning to the citadel, yet she'd never once wavered in her resolve to go.

"You take our hopes with you, Conrí," Kara said, his sere face grave.

The words with their unfortunate evocation of the grave echoed in my head as I rowed our small boat to shore in the relatively calm cove. I felt on my shoulders the weight of the hopes of thousands who'd fought with me, supported our cause, often with their lives. I took them with me, yes, to their final end.

Vesno's mournful howl followed us across the water.

Agatha hadn't exaggerated her knowledge, or endurance. We made it to the slumbering township outside the citadel walls faster than Kara had estimated—me pushing myself and my straining lungs, she keeping to a considerately slow pace. She guided us through stinking back alleys and down footpaths used by servants and slaves.

I mostly managed not to think about what we'd find left of Lia, and if Sondra shared her fate.

In deference to our disguises, I'd left the rock hammer behind. The bagiroca hung from its hook on my belt, looking like another of the burdens we both carried, and we wore rough and dirty clothing. For once I appreciated my scars and beaten appearance, because the Imperial Guards at the citadel's Slave Gate barely even glanced as they admitted us.

As Agatha had observed, getting in wasn't so difficult. Certainly not for invisible folk like us.

We trudged through the bowels of the place, making our way through a warren of poorly lit corridors. "Why do I smell burning vurgsten?" I asked her quietly.

She didn't hesitate. "His Imperial Majesty has it burning on the walls at all times."

That meant he had stores to squander, even without Vurgmun. Of course he'd have other sources, other mines. More slaves to mine his rock. We'd been doomed all along. I'd been the only one not to get that through my thick skull.

The kitchens weren't far in, venting another sort of smoke from their many ovens. A few low-tier souls were awake, tending the fires, some making dough for the breakfast breads that would be required in a few hours. A place as vast as this had servants awake and working at all hours.

"Wait for me here," Agatha said clearly, treating me like someone slow of mind. "Put down the sacks, unload the meal, and sit. Wait. Understand?"

I nodded dully, and she slipped off into the smoky shadows. Keeping to my role as draft mule, I unloaded the surface contents of meal the guards had barely glanced at, surreptitiously readying the supplies for our true mission. Checking on the remarkably compact vurgsten weapon at the bottom.

Then I waited for Agatha, trying not to reveal my simmering impatience. Being inside the citadel made my hair stand on end, and being so close to Anure . . . well, the wolf in me didn't much care for the good reasons to wait. I wanted to rend and tear, to annihilate the man who killed my beautiful Lia.

One of the bread makers offered me hot tea, and I accepted, figuring it fit my role and it gave me something to do with my hands.

The tea was gone all too soon, and Agatha still hadn't returned. What would I do if she'd been caught? Taking someone hostage and forcing them to lead me to the prison cells could work, but I'd need someone of high rank and low courage.

"Who are you and why are you in my kitchens?" a woman's voice demanded, startling me from dark thoughts of charging through the citadel, slaughtering everyone I came across.

Fortunately, the surprise worked in my favor, and I blinked at her in dull confusion—not easy with my nerves singing at high alert—and changed my instinctive grab

for the bagiroca into an uncouth scratching of my ass.
The woman glared at me. "Who let you in here? What is
this stuff?" She kicked the sacks and I tensed, hoping the
vurgsten bomb didn't explode.

"Sorry, madame," Agatha said at my elbow, just about
making me jump out of my skin, again. "My brother.
Good for carrying things. Not so bright. We'll get out of
your kitchen now."

"And you are?"

Agatha ducked her head and bobbed a clumsy curtsy.
"Crawya. I brought the grain and delivered messages to
the Guests."

"I don't know you, but you look familiar . . ." The
woman frowned in thought. I slid my hand surreptitiously
to the bagiroca, just in case she recognized Agatha.
Whatever Agatha's history at the citadel was, I doubted
she'd left under friendly conditions. *What will you do,
wolf?* Lia's voice chided me. *You can't just bash them all
over the head.*

"I've been away, ma'am," Agatha was saying, "but I
grew up in Pekoe, down the road. I'm back to care for my
sick mother and idiot brother, here. Making some coin by
delivering things to the citadel."

"Hmm. Well, don't be leaving the likes of him stinking up my clean kitchens again."

"No, ma'am. Come on, brother."

I got to my feet, keeping my movements slow and dull,
picking up our much lighter sacks and following Agatha
out of the kitchens. She turned toward the Slave Gate, as
if we meant to leave, then turned off into a side corridor.

"Sorry it took so long," she said. "My contact was
asleep, and she had to wake someone else to get the information. But she found out where they're being kept. We'll
take the back way."

"Just tell me where they are. You go back."

She gave me a stony look. "All right. They're being held in tower five."

My frustration rumbled in my throat. "You can't give directions?"

Shrugging her bony shoulders, she shook her head. "Directions clear enough to keep you from getting caught? No. And what happens if someone else challenges you? I know how people think here. Let me do this, Conrí."

"You're risking your life," I felt I had to say.

Her expression went withering. "With all due respect, I know that better than you. I'm risking more than my life: I'm risking my freedom and sanity."

"Then why do it? Just point. Draw me a picture. You don't have to do this."

"Yes, I do. I owe Her." With that, Agatha turned and walked down the dim hall with the brisk, quiet pace of a longtime servant. I had no choice but to follow.

Taking the servants' passages made the journey circuitous and lengthy. Try as I might to track our relative location in the maze of the citadel, I soon got hopelessly turned around—and pathetically grateful for Agatha's unerring guidance. Occasionally we passed another servant. Some stared curiously; others ignored us as we did them. I arranged the heavy sacks over one shoulder and unhooked the bagiroca, tucking my thumb loosely in my belt as I held it at the ready.

Everyone else was asleep, the citadel as quiet as a tomb. Not like Lia's palace, where the revelry had continued all night and into the early-morning hours. These grim walls hadn't known anything like celebration in a long, long while. I hated everything about this place. Mostly I hated that Lia, child of sunshine and flowers, had spent her last days here.

A guard stood at the base of tower five—or so I assumed—as Agatha continued up to him, head bowed deferentially. I did my best to shuffle stupidly behind her, holding the bagiroca and assessing him with my peripheral vision, while trying to subdue the desire to take him out, just to vent the need to kill something.

"State your business," the guard said, stifling a yawn.

"Delivery for third floor, tower five guard station, syr," Agatha muttered in the same bored tone.

"Only one of you needs to go."

"I can't carry the sacks and he's too stupid to find his way alone." Agatha gestured to her head, miming a brain problem.

The guard studied me, and I did my best to look dull and ineffective. "Go. Be back in ten or I'm coming after you."

"Thank you, syr." Agatha scurried past him and the main stairs to a shadowed door, and into a narrow servants' stairway. I followed more slowly. My exposed back prickled with unease until I pulled the door shut again. Picking up the pace, we jogged up the stairs, well past the third floor. Finally we stopped at a landing, and Agatha pointed at the door, beckoning me to lean close. "Outside this door will be an antechamber, with doors to several cells. According to my source, they are in the second from the left. There will be guards."

"How many?"

"I don't know. I just know there will be some, because prisoners are always guarded. We could get lucky, but . . ." She shrugged fatalistically. Yeah, our luck had held so far, but we were stretching it thin.

She stepped back and huddled in the shadows of the wall, letting me handle this part. Setting down the sacks, I weighed the familiar heft of the bagiroca and eased the door open so I could see through the crack. Two guards, one relatively alert, the other sitting with his back against the wall, dozing. It would've been too much to ask that both would be sleepy, but the discipline of the citadel was clearly fierce enough for them to take shifts.

Going for surprise, I threw open the door and charged straight for the standing guard, releasing all my pent-up rage in a burst of speed. My bagiroca connected with his helmet, stunning him into staggering against the wall. His buddy leapt to his feet, sword swinging for me with admirable speed for a guy who'd looked sound asleep. Not fast enough. I sidestepped the blade, continuing my own swing to take out his knees. He fell with a cry of pain that became a grunt when I kicked him in the face with my heavy boot.

Sharp pain sliced my side and I spun, grabbing the other guard by the throat with my free hand and crushing the fragile cartilage there. His eyes in the narrow opening of the helmet bulged, and he dropped his sword in his panic—bad training there—and clawed at my fist. I squeezed harder and his windpipe collapsed with a satisfying crunch. Dropping his lifeless body to the floor, I checked his buddy, then strangled him, too. Not too much blood to betray a problem, and most of it not obvious in the grimy lighting.

I checked the other doors, finding one cell unlocked and empty, then dragged both bodies in there. With them out of sight of anyone who happened by, I searched for keys, finding none. Going back to Agatha, I found her huddled on the landing, arms wrapped around herself, face strained and eyes wide as they went to the blood on my hands. Nothing like having to wait to make fear grow. But she showed no signs of cracking.

"I took out two guards and don't see more," I said quietly. "But no keys. Am I missing something?"

"Probably whoever brings the food in the morning has the keys," she replied, looking stricken. "I didn't think of that."

"That's all right. I did." I got out one of Brenda's new toys and my vurgsten sparker. "What are the odds anyone is close enough to hear a small bang?"

"Low?" She frowned. "I hope. The doors are pretty thick."

"Keep hoping." Checking that no one had come up or down the main stairs, I tied the cloth bag to the handle of the cell Agatha had indicated. It didn't catch immediately, but soon began to smolder. When the flame licked into life, I slipped around the corner of the stairs leading up, figuring someone would be most likely to come from that way. My bagiroca in hand, I alternated between checking the burning bag on the cell door and bending my ears for approaching footsteps.

The bag blew with a considerable bang—louder than I'd hoped—and I ran for the cell door. The lock had cleanly blown, pushing the door nearly off the hinges. Shoving it aside, I pushed into the room. "Songrhhh . . ." My voice went to a garble, breath stopped by the forearm around my throat, crushing my own windpipe, Sondra like ferocious burr on my back.

"Conrí?" she whispered, astonished, and let go.

"Yes. Lia?"

"They took Her." Sondra stowed a makeshift knife and grabbed a few things. "I don't know where. They take Her every day, but this has been much longer. Conrí, I don't know if—"

"We'll find her." Sondra didn't know Lia had died. I

hadn't expected that they'd bring her corpse back to the holding cell. Still, I'd hoped . . . what? I knew she was dead. I needed to get a grip on that. "Let's go. This way."

Sondra looked only briefly surprised when I pulled her away from the main stairs and to the servants' door, but that was nothing to her shock when Agatha rose from her protective crouch. "Lady Sondra," she said. "Good to see you. Her Highness?"

"Not here. They took her away this morning."

"Who did?" Agatha asked sharply. "Be specific."

"Agatha knows the citadel," I supplied when Sondra slid me a sideways look.

"They were Imperial Guards. They've been taking Her to the wizards to be . . . interrogated."

I growled at Sondra's words, and she nodded. "Agatha was right. Four wizards. Guess you have experience with them, huh?"

"You have no idea," Agatha replied in a hollow voice. She turned to move down the stairs, but I stopped her.

"I'll take the lead to the bottom. We'll want to remove that guard. If he hasn't started up after us yet. We're close to that ten-minute deadline." Agatha nodded and followed behind us. "Are you hurt at all?" I asked Sondra.

"No. They didn't hurt *me*," she replied with enough emphasis that it would've told me all I needed to know regardless. "How did you get in—is Ambrose helping you?"

I shook my head and signaled for silence. We hurried down the stairs, short runs to each landing, then a pause at each to peer around the corner and listen for pursuit from above or below. At the final landing, I heard footsteps. One man, moving cautiously. That worked just fine for him to come to me. Signaling for Sondra to guard Agatha, I crept forward, keeping just back behind the curve of the wall. Waiting. Listening. Sondra drew her make-shift blade and held position.

The guard's drawn sword came into view first as he scanned the landing. *One more step. Come to papa.* He eased out, and I struck.

He ducked in time, agile on the steps, and shouted, "Esca—" His shout broke off on a gargle as Sondra's blade buried itself in his throat. My bagiroca connected with his skull a moment later—too fucking late to stop the warning shout—and he fell, careening down the steeply spiraling stairs, sword clattering.

"Run," I said. Sondra grabbed up the guard's dropped sword as she passed, ushering Agatha along. Cutting the man's throat with Sondra's blade, I left him there—not worth the time to hide the body—and chased after the pair of them. As soon as I caught up with them at the bottom, Sondra eased open the door, scanned the area, and nodded to me.

Taking the lead again, Agatha dashed out. "This way."

We ran across the open space, making no attempt to hide. Though she'd lost her armor and wore a shift, with her long hair and fierce mien Sondra couldn't pass as a servant, not even if she gave up the sword. She clutched it with such ferocity that I knew I couldn't ask her to relinquish it. We would be fighting our way out from here on.

The quiet back halls gave the illusion of safety, but we jogged along, ears pricked for the sounds of alarm or pursuit. We wound down, ever deeper, until I was sure we had to be well belowground. These halls were barely lit, with a feeling of stale disuse, and we passed no one else. "Where are we going?" Sondra hissed.

I shrugged, but Agatha glanced back, her face ghostlike in the dimness. "The wizards' workroom. Her Highness will be there. They always stored their experimental subjects where they could be easily accessed."

Sondra made a choking sound but said nothing else. I was glad of it, because I had enough trouble wrestling down the howling creature in me that wanted to rend and tear. *Like a caged wolf*, Lia's lilting words mocked me, and I missed her with the despair of a thousand deaths.

"Here." Agatha stopped by a door. "I can't—" She broke off with a strangled squeak. "I can't go in."

Figuring she meant the knob wouldn't turn, I tried the handle. "It's not locked."

"No." Her voice was small. "Nobody goes in there if they don't have to."

Oh, Lia. I glanced at Sondra. "I'm coming with you," she said.

"Get out now," I told Agatha, but she shook her head. "I'll wait. You'll never find your way. I can do that much." When her hollow gaze met mine, I realized she knew what we'd find in those rooms.

Sondra took a flanking position on the door, her makeshift blade in hand, and nodded her readiness. I eased the door open, finding the room empty of people, lit by a few shielded sconces. It looked like the alchemist's workroom, back in the tower at Keiost—tables and desks littered with documents, a few bits of scaffolding on taller benches with glassware and metal instruments.

Though the place seemed unoccupied, Sondra gestured to a doorway, moving silently in that direction. I followed along, keeping my senses alert. The place stank of . . . fresh blood, and bowels, and death. And also of something essentially green, like fresh leaves crushed on a garden path.

My heart broke all over again, knowing Lia had died in this horrible, windowless place.

Sondra looked back from the doorway, her face such a rictus of grief that I knew what she'd seen—and that it was worse than my imaginings. She cleared her throat. "Conrí, maybe you shouldn't—"

"I can handle it," I said, and pushed past her before I lost my nerve.

The sight nearly brought me to my knees. But I could hardly turn away from Lia. I should be able to at least witness what she'd had to endure.

She lay on a slab of stone, pale and still as cooled wax. Chains and straps dangled from the corners, but they'd done the courtesy of releasing her in death. Her left hand was gone at the wrist, her arm ending in a blood-soaked bandage stained brown with old blood. Just above it, the orchid that had been on her ring seemed to be fastened to her arm, but it lay wilted and limp, devoid of color. Dead as she was.

Lia seemed smaller than ever, no more than a dried leaf, and her beautiful face was both swollen and hollow, marred with terrible bruises. Devoid of makeup, her scalp bare, she'd never looked more vulnerable. Her real hair had grown in more, and the sight of it carved an even greater hole in me. The new tendrils and vines hung withered, breaking off like spring flowers killed by late frost.

"Oh, my love," I whispered, running tender fingers over her cheek. "What have they done to you?"

"They were trying to take the ring," Sondra said beside me. "I wasn't sure if I should warn you . . ." She couldn't finish, sounding as broken as I felt.

"It's all right." I couldn't say more.

"She asked—She made me promise that if She died, I'd do my best to burn Her body."

"No."

"Conrí, I *promised*."

"Then I'm overruling Her. She's going home to Calanthe." I pulled out the extra burlap sack we'd brought, and I gathered up her frail body, carefully sliding her into it, though she was cold and long since passed being uncomfortable. I tied the top and lifted her into my arms. She weighed even less in death than in life. "Come with me, love. Let's take you home."

As I turned, I saw something under a glass bell nearby. "Is that her hand, and finger?"

Sondra looked, too, and grimaced. "Apparently they saved them."

Something tickled at my memory, an odd impulse. I wouldn't leave any part of Lia here. "Bring them."

"Conrí, I—"

"Please, Sondra."

"Fine." She sounded like she thought I'd lost my mind, but she complied. She tucked the finger in with the severed hand, Lia's jeweled nails sparkling in macabre contrast, and wrapped them in cloth. She picked up the sword again.

"Sondra, we have to try to sneak out as servants if possible. You have to leave the sword."

She held it tightly, clenching her jaw. Then shrugged, as if it didn't pain her to be defenseless, and tossed the sword aside.

"I have the blade you made," I offered.

"No." She spotted what looked like a walking stick, solid and battered, propped in a corner. "This will work."

I didn't argue. We didn't have time, and at least it was a concession. Not the last one, either. "Can you cover your hair—or braid it?"

She stalked to a mirror, glowering at herself. Then picked up a knife and started hacking at her glorious hair.

"Sondra, I didn't—"

"It's hair, Conrí. She lost Her fucking hand and joked about it. She lost Her life. I promised I'd get Her body out of here. If losing some hair helps, that's the least I can do." She cut the hair off close to her scalp as she talked, then gathered it all up and tucked it into a sack with Lia's hand. Giving me her lethal grin, she faced me, looking so much like the girl back on Vurgmun that I nearly couldn't breathe. "Let's go."

Outside the door, Agatha took one look at Sondra's shorn hair, then at my burden, and nodded in grim resignation. "Any sound of alarm?" I asked.

She shook her head. "But we wouldn't hear, down here. Up on the main level is where we'll face the worst danger."

We followed her out, the winding egress seeming to take even longer. Though I hated to desecrate Lia's corpse, I had to put the sack over my shoulder as we came to the more heavily traveled sections of the citadel, so it would look like a manservant's burden. The vurgsten bomb bounced heavily against my back with her shifting weight, and I prayed that it wouldn't go off.

I could still use it.

The place was waking up, more servants in evidence as they carried heated water and, in some cases, platters of food. A group of guards, weapons drawn, jogged down a main hall, passing the doorway of an intersecting hall. "We need to hurry," I murmured to Agatha.

She didn't comment on my obvious remark, simply kept on at her same pace. Sondra shuffled along, head down, leaning on the walking stick. Still, she drew a curious glance or two, and I readied my bagiroca to fly and myself to run.

We made it all the way to the Slave Gate without more trouble than that, though I was soaked in a greasy, nervous sweat by that time. Unfortunately, there we joined a queue of servants, slaves, and tradesfolk lined up to leave the citadel. From my height, I could see over most of the heads that the guards were questioning each person, sometimes examining missives they presented—presumably identification or permission—and, worse, rifling through any bags. Beyond them, out the tantalizingly open gates, the sky showed dark still, but with glimmers of predawn light.

"Can we exit another way?" Sondra murmured.

Looking near tears, Agatha shook her head. "This is the least guarded gate. I'd hoped we'd be early enough that there'd be a short line. The cows need milking," she added for the benefit of anyone listening.

Sure enough, the man ahead of us glanced back, grimacing. "Something about a guard alarm. Dunno if it's real or a drill. But I hoped to deliver my catch and get back in time for early tide. Doesn't look good now."

I shifted my burden to my other shoulder. We'd have an easier time without Lia's corpse. Without that, I'd stay behind to kill Anure and let Sondra escape with Agatha. But I couldn't leave her body behind for those wizards to dissect. And the orchid . . . it might be dead along with Lia, but every instinct screamed at me that if those wizards had wanted it badly enough to do all this, then we didn't want them to have it.

Slowly—far too slowly—we crept forward. The line forming behind us in the narrow passage sealed our decision. We couldn't reverse direction without disturbance, and thus calling attention to ourselves. The light outside the open gate grew as the sun rose. Soon, someone would come to relieve those guards, maybe with Sondra's description. Or looking for Lia's corpse. If we could just get her out . . .

I didn't see how. We'd just have to break our way through. They delayed the fisherman in front of us for some time, questioning several things on his paperwork, then admonishing him at length for the lapses. Finally they let him go and it was our turn.

I shifted Lia to my left shoulder, acting wearied, and put my hand on my bagiroca.

"Your master and destination?" the guard asked, giving the three of us a frown.

"We answer to Lord Ryder," Agatha answered. "He sends us to convey these bundles and this slave to his family in the township."

"Where's your permission?"

"Syr Guard, our master was in his cups last night and sleeps still. He passed out before writing the permission, but he was most emphatic that we leave by dawn. I didn't dare wait for him to wake. Now we are already late and I fear his reprisals." Agatha peered up at the guard, her eyes anxious and hopeful.

"Hmph." He turned his gaze to me. "What's in the sack?"

"Syr," Agatha said, laying a beseeching hand on his sleeve. "Lord Ryder said it was private. I didn't dare ask. He gave me this coin, to pay the gate toll."

With a flick of fingers, the guard pocketed the coin Agatha produced. "I can waive the permission, but I have to examine your bags. You, oaf, lay that sack down here and open it."

I shuffled forward, eyeing the open air beyond the guard, bagiroca ready. Sondra, well acquainted with my thinking, shifted subtly, changing her grip on the walking stick, and edged Agatha with her, so they stood on the daylight side of the guard. I made a show of struggling with the bundle to give them time, making sure the other

guard was well occupied. I tensed to swing the bagiroca.
We'd have a few seconds to run, and a long open space to
cross.

We couldn't make it.

We had to.

"Hurry it up." The guard jabbed me with his metal ba-
ton. He peered at me more closely. "You don't look like a
manservant. What—"

"I assure you, he is," a smooth voice said. A golden-
haired man in elegant clothes and a jeweled walking staff
swept up from the outside. "These three are mine and
you're delaying them. Agatha—I specifically *told* you by
dawn!"

"Yes, Lord Ryder," Agatha murmured, head bowed.
She'd recovered faster than Sondra and I did, but we hastily averted our faces, covering our immense surprise—and
knee-watering relief—at seeing Ambrose.

The strange intervention had gotten the attention of the other guard, and I braced for a fight. Then they both nodded with calm expressions. Neither seemed inclined to question the outrageous possibility that an apparent nobleman had come to the Slave Gate to fetch his servants. "Of course, Lord Ryder. Apologies for the delay. Move along, you three."

Ambrose strutted off and we followed meekly behind. None of us dared ask the wizard where he'd come from. We hadn't had time to explain to Sondra how thoroughly Ambrose had disappeared in the aftermath of the battle at Cradysica, so she went along with the subterfuge easily enough. And Agatha, well, she seemed practiced at play-acting.

I tried to keep quiet, and did until we had passed the township, heading up the road to where we'd left the rowboat. Then I couldn't stand it any longer. I stepped up my pace to Ambrose's side. "Holy fucking Sawehl, Ambrose! Where have you been?"

"I was otherwise occupied."

"Doing *what*?"

He slid me a look. "Temper, Conrí. It's a very long

story. Do you really want to hear it now, or would you prefer I concentrate on making sure we escape?"

Cursing under my breath, I dropped back, taking up the part of dutiful manservant again. Sondra raised a questioning brow at me, but I shook my head and she subsided. It turned out to be a lovely morning, which got prettier the farther we walked from the citadel, the countryside of Yekpehr growing lush and well tended away from the jagged rocks of the point the citadel sat on.

I studied everything, laying it down in my memory so I could come back and retrace my steps once I gave Lia over to Kara's reliable care. That distracted me from dwelling on how I carried Lia's dead body. And that I might as well have killed the Queen of Flowers with my own hands.

My doom, to destroy every last thing of beauty and worth in the world. Anure and I were much alike, as it turned out. All I could do was understand that, and use it to kill him.

The sun had grown warm and high by the time we made it to the rowboat, where we'd hidden it under some driftwood on the beach. A flimsy and fanciful thing that matched the yacht, it would barely hold the four of them, no matter how light Lia's body. No surprise, Kara hadn't left, though it was well past the time I'd told him to leave us for dead. Stubborn fool. The *Last Resort* glittered at anchor offshore, where the fancy ship would surely draw attention soon. I wanted to curse Kara for the risk, and also kneel in gratitude that he'd stayed.

But he and I had already said our goodbyes.

I set down the sack with the vurgsten bomb, laid Lia's body in one corner of the boat, then helped Agatha in. Sondra steadied Ambrose, who settled himself next to the sack holding Lia. He hadn't asked, so I figured the wizard knew what had happened to her. Sondra helped me push the boat into the water. She hopped in, the thing sinking ominously low. Sondra held out a hand, but I shook my head, giving them another push.

"Conrí!" Sondra called in hushed, hoarse tones.

"I'm going back to finish this," I told her, shouldering the sack with the bomb, my own throat unexpectedly tight. "Goodbye. Take care of Lia."

"Get in the boat, Conrí," Ambrose said genially enough, but eyes emerald bright.

"It will sink." I pushed again, but the little boat didn't budge that time, the currents swirling around it in circles that looked all wrong.

"No, it won't," he corrected, as if speaking to a slow student. "Get in."

"I'm going back," I repeated, "to kill the toad."

Ambrose fixed me with that penetrating gaze. "You deserted Queen Euthalia once for your revenge. Will you repeat your mistake?"

"Lia is dead." I meant to say it flatly, but my voice took on a creaking hollow sound, sobs threatening to crack my chest. Vesno's howl came across the water, echoing me. I shoved futilely at the boat, ducking my head so they wouldn't see the fearsome Slave King weep like a child.

"We don't have time for your dramatics," Ambrose snapped. "Get in the boat now, or we're all in serious trouble."

"Conrí," Sondra said, her face ashen. "Please."

"No." I took a deep breath, steadying myself. "I'm here. I can get inside the citadel. There won't be another opportunity like this."

"Just like there wasn't another opportunity like we had

at Cradysica?" Sondra bit out. "I love you, Conrí, and I'll follow you to the end of the world, but you and I were wrong there. And Her Highness paid the price."

"Exactly. I got Lia killed. I failed you all. I have Agatha's weapon." I nodded at her. "This way I don't have to worry about the delay on the trigger."

"It will kill you," Agatha said flatly.

"I know." I looked forward to it.

"Conrí." Sondra gasped my name. "Don't do it. We'll find another way. There are things still to live for."

I shook my head. She wouldn't understand that a world without Lia had lost all its color. Even the driving need for vengeance had vanished. I was already the walking dead. "The least, last thing I can do is go back and take Anure out."

"The least you can do," Ambrose declared, "is get in this boat. Please join us, Conrí."

Before I realized it, I'd heaved myself over the side of the little boat, feeling the flimsy craft shudder under my weight. Ambrose returned my glare. He'd magicked me. Wonderful. "Happy now?" I ground out.

"I will be when you start rowing," Ambrose said, much more cheerfully. "I'm the talent, not the brawn."

So I rowed. Which didn't take much work, as the boat that should've sunk an arm's length from shore not only floated just fine, but glided straight for the *Last Resort* at a remarkable clip. Ambrose, seated in the stern, hands wrapped around the jeweled staff between his knees, watched me row. Sondra held her walking stick in both hands, vigilant gaze scanning the shore, the ragged tufts of blond hair glistening in the morning light, while Agatha huddled to the side, making herself as small as possible.

"That's quite the artifact you've acquired," Ambrose said to Sondra, keen gaze on the walking stick.

She barely glanced at him. "It's not much, but I didn't have anything else, so I grabbed this."

"Ah. Grabbing things from wizards can result in surprises," Ambrose noted cheerfully.

Now she reacted, looking at it like she might be holding a snake. "What—is it dangerous?"

"Not to you, child," Ambrose soothed her. "Though I know of a certain red wizard who will be most put out to have lost it."

Sondra opened her mouth, but caught sight of something that made her go alert. "Company." With my face also to the shore, I kept an eye on the mounted Imperial Guards galloping along the shore path. They never glanced our way, continuing up the coast.

Ambrose gave me a little smile. "I *am* a wizard," he reminded us. "I can distort what people do and don't see."

"Except when our invisible ship was perfectly visible to the Calantheans," I grumbled.

"You'll never let that go, will you?" Ambrose patted the burlap sack with Lia's body in it. "I explained that the laws of magic and the natural world aren't the same when Her Highness is around."

"Don't touch her," I growled, wanting to lunge at him. "And it's *was*. She's gone."

"Is, was." Ambrose waved a hand. "Language applies tenses in black-and-white lines where time flows in grayscale."

"We're there," Sondra broke in, giving me a warning look.

Vesno's howls had become excited barks, and we immersed ourselves in the business of getting Lia's body aboard, the skiff reloaded, and the *Last Resort* under way. Any thoughts I'd had of rowing myself back were thwarted by Ambrose. When I gathered up the sack with

Lia in it, intent on storing it below in one of the many unused cabins, Ambrose stood in my way.

"Where do you think you're taking Her Highness?" He didn't wait for my answer, but pointed to a lavish couch under a silk awning near the front of the yacht. "Put Her there, in the sunlight. And for Ejarat's sake, take Her out of that tacky burlap sack already. Ah, Lady Ibolya, your services are required."

If I hadn't held Lia's corpse in my arms, lax and wilted, I would have throttled him. Instead I put the sack on the couch he indicated. Sondra helped me, extracting Lia's body from the rough material with a gentleness I didn't think I'd ever seen from her. Ibolya asked no questions, arranging Lia's limbs so the remaining hand covered the space of the missing one. The dead orchid clung to her skin, as bruised and limp as Lia, both of them decaying.

"She was so brave," Sondra said to me, hoarse voice quiet, as we watched Ibolya gently bathe Lia's body with a damp cloth. "Courageous. Even after everything they did to Her. I understand now why you fell in love with Her."

"Kara is making full speed for Calanthe," Ambrose informed us, walking up. "With luck and a bit of nudging, we should make Her waters before sunset. Not a lot of extra time, but enough."

"It hardly matters what time we get there," I commented dully. With the urgency of rescue and escape fading, the strength left my body, too. My legs gave way of their own accord, and I sat heavily on the deck, my back against the sofa abutting the one Lia lay on. Vesno wormed his way around a low table to stretch out beside me, head on my lap, gaze fixed on Lia's body. Ibolya ignored us all, tending her queen's body, humming a quiet song.

"Of course it matters," Ambrose chided. "What time yesterday did you feel Her die?"

I glanced up sharply. Sondra and Agatha gave me strange looks. Deciding not to bother asking how the wizard knew, I admitted, "About four hours before midnight."

Ambrose nodded in satisfaction. "I thought so, but I needed to be sure. These things aren't always easy to pinpoint from a distance."

"You knew Her Highness was dead before we even went ashore?" Agatha asked.

"I felt it, yes," I said. "I apologize that I didn't tell you."

"Why didn't you?"

I met her gaze evenly, letting her see the ruthless bastard I was. "I was afraid you wouldn't want to take the risk."

She nodded to herself, looking thoughtful.

"I'd say it was wrong of me, but I'd do it again."

"Not wrong, but you should have trusted me, Conrí."

"I see that now. But I also thought I'd be staying behind." I gave Ambrose an accusing look, which he returned with a cheerful smile.

"Just as well, eh?" He glanced at the sun and back at Lia. "You both would've been unhappy if you hadn't been here when Her Highness wakes."

I stilled, unable to bear the pain of the sudden hope and crushing certainty of grief.

"That's not funny, Ambrose," Sondra growled, grasping her walking stick.

"I don't mean to be," he replied in all seriousness. "If we can get Her Highness back to Calanthe's waters in time, I can bring Her back."

"You told me there's no bringing back the dead," I grated out.

"Why, Conrí! You *were* listening. Honestly I can never be sure." Ambrose beamed at me, then tipped his staff in my direction. "However, your listening skills could use improvement. I said that with people who've been dead a long time, it almost never works out well. That's not at all what we're dealing with here. Her Highness hasn't been dead for a full cycle of Sawehl's journey around Ejarat, and our beloved queen isn't fully human, as you well know."

Sondra and I exchanged a long look, her face showing the same contorted longing I felt. When you've resigned yourself to the worst, hoping for anything else can be agonizing.

"Are you saying she's not actually dead?" I asked carefully.

"The concept of death is another of those lines we draw that we pretend is a finite threshold, but is truly more of a spectrum. There's a fascinating treatise on the topic that . . ." Ambrose trailed off, smile dimming at whatever he saw in my face. "Something to discuss another time. I believe the answer you're looking for is, yes, Her Highness is dead, but She's not so far along that we can't pull Her back. Speaking of, you did get Her hand, didn't you?"

I glanced at Sondra.

"Yes, Conrí insisted." With an odd expression, she dug in her bag and pulled out the wrapped hand we'd taken from the wizards' laboratory.

"Excellent." Ambrose beamed at us. "Everything is falling into place."

"Are you going to reattach Her hand, and finger?" Sondra inquired blandly, making me grateful she'd asked the question I couldn't. I still didn't know how to think or feel. It was all I could do to sit there and not fall apart.

"Good Ejarat, no! Conrí will need them."

I stared at him, unable to muster any kind of reply.

Ambrose shook his head for my denseness. "At least you remembered what I told you. *Claim the hand that wears the Abiding Ring.*" He pointed at the wrapped, gruesome package. "And so you did."

"That severed hand *wore* the Abiding Ring," I said, my voice sounding as dangerous as I felt. *Caged wolf.*

"Really—you're going to parse verb tenses again, and now with a prophecy. Humans. So nitpicky about past and future. Someday I'll learn."

"Then, we wait," Sondra finally said, when no one else spoke.

"Waiting and sailing, yes," Ambrose agreed.

"Where is Merle?" Sondra asked, looking around. That's right, I hadn't seen him at all.

"Oh, he's busy."

"Busy doing *what*?" Sondra frowned.

"Making sure there's a Calanthe for us to return to. Let's hope he's successful. We thought about having him come after you all, and me stay behind, but the whole lack of thumbs and human speech becomes a problem. You understand."

Sondra and I exchanged a look. "No," she said. "We don't."

"Ah, well. And now I must concentrate." He wandered off.

I sat there on the deck and rested without sleeping, half listening to Ibolya's wordless song. I couldn't remember the last time I'd slept for more than a short nap, and the lack of sleep gave everything a surreal quality. The glittering yacht, the scent of sea spray, the cloudless blue sky with a hint of oily smoke coiling in the distance from the burning citadel, Lia's dead body that maybe wasn't entirely dead lying in state while Ibolya tenderly cared for her. Vesno held vigil with me, the faithful companion Lia had promised he'd be.

Steadying my hand, I stroked Vesno's silky head. The wolfhound flicked his brown eyes to me, then once again trained them on Lia.

It might all be a dream, like those nightmares of my father's death, and I'd wake from the fragments of believing Lia lived and have to face that crashing awareness that I'd lost her all over again. Sondra went to bathe and came back in her favorite fighting gear that we'd brought along for her. She sat with me awhile, tried to get me to eat, then left again. Ibolya finished cleaning up the blood and other marks of the torture Lia had endured, as best she could, and she sat nearby, holding vigil also.

Kara came by, and reported on progress. He laid a dark hand on Lia's forehead and murmured some prayer I didn't know, before departing as quietly as he'd arrived.

And we sailed on.

I might've slept, because Vesno's stirring startled me. He lifted his head abruptly, then let out a long howl, reminiscent of wolves at night, calling to one another under the moon. Ambrose appeared as if from nowhere—for all I knew, he had—wearing his robes as court wizard of Calanthe. He smiled at me, eyes alight. "Calanthe."

Coming fully alert, I looked to Lia. She seemed the same. If anything, her skin had sunk more over her fine bones, her closed eyes dark pits in her delicate skull. Ibolya watched her queen, tremulous hope in her eyes. She hadn't said anything to us, but I felt sure she'd heard every word.

Ambrose slowly spun his staff, the lowering sun catching the faceted emerald atop it, shards of brilliant green flashing. I recalled how I'd described the color of Lia's one eye as like that. "Call her," Ambrose murmured.

"What?"

"Call her. Give her a kiss. She needs something to follow back to this body."

Aware that the others had gathered round, I knelt up. Vesno moved with me, laying his chin on Lia's lap, eyes still fixed on her face.

"Lia, my love," I said, stroking my hand over her scalp, the soft, crisped and wilted growth there tickling my fingers. "Come back, Lia." Bending over her, I pressed a kiss to her lips. Not cold, not in this heat, but not warm, either. And waxy, lifeless. A shudder ran through me, not of horror, but the final shattering of hope. I shouldn't have allowed that seedling to take root. This final loss would break me and I'd collapse, without even touching Anure.

I might as well have stayed in the mines.

Sondra put a hand on my shoulder, then Kara, too, on my other side. Ibolya hummed her song. The emerald shards caught the lowering light, dancing in a circle and bouncing against the blue sea.

"Lia. I love you. Come back, please. Calanthe needs you. I need you." I kissed her again, remembering how she'd felt in life, so vivid and shining, her mischievous humor and simmering passion. The way she smelled of green life, her courage and determination. And flowers, how she felt and smelled of the lushest blossom.

Her lips moved under mine, breath flowing cool as dark earth. I lifted my head, half in terror, half in wonder. And she opened her eyes. One blue, one green.

~ 24 ~

"Are you dead, too?" I asked Con, surprised to see him smiling at me. Maybe he was laughing at my final joke, that I'd put him first in my last thoughts. But no, his golden eyes filled with tears, his face crumpling in an agony of feeling, and he dropped his head to my breast, his dark hair spilling against my skin.

I wanted to lift a hand to comfort him, but only my fingers wiggled. Calanthe's vitality thrummed through me, though, prickling my tissues with pins and needles, as if I'd been lying still far too long. I wanted to stretch but couldn't.

My gaze went to Sondra, her blue eyes also full of emotion. "I see nothing has changed," I commented, my voice as creaky as hers ever was.

"Quite the opposite, Your Highness," she replied, bowing deeply. "I think You'll discover this third awakening finds us in vastly improved circumstances."

"Except for your hair," I noted with compassion. "I'm sorry."

"I'm not." Her rough voice wobbled. "A small thing."

"How do you feel, Your Highness?" Ambrose's gaze was as deep and old as an ancient forest, and I recognized his magic winding in my bones and blood, blending with

Calanthe's. Someone else's magic there, too. Something wilder, fierce, and feathered.

I let the mystery go for the moment. "Stiff. Sluggish." I finally managed to move my arm, and Con lifted his head, sitting back on his heels and wiping his face on his sleeve. The orchid on my wrist rustled, unfurling its petals, color leaching into it. Below that, the stump of my arm itched as if fire ants had gotten under the bandage. "Itchy."

"Welcome back to the world of the living, Your Highness," Kara said, giving me a salute and a rare smile. "You were greatly missed."

"Very much, Your Highness," Agatha added.

I nodded, surprised to see her there, too. And Ibolya, who bowed her head to me. The terrible itching of my stump distracted me from asking her about it.

"Don't scratch, Lia," Sondra scolded gently. "You have to let it heal."

Con looked from her to me, clearly bemused. I managed to lift my good hand, reaching over to stroke his cheek. He was as unkempt as I'd ever seen him, beard wild and hair hanging in ropes, dark circles under his golden eyes. He was the most beautiful man I'd ever seen. "How's My wolf?"

He smiled a little, pressing a kiss to my hand, then covering it with his big one. "Rough. Better now."

"And Calanthe?"

A hoarse laugh coughed out of him, and his smile widened. "Did you just ask about me *before* Calanthe?"

"Yes," I replied gravely. "I did. Somewhere in all that happened—" A shudder racked me and he squeezed my hand. "You were what mattered most in the end."

"Lia, I let you down. I'm sorrier than you can know. I shouldn't have—"

"Shh." I moved my fingers over his lips. They were

cracked and peeling. "When I get my strength back, we can have a huge fight about it."

He closed his eyes and nodded. "Fair enough."

"In the meanwhile . . ." I let go of him and picked at the bandages on my wrist. "This is making Me insane with the itching."

"Lia!" Sondra started forward. "Leave it—"

"Allow me, Your Highness," Ibolya said, gently inserting herself. As deftly as she'd tended me all those times, she unwound the bandage, soaking the dried blood away as she worked.

When she pulled the last of the bandage from the stump of my arm, we all stared at the skin there, pink and smooth, tendrils of the orchid wound around it. And the tender twigs of new fingers, green with blushing petal tips, growing out of it. I wiggled them, and they curled and uncurled again.

Con turned his molten gaze on me, the dimple in his cheek appearing like the first star of evening. "I guess I get to keep the one I found, huh?"

"And the empire falls," Ambrose said with good cheer.

"Still?" Con nearly growled the question.

Ambrose rolled his eyes. "You're not giving up now? Not with all we've overcome. You've completed some of the prophecy. We must finish." His gaze unfocused. "Besides, Anure's wizards came much closer to succeeding than I care to contemplate. Knowing them, those four will only try harder now."

"You know them?" I demanded, unable to suppress a shudder at the memory of my torturers.

"There aren't so many wizards in the world," Ambrose replied, as if stating the obvious. He heaved a sigh of exasperation at us. "And I didn't spring full-grown from

Sawehl's forehead, staff in hand. I had to study *somewhere*."

Con made a sound deep in his throat, and Sondra scrubbed a hand over her face. "I don't understand."

"No." Con made a face. "None of us do, but we'll work on that. To answer your question, Lia, Calanthe was all right when we left. I'll give you a full report on the damages and casualties at Cradysica."

I raised a brow at Ambrose, that side of my face still swollen and aching. It would be nice if that healed, too. Though I supposed coming back from the dead and regrowing a hand should be enough. "Any aftereffects?"

"Unfortunately, yes," the wizard allowed. "Merle and I did what we could, but we made a bit of a hash of it."

"What?" Con snarled at him. "What are you talking about?"

I closed my eyes, feeling the vibrant response of Calanthe. Oh yes, She was awake, all right. Restless and angry. And Merle . . . "The raven is holding Her?" I asked.

"He was. He says he's losing his grip."

"I specifically told you that if it came to choosing Me or Calanthe, to choose Her."

"Yes. Well." Ambrose actually looked chagrined. "I thought we had Her settled, but then She started breaking free when She felt You die. We decided I'd better get You after all."

Con made an incoherent sound, raking a hand through his hair and gripping it. "Would *one* of you explain?"

"Blood shed in violence," I said. "I warned you that it could be received by Calanthe as a blood sacrifice."

"So . . ." He frowned. "Calanthe is a monster inside the island?"

"No. Calanthe is a monster who lay down to sleep in the sea and became an island we live on."

Sondra made a little sound. Kara looked as if a light had dawned, and Agatha wrapped her arms around herself. Ibolya nodded, smiling ruefully.

"So the earth tremors," Con said. "If the monster is the island, and She wakes . . ."

I met his gaze. "No more Calanthe. Everyone on Her falls into the sea."

"Maybe we should go back to Yekpehr," Con said, only half joking. "Or . . . *anywhere* else."

"Percy will haunt you if you take his life raft and leave him to die," Agatha said quietly.

"*This* is Percy's yacht?" I asked, incredulous. "How did you pry it out of his grasping hands?"

"We needed it," Con replied grimly. "I managed to destroy every other seaworthy vessel and we had to come after you. How did *you* get to Yekpehr?" he asked Ambrose.

He smiled, terribly pleased with himself. "It's a long explanation, full of fascinating theories concerning time and space. You see—"

Con held up a hand. "Maybe later. If we haven't drowned under Calanthe's fins."

"Lord Percy loves Your Highness, too," Agatha said with a shrug. "You saved us. So did Calanthe. How can we help save Your island?"

"I don't know yet." I turned back to Con, squeezing his hand. "I have to try."

"I'm not arguing," he said, shaking his head. I could see the hollowness in him, how utterly he'd exhausted himself. "I'm not arguing with you ever again."

"What?" I demanded. "Did Ambrose steal My wolf and put someone else in your body?"

He looked startled, then grinned crookedly at me. "I'm just so glad to have you alive again, Lia."

"I'm just so glad to be alive. And to be with you," I replied softly.

"Good." He took a breath. "If you ask, I'll give up my vengeance for you."

"You'd let go of killing Anure?"

"For you, yes."

I didn't know what to say. "Well, let's think about that. I doubt those wizards will let Me go easily. We may yet have to fight."

"Oh yes," Ambrose put in. "And now we have renewed connections inside the citadel."

Agatha nodded. "Lady Rhéiane promised to help in any way possible."

My heart shivered in my chest, cold dread making it stutter in its newly recovered beats. That was nothing to the look on Con's face.

"Rhéiane?" he asked, very carefully. "A woman named Rhéiane was your contact at the citadel?"

Agatha hesitated at the thin scratch of his voice. "Yes. She was my mistress when I lived there. She's about Lady Sondra's age and . . ." She trailed off. Sondra looked like she might vomit. "You know her," Agatha finished flatly.

"We didn't know, Conrí," Sondra said, pleadingly, her expression aghast. I was sure if she was excusing him or us.

"No, we didn't." He lifted his head, the ocean breeze catching his dark hair and tumbling it around his face, eyes blazing gold with renewed fervor. "But we do now. We're going back for her."

"Not yet," I cautioned. "After careful planning."

He smiled at me, ruefulness and amused affection in

it. He smoothed a hand over my skull, warm and rough, achingly familiar. "First we save Calanthe. Then we can plan."

I nodded and, when Vesno nudged my hand with his cold nose, I stroked his head. The scent of Calanthe, lush with blossoms, floated by on a warm breeze, and I allowed my eyes to drift closed. Con pressed a kiss to my temple.

"I need to sleep a few moments."

"Then do."

"Wake Me when we get to the reef, and I'll guide us through."

Kara snorted. "I can do that, Your Highness. I solved that riddle."

"And I can assist," Ibolya volunteered.

I smiled at them. "Then wake Me at the dock. I have to see about Calanthe."

"Rest now, Lia," Con murmured. "I'll see you safely home."

Wrapping the dreamthink around me, I trusted that he would.

Read on for an excerpt from the next spellbinding
book in the Forgotten Empires series

The Promised Queen
By Jeffe Kennedy

Available Summer 2021 from
St. Martin's Paperbacks

~ 1 ~

"Lia? Wake up."

The voice reached me deep in the dreamthink, where I slept wrapped in the verdant cloak of Calanthe's maternal embrace. For a moment, I thought all was well, that my realm was at peace, safe and protected—and that I was, too. That things were as they'd always been, and my ladies had arrived to wake me for the morning rituals.

But no . . . that wasn't true at all. Calanthe roiled with restless anger and furious hunger. All that blood, violently spilled in battle saturating the waters and soaking into the very bedrock of my island kingdom, had awakened Her. And that same ravenous rage filled me. That and pain. So much death, including my own.

I screamed. The bloodcurdling shriek ripped itself from Calanthe's bones to rise from my stomach and rake my throat with rending claws as it tore from me.

Con wrapped himself around me—a man, not an island, made of sinews, muscle, and hot skin—stilling my thrashing limbs with his overpowering strength. "Lia. Lia, no. It's me. You're home. You're safe. It's all right now."

I nearly laughed at how wrong he was, but it came out as a moan. None of us was safe and nothing would be all right ever again.

"Lia, wake up. You—"

"I'm awake," I said, cutting off any further empty reassurances and opening my eyes.

Con held me on his lap, cradling me there. Beyond the flapping awning that stretched overhead, full night had fallen, blackness severed by lightning-streaked skies. Rain poured, the wind howled, and waves rose white-tipped in the torchlight. Calanthe had tasted blood and wanted more. Her longing was mine, intertwined. The insatiable craving filled me. The orchid burned on my arm, drawing life from me, the spindly new fingers of my regenerating hand clicking as I flexed them. They itched and needed flesh.

I had starved, suffered, lost my ring finger, and then my hand. Drained of blood, I'd died . . .

No, I wouldn't think about that time when I'd been dead. Besides, I needed to feed. Or Calanthe did. It didn't matter which—no other thought could withstand that ravening appetite.

"Lia?" Con sounded uncertain, shadows haunting his face from the last few, eternally long days. He'd come for me, and saved me—and he'd never looked more beautiful to my eye. Longing for him filled me, and I *wanted*. My husband, my love. Mine. I was famished for him. I'd died thinking of him and here he was, for the taking.

His eyes caught the golden light of the torches as he studied me, concern turning to wariness. A blast of wind-blown rain shattered over him, but he didn't seem to notice. I laid my intact hand on Con's cheek, his pitted skin rough over his snarled beard, and I trailed my nails over the water droplets on his skin. He flinched slightly. That's right. My nails had all broken. Untended, they'd been reduced to brittle nothingness, all ragged, sharp edges.

Just like me. An orchid can't live on its own. I needed and I would have.

"Kiss Me," I commanded him.

Con might have hesitated, his keen instincts whispering of danger, but I wound my fingers in the hair that trailed over his shoulder, pulling him to me. He lowered his head, arms easily lifting me at the same time, brushing my lips with his. Sweet, hot, so tender. Alive.

I bit. Like a snake striking, I had his lower lip in my teeth, hot blood flowing into my throat. He jerked, but I had him, holding him tight as I drank the salt of him.

Then, instead of fighting me off, he growled deep in his throat, and moved into me. Tongue coaxing me to open to him, he kissed me, sending life and heat into the damp chill that lay still in the marrow of my bones, the heat a melting caress. Needing me in return, he kissed me like a man desperate for a deep breath of air only I could give. His arms powerful around me, he held me against the furnace of his body, kissing me as if our lives depended on it. Maybe they did. Because somewhere in there, sanity returned—and I remembered who I was.

Euthalia, Queen of Calanthe. I was Euthalia, not Calanthe. A flesh and blood woman, not an island made of soil and sea.

"Enough, Lia," Con murmured against my lips. His big, rough hand gripped my jaw, gently but insistently coaxing me away from my prize.

Relaxing into humanity again, I unclamped my teeth, and broke the kiss. Con pulled back enough to search my face. Blood ran from his lip—swelling rapidly—and smeared in his beard. Abruptly, astonishingly, he grinned at me. "They warned me you were a maneater, but I never thought they meant it literally."

"Bringing the dead back to life can be a tricky proposition," Ambrose observed, leaning over Con's broad shoulder to peer at me. The wizard's sunny curls were plastered with rain around his face, making him look even younger than usual. That deceptive youth made for an odd contrast with his eyes, which held the wisdom—and sorrow—of centuries. The clinical interest in them reminded me of the four wizards who'd tortured me so cheerfully in their pursuit of knowledge, and a shudder of animal terror shook me. "I do hope that there won't be a problem with—well, no sense worrying about it now."

"Explain," Con demanded.

Ambrose smiled wistfully. "We'll see if such explanations become necessary—or useful. Suffice to say, Your Highness, that it will take time for Your spirit to recalibrate to being in flesh again."

"Unfortunately, time is what we don't have at the moment." General Kara, dark and lean, stepped into my line of sight and bowed from the waist. "Your Highness, we need Your assistance." He grimaced, looking away to something. "Rather urgently," he added.

A startling lurch threw us to the side, another wave splattering us with chilly salt water, though Kara, a long-time sailor, absorbed the motion easily. That's right: we were on a boat. *The Last Resort.* The name came into my mind. Percy's pleasure yacht that they'd sailed to Yekpehr to rescue Sondra and me. Though I didn't remember that part. I only recalled awaking on a couch under this awning, to sunset skies and Calanthe's flower-scented breezes.

Now waves tossed the ship about, a storm raging. I frowned in puzzlement. There shouldn't be a storm this violent near Calanthe, should there? But we were near

Calanthe's shores; I knew that like I knew my hand moved at the end of my arm.

"We might be fucked." Sondra strode into view, her smile nearly gleeful. "It's total chaos out there. Your Highness—good to see You awake. And alive," she added as an afterthought. Self-consciously, she ran a hand over her shorn head, the tufts of pale hair uneven, a few darker lines marking scabbed-over cuts. I didn't know how she'd come to lose her beautiful hair.

I couldn't remember much at all, except the pain, and that dreadful, nauseating weakness as my blood and very life drained away. And then I died. Remembering that *nothingness*, the sense of my self dissipating, had me spinning down and away, the clammy claws of death reaching for me . . .

"Stay with me, Lia." Con's hand still on my jaw, he turned my face toward his. "We need you to get us home."

Home. To Calanthe. I should never have left.

"What's going on?" I asked, my thoughts clearing as I levered myself up. I had a duty, a responsibility. There should *not* be a storm like this. Not restraining now, Con helped, steadying and supporting me. I tried to see past the pitching deck that filled most of the scene, but couldn't. "I need to stand."

I pushed to my feet, but my legs gave way like wilted flower stems, and I collapsed back against Con. How humiliating. I hated being weak in any way and now I was only that.

"Let me," Con said, sweeping one arm under my knees and lifting me in the cradle of his arms as if I weighed nothing. Probably I did, after all that I'd been through. He tucked me against his chest—a comforting place to be— and braced against a pole that held up the awning that had sheltered us from the storm. I scanned the night-dark sea.

Our torches made a pitifully small circle of flame in the swirl of wind and water. Rain drove sideways outside our flimsy shelter on the deck.

In the distance, Calanthe shone with drenched light, crowned by the glittering jewel of my palace high on the cliffs. The home I thought I'd never see again.

Lightning forked through the sky with an immediate *crack*! of pulse-jumping sound, illuminating everything in a harsh, ruthless glare, thunder rolling after as Calanthe groaned of her pain and hunger. Not far away—entirely too close—sea spray fountained dramatically from the waves churned into fury by the massive coral reef that protected Calanthe.

"*That* is our problem," Kara shouted over the wind, pointing, in case I'd failed to notice.

"Why are we so close? Your boat will damage My coral reef." Con snorted out a sound suspiciously like a laugh.

Kara looked pained, but inclined his head. "My apologies, Your Highness, but it's true. Unfortunately, we may not survive the encounter either."

"I thought you said you knew the trick of navigating My reef and harbor." I could remember at least that much.

He grimaced, wiping rain from his face. "It seems to have . . . shifted, Your Highness. And the wind is driving us straight for it."

Oh. Of course. Calanthe had changed the conformation of the barrier reef. Not only was the coral a living entity, but so was the entire island, though in a different way. And where I'd thought of my connection to Calanthe before as trying to coax a sleeping cat to do my bidding, now She was awake, a raging lion savaging all in her quest for more blood.

The storm was like a living thing, too, ravening and

full of inchoate rage. Even when I understood little else of my abilities, I'd always been able to steer the worst storms around my island kingdom. Allowing the gentle, nourishing rains and sending the rending winds and waves out to sea had been as natural as breathing.

This, however, was no normal storm. Birthed by the thrashing of Calanthe's abrupt awakening, the ferocious surf and driving winds ignored my call. And . . . something else contributed here. A magic not my own. But one I recognized.

"I need to see the other direction," I told Con.

He turned, stepping out from our dubious shelter, his body flexing, briefly shifting me in his arms as he looped an arm around the post and braced against the pitching of the ship. I peered into the gloom, seeking through the violent chatter of Calanthe's ravings for information on what disturbed Her waters.

"Lia, I don't know what—" A flash of lightning cracked, illuminating the night. "Great green Ejarat," he breathed in horror.

Rearing against the horizon, an enormous wave chased us. Kara and Sondra shouted orders and—absurdly—Ambrose laughed. "Now, *that* took some doing!" he exclaimed.

Anure's wizards, chasing us. No. Chasing me.

"We have to get below," Con shouted in my ear.

"No." I loaded my voice with all the authority I could, ridiculous as it might be from a bald, barely clothed, and sodden heap who couldn't stand on her own. "I can stop it." I hoped.

"Then do it fast," he answered without further argument, then shouted something back to Kara and Sondra.

I concentrated, feeling my way. These were my waters, mine by right of birth, responsibility, and through long familiarity. This sea belonged to me as much as my own blood did. Not a great analogy, as those wizards had tried to steal that, too. But it had done them no good. They'd ultimately failed to take the orchid ring, and they'd fail in this, too.

The waters were mine, but the wave came from elsewhere. As wizards, they couldn't bend my elemental magic to their will; they could only try to disturb it. Like dropping a rock in a still pond. The rock wouldn't change the water, only displace it. The wizards no longer powered this wave. They'd started it—dropped the rock to swamp us—but it traveled on its own now.

The yacht plummeted down a slope, following the irresistible current made as the powerful wave sucked the sea toward it. A roar of the tumbling water filled my ears. Con's arms tightened on me and he shouted some kind of prayer or exhortation.

Be still, I told my sea. *Shh. Lie down.*

The wave stalled, shifted and simmered, blacker than the sky as it reared above us. Then, like a dropped bowl of water, it *splooshed* down and outward. The swell caught us, lifting us high and tossing the yacht down again. Con bent over me, holding us against the post as the ship hurled up one wave and down another—and shuddered to a screeching stop.

We'd hit the coral reef.

Another swell—smaller, but still huge—hit and the boat leaned to one side, grinding against the rocks ominously. *The Last Resort* shuddered, as did my bones, the living coral beneath us screaming of their small deaths as the yacht crushed them.

The boat lurched again. Something broke beneath us with a loud bang, *The Last Resort* tilting precipitously. Agatha and Ibolya had joined us, clutching each other for support, their faces pale, but calmly turned to me, trusting in me to save them.

"We need to get off this boat, now," Con barked in his rough voice. Not so much trust there. "Can you swim?"

I needed to be firm and I couldn't do that while cradled like an injured babe in arms.

"No, but I don't need to. Take Me to the prow."

"What? No. We'll be swept over onto those rocks."

"Take Me now or put Me down so I can walk," I commanded coolly.

Con muttered something but began forging uphill toward the leaning prow, powerful muscles working against the incline. Sondra came up beside him, using an odd-looking walking stick to dig into the wooden planking of the deck, steadying herself and then Con with a grip on his arm.

"Close enough, Your Highness, or would You prefer I dangle you overboard?"

I ignored Con's sarcasm, concentrating on reaching through the tempest to the waters of Calanthe.

"I have to stand," I told Con.

He huffed out a sigh, but set me down, bracing me between his bulk and the railing, one arm around my waist—and pretty much supporting my entire weight still—his other hand gripping the rail. "Whatever you're going to do, do it now. If the ship breaks apart, it will get ugly."

A smile stretched my lips, the dry skin cracking painfully. Being dead left a body in less than ideal condition. Layering metal into my spine, I reached out to Calanthe's churning seas once more. They responded less sluggishly this time, and I directed the currents to calm, to follow my bidding. With a mental twist, I reversed the direction of the waves. No need to be anything they were not. They need simply do the same in the other direction.

The Last Resort lifted, shifted, then shot off the coral reef. A wave curled over us, dousing the spontaneous cheers as we hit a trough. I had the sea catch us, encircling the yacht in a pool of calmer water. Con laughed, a belly deep howl of relief and delight.

"We're on the wrong side of the reef still!" Kara shouted over the wind as he clutched the rail on our left.

"Shut up. She knows what she's doing," Sondra, on our right, yelled back.

I wouldn't put it that strongly, but I did have a plan. During my abduction and imprisonment, I'd spent so much time and effort trying to reconnect to my lost Calanthe that she roared into me now, as if I'd thrown open every portal in my seeking. The dreamthink flowed like blood, infused my lungs like air, and the coral reef spoke to me. Millions of small voices created a symphony of information, singing of their place. I let them inform the waves, who then took us around and between the crevices.

Calanthe wanted me home as much as I wanted to be there. And with the sea carrying us into the harbor, I diverted my attention to the storm, inviting it to turn its savagery on the open sea, away from land.

The fury of it lessened. Not abating entirely, but the rain no longer slanted sideways, the wind no longer howling. *The Last Resort* glided into the harbor without sails, more or less upright, though with a definite list to one side.

"We're still taking on water," Kara reported, "but we should make it before she sinks."

Percy would never forgive me if I sank his boat, so I encouraged the sea to flow back out again. Slowly the yacht righted. Kara glanced my way but said nothing.

The harbor sat quiet in the drumming rain, the docked ships tossing in their berths, lights on in only a few houses that wended their way in spirals up the hill. No one waited to greet us. Not surprising, I supposed, as the hour was late and everyone would be hunkered down to wait out the storm. Still, returning from the dead seemed like an occasion for a bit of celebration.

"Your Highness." Lady Ibolya stepped into the place Sondra vacated, curtseying deeply. "I brought a cloak for You, in case You wanted to return without fanfare." The cloak had a deep cowl and long sleeves with draping cuffs that would cover my hands—and lack thereof. My nobles and courtiers often wore that sort of thing to secret assignations, and I'd worn this one before to sneak out and visit Con in the map tower, back in another lifetime, before I died.

"They don't know, do they?" I asked Ibolya, then tipped my chin up to Con. "What did you tell everyone?"

"We kept the news as quiet as we could," he told me gravely, a hint of doubt in his face. "I know how hard you've worked to keep your—our—people from panicking. Not many know you disappeared from the Battle at Cradysica."

"What do they think happened to Me?"

"That you were injured and needed time to recover," Con replied.

"Your other ladies went to the Temple, Your Highness," Ibolya added. "They've gone into seclusion and we let everyone believe You went with them. To heal."

The way she added that last, so tenderly and hopefully, sorely tested my precarious poise. *To heal.* It sounded as far beyond me as the sky.

"Lia." Con at last let go of the rail, and gazed down at me very seriously as he ran a gentle hand over my bald scalp. "You should know—Tertulyn is with them."

I nearly staggered. Would have, if Con hadn't been

supporting me still. "I didn't see her," I managed to say, "at Yekpehr. Because she was here all along."

Con nodded, then shook his head. "It's a long story, and you're weaving on your feet. Let's get you inside and take this slowly."

I looked past him to the horizon I couldn't see, the night and storm obscuring it all. But it seemed I felt the gazes of those wizards streaming through the distance, the hot glare of their obsession following me. I'd vanquished their wave, but they'd be back with more and better.

"I think taking things slowly isn't an option," I observed. Ambrose stepped into my line of sight and inclined his head. "Unfortunately," I added with a nod to Kara, "time is what we don't have."